DEATH LOOT & VAMPIRES

THE VAMPIRE VINCENT
BOOK ONE

BENJAMIN KEREI

This is a **work of fiction**. Names, characters, businesses, places, events, and incidents are either the products of the author's imagination or used in a fictitious manner. Any resemblance to actual persons, living or dead, or actual events is purely coincidental.

ISBN 978-0-473-68030-5

ACKNOWLEDGMENTS

I never planned on writing this book, so I would like to start by thanking my muse for visiting me in January. Until I wrote this book, I didn't know I had one, let alone that they were any good at their job. Feel free to visit whenever you like muse, because you do good work, which comes together a lot faster than when I'm out here working on my own. I mean a lot faster.

I would also like to thank my editor Ellen Klowden for all her wonderful help, my cover artist Luciano Fleitas for another brilliant cover, and my typesetter Nikko Marie for making everything look professional.

As always, I would like to thank my family and friends for being so supportive. You're all wonderful people and I love you dearly.

PROLOGUE

To a starving vampire, the sound of a human heartbeat is a symphony. The *thump, thump, thump* echoes through the world like a joyful trumpet, announcing the opening of the hunt. The aroma of blood quickly follows, sweet ambrosia overflowing with life. Either one is tantalizing, but together they are enough to drive you to madness.

Thirty-three days ago, I was a happy father of two. My friends called me Vinny, instead of Vincent, and I worked a job that paid too little, to provide for a wife and children who showed me nothing but love and affection. It was honest work. The kind that made the world a little better with each passing day and gave me a sense of satisfaction that I was doing good.

Then *they* shattered that life.

If you had told me watching anime with my son, Luke, would one day let me understand the most bizarre experience of my life, I might have laughed. Those silly shows were too ridiculous to offer more than the simple pleasure of spending time with my boy, or so I thought.

Thirty-three days ago, I was isekaied, summoned from our world to another like some tragic anime cliché, but instead of some noble king needing a hero to save his kingdom, I ended up in the middle of a dark cult, hellbent on becoming vampires.

They made a *literal* deal with the devil, while they held me in chains. It was a creature so foul that its presence nauseated me in a way I cannot adequately describe, making me want to curl into a ball and tremble as I tried to scrub away the filth crawling under my skin from being in its presence.

The ones who summoned me called me 'hero', another cliché. Then, as newly turned vampires, they feasted on me, which was the only part of the experience that was remotely original.

I *died* in the same room where I was summoned, where the demon was summoned, where they blunted their new fangs on my flesh and drank the life from me. Then thirty-three days ago, I returned to the world of the living. And I did not come back as the same man who left.

I once viewed life through an emotionless haze, due to a concussion. Being a vampire was a little like that. My emotional range and interests were smothered when compared to what they once were. My objective morality was skewed, and my compassion was so limited as to be non-existent.

The loneliness of the small, damp cell I'd woken in would have driven me insane in the past. The screams of my neighbours in the other cells by me would have left me in tears. Now, the only thing I cared about was the fact that no one had fed me. So, I sat in the cell I couldn't escape and allowed time to flow by as my hunger grew.

My thirst for blood had me aware of the party of adventurers the moment they arrived.

They came through sewers, wading through the filth and muck, heartbeats erratic and fearful. They entered via the pipe where they disposed of the subterranean structure's waste, likely thinking it would disguise their entry.

There were four of them. The men wore leather and steel, while the women were dressed in soft fabrics.

Through the barred window in my cell door, I watched them skulk down the brick-lined hallway with great caution. They were not half as quiet as they thought they were, and they were not ready to face what awaited them in the darkness down here.

So, I did them a favour, possibly the last favour of my life, and told them so. "You're all going to die down here."

My voice had changed during the transformation. It was deeper, smoother, filled with confidence and predatory intent, giving me the sort of eloquent articulation, you only see in movies.

My wife Sandra would have loved it.

The young blonde woman, in her early twenties, who was dressed in a pristine white robe spun, raising the head of her staff in my direction and muttered a single phrase: "*Holy Shot.*"

A blast of radiant light burst from the end of the staff, engulfing my head with the intensity of a lighthouse at night.

I blinked away the stars I was seeing, otherwise unaffected, but a little surprised by her actions. "Did you just say holy shit to blast me with magic, miss? I'm not going to lie, but never in a million years would I have thought that those would be the words that someone used to kill me. Do you get some sort of perverse pleasure from making the last words people hear profanity? If so, you should talk to someone about it. That *can't* be healthy." My words came out in a disjointed rush as I tried to distract myself from the thirst clawing at my throat.

The four-member party of adventurers stood in the middle of the hallway, staring at me with their weapons raised. They had been on edge as they made their way here; now they were ready to swing at anything that got too close.

The burly-looking young man in the steel breastplate seemed to be in charge, because he took control of the situation. "Lela, it didn't work. Hit it again."

"*Holy Shot.*"

Another burst of light hit me in the face, but this time I had enough experience to close my eyes. I also heard her properly this time. "Oh, you said Holy Shot. My mistake, miss. Sorry for the accusation."

"What the fuck?" Burly said.

"Language," I growled. "There are ladies present."

Burly took offense to my suggestion. "Look, I'm not going to be fucking lectured by a bloody blood-sucker. Kindly shut up and die."

"Holy Shot."

Light enveloped my head a third time.

"It's not working," Burly said.

"I noticed," I said, trying to be helpful as I ignored the hunger demanding I tear their throats out and drink their blood. It was difficult.

I was ready to die, ready to step beyond the veil.

Living as a monster for a chance at a few more lonely years didn't interest me. I wasn't safe to be around. And I still remembered what it was to be a good man, and I'd rather die with dignity than live like this.

These new instincts were pushing me to hurt people, and it was taking everything I had not to throw myself against the door and try to break through with my fists, even though I knew it was pointless. The door was too strong. Every attempt I had made to escape had utterly failed.

Burly ignored me as he focused on his allies. "Lela, why isn't it fucking working?"

The young woman blushed and took a tentative step forward, peering through the bars at my face, holding her lamp higher. "Um, excuse me, ah, sir. Have you killed and eaten any people since becoming a vampire?"

It was an odd question. "Would you believe me if I said no?"

"*Of course,* we won't believe you if you say no," Burly hissed. "We need to stake this vampire and move on. Peppy, shoot an arrow into his chest."

"The door's kind of in the way," I pointed out as I turned to the archer, who had nocked an arrow. He was a big man with dark hair and a mischievous face. "Also, is your name really Peppy?"

"It's a nickname," he replied.

"Is it because you pepper your enemies with arrows?"

He nodded.

"Good nickname."

He released the draw on his bow and scratched the side of his head. "Thanks, I think."

I turned back to Lela, ready to die. "Did you want to give your Holy Shot another go? Perhaps it's just performance anxiety. You probably just needed to warm up your staff."

Peppy chuckled.

Lela looked confused, squinting through the darkness at me.

The other woman snickered.

Burly did not look happy.

Peppy quickly stopped chuckling. "Don't look at me like that. It was funny."

"*What* was funny?" Lela asked.

Peppy tried not to grin and failed. "He made a sex joke."

"When?"

A small chuckle escaped me over her apparent confusion. "You're a *priest* priest, I take it. Do you wear a chastity belt?"

"Could everyone stop talking to the vampire?" Burly snapped in a hissed whisper. "We need to kill him so we can finish investigating the complex for whatever is creating all that unholy energy."

They had no clue what they had walked into. "It was probably created by the demon-summoning ritual and the hundreds of vampires down here."

"Did you just say *hundreds* of vampires?" Peppy whispered.

"There are forty-seven in the cell next to me, if you want to check."

Peppy shuffled down the corridor, disappearing from view. He was back in a few seconds, much paler than before. "There are ghouls down here," he whispered.

"How many?" Burly asked.

"I didn't stop to count, but I would guess as many as he said."

"My apologies; I assumed they were vampires by their smell. But I also may have been misled by all the screaming for blood. If I could blush, I'd be embarrassed."

"Ghouls are created when a newly turned vampire is starved for blood," Lela explained, after hearing my confusion. "They *were* vampires; *now* they're ghouls."

That was sort of interesting. "What's the difference?"

"Ghouls eat everything, not just blood."

"Would everyone please stop talking to the vampire and kill him?"

"We can't kill him," Lela said.

I realised I'd been too friendly. "Look, it's nice that you've grown so attached to me, but if it's all the same to you, I would prefer to die."

Burly raised his hands, finally finding the support he was looking for. "See, he wants to die."

"Technically, he's already dead," Peppy said. "Vampires are soulless demons that animate dead flesh."

"Wait. I'm soulless?"

"Technically, he's *not* soulless until he takes his first innocent life," Lela corrected. "Currently, he is a disembodied soul, tethered to his animated corpse, which is possessed by a demon."

"What's the difference?" Peppy asked.

"Holy magic doesn't work on a righteous soul. Even though his soul isn't bound to his flesh, it's still tethered, so I can't harm him. Actually, he's still at the stage where his vampirism can be reversed."

Everything in the world disappeared, except her face. "Wait. You can *reverse* this? If that's possible, *I would rather not die*."

"How can you be sure?" Burly asked.

"Holy Shot."

Light enveloped me for a fourth time, and I returned to seeing stars.

"Either he has not killed anyone, or he's an ancient vampire," Lela said. "And if he's an ancient vampire, we're already dead, and he's just toying with us before he kills us."

The others took a step back from me.

Their fear amused me. "Is there something on my face?"

"How would we tell if he's an ancient vampire?" Burly whispered.

"I can hear you."

"Holy symbols will burn in his presence."

Burly glanced at the amulet around Lela's neck. "How close does it need to be?"

She squinted at me and then at her amulet. "This would probably be close enough."

"It's not doing anything. Shouldn't it be burning?"

"It won't harm him or burn if he hasn't killed any innocents. But he wouldn't be an ancient vampire unless he had."

"Just to be safe, maybe you should put it a little closer to him."

I glared at Burly, upset by his suggestion. I was doing my best to remain a good person, and he wasn't trying at all. "Are you seriously trying to delegate what could potentially be a suicide mission?"

He scowled, not liking someone questioning his orders. "Shut up. It's the cleric's job to deal with unholy abominations."

I frowned, considering his statement. "That's actually a pretty good justification."

Peppy chuckled. "He's full of pretty good justifications."

Burly groaned. "Please don't undermine me in front of the vampire, Peppy."

"Yeah, he's doing a fine job on his own." I gave Burly a thumbs up through the window. "Don't worry, I've got your back."

Peppy was wise enough to bite down on his next chuckle.

Lela finally gathered her courage. She grasped her amulet and stepped forward, holding it out, stopping just outside my reach.

"Closer," Burly instructed.

I was about done with his attitude. He seemed like a six-letter word that rhymed with banker, so I slid my arm between the thick metal bars and held out my palm only a few inches from her amulet, glaring at him. "You happy now?"

"So, he's not an ancient vampire, just a vampire that hasn't fed yet," Peppy said. "What do we do now?"

"Well, we can't free him," Burly said. "He'll just try to eat us."

"You wouldn't do that, would you?" Lela asked. Her tone suggested that she believed I wouldn't.

"Would you like an honest answer?"

She nodded, far too doe-eyed and innocent for this place. "They are the only ones worth listening to."

"I give it a fifty-fifty chance that I try to eat you. I've been locked in here for thirty-three days, and you all smell like cold beer on a hot afternoon. I think the only reason I haven't gone mad from the hunger is because my wife made me do a weeklong water fast with her once, and that hellish experience taught me how to tolerate hunger."

She grinned. "You're pious."

"No, I was fat."

Peppy snorted.

It was good to have someone to make jokes with again, but this had to end. "Look, there are several hundred ghouls down here, along with the thirteen vampires that turned me. You all seem like nice people, so I suggest you climb back down that hole you came out of and get as far away from here as you can. Actually, that brings up a question I've been wanting to ask this entire time. How are you all so clean? I know what you climbed through."

"It's a spell," the second woman said.

"Rena can't stand being dirty," Peppy added.

"Cleanliness is next to godliness, they say."

"I like that," Lela said. "Do you mind if I use it?"

"You're welcome to it. Now if you would kindly head back the way you came, just look for the filthy tunnel that leads to a long, happy life."

"He's got a point," Peppy said. "We aren't equipped to deal with a vampire nest. If these ghouls wake up, we're dead."

"I'm personally surprised they haven't woken up already. You lot aren't exactly quiet."

Lela frowned. "That is odd. By now they should have broken out of their cell and torn us apart." Her head tilted to the side the way, Kathrine, my daughter always tilted hers when she was thinking. "You said you've been in here for thirty days."

"Thirty-three, but who's counting."

"Did these vampires summon this demon to become vampires, by any chance?"

"Yes. They then ate me and the entire nearby village, from what my old neighbours complained about. Apparently, they thought they were being invited to their lord's manor for a feast, only the invitation didn't specify that *they* were the feast."

"They're slumbering," Lela whispered.

"For your sake, I hope so."

"No, you don't understand. Vampire spawn need to eat and then sleep to transition into *full-fledged* vampires. Then those vampires need to eat and then sleep so they can transition into elder vampires. Elder vampires then need to eat and then sleep so they can transition into *ancient* vampires. When they go through this transition, the only thing that will wake them is the death of a nearby vampire. Right now, they're vulnerable."

"How vulnerable," Burly asked.

"They won't wake up even if we stake a vampire right next to them?"

I scratched the side of my chin. "I thought you said killing one would wake the others."

"That's right."

"Why would you stake them, then?"

"To paralyze them."

I raised an eyebrow. "Staking vampires doesn't kill them?"

Lela looked at me perplexed. "Why would staking vampires kill them? You need to cut off a vampire's head to kill them, and an elder vampire will come back to life if someone then reattaches it."

"My apologies. I'm new to the whole vampire business. Anyway, it won't do you any good. You won't be able to find them. They're in a hidden room."

"You expect us to believe you?" Burly asked.

I could see he wasn't going to listen to reason. "Since you're committed to dying young, see for yourself." I pointed in the direction I sensed my makers resting. "They're that way. I'll be here when you come back for help."

The party made a quick plan that would lead to all of them dying, and then disappeared for an entire day. I listened to them stomping around the complex from my cell as they searched for the secret room. Lela was right. The vampires that had turned me wouldn't wake up for anything.

Tired and despondent, the party returned to my cell.

"This is how it's going to work," Burly said the moment they appeared. "Peppy is going to unlock your cell door, then I'm going to get in the cell *with* you. If you can fight the impulse to feed on me for a reasonable amount of time, then we're going to let you out so you can help us. If you try to kill me, I'm going to knock you senseless, and then we're going to get the hell out of here."

"No," I said simply.

He frowned. "No?"

"No. I don't like you. If you waltz in here, I'm going to try to eat you. I might not even try to fight the impulse. If you want to make this work, then you have to do it my way. And my way involves using the most likely to survive, and that is Lela. Second most likely is Peppy. Then the clean one, Rena. Then some random stranger you manage to find. Then a sewer rat. *Then* you."

"I'll go," Lela offered.

"No, you won't," Peppy said. "Without your holy magic, you won't be able to keep him off you long enough for us to save you. I'll go."

Lela shook her head. "I'm our best chance of ridding the world of this evil. It needs to be me. A higher chance of success is worth risking my life."

"Her odds are much better, Peppy."

He turned to me frowning. "Why?"

"She reminds me of my daughter."

"And that's enough to protect her?"

"It helps that she's the one who wants to help me become human again, but it's *mostly* the reminding me of my daughter."

Every word I said was true. The natural impulse to value human life was entirely gone. I was a monster.

"I'll be fine," Lela said.

"I wouldn't be that enthusiastic. Let's go with you might be okay."

"Very comforting," Peppy muttered as he approached the lock on my cell door.

I stepped back and gave him room to work. In only a few seconds, he had the lock turned and door open. Lela stepped into my cell, a room barely larger than a bedroom, and placed her back to the entrance, taking a defensive stance. The door closed behind her, then it locked.

Lela became my whole world as my instincts and hunger focused on her with hyperintensity.

Hunger is painful.

I'm not talking about the dull ache you experience when lunch is four hours late. I'm talking about the hunger you experience when your last meal was three days past, when your body has you looking for any source of sustenance. When you have a conscious awareness that your body is eating itself, and that you need to do something --anything --to stop the process.

The key to controlling yourself in such a situation is to accept that hunger is painful. Accept that you are allowing this pain. That this pain is what you want. If you don't, if you try to deny it, instead, you're in for a world of misery.

I told myself I wanted to feel the hunger, because if the hunger remained, I wasn't a monster. I was still the good man I had always been.

When I'd joined Sandra on her water fast, the hunger had gone away after three days. The hunger had never gone away as a vampire. Every minute was agony, more intense than anything I experienced that week.

People think when you're starving you dream about eating the entire McDonalds menu, but that's the sort of thing you dream about when you're hungry. When you're starving, your body is eating itself, and all it wants to do is stop eating itself.

In this state, you dream about things that will stop this slow death, even if it is only for a little while. The thought of eating a single ripe raw tomato without anything else is enough to leave you salivating for hours. It's intense and different to anything you experience with normal hunger.

Starving as a vampire was nothing like starving as a human. There was no slow reduction in expectations. It grew with each passing day. I wanted the entire McDonald's *staff* and the people coming through the drive-through. It was like the worst sugar crash met the worst cravings of my life, and gave birth to something that would see me driving my car through a supermarket window at three in the morning just so I could get a Snicker's bar.

It was the kind of hunger that stopped you from being human, like your entire body was on fire and the water was only a few feet away. All you had to do for relief was feed.

I scratched the back of my head and gave a dry chuckle. "Well, this is awkward."

Lela frowned, her back pressed against the door. "Why is this awkward?"

"I thought I was only able to control myself because you were out of reach, but it's the same."

"You're not struggling?"

I shook my head. "No more than before."

"Can I come closer?"

"Sure."

She got a lot closer than I expected, standing only a few inches away. "Are you okay with this?"

I nodded. "No change."

"What about this." She turned her back on me.

I felt my fangs descend and threw myself backwards, slamming into the wall. "Turn around."

She spun.

If I still had a heartbeat, it would have been hammering. Certain predatory instincts that I didn't know I possessed had kicked in when she had left herself exposed. It wasn't hunger. It was something more primal. Something I hadn't needed to deal with yet.

"Are you okay?"

I held up my hand, hoping she would stay back. "Give me a minute." It took longer than a minute, but I eventually settled down. "Okay, I'm good. New rule. No one shows me their back."

"Try standing close again to see if anything has changed," Burly suggested.

Lela nodded and then walked way too close, getting in my personal space.

"It's the same."

"Let me circle around you to see if that makes a difference."

She circled around me, making sure she remained facing me.

"It's fine."

Lela exited the cell, and then their party discussed how they would work with me. Having me at the front of the group was a must, but they also discussed how they would have to move if they got into a fight.

Eventually, they came up with a method they were happy with and released me. Then they let me march through the hallways at sword point.

The subterranean structure we travelled through was just more of what I had already seen. Smooth brick walls and cells. It was a world without change and appealed to my new aesthetics. I found it comforting.

I knew I shouldn't have, but I couldn't help the way I felt.

The ghouls I saw in the cells no longer looked human. Their fingers had become claws, and their eyelids had fused together. They were emaciated creatures with sharp teeth, and they hung from the ceiling by clawed feet.

After a few false turns, I found the right hallway and stopped in front of the false wall the vampires were sleeping behind. "They're behind this wall."

"This wall," Burly said.

"Is there an echo in here? Yes, this wall. Try to find a secret switch or something."

"It's an enchanted lock," Rena said. "Without him pointing it out, I wouldn't have noticed it."

"There's actually something here," Burly said.

"Yes."

"Told you."

Burly ignored me. "How quickly can you open it?"

Rena waved her hand and muttered an incantation. The wall immediately swung in. "That quickly."

The room beyond was a large, open space filled with expensive-looking trinkets, wall-to-ceiling tapestries, several large chests, and thirteen standing sarcophagi. All but one of the sarcophagi were made from stone. The largest appeared to be made from lead and sat in the middle of the far wall in a place of prominence.

I shook my head in Rena's direction. "You know, you should warn your party when you're going to open the door to a room filled with vampires. Not only is it common courtesy, it's also common sense."

Burly continued to ignore me. "Vampire, take the lead."

I looked into room. There were two ritual circles made from old blood in the centre, one of which was made from *my* blood and had been used to summon the demon. The other had been used to summon me. Red crystals sat in small alcoves, providing an ominous light that made everything look like it was bathed in blood.

This was where I had died. That meant it should have bothered me. It didn't. It felt like *home*.

The room didn't bother me, but it was still dangerous. "Peppy, can I get some support up here? I don't want to discover a trap with my intestines."

"We should leave," Lela whispered.

"What is it now?" Burly whispered back.

Lela raised her hand. "That's a lead coffin. Only *ancient* vampires require lead coffins. If it's further along in the transformation than we think, we won't be able to kill it."

Burly scowled. "But if we do, we will save the kingdom from suffering unimaginable evil."

Wanting to get out of the situation I had found myself in and return to the world of the living, I tapped Peppy's arm. "They're going to go back and forth until they eventually settle on going in, so we might as well get started on sorting the loot. Remember, tell me to stop before I step on a trap."

I crossed the room. Peppy didn't follow.

"But I don't know how to recognise traps."

I turned and glared over my shoulder from the opposite side of the room. "You waited to tell me that until after I crossed the room, didn't you."

Peppy began walking forward. "You're the only one that won't die if they discover what their intestines look like. Seemed wise to wait."

"You just moved down the survival list, Peppy. Not smart."

He shrugged.

While Burly and Lela argued, the rest of us investigated the room. For obvious reasons, we started with the chests. Peppy undid the locks, and then the three of us whistled appreciatively.

"That is a lot of silver and gold," I said.

Rena didn't agree. "It's mostly silver. We'll be lucky if there are a few thousand gold pieces between the chests. After guild taxes, crown taxes, and the lawyers take their cut, we'll only see a thousand gold from this. The bounty on the vampires is bigger than that."

Peppy closed the lid and looked back to the entrance. Burly and Lela had finished their argument and noticed they were the only ones still in the corridor. They quickly hurried into the room.

Burly glared at me and pointed to a spot beside the lead sarcophagus. The sarcophagi were aligned in a semi-circle, feet facing the door. There was a gap beside where the lead sarcophagus and the wall met that was just big enough for me to fit.

The party gathered around the lead sarcophagus, and then together we grabbed the lid and slid it open. Inside stood a pale, regal looking man with short-cut hair and a dense beard. His body was covered in thick muscle, giving the impression of a sleeping knight.

Since becoming a vampire, I'd been able to sense the life in living things. The life energy that radiated from his body was dozens of times stronger than the group I was with, like dozens of undigested meals. My fangs extended as my hunger grew.

The only reason I didn't jump on him immediately was there was no sweetness to his blood to entice me. He smelled like a corpse. Or perhaps a salad. There was certainly nourishing life within him, but it was not the sort of life that left me salivating.

Peppy nocked an arrow, crouched, and then fired it up at an angle, going through the vampire's diaphragm and under the rib cage, before piercing the heart.

"Lord Denton," Burly growled. "At one point, he was the king's guardsman. Now, he's a mass-murdering fuck stain. We'll stake the others. You stay where you are, vampire."

Burly led his party to the next sarcophagus, where they repeated the process. Then the next. Then the one after that. When the last vampire was staked with an arrow through the heart, it was safe to kill the vampires, and wake their paralyzed neighbours. Thus, Burly drew his shortsword without ceremony and brought it down on the neck of the first sleeping vampire.

From deep within the dungeon, the ghouls began to howl. They had sensed the death of their master and woken. The vampires in the room had not.

Lela calmly drew her dagger, stepped to the side, and thrust it through Rena's kidney, giving the knife a vicious twist with a grin on her face. The sorcerer collapsed, with a soft whimper.

Peppy nocked an arrow, muttering a word that caused the tip to glow green, and then fired it at Burly's head.

Burly shouted a word and raised his bracer, knocking the arrow aside, before pivoting and thrusting with his shortsword, forcing Peppy to block with his bow. The wood barely held, stopping the blade long enough for Peppy to take a step back. Then it snapped along the cut.

While Peppy went for his shortsword, Burly changed his grip, holding his sword like a spear. He launched it at Lela, who had picked Rena up by her hair, so she could slit her throat. The tip of the sword went through one side of Lela's neck and out the other, killing her instantly.

The smell of so much fresh blood pushed me over the edge, wearing away my failing resistance. With the last of my will, I dove into the lead sarcophagus and slid the lid closed behind me.

The madness of thirst took me while I was alone in the darkness, and I sank my teeth into Lord Denton's throat. Sickly cold blood filled my mouth as my hunger made the world vanish.

When I came too sometime later, there was no Lord Denton, just a pile of ash at my feet and an absence of the pain that had been plaguing me for thirty-four days.

I could sense only one life outside the sarcophagus. It was weak and growing weaker.

I pushed the lid aside.

Burly sat with his back against the entrance, holding his bloody side. He gave me a red grin as he saw me. "Come to finish me off?"

The smell of blood assaulted my nostrils, making me salivate, but its attraction was nothing compared to before I ate. It didn't overwhelm me, only made me feel like I was missing out on the best meal of my life. Behind him, the ghouls pounded at the door, howling madly.

I glanced at the three dead bodies, curious about what had happened. "Do you know why they did it?"

He scowled. "I'm guessing, but I would say they were members of the cult. One of the vampires likely promised them they would become their second in command if they broke in here while they were sleeping and killed their competition for them."

"Is there anything I can do for you?" It seemed like the right thing to say. The kind of thing I would have said in the past.

He nodded. "Finish the vampires off for me."

"Besides that."

"There is no getting out of here alive without my party. There's a horde of ghouls between me and freedom. It would be suicide to try, and I'd rather die as I am than see myself become one of those creatures."

"I think we can take them."

He started to chuckle and then winced. "Your average ghoul can tear a vampire spawn limb from limb. You stand even less of a chance than I do."

That surprised me. "Why would they attack me? Aren't we related or something?"

"You wish. Ghouls only obey their creators. You're nothing but food to them."

"That's unfortunate."

"You're a very odd vampire." He paused and then sighed. "How did you end up here?"

"I was summoned from another world. They beat me to a pulp when I arrived, tied me up, summoned a demon with my blood, became vampires, feasted on me, turned me into a vampire, and then threw me in the cell and forgot about me."

Burly suddenly smiled. It was the first real smile I'd seen from him. "You're a Hero?"

"So, they keep telling me."

"In that case, I pledge my life and my soul to the Hero. Let his path be my path and his fate be my fate."

A very holy-looking light enveloped Burly, and his smile grew. A feeling settled in my chest. It was a tether between us that told me he was mine. Somehow, I knew harming him would now be impossible.

"I dreamed about doing that as a kid," he said, content. "Didn't think I would ever get the chance. Didn't think I'd be worthy."

I scratched my chest, trying to remove the uncomfortable sensation. "You change your mind about breaking out of here?"

He shook his head. "That would be a death sentence. However, you might survive. I take it that you ate Lord Denton."

"I believe so."

"Good. Eat the others. Then climb into his sarcophagus and go to sleep. Vampires bear the Curse of Sloth. You won't awaken until you grow hungry, or until someone disturbs your slumber. You should wake several months from now, which might give you a chance of making a run for it. Find the church and ask them to lift your curse."

I stepped out of the sarcophagus, walked across the room, and offered Burly my hand. He took it, clasping my wrist. "What's your name?"

"Denton, son of Denton."

I glanced behind me. "That was your old man."

"Yes."

"You're a better man than he was."

"I like to think so."

Denton, son of Denton died with a smile on his face. I closed his eyes to this horrible world and then did as he instructed, putting the head back on the elder vampire who Burley had decapitated, so I could consume him. Without the hunger, drinking vampire blood was a horrible experience. But one by one, they turned to ash. Bloated from a sickening amount of cold blood, I gathered the ash in the lead sarcophagus and the ones next to it into three separate coin pouches and then placed Denton and Rena's bodies inside them, leaving the other two on the ground to rot. Denton and Rena had saved my life. I owed them.

I climbed into the lead sarcophagus, closed the lid, and prayed I'd wake to a safer world.

1

TEN YEARS LATER

Vampires do not dream. Only the living dream. For vampires, the world falls away, and a sense of peace engulfs everything we are, wrapping us in warm, loving arms that promise to never let go. The tranquillity this brings consumes us. It is a thick blanket we do not want to leave on a cold winter's day, so necessity must force us from this peaceful slumber. Usually, hunger drags us to the waking world, but hunger never bothered me.

I woke ten years later, to someone tearing the lid from my sarcophagus. How I knew I had slept so long was not my immediate concern as the lead lid of my sarcophagus was flying across the room and my new instincts warned me there was a threat capable of killing me nearby.

I flung my body towards the ceiling. The small cracks in the stonework were enough for me to find purchase with my fingertips, and I scurried along the roof like a cockroach, moving by instinct, and heading for the closed door.

Radiant light enveloped the room a second later, and I snapped my gaze to those below.

A familiar young man stood in the middle of the room where I was turned. The blood summoning circles beneath his feet had faded with the passage of time, becoming dust, and the red glowing crystals in the small alcoves had lost their light, leaving the room less ominous. At the edge of the room stood three robed women: a blonde, a brunette, and a redhead. They each held a staff in their right hand and looked to be in their mid-twenties. They were in the process of moving their heads to track my movements, while the familiar-looking man held me firmly with his gaze.

"Dad?" he called, tentatively and full of surprise.

I froze, shocked as his voice and features took on new meaning. "Luke."

Horror replaced his surprise. "Are you a fucking vampire?"

Older instincts kicked in, brought on by years of habit. "Don't swear, Son."

The three women's heads finished turning and they lifted their staffs. All sorts of magic bombarded me, knocking me from the ceiling with thunderous cracks. My back hit the ground, and more magic piled on top. It stung a little, as my flesh was torn and burned, only to immediately reform, unharmed.

"My spells aren't working," the brunette shouted. She reached into her white robe and lifted a strange prism-shaped object, pointing it in my direction.

As my shock faded, joy filled me. Ignoring the spells, I jumped to my feet and ran towards my boy. While I was trapped in my cell, I had made peace with never seeing him again, but now that he was here before me, I wanted nothing more than to embrace him.

His sword pierced my heart as my arms wrapped around his shoulders. I didn't care. "My boy. My beautiful little boy."

"Dad," he said weakly.

"The vampire's got Luke! Restrain it."

Mystical chains wrapped around my limbs as I hugged him tight. "You were sixteen the last time I saw you. I'm so sorry I wasn't there for you."

"Dad." It seemed to be the only thing he could say.

"Luke, that creature is not your father," the brunette shouted. "Kill it."

Those words seemed to snap him out of his stupor. Then I discovered I was hugging a shark and my instincts that he was dangerous weren't lying. Without any effort, Luke picked me up and held me at arm's length. My feet dangled above the ground as he manhandled me as easily as I had handled him as a toddler.

A murderous rage transformed his features, filled with years of pain and loss. He'd grown into his features, with a strong jaw and soft hazel eyes. He was classically handsome with his light brown hair cut short and styled back. He must have become attached to the gym, because the size of his muscles was apparent through his sapphire blue plate armour.

"I've got him," he warned. "Kill him quickly."

I needed to de-escalate the situation.

When I failed to break free with strength, I tried talking. "Son, I know you're upset with me. But killing your old man isn't the right way deal with these emotions."

"Fuck off; you're not my dad."

Several ice spears penetrated my chest, shattering against a barrier that covered his breastplate. They stung a little as the exploded from my ribcage. But the ice quickly melted, and the stinging went away.

"Language, Son."

"I don't have to listen to you." Clearly, he was in denial.

More spells hit me. They had very little effect.

I could tell he didn't believe I was who I claimed to be. So, with my best James Earl Jones impression, I said, "Luke, I am your father."

"Noooooo," he screamed, reflexively.

We had been doing this ever since he was four and I'd shown him the original Star Wars trilogy. He used to love it because it was the only time he was allowed to scream in the house.

"The vampire's hurting Luke; do something."

"My holy magic won't work on him," the brunette said.

I glanced over my shoulder at the brunette in white. "I've never killed anyone. I'm still one of the good guys."

"We're dead," she whispered, catching my meaning. "We're all dead."

"That's a little dramatic, don't you think. I mean I haven't harmed anyone."

"Do something," Luke shouted. "I can't hold him forever. He's a tough sonofabitch."

"Please, don't talk about your grandmother that way, Luke."

"You can't kill an ancient vampire without holy magic. They heal too quickly."

A pillar of fire engulfed the centre of my body, and for the first time since awakening, I experienced actual pain. My body thrashed for who knows how long, until Luke's grip weakened. Several seconds later, I managed to fling myself from the inferno. I bounced along the floor, and the pain vanished. Sensing another spell coming for me, I leapt to the side as three ice spears slammed into the wall.

I bounced back to my feet with unnatural ease and turned back to my son and his friends. "Would you please stop trying to kill me?"

Luke drew his sword and flashed towards me. I managed to sidestep his first swing, but the second cleaved my arm off, which immediately pulled itself back to my body, where it repaired itself.

I stared at my arm for a fraction of a second. "That's new."

Luke used my distraction to cut off my head. *The same thing happened.*

Feeling a whole lot less worried about imminent death, I decided to do what all parents do with grumpy, misbehaving children. I ran them around in circles until they tired themselves out.

The cleric went through her repertoire of spells, before collapsing. The blonde throwing the ice collapsed next. The redhead throwing fire followed a few moments later. Luke took a little longer, but he eventually dropped to his knees, so out of breath he couldn't speak.

Seeing an opportunity, I sat beside him and explained what had happened to me. He was several inches over six feet, much taller than when he was a teen, and far more muscular, with thick biceps and thighs. He wore his set of sapphire blue plate armour like a second skin; but through his open face helmet, his features still reminded me of the boy he had been. He listened to me talk about my experiences, and as his breathing slowed, he didn't go for his weapon.

"You were summoned here by a cult of vampire wannabees?"

"Yep."

"That must have sucked."

I smirked at him. "You know how I feel about puns, Son."

"The lowest circle of Hell is reserved for traitors and those who use puns."

I chuckled, feeling more alive than I had since arriving in this world. "I'm glad you remembered. Now be honest with me, am I or am I not a sexy vampire?"

He scrunched up his face. "I'm not going to answer that."

I grinned back. "I'll take that as a yes."

"I didn't say that."

"You didn't need to. The envy is evident."

He smirked. "You can keep believing that, old man."

"I hope I don't sparkle."

He chuckled.

I glanced at his three female companions. "I knew letting you watch those harem anime wasn't good for you."

He groaned. "I don't have a harem, Dad."

"That's exactly what a son with a harem would tell their father."

"They're married."

"To each other? That's even weirder."

"To their husbands."

"I'm beginning to feel uncomfortable about this harem of yours, Son."

He ignored me. "Men are predisposed to becoming warriors. We get more benefit from strength, endurance, and constitution than women do. I don't have any magical ability, so the king filled my party with the strongest mages of my generation."

That wasn't something that could happen quickly. "How long have you been here?"

"As long as you. Mum and Kathrine are here, too, but I didn't find out until five years ago. Mum was summoned by the church in a distant land to fight a lich king. Kathrine was summoned to help fight a dark lord terrorizing another kingdom. I was brought here to deal with the chaos that has been plaguing this kingdom since they closed the hellmouth."

I felt myself smile. "You're all here."

He gave a grim smile. "We're all here."

"We should go find them."

Luke sighed. "Mum remarried. His name is Marcius."

"She what?"

"You've been gone a decade."

I frowned, a little bothered by the news, but less than I knew I should have been. "When did she remarry?"

"A couple of years ago. They started dating four years after she got here."

I shrugged, no longer bothered.

"You're not upset."

"Your mother and I agreed a long time ago that if the other died, we would wait two years and start dating even if we didn't want to. Is she happy?"

"She is."

"Good."

"This isn't how I expected you to react."

"I'm a vampire. We seem to think differently."

"How differently?"

"Things I know should bother me, don't bother me anymore. I also seem to have a limited range of emotions. I can feel love. I can feel amusement. But I don't feel lasting happiness or sadness. I can grieve, though. And I do get angry and frustrated."

"Vampires are depicted as blood-thirsty fiends in this world."

"That apparently happens when we take our first innocent life. Until then, we're sort of in between. Speaking of in between, I need to find a cleric to lift this curse."

"That won't work," Luke's white-robed companion replied, while slowly sitting up.

I turned to her. "Why not?"

She began brushing herself off. "You're an ancient vampire. Any cleric worthy of the name can excise the demon inside a vampire spawn, but it would take a *saint* to remove the one in you. And there are no saints left in this world."

"Dad, this is Mara. Mara this is my dad, Vincent."

"Mara, why do you keep calling me an ancient vampire?"

"Because that is what you are."

"Last time I checked I was a vampire spawn. How did that change?"

"Older vampires feed younger vampires their blood to strengthen their bloodlines before their first kill. You said you sucked an ancient vampire and then an entire room full of elder vampires dry before feeding on your first kill. Your bloodline is now stronger than all of theirs."

That was annoying, but the annoyance quickly passed as I adjusted to my new situation. "Does being an ancient vampire come with any benefits?"

"Besides a whole host of attributes, you don't share most vampire weaknesses. You can walk in daylight. Silver and garlic don't bother you. Dead man's blood isn't an issue. This isn't because you are immune to them. You just heal so fast that they don't bother you. Staking you through the heart won't work unless you're already asleep, so the only things that can stop you are natural running water and holy magic. But you haven't killed any innocent people, so holy magic is out. You're basically unkillable, unless we can carry you to a large-enough river." She paused. "I've got a book on vampires if you're interested."

She was trying to distract me, but I couldn't turn down her offer. I needed information. "If you wouldn't mind."

Mara reached for the pouch on her belt and opened it much wider than I would have suspected was possible, before pulling out a book that shouldn't have fit inside.

"Bag of holding?" I asked Luke.

"They call them storage pouches, but same principle."

"Cool."

Mara tossed the book across the room to me.

I caught the book and turned to Luke. "Do you mind calming your friend while I read this?"

Luke nodded.

I started reading.

Most of the book revolved around the ways to kill a vampire, but there were several sections that explained what a vampire was, and what they were capable of doing. I was apparently a lesser demon. A servant of Hell. There was only one stage above an ancient vampire, and that was a primordial vampire. These creatures were *actual* demons, the kind that caused angels to descend from Heaven to do battle as their presence wasn't tolerated in this world, only lesser demons were tolerated.

While I wasn't the peak of my species, ancient vampires were considered the bane of civilisation. All lesser vampires would submit to our command. On top of this talent for leadership, we had the power to raise elder vampires, who could create stronger vampires, allowing us to construct and command the armies of Hell quickly, if we so chose.

We also didn't need to drink blood to sustain ourselves. Our hunger pulled life from the environment around us, and when we directed it, we could pull the life from someone with a touch.

The book was a rather depressing read. From what I could tell, I was bound to this location. I could leave, but once I did, I wouldn't be able to rest, which explained why I hadn't slept in the cell. So, no matter what happened, I would eventually have to return to this room. If I didn't return quickly enough, then upon arrival, I would fall into a slumber from which I could not awaken until I recovered. It would leave me vulnerable.

I closed the book and looked up to see Luke walking towards Mara. "Oh, so *that's* what it meant by vampire cunning."

Apparently, I could digest information almost instantaneously. It explained why I was able to process new experiences so quickly.

Luke glanced back and frowned. "I thought you were going to read the book?"

"I've read it already." I tossed it to Mara.

The book launched across the room at alarming speed. Luke's hand shot out and caught it inches from Mara's face. "You need to learn to control your body, Dad, or you might accidently kill someone."

"My apologies," I said, as I climbed to my feet.

She averted her eyes. "Would you mind putting some clothes on?"

I glanced down at my naked muscular form. It was all long limbs and abs, like a buff swimmer. My skin had a pale tone to it, like flawless ivory instead of sickly white. It was not the body I was used to seeing.

"You don't feel embarrassment, do you?" Luke asked.

"No." I knew I should have, but I didn't feel embarrassed.

"Give me a second, I'll find something for you." He reached for the storage pouch on his belt and withdrew an old shirt and a pair of trousers. Both were too big for me, but I put them on.

I had to hold his trousers up with one hand. "You have a belt?"

Luke threw me a piece of rope.

I put it through the loops. "So, what are the names of your other companions?" It seemed like something I should ask.

"The sorcerer is Diva, and the druid is Sharani."

"I don't know how to tell a sorcerer from a druid."

Luke pointed to the blonde passed-out woman in the red robe, stitched with mystical symbols. "Diva."

I glanced at the redhead in the green robe. "Which would make this one Sharani. Nice to meet you both. No, don't get up on my account. I can see you're both tired."

The two women remained unconscious.

"Does he think he's funny?" Mara asked.

"Yes," Luke replied. "And this isn't because he's a vampire. He's always had a terrible sense of humour."

"Your mother loved my sense of humour."

"Mum was brainwashed into thinking you were funny by grandpa."

"That man's jokes were a national treasure."

"They were terrible."

"What are we going to do about you-know-who," Mara whispered.

"I can hear the worms burrowing through the soil around us. The worms that are through several hundred feet of solid rock. Whispering won't help you. Also, I'm coming with you."

She shook her head. "We can't unleash this evil on the countryside, Luke."

I crossed my arms and rolled my eyes. "Everyone's a critic."

Luke gave a single chuckle and then his face turned grim. "We can't stop him until he kills someone. Traveling with him is our only option. Besides, he's going to need to go to the guild, if he wants to get out of the province to find my mum and sister. They're the only ones outside the army who could stop the rivers long enough for him to get out."

Mara placed a hand on Luke's shoulder. "I know he was your father, but you shouldn't trust him."

"Would it ease your mind to know I'm a hero?"

She blanched.

"Apparently not. Forget I ever said anything."

Luke frowned as he glanced at me. "You're a hero."

"It's why they summoned me. They needed special blood to make their ritual more powerful."

"Can you confirm this?"

I pointed to Burly's coffin. "The dead gentleman in there swore himself to me before he died, and this holy light enveloped him. Does that count?"

Mara scrunched up her face. "Shit."

"A lady shouldn't curse. Neither should a priest."

"I'm a cleric, and I've taken no vows barring me from swearing, so I'll say whatever the fuck I like."

"He's bullshitting you," Luke said. "He's been calling people out over swearing ever since the second Avengers movie. He thinks it's funny."

"No. I think it's hilarious. It also just so happens I prefer not to swear or listen to others do so."

Luke smiled and then sighed. "People aren't going to like it that you're a hero, Dad."

"Why not?"

"Heroes are the strongest warriors this world has. If the public finds out there is an ancient vampire hero, they will panic. They'll think it's the end of days."

"You seemed to handle me just fine."

"That's because you haven't unlocked your class. You don't have any levels, and I can only barely contain you."

"Dumb it down for me."

"If I'm Captain America, you could become Thor."

"Evil Thor. I can see why everyone would panic. I won't say anything."

"That would be for the best."

I glanced around the room and saw nothing to keep me here any longer. "Anyway, I've been asleep for the last decade, so do you kids want to get out of here? I've got a wife and daughter to reunite with, so if you don't want to come, I'll get out of your hair."

Luke glanced at his unconscious companions and then shrugged. "We just need to collect the loot, and then we'll get out of here."

"Amateur mistake, Son. You should always loot as you go. That's why I keep my loot with me."

Luke raised an eyebrow looking around. "Your loot?"

I pointed to the chests. "I killed the vampires, so it's my loot. Well technically, Denton and Rena helped, so it's a three-way split, but I'll have to hunt down their families in order to give it to them. Do you have a problem with that?"

Mara's eyes widened. "Is this where your loot fixation came from? I always thought it was strange after I met your mother and sister, but this makes a lot of sense."

"I'll arm wrestle you for it," Luke offered.

I grinned.

2

STREET MEAT

"You cheated," Luke muttered as we rode away from the manor. We were in the back of his party's wagon. It looked like one of those pioneer wagons with the hoops for the canvas cover that provided shelter. There were crates filled with food and a chest of draws that held clothing, along with what looked like a functional kitchen.

Petrified trees surrounded us. Suffering from the effects of my prolonged sleep. I would have found them a depressing sight in the past. Not anymore. They felt right, and they whizzed by surprisingly fast thanks to the enchantments on the wagon and the odd, blue horses that pulled it.

These enchantments also made the wagon bigger on the inside, nearly the size of a large living room, so there was plenty of space for everyone to stretch out.

I shrugged as I lounged on a pile of cushions. "You used your abilities first, so it was fair."

"You sucked the life out of me."

"Only a little."

"Mara says I lost a month of my life."

"I did apologise for that."

Escaping the castle had been as simple as a walk in a dog park where no one cleaned up after their pets, emphasising the age-old wisdom of the book Everybody Poops, even ghouls. Luke and his party had already killed all the ghouls on their way to the hidden room, so there was nothing in our way as we left, except the aftermath of too many mindless beasts living in a confined space.

The ghouls Sir Denton created had been plaguing the countryside for the last decade, and their numbers had tripled since their original creation. That's why my son and his party had been called in. The nearby village had been eaten, and the scourge was growing large enough to threaten towns.

Testing whether I would explode in sunlight only took a few tentative seconds as I put my finger directly into a beam of light. When nothing occurred, I happily walked out into the sun and freedom.

"A proper apology would be half the loot," Luke grumbled.

I shook my head. "That would just encourage you to be a sore loser."

"You missed like a decade of my birthdays and Christmases."

I winced, feeling that blow. "You missed just as many Father's Days."

He cringed.

"Would you two stop it," Mara shouted.

"We're negotiating," we both replied.

"I can't believe there are two of you. Guild regulations states that loot is the property of the party who makes the kill, so we don't have any rightful claim, Luke."

Luke cleared his throat. "Technically, the party died during their quest. Then the loot was claimed by the ghouls, which means we do have every right to claim it."

"You're forgetting the fact that it's *my* loot," I pointed out.

"You aren't a member of the guild. You don't get to claim it. Also, you're technically hellspawn."

"What I'm hearing is I'm a monster, and that's my loot, and you don't get to claim it until you've killed me."

"No, if you can steal something from a monster without dying, you still get to claim it," Mara replied, then she groaned. "Ignore me. I'm not involved in this conversation."

It occurred to me that I needed better material to argue with. "Mara you wouldn't happen to have a copy of the guild rules, would you?"

"Don't give it to him," Luke shouted. "He's evil. He's trying to take my loot."

Mara reached for her pouch. "The only reason I'm giving this to him is because you are more upset by the fact you might lose your loot than you are by the fact that we are aiding a creature of darkness."

I took the book and read through it in a few seconds. "Section 284, sub-section C. Loot cannot be claimed by a party or sold off, if the loot is subject to retaliation. All loot must then be transferred to the nearest guild headquarters' vaults until such time as the cause of this retaliation is vanquished. Basically, if I threaten to kill anyone you sell my loot to or use my money to purchase anything from, you can't keep it."

Luke glared. "I'd still get it eventually."

"Section 284, sub-section G. The guild reserves the right to return, destroy, or dispose of loot in the ocean, if the threat posed by the loot is greater than the guild can cope with. Threats such as this are greater dragons, liches, ancient vampires, demi-gods, ancient evils, ghost kings, and demon kings."

"It doesn't say that."

I flipped through the book and pointed to the page.

Luke took it and read. "This is bullshit. I know there is a set of rules here for heroes and loot."

I kept my expression neutral as he began thumbing through the pages. There was in fact a section on heroes and loot, and it let him claim whatever he wanted to, so long as he could prove he was strong enough to keep it safe, which he could.

I needed to distract him. "Any idea when your friends will wake up?"

"It's mana exhaustion," he said without looking over. "They'll sleep for about twelve hours and then be fine. Mara can force them to wake up if she has to, but they'll be in so much pain that there's almost no point."

I tried a different tactic. "You mentioned levels and classes earlier. Did you mean what I think you meant?"

Luke lifted his gaze and nodded. "This world is like the anime I used to watch with you. Classes are controlled by class stones. A blacksmith forge will have access to a blacksmith class stone, and a bakery will have access to a baker class stone. Touching the stone will give a person access to the class, and then they have to return and touch it again every time they level."

"You had to touch a hero stone, then."

He shook his head. "There are no hero stones. But adventurer guilds have a class hall with a universal stone that any class can use. I visited one to gain my class, and I have to visit whenever I want to level."

"Then what happens?"

"Don't answer him," Mara said.

Luke scowled, closing the book. "He could find this out from a random stranger, Mara. It's not exactly a secret."

"Let him find out from them."

"I'm not putting someone's life in danger for something everyone knows."

I smiled, proud of him and his choice.

Luke seemed to understand, because he returned the smile. "Every time your class levels, you gain attribute points. These points can be used to make you stronger, and the number you receive varies from class to class. Classes come with a few basic skills when you acquire them, and then you receive a new skill every fifth level.

Skills have their own leveling system, independent of your class system, but all you need to know right now is that every tenth class level, you can upgrade one of your existing skills to a higher tier. Occasionally, your class will receive a bonus skill when you level, but that's rare, only occurring about one in ten levels."

"Heroes aren't like other classes, I take it."

"No. Some classes lead to other classes, like most of the time you need to be a level 10 warrior to become a knight, but even the rarest and strongest classes don't give more than fifteen attributes and one skill every five levels. Heroes receive twenty attributes every time we level, along with a skill that is related to something we did during the time that it took us to level. Because of this, visiting guilds regularly is important."

"Why?"

"Skills build on each other. If you have the general swordsmanship skill, then you have a chance of gaining an advanced sword skill, like longsword. Having that advanced skill opens you up to gaining specialized skills, like parry or deflect. Which means, if I go ten levels without visiting a guild, I could miss out on a lot of potential progress."

"How do you level?"

"I kill evil."

"That's all?"

He shrugged. "Mostly. My first few levels came from training, but after level 5 that didn't help anymore. Mum leveled a lot from doing good deeds, but she has divine gifts I don't have access to. Kathrine also has more room for growth when it comes to training, so she reached level 15, before she had to fight."

"Hypothetically, how high would your level be if you killed an ancient vampire and a bunch of elder vampires."

"Mercy above," Mara whispered.

Luke leaned back, elbowing the pile of pillows behind him, as he scowled. "That depends on a lot of things. You've got the level difference between you and what you kill, but also the power difference. You've got how evil they were and how much destruction they caused. You haven't even unlocked your class, so you could potentially be a higher level than I am once you unlock it, which is why I'll stop you if you try."

"You still don't trust me?"

"I can't. And I don't want to. Life has taught me there is real evil in this world. The things I've seen don't leave me the option of trusting a vampire. Even one that was once my father."

"We're approaching Braywood," Mara announced.

"Bypass it," Luke replied.

"We need to inform the mayor that it's safe for people to leave."

"I don't want to give my father the chance of causing a massacre."

"Diva and Sharani need a proper bed to help them recover."

"And I can control myself more than you think."

"Vampires can't control their hunger," Mara retorted.

"I'm hungry right now and I'm in complete control."

Luke frowned at me. "You literally just sucked the life out of me. How can you be hungry?"

I frowned back, because that was true. I'd only taken a nibble, but Luke's life force was much stronger than anyone else's I had seen. So that small bite was more than some people had altogether. "I don't know."

"It's the sunlight," Mara said. "He's constantly healing, so he needs to eat more often."

"How often?" Luke asked, concerned.

"Vampires usually only need to feed once a month, but the frequency increases after injuries. He might need to feed once a week or every day like this."

Luke swore as he went for the pouch on his belt, tossing me a cloak, a pair of gloves, and socks. "Put those on. We'll stop in Braywood and find you somewhere out of the sun. You should have mentioned this earlier, Mara."

"I'm adequately familiar with the vampire literature, not an expert. You can't expect me to think of everything."

I kept plying Luke with questions to distract him until Mara slowed the wagon. At which point we both turned to look at the village. Braywood was not what I expected. It had a fifty-foot stone wall, which was twenty feet thick. The gate was several wagons wide, and a pair of shoddily dressed guards stood above it.

"That's a big wall."

Mara snickered.

Luke chuckled. "They use geomancers for construction here. Builders only need to dress the interior. A penniless peasant has a house larger than your average well-off suburban family back home."

"Is that why the subterranean structure was so big?"

"Yeah, small palaces tend to be the size of theme parks here, and large ones are the size of inner cities. They don't have our technology, but magic and classes make them more productive than we were back home. There is very little poverty, and no sickness thanks to clerics. Gold is also worth a lot less."

"How much less?" I asked, eyeing my chests unhappily.

"A gold coin is the equivalent to about fifty bucks. A silver piece, is worth one."

I stared at the chests, doing the math. "So, this is close to sixty grand."

"About that."

"How?"

"Geomancers can throw up a wall like this in less than a day. They can extract gold just as quickly. Without all the hard work and machinery involved, gold is more common."

"Who has approached the gate?" one of the guards yelled down.

"The hero's party," Mara shouted back. "Open the gate; we need to talk to the mayor."

THE MAYOR'S house had eighteen bedrooms, three floors, and several lounges. It was massive, but far from the largest house in the village. His study, while large, held very little in the way of furniture and decoration, denoting the difference between architecture and wealth on this world.

He was also quite rude and quite possibly the evilest man I'd ever met.

"Who's the funny-looking stranger?" he asked, the moment we entered.

Black smoke oozed from his eyes, as a web of black veins crisscrossed his skin. There was a slight ting of sulphur in his scent, and an aura surrounded him that told me he belonged to the night.

His appearance surprised me so much, I reacted sarcastically. "Not an ancient vampire if that's what you're thinking."

Mara's mouth dropped open as Luke groaned.

The man scowled. "Oh, you're a bard."

"I prefer the term comedian."

"That generally requires you to be funny."

"Maybe you just aren't cultured enough to understand my humour."

"You think highly of yourself for someone who is a walking cliché. Wandering around after the kingdom's hero in order to write an epic ballad. That's something only a talentless hack would do."

"Do you mind not insulting my bard," Luke snapped.

The mayor blanched. "My apologies, hero. I take it you've dealt with our problem."

He nodded. "There can't be more than a handful of ghouls left. If you want them gone, post a quest with the guild. I don't deal with problems that small."

"Thank you. Is there anything I can do for you?"

"We need a place to stay. Two of my party are suffering from mana sickness. We'll leave the moment they recover."

"I'll ask my wife to prepare your rooms. Will you join us for the celebration?"

Luke gave a begrudging nod.

SINCE NO ONE else seemed to care about the black smoke gaze of the mayor, I didn't either. Maybe it was a cultural thing. Maybe he was a different species. I didn't care enough to ask. I spent the day resting in the cellar, being guarded by my son. Then we went to the celebration.

There were speeches and cheering and then food and beer. People sang in the streets while children ran about playing games. It was rather dull.

The village housed fewer than two-thousand people, and the average family seemed to have a dozen kids, so it was a tight community. I spotted several black-gazed individuals, along with a few gentle, white-gazed individuals, as I wandered through the crowd. As the night lengthened, Luke grew less concerned, allowing me to wander further and further away.

Regular food didn't have the same pull as it once had. I felt no hunger for it. But not being hungry had never stopped me from eating, so I sampled anything that looked particularly interesting, enjoying it as much as I had in the past. Their beer was surprisingly good, but it had no lasting effects; a little tipsy was the furthest I could go.

A few hours after the party started, I watched a boy run down a barely lit alley, fleeing from another child who was counting. Then I watched a man with black eyes, sneak off after him.

My instincts told me he was hunting.

Intrigued, I followed, slowly blending into the crowd, before entering the alley a few minutes later and moving faster. I blurred past the man as he exited another alley and found the boy dead, neck snapped in a clean, precise way.

The alley was filled with trash, piled high to hide the body from the street. It smelled atrocious despite the cool night air. I felt no hunger, no excitement at the sight of his dead little body, only rage. It was an all-consuming fury that could not be denied.

I did not think.

I did not plan.

I just pivoted and rushed his killer, like a father who had found his own son would.

The man crumbled to dust as my fingers wrapped around his throat and I tore every ounce of life from his body, satisfying the hunger within. As quickly as my rage ignited, it was sated. Then my son ran me through with his sword, pinning me to the wall with his strength.

"I can explain," I said, nervously.

"Mara, hit it with a holy magic. I can't contain it for long."

"You-" Holy light enveloped me. "-don't have to do that."

Luke lost his glare and began to frown. "Why aren't you burning? You just killed a man."

"I'll let the evidence speak for itself," I said, pointing further down the alley.

Mara rushed past and then swore, dropping to her knees behind the pile of rubbish. Holy light filled the alley, it was warm and caring, overflowing with love and life, then the boy began to cry. Mara picked him up and he clung to her. "It's okay. You're all right. I've got you."

"He wasn't exactly an innocent. But I mean who could have realised with all that black smoke coming from his eyes, right."

Mara's gaze snapped towards me. "Did you say you saw black smoke coming from his eyes?"

"I take it you didn't?"

"No."

"I need an explanation, Mara," Luke growled. "What's going on. We just saw him kill an innocent."

"Evidence would suggest otherwise," she said, unhappily. "My spell didn't work any better than in the past, so what we thought was a man was either a monster in disguise or an Unseen."

"You can remove the sword now," I said, patting Luke on the shoulder. "No hard feelings."

Luke stepped back and pulled his sword from my stomach.

I glanced behind me, to confirm what I suspected. "You can cut through stone."

"It's less impressive than it sounds," he said. "Mara, any clue what he means by black smoke coming from his eyes?"

"He might possess the evil eye, but that's only a guess."

"What's the evil eye?"

"It's the ability to see good and evil. If that wasn't a monster, then he was Unseen. I think I remember reading a description of Unseen having black smoke oozing from their eyes when viewed by those with the evil eye."

"What's an Unseen?" I asked.

Luke sighed as he sheathed his sword. "Good and evil are tangible things in this world, Dad. They aren't constructs like where we come from. Unseen are people who have done so much evil that it has seeped into their souls. There is no saving them or changing them; they will keep causing harm until they're stopped. They're walking abominations."

Mara nodded. "Holy magic won't harm a murderer, but it will harm the Unseen."

I absently scratched the spot where I'd been stabbed. "Is that why guild rules say they have to be killed or apprehended on discovery?"

Mara nodded again as she clutched the whimpering boy.

"Do you want me to get rid of the rest of them?"

Luke frowned. "There are more?"

"About a dozen."

"I can test them," Mara said. "Let me return the boy to his parents, and then we'll see if you really can see Unseen."

"And if I can?"

"You can eat them."

For the next fifteen minutes, I couldn't stop smiling. Mara returned the boy to his parents, and then I pointed out an Unseen to

Luke, who grabbed the woman off the street without anyone seeing. In a side alley, while Luke held her mouth closed, Mara cast a spell that burned her skin clean off.

"She's Unseen," Mara said. "You can eat her without consequence."

"Why?"

"She's evil. Even Heaven won't judge you for this."

"Why not?"

The woman continued to thrash in Luke's grip, releasing muffled screams. "Think of the Unseen like outlaws," he said. "They have strayed so far from Heaven's path that they no longer receive Heaven's mercy. They are viewed as demons, and there are no consequences for harming demons, only for helping them."

"That seems a little harsh. God's supposed to be about mercy."

"Talk to mum if you want a religious lesson. All I know is there is no saving the Unseen. Eat her or don't eat her, either way she's dying here."

"Really?"

He gave a grim nod. "The Unseen are like psychopathic serial killer, rapist, pedophiles that think the guards at Auschwitz were amateurs. It doesn't matter what led them to this point. All that matters is that there is no coming back."

I wasn't about to turn down a free lunch, so I reached out and grabbed her wrist and ate. Her body began to wither as the life drained from her. Her flesh wrinkled and then grew dry before she finally crumbled to dust.

Luke began brushing himself down.

"That was slower than before," Mara said.

I shrugged. "I'm not hungry or angry."

"Why didn't you drink her blood?"

I smirked. "I'm abstinent."

"What?"

"You can't get addicted to crack if you don't try it."

"What?"

I rolled my eyes. "Human blood has the most inviting smell I've ever experienced. It's hard enough controlling myself around the scent without knowing what it actually tastes like. I would prefer to remain in control, instead of tempting myself. So, no blood for me."

"How long do you think you can maintain that?"

I turned around and started walking away. "No idea; but eating the rest of the Unseen should make it easier."

3

ACCUSATIONS

Luke and his party had no problem with me eating Unseen. However, they didn't like having to explain the death of the mayor and his wife to the village. Nor all the other deaths that occurred through our brief stay. When I suggested we just dine and dash, they looked at me funny and went back to dealing with the panic.

With a viable source of food for me, Luke and his party didn't care about keeping me on a leash, preferring to have me wear a holy symbol as proof I hadn't strayed, so every town and village we passed through over the next few days found itself with a few less citizens.

There was a surprisingly large number of Unseen wherever we went. Mara said that was because the province of Hellmouth was on a hellmouth. The unholy aura it produced attracted Unseen to the area. Crime rates were several times higher here than anywhere else, and people were more prone to violence.

Thirty years ago, when the hellmouth opened, the province's entire population and most of the army and adventurers were killed, throwing the kingdom into chaos. Cheap, fertile land and overcrowding in the other provinces, mixed with monster threats, were the only reasons people lived here now. The nation was still recovering from the event, trying to stitch together the shredded tatters that had once been a mighty kingdom.

Luke and his party were on loan to the local guild headquarters to help the province deal with the larger threats that normal adventurers couldn't handle but were still too small for the army. They had been moving from place to place for the last five years, like they were here in Hellmouth, cleaning up the kingdom. And they were finally seeing progress.

It was nice to know my son was a good man.

Mara stopped the wagon behind an inn as the dawning sun rose. I jumped out the back, landing effortlessly on the cobblestones. A stableboy, perhaps ten years old, dashed forward to help, eyes smoking black. I was so used to eating Unseen by this point that I didn't give it a second thought as I appeared behind him, grabbed him by the scruff of the neck and drained him.

As Luke climbed out, the boy crumbled to dust.

Mara's mouth hung open.

I patted my stomach, appreciatively. "That was different. A little more zing than I'm used to, but in a good way."

"That was a child," Mara hissed.

"And he was delicious."

Diva and Sharani exited the back of the wagon and looked around.

"What happened?" Diva asked.

"Dad ate some Unseen kid," Luke replied, throwing a dressed boar over his shoulder. "I'll see you all later. I've got to take this to the butcher."

"You're not going anywhere," Mara snapped. "You're staying here and watching him. We need to investigate this."

"What's there to investigate. Dad's wearing the amulet and it hasn't melted, *ergo* the kid was Unseen."

Mara gritted her teeth and counted to ten, then jumped into her rant. "Don't you find that a little convenient. He's been eating someone at every village. Either the church isn't doing its job properly, or he's somehow eating innocent people without suffering the consequences. The child is the last straw. I'm not comfortable letting him roam free until I find evidence that the boy was evil."

Luke sighed and handed the boar to Sharani. "I want decent steaks for this. You know the cut."

She scowled. "Why do you always have to trade for steaks? Chicken is just as good."

Luke glanced at Diva. "Make sure she gets steak." Then he turned to me. "Come on, I'll let you buy me a beer."

I chuckled and followed him into the inn. The back hallway led to a massive tavern that could seat three hundred, but only a handful of people were present. We'd stayed at places like this over the past few days. Buildings that could house a crowd, but only catered to a few.

Luke walked up to the innkeeper, a portly gentleman with impressive arms, who seemed to recognise him. "What can I do for you, hero?"

"We need rooms for the day and space in your cellar. Also, your stableboy was found to be an Unseen."

The innkeeper blanched. "You're certain?"

Luke nodded.

"I never suspected a thing."

"We're investigating the cause."

"Investigating?"

"Unseen children aren't common. We need to investigate whether someone created him or if he was born that way."

"I don't know which sounds worse."

"Created is definitely worse, in my experience."

The innkeeper didn't know what to say to Luke, so he changed the subject. "I'll begin preparing your rooms. Is there anything else I can do for you?"

"Beer. It's been a long night."

The innkeeper hurried off without saying another word, and we took a seat at a nearby table. We sat in silence until the beer arrived, then we drank.

"You're less talkative than you used to be," Luke said an hour later.

I considered his words for a moment. "I don't feel the urge for small talk anymore. There is no awareness of the slow march of time, no need to make everything of the present."

"You're immortal."

"Perhaps. Or perhaps my life is now just that much longer that I don't care."

"What will you do when I'm gone?"

It sounded like an innocent question, but his elevated heartrate said it wasn't. "Who said you're going anywhere?"

He took his tankard between his hands and stared into the amber liquid. "The life of a hero isn't safe; and if I somehow survive, I will still grow old and die."

I gave him a small smile; anyone who saw it would have thought it cruel. "You make the assumption that I will allow that to happen."

He didn't look up as he continued to stare at his drink. "I don't want to be a vampire."

"I know."

"Yet you're going to turn me."

"Not for a long time."

"Why wait?"

"Because I love you. I want you to be happy. I want you to have a wife and children, and the love and kindness they will show you. I want you to bounce your grandchildren on your knee, and when that's all over, I want you back."

"You know I'll stop you."

"I know you will try. But I will try harder."

"You think so?"

"There aren't many things I care about anymore. You, your mother, and your sister are at the top of the list."

"Mum remarried."

I shrugged. "Only because she thought I died."

"You're seriously going to try to win Mum back?"

"She's the love of my life."

"And if she doesn't love you anymore?"

I gave a weak, dry chuckle. "That's not how love works, Son. When someone dies, you don't stop loving them. You just grow your heart so another can enter."

"What if we don't have your strength? What if we can't control ourselves?"

"I've got a lifetime to figure out how to help you with that."

"And if you don't find an answer?"

"Then I'll do my best to follow you beyond the veil."

He finally looked up, reached out, and squeezed my hand. "Thank you."

I could see I was upsetting him, and I didn't want to upset him. Not for something that was still decades away. "When do we reach this guild of yours?"

"Running water is your Kryptonite, so we can't travel directly. We're still a few days away."

"You don't sound too happy about that."

He shrugged. "I'm not sure how they will react, and I don't want them to kill you."

"You must have some pull."

"Less than you would think. I'm a commodity to them, something to be traded and used until I'm spent. Don't get me wrong. They respect me and are thankful for what I do, but that thankfulness doesn't come with any authority."

"Ever think of quitting?"

He chuckled. "No. I do too much good in this world to stop. I'll keep going until it kills me."

"Is that why you're not married?"

He groaned. "Not you too."

"I take it your mother also shares my concern."

"Look, I'll tell you the same thing I told her. I. Don't. Want. To.

Get. Married. I might be twenty-six, but I'm perfectly happy with the way things are."

It was time for some desperately needed fatherly advice. Advice I should have given him years ago. "You're clearly planning to let your job kill you, which, I take it, is why you don't want to get married. But I think you're missing something important."

"What?"

"What if, despite your best attempts, being a hero doesn't kill you? What if you overcome every obstacle and conquer every enemy, only to then grow old and die in bed? What if what you fear never comes to pass?"

"And what exactly am I afraid of?"

"The same thing most men are afraid of. That you will die early and leave your wife and kids to fend for themselves."

"Like you did."

I winced, hearing his pain. "Yes, like I did."

He sipped at his beer and then sighed. "It's more likely than not that I'll die young."

"Living for the worst possible situation is no way to go through life, Luke. Plan for the worst and live for the best. Find yourself a wife who understands that you might die out here and accepts this part of who you are."

"That seems cruel."

"Soldiers go to war every day. Sometimes they come home and kiss their partners, sometimes they don't. Some of us have to be in danger, so the rest of us can be safe. That doesn't mean they have to be a martyr, sacrificing every aspect of their lives. It doesn't mean *you* have to be a martyr either."

"I've missed you," he said quietly.

"I'm sorry for that."

Our conversation turned away from heavier topics after our little heart-to-heart, and Luke began telling me about his life since coming here. The loneliness and distress he felt upon arrival had been with him until he found his sister. The happy childhood and adult life his mother and I wanted for him had been disrupted by a need to train and a harsh new world.

It was hard to listen to.

He'd felt so alone, so cut off from everyone.

He only stopped sharing his story when tears began trailing down my cheeks. I didn't even know I was crying until he handed me a handkerchief. All I could think was that I had failed as a father.

We drank in silence.

His party showed up around lunchtime. The three women were shockingly pale, almost green. Sharani took the tankard from my hand the moment she sat and guzzled its contents. Mara met my gaze and then burst into tears.

Diva gently patted my shoulder. "You did a good thing."

Luke sighed. "That bad, huh."

"Don't make me talk about it. I don't want to remember."

4

RULES LAWYERING

Giving Luke and his party the slip was easier than you would think. My little hunting trips were no longer just tolerated but actively encouraged, making it easy for me to jump the town wall and make a run for it when we were finally close enough to the city of Hellmouth. Yes, they called the new capital Hellmouth, after renaming the province Hellmouth. It seemed like anyone with an ounce of creativity was killed when the hellmouth opened.

Crossing the nearby stream, so I could arrive faster, was much more difficult than I imagined. That single step across running water cost me the life force of two people, draining away my substantial reserves. But it didn't deter me or slow me down as I raced for my target.

The early morning sun was at my back as I carried my loot into the adventurer's guild's headquarters. The large lobby greeted me as I entered, identical to all the other adventurer guilds I'd visited along the way with Luke and his party. To my left was an even larger tavern. I could sense people sleeping on the floors above, as I wandered up to the front desk.

I gave the young lady waiting there my best smile, ready to bluff my way through our conversation. "I'd like to apply to join your guild."

She blushed, because I happened to be a sexy vampire, not your run-of-the-mill vampire. "I don't mean any offense, but you're a little old to sign up for the guild."

I clutched my chest dramatically. "You wound me. Here I am ready to throw myself at adventure and you bring up petty things like my advanced age and my bad hip. I'd like to speak to your manager."

"I'll get her for you." She turned to leave.

"I'm joking."

"And I don't have a manager," she replied turning back.

That earned a chuckle. "Can I please have forms 1A3 and 27D."

She smirked as she reached below her desk. "Most don't bother to read the guild rules before they come. I'm Heather, by the way." She handed me one of those magical pens I'd seen Luke and his party use, along with two forms.

"Who wants to spend a month going through basic training, when you can just come to the regional headquarters and pay a small fee."

"Most appreciate the experience."

"Well, not me."

I quickly filled in the form. Not so quickly as to attract unwanted attention, but quickly enough. In less than a minute, I handed her back the forms. She read through them and then stamped them both, accepting the ten gold pieces.

Then she handed me a wooden chit. "Welcome to the guild, Vincent. Is there anything else I can do for you today?"

I bent down and lifted the chests. "Can you convert this silver to gold while I use your class hall, Heather."

She frowned. "How much is in there?"

"No idea," I lied. I knew exactly how much was in there, but I needed to keep her distracted for a few minutes.

I walked past her, into the tavern, following the signs on the wall pointing to the class hall. I made my way down several hallways, to a room with no door across the entrance. In the middle of the larger-than-average room was a pedestal with an ordinary stone on top, the kind you would find on the street.

I walked over to it and placed my hand over it.

Congratulations, you have unlocked your ancient vampire race and your hero class.
Your class has leveled.
Your class has leveled.
Your class has leveled.
Your class has leveled.
Your class has leveled.
You are now a level 5 hero.

Anger filled me as my plans were suddenly dashed. "Level 5! I killed an ancient vampire and all I get is level 5! This is bull!"

I touched the stone again.

Nothing happened.

Well, one thing did happen. Someone used my distracted state to bisect me down the middle. My shirt parted and my pants dropped to my knees as the steel blade sliced them in two. Then a bear of a man leapt at me, sweeping my legs and pinning me to the ground.

I glanced over my shoulder as holy light enveloped me, to see a half-naked man on top of me. "Do you mind, I'm kind of going through something right now."

"Hit it again," the big man shouted in my ear.

I could tell he wasn't anywhere near as powerful as my son, so I grabbed his bicep to pull him off me. He fought me with everything he had, which was unfortunate, because it caused me to tug too hard.

His arm separated at the shoulder. And not the nice kind of separated at the shoulder. It wasn't a dislocation. It was a dismemberment. Blood quickly began to spurt from the wound as I stood up holding his torn-off limb, with his sword still clutched in its grip.

The guy didn't seem to notice as he leapt after me, swinging his fist.

I calmly stepped out of the way and put him in a headlock, overwhelming his skill with speed and strength. "Behave yourself, sir."

Footsteps came from all directions, and then more mages filled the doorway, staring at me and the man I was holding, unsure what to do. They had their staffs and wands raised, which gave off an ominous glow, but none of them moved to attack.

I smiled at them, trying to deescalate the situation. "Would you believe me if I said, I come in peace?"

"Kill it," the man shouted from the headlock.

"Section 81, sub-section P. No guildmember may knowingly harm another guild member, except in self-defence." I reached into my pocket and held up the wooden chit. "I might be a junior guild member, but I am in fact a guild member. Whoever the heck this is, attacked me first, so I had every right to defend myself and I am perfectly willing to hand them over and submit myself to the guild master."

One of the female mages began to tremble. "You're holding the guild master hostage."

That was unfortunate. "Section 74, sub-section G, if a guild master should harm a member of the guild even in self-defence of themselves or others, the guild master loses the right to pass judgement and is required to call in another chapter's guild master to provide impartial judgement."

"Um, before we take this any further," the female mage asked. "What are you?"

"An ancient vampire that's immune to holy magic."

She paled. "Is he lying, guild master?"

"He's an ancient vampire. I'm not entirely sure about the other part."

All the mages began to tremble.

The one that had been speaking sucked in a breath. "Why are you here?"

"I needed to use your class hall, before the hero stopped me. Not that it did me any good. I'm only level 5. Can you believe that! I killed an ancient vampire and a nest of elders and all I got is level 5. Life is so unfair."

"That is rough," one of the male mages muttered.

The satisfaction I got from someone understanding my frustration was much greater than I expected. "I know, right? How peeved would you be if you killed a threat to civilisation and only ended up level 5."

Several heads nodded in agreement.

Which gave me another wave of satisfaction and resulted in me monologing.

It was several minutes, before the female mage interrupted me. "Um, sorry to interrupt you, but the guild master just passed out from blood loss."

I glanced down. "Oops. Ah, you've got clerics around, right?"

She nodded, waving someone forward.

A young man in a white robe hurried through the group, pale as a sheet. "Can I have the arm?"

"Sure." I passed him the arm I'd been using to emphasize my points and dropped the guild master. "Where was I?"

"You were explaining how nothing in life is fair and how losing a decade of your life to kill an ancient vampire resulted in only being level 5," another mage replied.

"Exactly," I said, diving back into my monologue.

I was still going at it an hour later when Luke pushed through the crowd and entered the room. Everyone seemed to relax as he appeared, even the guild master, who had regained consciousness, but I was too caught up in the injustices of life to stop just because my son had appeared.

Three hours later, I ran out steam finally finishing with. "And that's why there is no Santa Claus, no Queen of England, and no justice in life. Freaking level 5, am I right?"

Everyone agreed.

"I need beer."

No one moved.

Luke waited a few seconds before he started speaking, making sure I was done. "It's okay, everyone, you can go back to your business. I know he was monologing, but he won't harm anyone."

"Are you sure?" the guild master asked.

"He's managed to keep his soul by only eating Unseen."

"Fuck. I was praying our clerics were too weak. How the hell are we supposed to kill an ancient vampire that is immune to holy magic?"

"I would prefer it if you didn't kill me. Also, could I trouble your guild to help me leave the province?"

The guild master scowled. "You want us to help you?"

"I can pay."

Luke walked over and placed a hand on my shoulder. "Give him time to adjust. Come on, let's get a beer." His grip tightened as he dragged me from the room and forced me into a seat at the back of the tavern.

I was still naked.

Luke didn't seem to care. "You ran off."

"I wouldn't have bothered, if I knew I was only going to be level 5."

"What did you get?"

"Level 5, I just said."

"I mean skills."

"Oh, I didn't check. I don't know how to check. How do I check?"

Luke walked me through the process and another cascade of messages appeared before me.

You have unlocked your racial skills:

Vampiric Touch
Vampiric Aura
Vampiric Thirst
Ancient Vampiric Regeneration
Ancient Vampiric Physique
Ancient Vampiric Bloodline
Evil Eye

You have unlocked your class skills:
Willpower
Prodigy
Magic

Your class has leveled and unlocked new skills:
Vampire Hunter
Swordsmanship
Armour
Unarmed Combat
Tracking

You have reached level 5. You can upgrade one of your existing class skills.

You have 100 attribute points to spend.

I frowned as I read the last prompt. "I thought you could only upgrade class skills every tenth level."

"That's normal classes. Heroes can do it every fifth level. I must have not mentioned that. Tell me what your skills are, and I'll give you the best advice I can."

I read him the list.

"That explains a few things."

"Going to need a little more information than vague comments, Son."

"The skills heroes receive as part of their class are different than what other classes receive. For us, they're a reflection of who we are at our core, which means we can skip having to gain the general and advanced skills. You're the most strong-willed person I've met, Dad. And the fact that you have the willpower skill proves it. It's a specialized skill, rather far down the skill tree. So is the prodigy skill. Having the willpower skill explains how you can keep your hunger under control, when others can't."

"Do you have the willpower skill?"

He shook his head. "I have the stalwart skill. I have the prodigy skill, too; so does Mum and Kathrine. Weirdly, you have the same starting skills as Kathrine. But I don't think you should follow her path. Vampires can only perform necromancy, from what I'm told, and it isn't that helpful to someone as strong as you are, so I'd ignore magic."

"One doesn't go to a magical world and ignore magic, Son."

"Suit yourself, but don't use your skill upgrade on it. Prodigy and swordsmanship are both better choices for your upgrade. The first will make it easier for you to learn everything, and the second will make you more talented with a sword."

"What about willpower?"

"It's a double-edged sword. It will help you control your thirst, but it will also make you harder to stop once you lose control. There's no off button with skills."

"Well, swordsmanship sounds dumb, since I haven't held a sword since I got here. Unarmed combat makes more sense, but I'm not interested in becoming a kung fu master. Prodigy it is then."

You have upgraded your Prodigy skill to tier one.
This skill can be upgraded two more times.

Luke walked me through how to open my character sheet and I read off what I could see.

Race: Ancient Vampire
Class: Hero
Level: 5
Strength: 240
Agility: 320
Endurance: ∞
Constitution: ∞
Cunning: 240
Perception: 480
Recovery: ∞
Mana Regeneration: 0

Luke frowned as I finished. "You have an infinity sign next to your endurance, constitution, and recovery. That's odd."

I shrugged. "It makes sense, though."

"How does that make sense?"

"I immediately heal from any injury I take; so those attributes are essentially infinite."

"I suppose. Your base stats are still insane."

"How insane?"

"Humans only have 10 across the board by the time they turn sixteen. They can boost those numbers through hard work, but only a freak of nature would get above the low 30s."

"Is it weird that I don't have a magic attribute, only a mana regeneration attribute?"

"Mages don't have a magic attribute. They only have mana regeneration. To store mana and cast spells, mages need to build a core and a mana network, which is a painful and lengthy process."

"I notice there is no wisdom or charisma."

"Only nobles have charisma, and only holy classes have wisdom. I'm surprised you don't have dexterity, though, since it's a basic attribute that all people have. It might explain why you don't have such a wide range of emotions."

"Do you have cunning or perception?"

"No. But I would guess that cunning has something to do with why you can read so fast. Perception seems self-explanatory."

"Any recommendations for where I should spend my attribute points?"

"Strength. But don't do it all at once. I made that mistake and spent the next week stuffing my face, so my body could fuel the growth. I don't get any bigger anymore when I grow stronger, but I'm not sure if the same will apply to you."

"I'll wait until I find something to eat, then."

"Go one point at a time, and give it a few minutes to kick in."

"Will do."

"Now you listen to me."

He was upset with me, but I always knew that would be the outcome of breaking his trust. He'd left me with no other option, though. If I didn't break it, I wouldn't grow stronger, and if I didn't grow stronger, I would eventually lose him.

"What do you want me to say, Luke? You want me to apologise? You want me to say it won't happen again? It will. You've got your duty and I've got mine."

Luke scowled. "I needed you ten years ago. I don't need you now."

"I'm not here to hold your hand, but I will have your back whether you want me to or not. It's who I am. And if that means barging in here to get stronger, I'm going to do it."

"They're not going to let you leave the province."

The change in the conversation didn't faze me. "I never thought they would."

"Why did you bring it up, then?"

"Because that's how you negotiate."

"Negotiate?"

"Going and seeing your mother and sister is one option, having the guild bring them here to keep me in check is another."

He snorted. "You think they will go for it?"

I grinned. "You'll see."

I turned as Heather, the young lady from the front desk, approached our table. Her friendly, flirtatious attitude was gone. Now, she was looking at me like some sort of disgusting insect.

The tavern was completely empty. Almost everyone had evacuated the building, which made it much easier to listen to everything that was going on. I knew why she was here.

"The guild master would like to speak with you both." She held out a pouch. "I've converted your silver to gold like you requested. There are 982 pieces."

Luke scowled. "Is that my loot?"

I ignored him as I took the pouch. "Would you be able to track down the next of kin for a pair of adventurers from a decade ago? Denton son of Denton and his sorcerer party member Rena."

Heather paused. "That's not a lot to go on."

"Denton was the son of the lord who previously owned the manor that Luke and his party were sent to clear out."

"That should be much easier, though I have to know your intentions towards them."

"They saved my life. I want to pass on their share of the loot and tell their families where their bodies are."

"I'll see what I can do, but I'll have to get the guild master's permission. And don't bother quoting the rule book at me. You might be a guild member, but I can request oversight at my own discretion."

"I know you can." I stood up as she started to walk off and clapped Luke on the shoulder. "Let's not keep the guild master waiting. He's having a bad day. Someone accidently ripped his arm off."

We started walking to the staircase.

"*You* ripped his arm off."

"Accidently. And it's not my fault that the only person I've wrestled with is you, so I didn't realise how freakishly strong I am."

"In that case, we need to make a short detour." Luke turned and we headed for the class hall. "I'm probably going to get kicked out of here, so I need to do this now."

He walked into the class hall and slapped the stone.

"What the actual fuck is this bullshit! Fifteen levels in one freaking go. What the hell!"

My calm, peaceful tranquillity vanished, and I started monologing about the injustices of the world. Luke began swearing about the lost opportunity, about the advanced skills he was missing out on by leveling all at once.

Our voices grew louder and louder until we both shouted, "This is your fault!"

"My fault!" we both said.

"Yes, your fault!" we both replied.

"So, he is your father," the guild master said.

We both turned to glare at him, and he took a step back. He was dressed in a fashionable blue suit with red trim, which made his massive size even more imposing.

"I am," I said.

"He is," Luke added.

"Fuck. Come on, we can talk in my office."

He turned and walked out of the room.

We followed.

"Did you seriously go up fifteen levels, when I only got five for killing an ancient vampire and its posse?"

"Yes. And I'm not happy about it. Two levels are okay. Three kind of sucks. Four is bad. And five is terrible. But fifteen is a fucking shitshow."

"Don't swear."

"Bite me."

"Not until you're old and grey."

The guild master stumbled a step, catching himself by grabbing the wall. Then he pushed himself up and kept on walking, pretending he hadn't heard what I said.

His office was a large room, filled with books, a sizable desk, and five chairs. Magical symbols covered the walls and bookcases, giving it an otherworldly quality. He took a seat behind his desk and then invited us to sit. "We haven't been formally introduced. I'm guild master Riker."

"I'm the vampire Vincent."

"I take it you're here to invoke section 817 of the guild rule book."

"Yes, I would like to assist in wiping out a threat greater than myself to receive a neutral status from the guild."

"Are you, in fact, in control of your appetites?"

Luke nodded. "I've travelled with him for several days, and by all appearances he is. He possesses the evil eye, so he can limit his feeding to Unseen, which is something this province has in abundance."

Riker leaned back and crossed his arms. "No guild has ever invoked section 817 with a vampire, let alone an ancient vampire. Why should I do it now?"

"Because I'm asking you to," Luke said. "No, I'm *telling* you to."

"I know he's your father, Hero, but he's also an ancient vampire. I can't just set a new precedent for him."

"But you can *for a hero*."

"No, I can't. You get special privileges, but they don't extend to those you chose."

"I wasn't talking about me."

"Fuck." Riker met my gaze. "You're a hero."

"A hero summoned by vampire cultists, during the holy convergence like the rest of my family. Well, unfortunately, *not* like the rest of my family; they got to go to nice kingdoms, and I got eaten. Do you want me to start quoting the guild rules to you?"

"No." He sighed. "So, we've got a cursed hero on our hands, who is holding out for a saint to save him."

Luke frowned, clearly confused by the guild master's statement.

I quickly put my hand over his mouth. "This is called bureaucratic bull, Son. It's used to get around difficult things like the truth. Pointing out bureaucratic bull that works in your favour is not a wise action to take."

Luke snorted and pulled my hand away. "Yes, my father is suffering from a curse and waiting for a saint to save him."

Riker sighed again. "I suppose I could give him a neutral status if he were to prove himself worthy of it."

"And keep my status as a member of the guild?"

"No."

"Why not?"

He glared at me. "Why do you want to be a member of the guild?"

"Loot rights."

"Excuse me."

"As hellspawn, I have no rights to any loot I collect, and I can't claim any bounty on the things I kill. If I stay a member of the guild, no guild member can steal my loot, and I get paid for the things I kill."

"You want to get paid."

"And keep it."

"You would be required to follow our rules. That involves not involving yourself with hellspawn."

"I can do that."

"You are hellspawn."

"But I'm soon to be neutral hellspawn, and guild members are allowed to be involved with neutral parties."

"That's a stretch."

"No, it's bureaucratic bull."

"Fine, you can remain in the guild. But I'll treat you like the guild, which means you'll be paying taxes."

I winced. "Fine."

"What do we need to do?" Luke asked.

Riker took a deep breath as his face turned grim. "Kill the lich, Contessa."

"That's suicide."

"You just went up fifteen levels," I said, not understanding.

"It's still suicide."

"The lich is the only threat in the province clearly stronger than an ancient vampire, and the only way I can claim to the king that this is even remotely by the book."

Luke scowled. "We'll need a month to prepare."

"I've only got you for another month, and I need to deal with other threats. I'll give you a week."

I could see we weren't going to budge him by much, but we had to try for my son's sake. "Make it two weeks, and I'll help with the other threats."

Riker frowned and then nodded. "Two weeks."

Luke grabbed me by the shoulder, shoved a pair of pants into my hands, and hauled me out of my chair. "Come on, we need to train."

I smirked as I began humming.

"Is that Eye of the Tiger?"

5

SIR BRANDON

My son hadn't changed all that much since he was a teenager. He was still impulsive, prone to action without thought. It wasn't until we reached the empty tavern that he remembered the entire guild had fled the building, terrified by my company. He left me alone in the corner off the tavern as he marched back to the guild master's office to make everyone return.

By myself and without anything to do, I simply sat there wearing a borrowed pair of pants. I wasn't bored. I wasn't unhappy. Doing nothing didn't bother me in the least. People slowly entered and exited. I barely noticed. They weren't important. Few things in life were, anymore. So, I waited, letting time flow by unconcerned, until something important enough to warrant my attention perked my interest.

That occurred after sundown.

A terrified young man, whose name I didn't bother to get, led me through the building to a large courtyard out back. People lounged at tables dressed in armour, ready for a fight, sharing whispered conversations that I heard every word of. The sound of hammers came from the building to the right; magical words came from the one to the left. The building on the far side lay quiet, though I could sense three people within.

We made our way through the centre of the crowd to the far building, and the young man held the door open for me. A handsome, middle-aged knight in full armour waited on the other side, next to a similar-aged woman dressed in a white robe. A third older man, dressed in a dark coat covered in pockets, sat on a bench at the back of the room with a collection of books beside him.

The door closed behind me after I entered.

The knight gave me a brief nod. "I am Sir Brandon, weapons master for this chapter of the guild. I will be instructing you for the foreseeable future." He turned and pointed to the woman behind him. "This is my wife, Tora. She'll be observing."

Tora scowled at me.

"I'm immune to holy magic, madam."

Sir Brandon gave a nervous chuckle. "She heard about your little accident with the guild master and insisted she be here."

"Little accident," Tora grumbled. "He tore the guild master's arm off, because he doesn't know his own strength, and you wanted to train him without a healer. Heaven save me from sinners and foolish husbands."

Sir Brandon gave another nervous chuckle and then waved for me to follow as he began walking towards a table covered with swords. "Your son informed the guild master of your full capabilities. Riker chose to extend this information to the heads of staff, so I'm aware you're a hero, which is why this training session is private."

"What exactly will we be training?"

"We'll be focusing on your swordsmanship skill for now. Have you begun distributing your attribute points?"

"No."

"I would suggest you hold off. A hero's path is unique; and while your race might give you advantages to build from, you shouldn't shoehorn yourself down a path until you are aware that it is right for you. Which brings me to the first part of your training. Your son tells me you're completely unaware of how skills work."

"Completely."

He waved to the table of blades beside him. "I'll begin by explaining the swordsmanship skill to you, then. At its heart, the swordsmanship skill shows your proficiency with a sword, *any* sword. It is the foundation for more specialised sword skills, such as longsword, bastard sword, claymore, katana, and shortsword. All skills have twenty levels to them before they're mastered, and if you master the swordsmanship skill, you will reach level 10 in a specialised sword within the first day of receiving it."

"Why's that important?"

"Skills affect how you operate under stress. If you're exhausted, injured, starving, or distracted, you will fight with the minimum level of technique that your skill level offers. A soldier on a battlefield might be terrified out of his mind, but his skill level will keep him fighting, even if his brain has him too shocked to think."

"It's like muscle memory?"

He scratched his chin. "It's more effective than that. Muscle memory is a reflexive response. Skill levels are an *intentional* response you don't fully control. Put another way, you won't be able to fight below your skill level unless you intentionally force yourself to do so."

"Is there a big difference between skill levels?"

"Yes. We call it the five-level canyon. If someone possesses the same skill as you, but they are five levels higher, you will have to have double their relevant attributes to keep up with them."

I whistled. "That's a big difference."

"That's why you don't neglect your skills."

"Even if they're not relevant?"

He crossed his arms. "What do you mean?"

"I've never used a sword. I've never needed to. I can't be killed, and I can rip a person limb from limb with my bare hands. Learning to use a sword seems kind of pointless."

He chuckled. "And it would be if I were training *you* to swing a sword, but I'm training you to understand how *someone else* swings a sword, which is just as important. Your son can slice and dice you anyway he pleases, despite you being faster than he is. This leaves you vulnerable, as these injuries slow you down in the moment. If something stronger than you got hold of you in that momentary pause, you would be out of the fight."

That made sense to me, which meant I needed to learn. "Where do we begin?"

"I'll get to that. First, I need to explain how your skills interact. The prodigy skill is an extremely rare skill and one of the hardest to train, because the only time you can train this skill is during the first training session you have with another new skill. During our first sparring session, you will gain one level of the swordsmanship skill, thanks to your first-tier prodigy skill, but any additional skill levels you gain will help you to train your prodigy skill along with your swordsmanship skill. This is important, because the prodigy skill is the most useful skill you have. Not only will it make it easier for you to train *every* skill, but it will also modify your base skill level as its level rises."

"In what way?"

"Each level of a skill has a technical range to it. Your level assures you that you will have a minimum standard going forward, but you can also fight above this level by being in peak condition and by focusing. The prodigy skill raises your minimum standard for your skill level by around fifty percent when the prodigy skill is mastered, and it raises the level cap on mastered skills by up to three levels when the skill is raised to tier three."

"Half of a single level doesn't sound like a big improvement."

"It's often the difference between life and death. It also makes it much easier for you to train your skills, because it shrinks the training gap."

"You haven't mentioned that part yet, dear," Tora said.

Sir Brandon frowned. "I haven't?"

"No."

He chuckled nervously. "I should have said this at the beginning, but the way you raise any skill level is to perform at two levels above your current level. If your skill is level 1, then performing at a level 3 standard will raise your skill's level to 2. My swordsmanship skill is level 15. This is important because I'll be able to draw out your potential, causing you to unknowingly react at a higher swordsmanship level than you would otherwise be capable of performing. I'm hoping to have you at level 5 by the end of our first sparring session."

"Should we begin, then?"

Sir Brandon paused as if considering my question.

"Make sure you've educated him properly, sword-for-brains," Tora growled.

Sir Brandon sighed. "Yes, dear."

"I think I've got the gist of things," I said. "I need to perform two levels above my current skill level to level a skill. My first-tier prodigy skill will automatically have me performing any new skill at level 2 by the end of my first training session, making the skill level 1; however, I need to do this training session properly, because this is the only way to train my prodigy skill. Also, when I master a skill and have mastered my prodigy skill, I will have effectively raised the level cap for this skill by one level, or a maximum of three levels when I have upgraded the prodigy skill twice more. You are my trainer, and because of our level difference, you can help me to perform at a higher level than I could otherwise perform at on my own, because of the five-level canyon, which is in fact a fifteen-level canyon currently."

Brandon grinned. "That seems good enough."

His wife cleared her throat.

He sighed. "What do you know about swords?"

"Pointy end goes in the other person. If it's a one-sided blade, you can hold the back to block and gain leverage. Blocking with your blade is a great way to damage your sword, but it's better than dying.

And don't stop stabbing your opponent just because they stopped moving. Just because you've impaled their kidney, it doesn't mean they can't still kill you."

He seemed to be satisfied, so he pointed to the table. "Can you name these swords?"

I went through their names. I couldn't remember where I'd heard them, but the names came easily.

"Correct. Now which of them is the most lethal?"

"Whichever is closest."

Sir Brandon froze. "Say that again?"

"Whichever is closest."

He frowned. "Have you trained with a sword?"

"I'm not sure. The more we talk about them the more familiar they seem, but I've only ever picked up a sword a few times in my life."

He ran his gaze over me, in a detached, clinical way. "Your stance has changed since you arrived. You're holding yourself like someone who's spent their life with a sword on their hip."

I frowned, looking down at position of my feet. "I am, aren't I? How do I know that?"

"You should be able to answer that better than me."

"I have no clue. So shall we continue?"

Sir Brandon nodded. "Let's go through the safety protocols for our sparring match." He walked down to the end of the table and pointed at a pair of wooden swords. "We'll be using these. Wooden swords are all you need to progress to level 5. If you begin fighting at a higher level, I won't stop fighting, but I'll summon a real sword to my hand. If you progress further, I'll summon a second sword and toss it to you mid-fight. Repeat it back."

"We'll fight with wooden swords. If I progress far enough, you will begin fighting with a proper sword. If I progress further, I will fight with a proper sword."

"This sort of training isn't about lethality; it's about control. The more you control your strength and agility, the more progress you will see. A small tap that causes my armour to ding, will cause your skill to grow more than a full-blown swing that shatters my arm. However, if there comes a time where I think it is warranted, I'll tell you to cut me. From then on, you need to cleave through my armour and only go a finger's width deep."

"Anything else I should know?"

"The slower you fight, the better. If you can block my swing with a small turn of your blade or dodge a thrust with only sucking in your gut, do so. This is skill. Winning the fight isn't your goal; showing your skill is. And if you don't slow down, you won't be able to learn anything."

"What do you mean?"

"You've got almost four times my agility. I'll be fighting at full speed, but if you do the same, I won't be able to follow your movements and direct your technique. So, you need to go as slow as possible, even if that means taking a hit. This sparring session will be different to the way I teach others: There will be no holding back, and we will go until I collapse. Don't stop, even if I call for healing."

"Is this safe?"

He grinned. "Probably not. But this is the only opportunity I'm going to get to train a prodigy that is indestructible." He picked up a wooden sword and passed it to me. "Swing this around until you feel comfortable with it."

I stepped back and gave it a few practice swings. It felt like I was holding a cardboard tube. There was no weight to it, and it felt fragile in my grip. "I'm good."

"Swing it at me a few times, but slow down at the last moment to cause a light tap."

Ding, ding, ding.

He sucked in a sharp breath. "That was terrifying. I didn't even see your arm move."

"Could you have stopped me?"

"Not comfortably."

"But you could have stopped me."

"That's the power of skills."

"I think I'll take this more seriously, then."

"It's to your benefit. Now give me a moment. I need to drink a potion and let my wife buff me. You can wait over there in the circle."

I walked over to the nearest circle.

The training room was larger than a basketball court, with enough space for a dozen groups to train at once. There were empty racks for weapons along the walls and jugs of water. A stack of towels waited nearby, and there was weight equipment down the end. It was a mix of modern and old that looked out of place to my eyes, but I quickly adapted.

The old man at the back of the room hadn't stopped watching or taking notes since I'd arrived, but he occasionally picked one of the books next to him and flipped through. He gave off an aura that was more threatening than Sir Brandon's but was far from threatening to me, so I ignored him.

Sir Brandon finished chugging a potion as his wife completed casting her spell. A nimbus of green energy flowed around his body and then entered his mouth, causing his vitality to swell. It was a four-fold increase to the life energy I felt within him, which made me take notice.

I was beside the cleric before she realised. "What did you do to him?"

She jumped, releasing a small shriek. "What?"

"You just did something to him, and his life energy swelled."

She scowled. "Why do you want to know?"

"Because he's making me hungry. He went from being a meal to a feast."

She took a step back. "Are you have trouble controlling yourself?"

"No, but I want to know if you can do this to the people I eat."

"Excuse me?"

"You just turned your husband into something that could keep my hunger at bay for longer. Could you do it to an Unseen if I brought them to you?"

"I wouldn't be comfortable doing so."

"But you could, couldn't you?"

"Yes. But I won't."

"That's fine. You've been very helpful. If you happen to know a cleric capable of doing the same, but with more ambiguous morals, I would appreciate an introduction."

"I'm burning potion and buff, let's get started," Sir Brandon said.

"Sorry. I got distracted."

Sir Brandon moved to the circle, and I followed. We stood several feet apart and raised our wooden blades. The air in the training room was still, but I could hear a hundred conversations from the buildings around us.

Sir Brandon eyed my stance for a moment and then nodded to himself. "We'll take this slow in the beginning, so you can learn and then speed up, once I reach my peak and you need to match it, then slow down. Follow my rhythm."

He made a simple high slash from the right.

I blocked it.

He made a simple high slash from the opposite direction.

I blocked it, too.

Then he lunged and I stepped to the side.

Then he went back to the beginning.

After two more repetitions he began to speed up.

I barely noticed in the beginning, but by the time he shouted, "I'm at my peak," I was having to pay attention. I matched his speed and then forced myself to slow down, until I was only *just* blocking in time and stepping out of the way.

"You ready?" he asked.

"Ready."

The pattern of his movements shifted, and his sword collided with my chin, snapping my head backwards. I had seen the blow coming, but I hadn't been able to move in time at my current speed.

What followed was a series of humiliating strikes as my sword arrived a fraction of a second too late on multiple occasions. The blows didn't sting, but they did frustrate me. I could see the moment he changed direction, but by the time I moved to block him, it was already too late.

Then I began to find my rhythm, and a few less blows got through. It went from one in three getting through to one in four. Then he changed his rhythm again, and it went back to one in three. The second time was easier, and I went back to only having one in four get through rather quickly.

He changed again.

Every time I got a little more confident, a little more effective, he changed. On and on it went, until he threw out his hand and a metal sword flew across the room and into his grasp. It was a very cool trick.

He dropped his wooden sword before him, as he swung the real one, only to then jump and knee the wooden hilt, causing its blade to pierce through the bottom of my chin and come out the top of my head. He followed up by bringing his sword around, cleaving me in two at the waist.

The move left him open, and I swung for the side of his head. His arm came up and he dipped his chin, causing the blade to pass above him. The opening let me yank his wooden sword out of my head, and then we were back at it.

With only a wooden blade, I couldn't block, causing four out of five blows to get through, shredding my pants and leaving me naked. But quicker than I would have expected, I got the hang of turning his weapon aside, and that number began to decrease. When I got down to one in two blows getting through, I was happy. When I reached one in three, I was ecstatic. When I reached one in four, I began challenging myself by slowing down further.

Whenever I reached that one in four state, I would slow down even more; but eventually I screwed up, and a foot of my sword fell to the ground.

Sir Brandon raised his hand, and another longsword flew into it, while he stabbed me in the heart. He tossed the second longsword to me while I dodged, and we continued.

With a weapon I could block with, things became much easier. It became so much easier that I had to force myself to stop turning aside his blade. Instead, I slowed myself further and further, until I physically couldn't slow any more without becoming unable to stop him.

Then I began blocking again.

Sweat began to pour off Sir Brandon as I slowly gained ground, stopping all but one in seven of his blows. Then something inside me clicked and his blows stopped getting through, and I realised I could now slow down further.

Sir Brandon began using footwork more often, pressing forward and retreating, throwing me off as I tried to keep up. My slower speed made it harder, because he was always moving ahead of me, but I had another breakthrough, and I was suddenly able to interpret where he was going to move, by the way he positioned his body. It let me begin my counter before he started, and I slowed myself down even further, taking strikes until I figured out what I was doing wrong and then changed.

I eventually reached another limit to how slow I could move, and after finding no defensive way to counter this problem, I went on the offense. Sir Brandon's sword was always there to meet me. It took me longer to figure out what I was doing wrong, but when I did, I heard the most beautiful sound.

Ding.

One *ding* was quickly followed by another, and then it was Sir Brandon who was struggling, so I dropped my speed further. When I gained more confidence in my ability, I did it again, always slowing down, always making it harder, until I reached a point where it was impossible to keep up with him. His sword flayed my flesh as I tried to find a way to compensate.

Then everything clicked again.

Where his sword was, I was a fraction of an inch away. My movements shrank, until I used the absolute least to achieve what I needed.

Sir Brandon noticed the difference immediately. "Cut me."

Everything took on a new dimension as I had to discover a way of cutting through his armour only to immediately stop as I pierced his skin. My first hundred strikes only *dented* his armour, causing me to give openings I never intended. It was like I was back at square one.

Sir Brandon threw punches and kicks, anything he could to throw me off, and it worked for a time, but I eventually got used to what he was doing. Which was always the point where he changed how he fought. When his injuries began to slow him, he called for healing. When his breathing slowed him, he called for healing.

On and on we fought, until his battle flow became as clear to me as my own hand. His sword no longer touched me. His fists no longer hit me. In frustration, I tried to slow further, but it wasn't possible. I was giving myself the shortest time to react that I could. Anything less was impossible.

My frustration at his inability to see his flaws and give me a proper challenge came through, and I unconsciously began to show him what he was doing wrong. I followed him around the training room, keeping him on the back foot, showing him how he could improve. I realised his armour was slowing him down, so I removed it piece by piece. Without it, he could move more freely. His performance improved, up to a point. Then his progression stagnated.

I forgot about why we were fighting as my frustration mounted and I began to growl like an annoyed dog. *If he could only see. If he could only understand. Then he would stop doing things wrong.*

His quick foot stance was hindering his progress. His lightning parry was sloppy. His over-reliance on his iron- breaker strike was failing him.

At some point, I began shouting these things at him.

He listened.

Then he improved.

Then he improved some more.

Then he collapsed.

And I stood there frustrated.

You have mastered your Swordsmanship skill.

"Get up, recruit. You think the enemy will let you sleep if you want to?" I glared at the cleric. "Heal him."

She glared right back. "No. My husband has reached his limit."

"Husband. Why the hell is one of my recruits bringing his wife to my training field! Where the hell is my master at arms?"

She frowned. "Where do you think we are, Vincent?"

"Vincent? My name's not Vincent, woman. It's…" Reality came crashing back down. "Vincent." I blinked several times as experiences I didn't understand collided in my brain. A lifetime of memories bombarded me, until one by one they faded away, leaving behind knowledge but no source. "I think I need to sit down."

I stumbled over to the nearest bench, mind whirling.

While I took a seat, Tora ran to her husband's side and poured a potion down his throat. His body was covered in blood from the hundreds of small cuts I had given him. He'd been healed dozens of times over while we fought, but that didn't do anything for the mess.

He wasn't a vampire whose body reabsorbed everything.

I took several slow, deep breaths as I tried to understand what had happened to me. None of it made sense. There were several lifetimes of sword knowledge bouncing around in my skull, and I had no idea where it all had come from. Everything from foot work, to focus, to grip position was all just *there*. It unnerved me. No, it *concerned* me.

My ability to control my bloodlust was based on who I was. I was not a master of the sword. I didn't want to be a master of the sword. Because it might make it harder to control my bloodlust. I wanted my family to be safe, but I was a liability if I couldn't control myself.

Sir Brandon came forward while my mind whirled and knelt

before me, looking into my eyes. "That was a good fight." He held out a small crystal. "Would you do me a favour and hold this?"

I picked it up. It glowed purple.

A smile transformed his face. "A master of swordsmanship and a hero. I pledge my life and my soul to the hero. Let his path be my path and his fate be..." His eyes suddenly rolled back midsentence, and then he fell facedown and began snoring.

Behind him, Tora glowed with an ominous red light, but she was glaring at her husband. She stalked forward, leaned down, and grabbed his ankle. She started walking away, dragging him behind her. "I will be taking my husband home now, vampire, where there will be many lectures on piousness and not trying to pledge our souls to hellspawn. Thank you for not mutilating him."

She dragged him to the door and pushed it open, then she dragged him out and closed it again.

I went back to wondering what had happened.

6

VAMPIRIC LIFE

A few minutes passed, then the old man from the back of the room wandered over with his books and took a seat beside me. "You seem to be wondering what just happened to you. Would you like me to enlighten you?"

I glanced at him. He was much older than all the other adventurers I'd seen, but he carried himself like he knew how to fight. His face was heavily wrinkled from spending time in the sun, and scars crisscrossed his exposed flesh. He'd placed his stack of books between us, exposing the cover of the top book: A Study in Vampiric Physiology and How to Hunt Them.

"You're a vampire hunter," I guessed.

"One of the best, and you can call me Hector."

"Is that why you're not afraid?"

"Knowledge is the antithesis of fear. It also helps that I have been in your position."

Hector finally caught my attention, dragging it away from my musing. "You were a vampire?"

"For three entire days. Not as long as you, from what I hear, but certainly long enough for me."

"What happened to me?"

He smiled. It wasn't a friendly smile. "That answer is going to cost you."

I paused, considering beating the information out of him. Sadly, Luke wouldn't approve, and I knew it was wrong, even though it would have been easier. "What do you want from me?"

"I would like to study you. You're the *only* ancient vampire to have *ever* maintained their soul. There have been several full-fledged vampires who have done the same, but none have made it to the elder stage, let alone the ancient stage like you have. To say you are an anomaly is an understatement of the highest order. You could singlehandedly double our understanding of vampires, making the world a much safer place. In return for your assistance, I will do my utmost to help you understand yourself and what you are capable of."

"You aren't worried that you'll be creating a monster?"

"No. I'll be stopping one from being born. Vampires are only dangerous when they're hungry."

"I'd disagree."

"That is because you're traveling with your son. Your love for him keeps you active, keeps you aware of the world around you. Left to your own devices, the Curse of Sloth would have you in its grasp, and you would happily laze away the weeks until your hunger prompted you to go out and eat. That tip was on the house; the next one will cost your assistance."

I had read about the Curse of Sloth in the book Mara had given me. Vampires found it incredibly hard to motivate themselves to do anything beyond feeding, and that only happened when they were hungry. His faith in this curse was misplaced in my eyes, but I'd never interacted with other vampires beyond feeding on them while they were unconscious, so perhaps my own experience left me biased. "What would you like to know?"

"To start, I would like to know the full extent of your racial skills. Just read them off to me."

"Vampiric touch, vampiric aura, vampiric thirst, ancient vampiric regeneration, ancient vampiric physique, ancient vampiric bloodline, and evil eye."

"Interesting. Have you leveled any of these skills?"

"No, but my ancient vampiric thirst began at level 2."

"That would explain why you have the vampiric bloodline and evil eye skills. You'll want to watch that first skill closely. If you ever master it, you will evolve into a *primordial* vampire and find yourself damned to Hell, soul or no soul."

"How do I make sure that doesn't happen?"

He waved away my question. "We're getting ahead of ourselves. Let's start from the beginning of the list. I take it you're aware of what vampiric touch allows you to do?"

"I can suck the *life* out of someone I'm touching, instead of having to drink their blood."

"Yes. The more you practice with it, the stronger it will become. The next time you feed, its level should increase substantially.

"Why do you say that?"

"Your son mentioned you were able to instantly drain the life from an Unseen in anger, after discovering it had killed a boy. That sort of emotional intensity is rare among vampires, because few have the emotional fervour to draw out their own strength."

"Anger is a strength?"

"Anything that can stop a vampire from succumbing to the Curse of Sloth is a strength. The only reason they haven't overrun the world is because they can't be bothered. A focused and driven vampire is a calamity waiting to happen."

"Makes sense, I guess."

"Vampiric aura is a similar ability to the previous one. Your presence draws in the life of everything around you to sate your hunger. Here in a city like Hellmouth, it means little as there are plenty of people. The amount you need to sustain yourself while sleeping would practically go unnoticed. If you stayed here for their entire lives, you would only shorten the population's lifespan by a couple of months. This is the safest way to deal with your kind, and there are more than a dozen ancient vampires interred below major cities. They went to sleep, and people moved in to keep them that way."

"No hunger or danger to wake them."

"Exactly. Now to answer the question that has you sitting here confused."

"How do I know how to use a sword?"

"That answer comes from your next skill. Vampiric thirst is a skill almost every vampire possesses and is a mutation of a demonic skill that allows demons to gain the knowledge of the demons they kill and consume. The basic idea is that when you drink the blood of another vampire you gain some of their knowledge. The more blood you drink, the more knowledge you gain. There is a limit to what you can gain from blood without drinking another dry, but that limit is pushed back significantly when you do."

"Then the reason I can use a sword is because the vampires I ate could use a sword."

"Yes. The skill won't automatically make you capable of doing what they could. You need intense focus to trigger it, and then something similar to what occurred here will take place. When vampires go to war with each other, the victor drinks the loser, gaining their knowledge and adding it to their strength. This skill is linked to your vampiric bloodline skill and is how you make it stronger."

"Is there any benefit to making it stronger? You said there were a lot of negatives."

"Your bloodline strengthens your other vampiric abilities, and gives you access to powers that aren't defined as skills."

"Like what?"

"Shapeshifting, hypnosis, control over the creatures of the night, shifting shadows around you, levitation, and a whole host of other abilities. I can't teach you to do any of that, so you will have to eat a vampire who knows how to do these things to understand them, or practice these abilities alone."

"Will eating other vampires affect my personality?"

"Only briefly. What you experienced and how quickly it vanished is all the personality intrusion that will occur. Demons wouldn't eat each other so readily otherwise."

"It's going to happen again, I take it?"

"I would expect so. You ate an entire nest of elder vampires and followed it up with an ancient. Their blood contained more knowledge than a regular vampire's would. And while they didn't know the first thing about being vampires, they were most likely all highly skilled individuals. Lord Denton only surrounded himself with the best, from what I have gathered."

"What can you tell me about my other vampiric abilities?"

"The only way you can level your ancient vampiric physique and regeneration is by killing demons. You're a demon. They're a demon. Killing each other leaves the winner stronger. Beyond that, the skills' effects are self-explanatory, so I won't bore you with the details. Your evil eye skill is also beyond my understanding. It's something both those touched by Heaven or Hell possess, and its leveling mechanism is, to my knowledge, unknown."

"Any advice for me?"

"You seem to still care for children, so you should open an orphanage and maintain it yourself."

His answer confused me. "What?"

"The Curse of Sloth is a vampire's biggest weakness. If you don't find something to pull you into the world around you every day, you will end up sitting there doing nothing for all eternity, occasionally getting up to eat. So, if remaining active requires you to have thirty rugrats that depend on you for food and shelter, you need to do it."

"That seems more like a long-term plan. Any advice for the short term?"

"Your son tells me you're trying to protect him."

"I am."

"Use that. You can't motivate yourself to do anything you don't feel passionately for, so use the love you have for your son to drive you forward. There has been more than one apocalypse in this world, more than one kingdom slaughtered overnight. Build a place that is safe for him and then maintain it. He fights monsters for a living; become the foremost authority on monster hunting so you can give him the knowledge he needs to be safe. Hell might come for him, so make yourself stronger than Hell. Protect your son. He won't stop fighting until this world is free from danger. He won't be safe until it's free from danger. So go out there and kill every monster you can find."

A low growl came from my throat. "Where should we begin?"

"Let's start by finding out what makes an ancient vampire tick."

I DIDN'T CARE about getting stronger, but I cared about protecting Luke. I wasn't interested in ridding the world of evil, not in a way that would send me halfway across the country, but I was interested in protecting Luke, and maybe getting my hands on whatever loot they had. Hector and I spent the entire night talking, trying to find the motivation for me to stay active, to stay present. He changed my thinking, tweaked how I viewed the world, showing connections between actions and behaviours that didn't mean anything to a regular person, but gave me hyperfocus.

He agitated me. He got under my skin in a way that wouldn't let me sit still. Then he took me to the restricted section of the guild library and showed me what real power looked like. There were creatures in this world that made me look like a plaything. They were an insurmountable mountain, and my family wouldn't be safe until I could climb to their peak and crush them with my foot.

Without anyone to train me, I was left with study. With over ten thousand books in the guild library, I had my work cut out for me, even at my prodigious reading speed, which I discovered slowed when I used it to excess. Reading a book in a second or two was something I could only do a few times, before the weight of the knowledge caused me to take a hundred times longer. That still meant I could finish a book in a couple of minutes, but that was far slower than a few seconds.

Without Hector's guidance, reading the entire library would have been an impossible task for me. The Curse of Sloth was not as easily overcome as I believed, and the repetitive, dry monotony of the literature and the effort I had to put in to continue reading kept making me want to put it down and let time pass.

In the early hours of the third day, Sir Brandon found me. "Psst," he hissed.

I forced myself to finish the book I was reading and then looked up.

"You ready for your next training session?" he whispered.

I hadn't expected to see him again. I had overheard guild gossip that his wife had banned him from interacting with me. I nodded that I was ready to continue.

"Meet me in the training room at noon. Don't let my wife see you."

He vanished behind the door, and I picked up the next book. A little before noon I made my way to the training room. It was easy enough to navigate around his wife. I could hear her heartbeat.

Sir Brandon was waiting for me in the training room, in a new suit of armour. A young man in a white robe stood nervously behind him while a group of a dozen even younger adventurers stood off to the side with bored expressions.

Sir Brandon glanced over my shoulder as I entered, smiling the moment the door closed. "Did she follow you?"

"No. She's in a meeting with the guild master."

"Good. Good." He shooed away the young man in the robe and waited until he was out of earshot. "Today, we're going to train your armour skill. This will be much simpler than training your swordsmanship skill, and I suspect you will have mastered it by the end of our sparring session. The reason I'm so confident-"

"Is because the armour skill is easy to train. All you must do is perform as well in armour as you would outside it. This is made significantly easier when you have already mastered a weapon skill, and even easier when you have the prodigy skill. My ability to perform above my skills' max level makes mastering the armour skill a simple matter."

I'd read literally thousands of books in the past few days, so my knowledge of this world was extensive.

"I'd heard you'd been studying. Good. We'll skip the tutorial and go straight to the questions. What don't you understand?"

"Why didn't my prodigy skill level when we fought?"

"Hector mentioned that. I'm guessing here, but I think you didn't use your prodigy skill while we sparred. You used that vampiric thirst skill instead, so the prodigy skill didn't earn anything from our session."

"Which means it won't level this time, either."

"It might, but probably not." He nodded over his shoulder to the table behind him. "Your armour's on the table. If you need any help, tell me. We need to do this fast. My wife is bound to catch on.

You have mastered your Armour skill.

7

SHOPPING SPREE

I closed that last book in the library with three days to spare. Over half of the books in the library were adventurers' accounts. These were books about their experiences with different monsters, tactics that had worked, tactics that hadn't. Much of it was repeated. Much of it contradicted each other. All of it was useful.

The other half of the library was made up of books on lore, history, training methods, and knowledge on skills. Much of it was repeated. Much of it contradicted each other. All of it was useful.

The guild's library wasn't something a scholar would appreciate, but an adventurer would. In it was the collected knowledge of how to deal with local threats.

It was a good start.

But it was also concerning.

A lich was not to be trifled with. They were the undisputed masters of the dead, and there would be an army of abominations between us and it. Vampire elders, ghouls, skeletal knights and mages, zombies, wraiths, revenants, ghosts, and all sorts of creatures out of nightmares would be waiting for us.

Luke was right. This was a suicide mission, though a much

different suicide mission than it usually would be. A lich typically softened its enemy with an endless stream of easily replaced cannon fodder. That would be impossible with my presence. Because of this, it would likely attempt a swarm tactic. Hitting us with everything it had at once.

It would try to draw me away, so it could weaken Luke's party enough to kill them. If that didn't work, it would bind me up with magic and hold me down. I saw only one tactic that worked in our favour. Kicking down the door and charging straight in, not stopping until we reached the lich and destroyed its body.

That would give us the breathing room we needed to dismantle its army. Then we could deal with it alone, after it reformed its body at its phylactery. It would still be a tough fight. It wouldn't underestimate us a second time, and it wouldn't need to hold back for fear of killing its minions. It could also do the opposite and attempt to flee. There were too many options, too many ways events could go wrong.

I heaved a sigh and pushed myself to my feet, sliding my chair across the floor and disturbing the silence.

I left the empty library and made my way to the guild master's office. I could hear him inside, shuffling papers as he went over the guild's paperwork.

I knocked.

"I'm busy," Riker shouted.

I opened the door and entered.

He scowled the moment he saw me.

I didn't care, taking a seat across from him. "I need equipment."

"Talk to the quartermaster."

"I want the stuff in your vault. The stuff at the back." I had begun sensing it through the building several days ago.

"That equipment is cursed."

"I know. I can feel it. It resonates with me."

"Just because you're hellspawn, it doesn't mean you're immune to the effects of all cursed items. There is stuff down there that would turn you into an actual monster."

"I can sense that. too. Look, I'm a reasonable vampire. I'll point out what I want, and you can decide if you're willing to give it to me."

"I'm not willing to give any of it to you."

I met his gaze. "We both know you gave my son this mission to deter him. You don't want me as a neutral party; and you thought giving him a suicide mission would make him see sense. But it didn't work. Nothing you or I have said over the last week has changed his mind. And you're about to be responsible for killing the kingdom's hero and his party."

Riker pushed his paperwork aside. "He missed you more than I imagined."

"I'm aware of that. He's emotionally compromised and not thinking straight. Give me what I need to protect my son."

I'd been listening to Riker's conversations for the past week, so I knew how frustrated he was. He'd tried everything he could think of to dissuade my son, talking to anyone who could help, but nothing worked. Luke was set on getting himself killed.

Riker sighed. "I'll let you look." He pushed his chair back and climbed to his feet. "Follow me."

We made our way through the building, to the basement, then went several levels lower, following a winding staircase to a large room with eight large, enchanted statues and a pair of stone doors. Riker held out an amulet, and the barrier at the end of the staircase vanished.

The adventuring party on the other side raised their weapons the moment it disappeared. "Password?" One of them shouted.

"Nobody knows the password."

They lowered their weapons, and Riker continued walking forward. One of the adventurers broke away from the group, and the two of them held out their amulets, before the doors. A second barrier I hadn't noticed vanished. Instead of opening the door, Riker began pushing a series of obvious hidden buttons. I memorised the sequence, only to realise it likely didn't matter. He hadn't cared that I could see, which likely meant the sequence changed.

Once he was done, he opened the door.

The vault beyond was split into five massive sections, each separated by arches. Gold and silver filled the sides of the first section, a literal fortune beyond anything I'd ever seen. Riker and the adventurers walked past the gold and went to the first arch and raised their amulets.

"How deep are we going, sir?"

"All the way."

"Is that wise?"

"The vampire could eventually brute-force his way through. This vault was never designed to keep his kind out."

That made me curious. "Who was it designed to keep out?"

"Thieves and those with a taste for power, but none of their own. We keep the gold at the front, so those who are only greedy don't take anything dangerous. Second section is for priceless artifacts that hold historical value but aren't easily sold. Third section is magical weapons. Fourth section is controlled knowledge. And the fifth section, is where we keep cursed objects and dark knowledge. Every object in that section is shielded, and it takes an entire morning and a team of mages to lower the shield on any object you want to retrieve."

The amount of magic required to maintain this had to be absurd. "What powers this?"

"The hellmouth. Its presence draws in magic. We have receptacles in the pit to syphon off the magic, so the portal doesn't reopen. Most goes into maintaining the barrier over the pit, but some is sent here to maintain the vault."

"Why don't you close the hellmouth?"

"You need a saint to close a hellmouth, and the process kills them. The world doesn't have a saint, and if it did, it couldn't waste it on closing our hellmouth."

"That's depressing."

"That's life. Our kingdom is lucky to have a hero. The world around us was a far darker place before your son arrived."

I had read their library, so I knew he wasn't exaggerating. Luke was changing this world for the better. Heroes seemed to have a cleansing effect. Where they fought and won, mindless evil didn't return for a very long time. Anyone else was a temporary solution, but heroes were a permanent fix.

The final barrier eventually fell, and the adventurer left the vault. The cursed section was by far the biggest of the five sections, and it was filled with the kind of display cases you would normally see in a museum. However, instead of being square boxes, they were half-spheres, etched with mystical symbols. I could now read most of the symbols and understood how they contained the objects housed within them.

Everything radiated evil to my gaze, giving off a black smoke. There were piles of bones, single broken horns, and every kind of weapon you could imagine, very few of which were designed to fit in a human hand. Numerous books caught my attention -- their voices whispered in my mind, calling me to open and read them.

"Oh, I have guests," said a girlish voice clearly and loudly above the others.

My head whipped around.

"Something talking to you?" Riker asked.

"Yes."

"It's probably Lilith. If you see a little girl walking around, ignore her."

A child giggled. It was a murderous sound. The kind you would hear at a tea party serving blood, while you lounge on a pile of squishy corpses.

I slowly turned my head, until my eyes landed on an obsidian obelisk. "She's in there, isn't she."

"Yes."

"What is she?"

"An anti-saint. An Unseen who managed to achieve demonhood without needing to descend to Hell. She's the one who opened the hellmouth. So long as it remains, she can't be killed."

I sniffed the air. "She's not full demon. I smell a touch of humanity in her blood."

"Fuck!" Riker reached for his pocket as he swore, and the obelisk exploded.

I took a step forward, sensing the most powerful threat I'd ever encountered. I mentally opened my character sheet and dumped all of my attribute points into agility, knowing it was safe to because of Hector.

+100 Agility

My next step was faster, and the one after that even faster.

The pieces of the obelisk met the glass barrier as I blurred forward. The glass containment barrier shattered, creating more shrapnel. It tore through me coming out the other side as I ran through the wave of destruction and grabbed the seven-year-old girl at the centre by the throat, squeezing as hard as I could.

Surprise sparked in her smoke-ridden gaze as I drove her little head into the far wall. A normal child would have been nothing but mush. She was unaffected.

Then I began to feed.

I hadn't eaten in nearly two weeks, and I had taken significant damage over that time from being around the sun. I'd gone hunting through the city, but Hellmouth was devoid of Unseen. The cleric and the guards on the gate made sure they did their job, unlike in other places.

Not wanting to go further afield, I had let the hunger grow.

Life rushed into me as claws extended from her fingers and she began tearing into my intestines. "You ruined my surprise. Naughty vampire."

My head rocked back as words slammed through my mind. Pain,

pain like I hadn't felt since arriving speared through my skull. I screamed. The volume and power of my voice caused Riker's eardrums to explode, and he swore.

"Release me," she commanded.

The words hammered through me, and I screamed again.

"Release me, demon."

My hands fell away from her throat as I collapsed to my knees, filled with life force, but overcome by pain.

Luke took my place, causing a windy vortex with his passing. He ran his blade through her heart, pinning her to the wall. He immediately followed up, delivering a punch to her face.

"Kill this hero for me, demon."

I screamed again, denying her request with every fatherly instinct I had. I launched myself to my feet and threw a right hook, connecting with her little face. "Thanks for the pep talk." I clapped my hands over her mouth and pulled on her life force.

Then I was reminded she didn't need to use her mouth. "Stop feeding, demon."

I started screaming again but held on, to protect my son.

"Fine, have it your way. Feel pain. Feel agony. Feel despair. Feel grief. Feel anguish. Feel suffering. Feel misery. Feel the loss of hope. Feel the torment that awaits you in Hell. Feel your mind peel back as the totality of what awaits you becomes your only reality."

The walls that were my psyche caved in and I descended into the depths of Hell. My soul began to scream.

I WAS fine when I came to. Vampires were demons, and the horrors of Hell only bothered demons when we were actively on the receiving end. When it was over, we didn't dwell on what happened to us. We didn't live in the past. We went back to being demons the moment the torment ended.

I'd learned that in a book.

And was grateful to discover it was true.

A human who returned from the mental Hell I'd experienced wouldn't have stopped screaming until their throat became so bloody and raw that they drowned in their own blood, but I was fine. Better than fine. I was a bubbling cauldron of life, and I had managed to train a few of my skills.

You have mastered your Vampiric Touch skill.
Your Willpower skill has increased to level 15.
Your Prodigy skill has increased to level 10.

Luke stirred in his sleep as I moved, opening his eyes and glancing down. He was sitting in a chair next to me, with his unsheathed sword resting across his knees.

We were alone in a room with no windows and only one door. The door had a barrier over it.

Luke gave me a concerned look. "Hector says you should be okay, but I have my doubts. Lilith is no joke. *No one* has *ever* survived her mental attacks."

He was concerned, but I couldn't pass up this opportunity to mess with him. This was a rare occasion, like waking from a coma. "Fudge on a popsicle stick. Meat in the microwave. Christmas at thanksgiving."

More concern filled his gaze. "Dad, you're not making sense."

I doubled down. "Fudge on a popsicle stick. Meat in the microwave. Christmas at Thanksgiving."

"Dad those words are nonsensical." Very slowly he said, "Can… you…understand…the…words…that…are…coming…out…of… my…mouth."

"Not when you say them slowly like that, Son. Talk like a normal person or there will be no Christmas at Thanksgiving for you." I started to laugh as his face transformed. "Your expression is priceless. I wish I had a camera, so I could show your mother."

Luke launched himself to his feet, glaring down at me. "You were messing with me!"

He swung his sword, but I saw it coming, and I was off the bed and out of his way before it was anywhere near me. The poor bed wasn't so lucky.

I laughed.

Luke took that personally, following me around the room, trying to land a hit. "Stop running."

I laughed harder.

Between my heightened agility and my swordsmanship skill, Luke couldn't touch me. And after the first minute, he started treating it as training, realising he had an opponent that challenged him.

Seeing the same opportunity, I began shouting out tips. "Stop relying on your strength. Keep your elbow tucked. Why aren't you relying on your strength? Go through the rubble, not over it. Don't kick the furniture, they could have repaired it."

Luke collapsed, heaving for breath after a few hours.

I stood over him, smiling. "Did you train your skill level?"

He nodded. "One level in longsword, and quick strike. You're the best damn training dummy I've ever had."

I offered him my hand. "Glad I could help."

Luke let me pull him to his feet. "You're really fine?"

"I'm not interested in going through it again, but now that I'm on the other side it doesn't bother me."

"You shouldn't be fine. You should be a raving lunatic trying to tear out your eyes."

"Demons don't go insane from torture. You can torture them for information, but the moment the torture stops, they're back to their former selves."

"How do you know that?"

"Read it in the library."

He placed his hand on my shoulder and looked me in the eye. "You're really fine?"

"Fine is relative. As a vampire, I'm fine. If I become human again, I will immediately turn into a screaming mess until someone puts me out of my misery. How did *you* survive Lilith's mental attacks?"

He held up his hand, showing me a ring. "It provides complete protection against all psychic attacks. It's standard issue for high ranking and powerful members of the guild."

"I'd have appreciated one of those."

"These ones only work on humans, but I'll see what I can do."

"Mention the fact that if anyone but you had come to help, I would have slaughtered them, and then they would have had to deal with a mad ancient vampire."

"Okay, that just moved up my list of priorities."

"I'm missing parts of the fight. Do you mind filling me in?"

"What's the last thing you remember?"

I told him.

"When you turned into a screaming mess, your body locked up like you were being electrocuted. You dug your fingers through her flesh and kept feeding while you screamed, which slowed her down enough for me to keep overpowering her. I managed to hold her long enough for the clerics to arrive, and then they hit her with enough holy magic to knock her on her ass. After that, Mara led half of them through the ritual that contained her the first time. Then they put her new obelisk on her podium and mages went off to forge a new containment shell. They're still down there watching her. The new containment shell should be completed sometime tomorrow."

"I suppose I can hold off on my shopping trip until then."

RIKER LOOKED EXHAUSTED as he led me through the vault. Lilith's new containment system was in place, but the guild was out in force, ready to react if anything else occurred while I was down here. Weapons, armour, multiple buffs; they weren't taking any chances.

I wandered through the pedestals without making a noise. There were all sorts of scents in the air. There were supposed to be none; that's what containment meant. Contained. It was why Riker had immediately reacted when I mentioned I could smell her blood.

I circled the room twice. Then I pointed to the biggest threat I could sense, and flashed towards the second, pointing towards the third, for Luke to cover.

Cursed objects and demons are perfectly willing to lie in wait until the precise moment they can cause the most chaos. Many of the containment systems had been perfectly functional when I came here last time; now, they *weren't.* Announcing that I knew this fact caused them to act early.

A cursed sword shattered its magical barrier as a set of demon bones began pulling itself together. The sword flew through the air, heading for a mage's head, only to be knocked aside by Sir Brandon. The distraction gave another cursed chain an opportunity to attack. It went for a different mage, only to be stopped by a barrier. A cursed axe used the opening to cleave the first mage in two.

A ghost rose from the crown before me, reaching down to pick it up. I got there first, smashing the glass and tossing the crown to Tora, who hit it with holy magic, making the ghost king vanish. I moved on to the next-biggest threat as Luke knocked the skeletal demon into the far wall.

It was a brutal and bloody fight for the guild, but a necessary step to take, before my shopping spree. Fifteen minutes after it began, I went shopping.

Riker wandered behind me, receiving updates from the guild administrator. "We have three dead. Two more unconfirmed; the clerics believe they can resurrect them. Eleven have already been resurrected and are in the infirmary."

Riker grunted his acknowledgement. "How many heavily injured?"

"Forty-three. Most have a mix of minor curses and hellfire burns."

I stopped beside a longsword. "What about this one?"

"No," Riker snarled in reply. "How many permanently crippled?"

"Eight so far, but that number might grow. Some of the hellfire burns are substantial."

I kept walking and stopped beside a kilij. I could sense its hunger. It matched my own. "How about this one?"

"Maybe."

I froze and stared at the black kilij. It was a brutal- looking weapon, made from some sort of tainted metal, with red veins through it. He'd shot down eighteen of my requests so far. "What's the difference with this one?"

"Slaughter was created by the ancient vampire Lavire from the blood of elder vampire sorcerers. It literally sucks the life and magic out of anyone who touches it, but it's not sentient or capable of acting on its own. If it doesn't suck the life out of you or increase your hunger, you can use it."

"Will it affect my magic items?"

"You have magic items?"

"I will."

"You should be safe. It didn't affect the magic items Lavire wore, so it shouldn't affect yours."

I kept walking. "What about this sword."

"No."

"This one?"

"Hell no."

"That one?"

"That's not a sword; it's a ghost of a mimic."

"What about the one over there?"

"That will open a portal and drag you to Hell. Feel free to grab it."

"I changed my mind; I want that one."

"You'll go berserk and kill everyone around you if you draw it from its sheath."

"I'm having one of those psychic immunity rings made."

"It's not a psychic attack. It's a possession. And I know for a fact vampires aren't immune to it."

"I'll only draw it when I'm surrounded by enemies."

"You won't suddenly come to your senses when they're dead. You'll go looking for more things to kill until you're stopped."

"We'll add it to the maybe pile." A few pedestals later another object caught my eye. "I like this armour."

"It's animated."

"What about this set?"

"That will also open a portal and drag you to Hell."

"Lot of things drag you to Hell around here."

"We're on a hellmouth. Most of this stuff is left over from the war and too powerful for us to dispose of."

"Ever thought of just opening another portal to Hell and chucking it through?"

"Tried it. They just reappeared where their masters fell. A seer eventually told us that they would keep returning to our world until their masters came to reclaim them. So, we locked them up here."

"What about that armour?"

"Another form of possession, except this time an angel appears to smite you."

"Then you get dragged down to Hell?"

"Then you get dragged down to Hell."

8

TALKING ABOUT WHAT'S IMPORTANT

"Food?" Mara asked, standing in the back of their wagon and reading from a list of provisions. We were outside the guild near the stables, preparing to leave.

"Check," Luke replied, loading a crate of non-perishables onto the back.

"Potions?"

"Check. I also raided the guild's stores, so we've got a few firebomb potions and a holy smite potion."

"Are they properly stored?"

"Ah…"

I walked over and took the box from his hand, flipping open the lid. "They are not. We need liquid mercury and ice phoenix tears."

"I'll get them," Diva offered, racing back into the building.

"I'm guessing the stuff I pulled them out of was important, then," Luke said.

"Only if you don't want your wagon to explode," I said, dryly.

"Weapons?"

I rattled Slaughter. "I'm set."

"I've got two dozen enchanted spears," Luke said. "I also grabbed another bow and a few hundred enchanted arrows."

"Undead enchantment?" Mara asked.

"We used all they had with that zombie plague. They're flaming arrows."

"Pity. How's everyone's armour?"

I pointed to the vampire cliché that was my armour.

I was dressed in a long, black, hooded leather coat and a pair of matching skin-tight leather pants, boots, and gloves. The outfit was called 'The Day Walker Set'. Lavire had made it for his elder vampire brother by flaying his own skin, turning that skin into leather, and then enchanting it with demon king blood. It provided the wearer with complete protection from sunlight and non-magical weapons, along with having high magical and elemental resistance properties. It would also heal itself when damaged.

The only drawback to it was if anyone but a vampire wore it, they would crumble to dust. The demon king blood and ancient vampire regeneration also made it close to impossible for anyone but a saint to destroy, so it had been sitting in the vault for over two centuries.

Mara glanced at my armour with distaste while Luke said everything was accounted for. "How are we for spell scrolls?"

"We've got a crumble undead scroll and a dozen lesser shield scrolls."

"Those should be greater."

"Riker wasn't willing to hand them over after recent events."

I pulled two from one of the storage pouches I kept in my coat pockets and passed them to Luke.

Mara glared.

"Don't look at me like that. They revoked my guild membership until we kill the lich. I'm not breaking any guild rule."

"You stole spell scrolls," Mara said, like it was something I should feel bad about.

"And anything else we needed, so we should get out of here sooner rather than later."

Mara glared at me. "Hand it over."

I sighed and removed one of the storage pouches from my coat pocket, like it was the only one I had. While Mara went to return the stolen goods, Luke and I finished going through the list. With our agility, we were done by the time she got back which was good, because I had a lot of stolen property I needed to hide in the wagon. Diva finished stabilising the potions, and we leapt into the back and left the guild headquarters without fanfare or ceremony.

Ironically, Hellmouth was by far the safest and most peaceful city I had seen in this world. The walls were a hundred metres high and fifty metres thick, reinforced with all sorts of enchantments. Guards patrolled the top at all hours of the day, and a cleric with white, glowing eyes hit everyone who entered and left the city with holy magic. The guild and the local lord spared no expense for security, so it had upset them to learn I had just walked in.

The tops of the buildings were flat with a two-foot-thick ledge around the edge, making each one an effective turret for fighting ground and air forces. Enchantments were also placed up there to make it easier for mages to raise shields to deal with threats from above.

The only thing that was strange about the city's design was the fact that it was built to fight threats from outside *and* within. The hellmouth pit sat in the heart of the city, so the city was constructed to fight an army getting in *and* getting out. With a population of over a million, the city was gigantic, but so was the world around it.

Most wagons could travel at close to fifty miles an hour. Even with all the back and forth we had to do to navigate around streams and rivers, the location where I had been summoned was still a thousand miles away. This province was the size of the North American continent. The second smallest of the kingdom's fourteen provinces. They didn't have an exact measurement for the planet, but it was safe to say that it was several times larger than Jupiter.

Mara took the wagon off the side streets and entered the equivalent of a freeway. The wagons there were moving at a similar speed, thanks to the enchantments built into them. Horses, a special magical breed with blue coats, were buffed by magic and could run for hours, before needing to take a short break to eat and drink. So, traveling in the wagon was very close to traveling in a car.

As we exited the city, Luke opened a tube-shaped case and unrolled a map across the small table they kept in the middle wagon's bed during the day. "This is going to be our last mission in this province. The extra time we need to take to navigate around rivers and streams is going to run out the clock, so Riker has asked us to deal with all the current threats along the way. So, we've got an important decision to make."

"Loot distribution," I said.

He nodded. "Loot distribution."

All three women groaned.

"I propose a five-way split," Luke offered.

His offer was so insulting I almost slapped him. "I was thinking a two-party split. However, since your party has a few extra members, I'll allow a 60/40 split."

"I'm insulted by that," Sharani muttered.

Luke covered his grin. "My party is insulted by your suggestion."

"Well, I'm insulted by yours. I could take all three of your companions in a fight. I'll admit Mara *is* needed to put down the lich for good, but the other two aren't pulling their weight."

Luke winced as Diva and Sharani scowled. "They pull their weight just fine. They might not have our raw power, but you and I can't counter magic. *They can.* If you find yourself trapped in a barrier, you're going to be grateful they are there."

I tapped Slaughter. "I don't need their help for that. I chose a mage-killing sword for a reason."

"You chose it because it was the one lethal weapon that Riker would let you walk out with," Mara shouted from the driver's seat.

"And that was a good reason to choose a mage-slaying sword. However, my point still stands. It makes their contributions less."

Diva frowned. "He has a point."

Luke groaned, knowing she had just handed me an advantage. "Don't agree with him." Then he turned back to me. "And you, stop making my party doubt themselves."

"I don't doubt their ability. I'm confident they have the skills needed to keep you alive, through most situations, but when it comes to actual contribution in a fight, their utility in a given situation is dependent on that situation. Hence, they are worth less loot in this case."

"How little is our contribution worth in your eyes?" Diva asked.

I didn't care about her feelings, so I replied honestly. "Fighting the lich, Luke and I are worth 40% each. Mara is worth 15%. You both make up the rest."

"That's 2.5%."

"I gave you an extra 2% since you're in my son's party."

"I'll give *you* an extra 2%," she snarled.

Her anger didn't concern me. "It's fair, believe me."

"How is that fair?"

"We're going up against the lich, Contessa. She has converted Kindling, which was the largest city this province had before the hellmouth opened, into her own personal kingdom. Estimates say there are over two million undead within the city walls. Our only winning scenario is to rush the palace, and that requires Luke and I to cut our way through an army of undead that has had thirty years to grow stronger. If any of you help in a significant fashion on the way in, you will be too exhausted to fight by the time we arrive at the palace, where the real threats are. Even when we get to the palace, each of you will only act in a support role, dealing with skeletal mages and abominations. Getting to the lich will be *our* job. Destroying Contessa's body, the *first* time, will be *our* job. Putting her down *permanently* will be *Mara's* job. Dealing with spells will be your job."

"Dealing with a lich is a mage's job," Diva argued.

"It is in a traditional confrontation, where an army would storm the city and slowly push forward, giving hundreds of mages a chance to battle the lich together. We don't have an army. We have a hero and an ancient vampire hero. We have two heavy hitters who can go toe-to-toe with the lich. This will be that sort of fight, not a traditional one, which is why you get 2.5%"

"You don't even know what we're capable of!"

That's where she was wrong. "You're a level 57 arch-sorcerer savant. You were a sorcerer until you reached level 10, so you received 70 attributes up until then. Your aptitude for magic shined through at that point, and you upgraded to the sorcerer savant class, giving you 12 attributes a level. At level 30, you became one of the lowest-level sorcerers in the last century to achieve the arch-sorcerer savant class, and you boosted your attributes to 15 per level. You have received a total of 705 attributes from your levels, putting you 335 attributes *behind* Luke. Until recently, you had more attributes than he did, but his extensive list of skills, and their high level, still made him twice as effective as you were. Now that he's fifteen levels higher, he is several orders of magnitude greater."

I pointed to Sharani.

"We get your point," Sharani said. "You're aware of what we're capable of. That still doesn't justify 2.5%."

"It does."

She calmly folded her arms and leaned back against the side of the wagon. "No, it doesn't. How much does our presence improve the odds of success in your mind?"

"Around 10%."

"Then you admit you're underestimating our significance."

"If Mara, Luke, or I left the chances would fall to 0%, so I'm not underestimating anything."

She smirked far too smugly. "That's where you are wrong. The three of you constitute the bare minimum of what's needed to kill the lich. We represent what you need to improve your odds. The two of us will accept 10% of the loot to improve your odds by 10%. That's fair, since if you fail you get nothing and will die horrible, painful deaths. Now that I've settled the matter, I'll leave the three of you to work out how much each of you are worth if you did this alone."

Diva opened her mouth to protest, but Sharani glared at her. "We will accept 10%."

Something had gone horribly wrong in my negotiation. I couldn't think of a reasonable argument to give that would counter her logic. Technically, for a 10% increased chance to save my son's life, their 10% of the loot was a fair trade. "What just happened?"

Luke grinned. "I don't know what you're talking about. No one here has the negotiate skill."

I groaned. "How high?"

Sharani grinned. "Level 15. Would you like me to continue, or would you rather I leave you with 35% of the loot?"

I ran through the knowledge I had recently acquired and immediately realised she was throwing me a bone. "I'll accept 35%."

"You will, of course, be helping us take care of the threats along the way, accepting a five-way split for these missions, in order to get your 35%."

I gritted my teeth. "Not the dragon."

"Including the dragon."

I squirmed.

"You could always wait in the wagon while we take care of it."

"Fine, including the dragon."

"I need you to say it."

"I…accept…your…terms."

LUKE and his party had taken care of any major threat within three days of Hellmouth, so the first few days passed uneventfully. With his high attributes, Luke could get by on only a couple hours of sleep, so while the rest of his party turned in for the night, I trained his swordsmanship.

As the sun rose, Luke slumped onto a log. "How am I

progressing so fast? I've been stuck at level 15 for years. I've reached level 16 in only three days."

"It's the five-level canyon," I said, holding off from mentioning that he hadn't been training the way he should have been these past few years.

"I accounted for that. But that gap disappeared when I reached level 15."

"No, it didn't. First-tier prodigy skill, remember?"

Luke groaned. "I forgot about that."

I took a seat beside him and threw my arm over his shoulder. He needed some more advice. "You don't like being in charge, do you."

He heaved a sigh, letting go of the hero persona he wore with others. "It's that obvious?"

"Yes. I mean, you aren't suited to it. You don't seem to enjoy it. And you kind of suck at it."

"How do you *really* feel?"

I chuckled. "Why are you the party leader?"

"The hero is always the leader. A party falls apart if they're not."

"Do you understand why?"

"You can't have someone as powerful as I am thinking they're being used. It breeds resentment. That doesn't matter if you're a nobody, but when you have the power to topple a kingdom, resenting those in power is dangerous."

"It is. Now, would you like some advice?"

"Not really."

I ignored his protest. "Stop confusing leadership with micromanaging. Mara is a logistical genius. She should oversee keeping your party equipped and come up with your battle plans. Sharani is a natural ambassador; talking to the locals and being the public face of your party is something she enjoys and is good at. Let them do what they're good at and stop sticking your nose where it doesn't belong."

"But people want to meet the hero. It reassures them."

"Screw 'em. Let your work speak for itself. Roll into town, be mysterious, deal with the threat, and then roll out. You waste hours of your day, placating people. That's time you could spend training to make the world safer. Which brings me to my other point: *Why* haven't you been training?"

He scratched the back of his head. "There's no time. We're always on the move. The two-week training break we just took is the longest break I've taken in two years."

"I know."

"You know?"

"You're a celebrity, Son, and they have newspapers in this world. People follow what you do in the same way people did back home, so I read the articles they wrote about you. Your early progress at the academy was impressive, but you stagnated when you began adventuring."

He winced. "You read the articles."

"I wanted to know everything I missed and to understand why you weren't stronger."

"I've got places to be."

"And I respect that. However, there is a better way."

He took a deep breath. "I'm listening?"

"There are people in the kingdom who have mastered the skills you possess that offer very little or no tactical advantage. You're important enough that you could ask the king to make them travel with you. Not to fight beside you, but to train with you in your downtime. You're not in a position where you can work around others' schedules, but you *are* in a position where you can make them work around yours."

"Seems kind of rude."

"To me, it seems like a good way to let people participate in the fight. They might not be able to slay a dragon themselves, but they can make the man who can slay them stronger."

"You used to tell me to be polite and respectful of others."

"You were a boy then, and that was the right advice for the

situation. But you're a man now. A man with the weight of a kingdom on his shoulders, so my advice has to change."

"I'll think about what you've said."

I patted his armoured shoulder. "You're a good son, even if you only give me 35% of the loot."

9

LITTLE MONSTERS

"This is going to be a busy week, people," Mara said the following morning over breakfast. "I've plotted a route that will let us make the most of our time. We're going to be in a minimum of five battles a day if everything goes according to plan, so don't expect much sleep."

"I don't sleep," I pointed out. "In fact, I *can't* sleep until I return to the place I was turned. Also, there shouldn't be that many major threats on the way."

"There aren't. We're hitting every mid-tier threat between here and the lich. If this is our last hurrah in Hellmouth, we're going to leave it a little safer than it is now."

"Loot rules still apply?"

She groaned. "Yes, the loot rules apply."

"I'm listening then."

She placed a small map in the middle of the table. "Today, we're dealing with small threats. This region has a drake problem. It looks like a nesting pair raised a clutch of eggs and they finally reached maturity over the last summer. There are around a dozen full-grown drakes spread throughout these hills." She pointed to another section of the map. "In this forest is an arachnid infestation, and over here on the plains there is a ground worm. When we reach the mountains, there is an earth elemental we can stop and take care of."

I did some quick math in my head, estimating various body parts and their value. "That's roughly 900 gold pieces' worth of pure loot. Not a bad day."

"We don't have enough storage for all this," Diva said. "Most will be left to rot."

I leaned over and flipped the top off one of the crates, yanking out the storage chest I'd hidden inside, and scattering the grain that covered it. "I borrowed this from the guild. I think we should be fine."

"That's the guild's master storage chest," Mara gasped. "Where is the rest of the grain that was supposed to be in there?"

I reached into my coat and pulled out a storage pouch. Then I removed the sack of grain and began pouring it into the crate. I put the lid back when I was done.

Mara glared at me. "You took more stuff."

"A lot more. You really should warn the guild not to store greater illusion projectors in their vault. It makes it rather easy to empty it without anyone noticing."

"You didn't."

"Didn't what?"

"Take everything in the vault."

"No. Only like a tenth. A lot of it wouldn't help us, but I mean if I wanted to take it all I could have, because they left greater illusion projectors right there."

"Perhaps we should focus on the missions we need to clear," Luke said, trying to keep the peace.

"We need to move on," Mara insisted.

I was waist-deep in drake guts, throwing aside anything that wasn't valuable. Luke and I had done a number on the dragon wannabee after Diva grounded it, so many of the organs were damaged. "I found the kidneys, and they look like they're intact. How are you doing with the hide, Luke."

"I'll have it off in a minute."

The body rotated as Luke moved it, causing an avalanche of organs to sweep over my head. "You did that on purpose," I shouted after spitting out a mouthful of offal.

"Sorry, I can hear you. I'm skinning a drake."

"That doesn't make sense."

"Do we need to do this every time we kill a drake," Mara yelled.

"Yes," we both said.

Earth elementals were created from an over-concentration of earth magic within rock. They had no thoughts, nor feelings, and they couldn't be reasoned with. Most weren't violent, happy to wander aimlessly for all of eternity. This one was one of the exceptions.

Shattered wagons lay everywhere, scattering the pulverised, rotting remains of the victims who didn't get the warning soon enough. The earth elemental had taken the form of a gargantuan chipmunk, thirty feet high, with bulging cheeks. It scurried between the wrecks and climbed the cliff walls of the mountain pass with equal ease.

"That is *not* a minor threat," Luke observed.

Mara scowled. "These mountains are known for generating earth elementals; there is a very good chance whoever they sent to investigate the disappearances didn't do their job."

"You think?"

I glanced at Sharani, unconcerned by the behemoth. "How long do you need to tame it?"

Druids were tuned to the natural world. They had dominion over it and its elements. This was one of those situations where she excelled beyond the rest of us.

"I'm not an elemental tamer."

"You don't know the spell?"

"I didn't say that."

"Good. I'll distract it. Luke, you're on loot scavenging."

"WHERE'S THE LOOT?" I screamed, scrambling through the piles of scrap metal. It had all been flattened and rubbed so hard it shined, but it was all copper and steel. At one point it had likely been pots and pans, now it was all just metal leaves.

Luke was on the other side of the cavern searching just as hard, knocking over piles of metal hoping to find the pile of gold we were searching for. So far, neither of us had had any luck.

The dragon's corpse sat in a pool of blood, with its head several meters away. The sword of dragon-slaying that I'd borrowed from the guild had made short work of it.

"Not all dragons go after gold and silver," Diva said far too calmly.

"But most do," I shouted back, kicking aside more copper and steel.

"We still have the dragon's carcass."

I ignored her. "Luke, you find the gold yet?"

"There's nothing over here. What about your side?"

"Can't you smell gold," Mara complained.

"I don't trust my nose."

"Why not?"

"Because it's telling me there's no gold."

LUKE HAD WARNED me cultists were a walking cliché, but I wasn't prepared for how right he was. Black robes. Black candles. Symbols written in blood. Meetings at midnight in a candle-lit basement. It was about as cliché as you could get. The most upsetting part was that I fit right in.

All it took for me to match the theme, was to raise the hood on my coat, and obscure my face in shadows. With my fangs out, the cultists took me for one of their own and invited me in.

I had come across the cultists by accident. We had stopped in the town of Tobil, because it held the last adventurer's guild before we reached Kindling. A week of wanton slaughter had earned the party another level and left them exhausted, so Luke and the others were taking a day to rest.

While they rested, I had stepped out for a bite to eat and quickly found an Unseen moving through the night. I was on my way back to the guild when I saw someone else wearing the same cloak. Figuring I might as well eat two Unseen, I doubled back and walked down the road towards them, only to find they were just wearing the same cloak. Figuring they shared the same tailor, I continued on my way to the guild, only to run into a third person wearing the same cloak, another Unseen.

Realising my instincts were right, I didn't eat her. Instead, I followed her to a manor in the middle of town, lifted the hood on my coat, and knocked on the door. The Unseen maid saw my fangs and invited me in.

Now I was mingling in the basement.

There were a lot of Unseen talking to each other and drinking wine. Thirty-three so far, with more coming every minute. I wasn't sure if I could eat them all, but I was going to try. A buffet was a challenge to a man's personal fortitude, after all.

"Night favour you, dark one," the sacrifice said.

She was young, maybe sixteen, and completely naked, the way most sacrifices tended to be. Someone had spent hours painstakingly covering every inch of her body in bloody symbols, going so far as to remove her hair and leaving her bald. The fact no one was guarding her surprised me.

"You honour me with your presence," the sacrifice continued, excitedly. "My ascension ceremony will be the talk of the cult for years."

I glanced at the runes covering her one more time and then realised why they weren't guarding her. She didn't know she was a sacrifice. It was mildly amusing.

"Those aren't the symbols for an ascension ceremony," I said, fighting a smile.

"You must be mistaken," she said, and began pointing to the symbols on her body. "These are all the runes of ascension."

"Except the ones around your belly button. Those are a mother-child convergence. The power from your ascension will go to your mother."

She frowned for the first time. "But the sacrifice is in the other room."

"You're the intermediary."

"The what?"

I had read about the sow reaper cult in Hellmouth. The guild ran into them every decade or so. "Your ritual only works once, right?"

"Yes, why?"

"Well, if you want to do it a second time you need the right sort of sacrifice. Flesh of your flesh. The mother-child bond is one of the strongest magical bonds in existence and is powerful enough to overcome the limitation of the ritual. You must have noticed that the women here are significantly stronger than the men."

She continued to frown. "That's because the ritual is more effective with women. It doesn't mean my mother is going to sacrifice me for power."

"Believe what you want to believe."

A thin film of sweat began to cover her. "Just because most of the newly ascended leave to join the other chapters doesn't mean that they were sacrificed."

"Certainly not."

"I receive letters from my siblings every other month. Their handwriting is a little different, but that doesn't mean the letters aren't from them."

"Of course."

"They still know all the relevant details."

"The kind of details your parents would know, but yes you are most likely correct."

"My parents are going to sacrifice me, aren't they."

"I believe I said that several sentences ago."

Panic set in, and her heart pounded in my ears. It was a whooshing, erratic sound I found quite pleasant. "If you get me out of here, I'll become your familiar to do with as you please."

The desperation in her voice satisfied me. "Anyone here would willingly do the same."

"But I have magic."

"You don't even have a class."

She held out her hand, making a small gap between her thumb and index finger. A tiny jolt of dark energy jumped between them. "See."

"Necromancy is hardly rare."

"My father is a lawyer."

"So?"

"Evil is in my blood. I'm a creature of darkness."

I chuckled. "You get points for amusement, but you fall well short of earning a place as my familiar."

"You probably couldn't get me out of here anyway."

I smiled. "Reverse psychology, the last attempt of a desperate teenager."

"I'm just saying it how I see it."

The girl wanted to live, but as she was, she held no value to me. That could easily change. This dark ritual did provide an opportunity.

"If I were to take you as my familiar, you would have to bathe yourself in blood."

"Are you not aware of what I'm covered in?"

"I was speaking figuratively."

"I'm okay with killing people."

That wasn't true. "You're here because you're afraid of disappointing your parents. These people repulse you, so much so that you would rather speak with a vampire than speak with them. You are not comfortable with killing people, and becoming my familiar would require you to kill a great many people."

"How many."

"Hundreds, maybe more."

"Hundreds."

"Hundreds."

The door at the back of the room opened, and two robed figures dragged another naked girl into the room. She was gagged, with her arms tied painfully behind her back; tears streamed down her cheeks as they placed her on the altar.

The runes on the altar immediately began to glow with a dull red light as the time for the ritual approached.

"Salina," the sacrifice whispered.

"You know her."

"She's my best friend."

"And a fitting sacrifice. Your bond will make the attribute transfer greater."

"Can you get her out too?"

I snorted.

"I'll do it if you save her."

"You're a loyal friend."

"Do you agree to save her?"

"You wouldn't be planning for me to save her, only to then kill yourself once she is free?"

She cringed. "No."

"You don't fit in here. You realise that's why they're sacrificing you right?"

"What?"

"Cults like this one need people who are loyal to their own self-interest, people who will willingly sacrifice others for that self-interest. Anyone with a shred of decency must go. Anyone who can't pretend to have decency must go. You don't fit that description." I glanced around one more time. "You wouldn't happen to know if everyone is here by any chance?"

She quickly scanned the room. "Alister is missing."

"Bald man with a large moustache?"

"Yes."

"Anyone else."

"No, everyone else seems to be here."

"Good. I accept your offer. Now swear you will serve me."

"I swear to serve you from this breath until my last."

My skin tingled. Oaths made by people with magic weren't binding, unless rituals were involved, but uttering those words would make her a little more open to my requests.

I blurred to the nearest Unseen and ripped her heart out, going through her spine to reach it. I was back beside the sacrifice before the woman had even realised she was dying. With a fresh dose of heart's blood, I used my agility to change many of the blood runes covering her body to the ones I had seen in the guild's books, while retracing others. This was dark blood magic, about the darkest you could get, but it seemed a waste to let the opportunity go by without taking advantage of it.

I placed the deflated heart muscle in her hands. "Eat that."

Behind me, the owner of the heart collapsed.

The sacrifice scrunched up her face. "What is this?"

"Human heart. It's the only way to save your friend," I lied. "Quickly now, freshness is important."

Her eyes darted to her captured friend and then she shoved it in her mouth and began chewing, scrunching her face up with disgust.

There were several concerning noises, including the words. "Is that a hole in her back?"

I picked up sacrifice girl and raced across the room to the altar. The two men holding down her friend were both Unseen, so I tossed the girl I was holding in the air, ripped their hearts out, shoved her friend on the altar off violently, and caught her, gently placing her down.

"Swallow," I instructed.

She swallowed, and the runes all over her body began to glow as the light coming from the altar intensified.

"Now stay put."

I picked up the still-beating hearts of the Unseen I had killed and squirted the blood over her. It was immediately sucked into the runes, causing them to glow brighter.

By now the cultists were starting to sense there was something wrong. It was too late. When the first scream filled the basement, the Unseen were all teetering on their feet, and I was covering sacrifice girl in the last of their hearts' blood.

Her runes began to burn, drawing every frightened gaze.

She raised her head to look at her body. "Am I on fire?"

"No."

"I think I'm on fire."

I picked up the ritual dagger, lying at the head of the altar, and gave a growl when I saw the poorly etched runes. "Cheap knockoff. Okay, I guess we do this the hard way."

A lot of bones snapped in the next few seconds, and then the remainder of the cultists were all screaming. It was vicious, violent, and bloody. It didn't bother me at all.

I made my way back to the altar and stood over the girl while she burned. "I did the hard part. Now you need to go finish them off."

Cultists writhed on the ground, with shattered arms and legs. Bones protruded from their skin as they cried out in pain. It was a beautiful sight and an exquisite sound. I didn't want it to end.

Their injures were serious, but not the sort that would kill them in the next thirty minutes. If I had to, I could race back to the guild and get Mara.

"Finish them off," she said dully, looking past me to the screaming cultists. "What's going on?"

"You're becoming useful to me. Now go kill them." I appeared on the other side of her and snapped the gag in her friend's mouth. Then I placed my bloody hand around her neck threateningly. "I held up my end of our agreement. Now you kill the people I want killed."

Her eyes darted to the screaming cultists and then back to her friend. "With pleasure."

She blurred across the room, and the first few cultists exploded from the impact. Because of the ritual, she temporarily had the combined attributes of *all* the Unseen I'd killed, so I wasn't exactly surprised by the display.

Her friend glanced up at me, while trying to cover herself. "You were with the hero when he arrived in town, weren't you?"

I removed one of the dead cultist's cloaks and handed it to her. "Yes."

She pulled it around her. "Are you a vampire?"

"Yes."

"But you were in sunlight."

"I'm an ancient vampire."

"Did you mesmerize the hero to grow your dark empire?"

"No. I'm working with him, so the guild will give me neutral status."

"Is that why you're here to save me?"

"No. This was an accident. I stepped out to feed on a few Unseen and wound up here."

"Is it all right if I pretend this is all just a dream?"

I reached into my coat and pulled out a vial filled with sleeping powder. I dumped it over her head. "Sure, kid."

Her eyes grew heavy, and she slowly dropped to the ground. "Thank you."

As the last member of the cult was torn apart, sacrifice girl turned her gaze on me, body coated in unholy fire. My instincts warned me she was about to attack; and in her current state, she might actually be able to kill me.

I kicked the altar, shattering it. The runes covering sacrifice girl vanished, leaving her a lot weaker, but significantly stronger than when she started.

I smiled as she charged.

10

MY MONSTER

Getting Salina cleaned and into her bed was the first thing the sacrifice, Angelica, and I took care of. Then we gathered up all the cult's occult paraphernalia and freed the victims locked in their basements. The sun rose the following morning as we entered the guild and approached the front counter.

The young man behind it, eyed me nervously. "How can I help you, your Dark Eminence."

I chuckled. "That's an old title."

"Would you prefer another?"

"No."

"How can I help you?

"I discovered a dark cult during the night. There were thirty-seven Unseen present. I dealt with them, obviously. Now, there's a wagon filled with occult paraphernalia out front, and a manor filled with dead people you need to take care of."

The clerk swallowed. "I think I need to get my manager."

"Give me the mission report paperwork before you go."

He quickly ducked below the counter and began riffling through papers. "Yes, your Dark Eminence."

"Can I sleep now?" Angelica whined.

"No." There was no compassion in my tone. She was a tool to be used and discarded as needed.

"Here they are." He placed them on the counter and then added a pen.

"Why not?"

I took the papers and nodded to the clerk. "I'll be in the tavern." Then I turned to look at Angelica and started walking. "Because you tried to kill me."

Angelica gave me the biggest smile she could, which was far less charming without any hair. "You wouldn't hold what someone does during an evil ascension ritual against them, would you?"

"Nothing about that ritual affects your choices. You thought you were stronger than me and decided it was a good time to renege on our agreement."

She stopped smiling. "Well, you *are* evil. What did you expect?"

Chuckling, I dragged her into the tavern. I spotted Luke and his party and headed for their table. I swiped a chair as I passed an empty table and slid it into the space between Diva and Sharani. "Take a seat, Angelica."

"Are you bringing your meals to breakfast now?" Mara grumbled. "She reeks of evil."

"I will not be insulted," Angelica said, raising her nose as she tried to walk away. This was just the latest attempt to flee, so I picked her up and placed her beside the chair.

"Sit.

"Yes, sir."

I grabbed another chair and sat beside Luke.

"You didn't answer my question," Mara said.

"She's not food, Mara."

Angelica perked up as I said Mara's name. Then her gaze immediately went to my son. "Are you Luke?"

He nodded.

"I'm your biggest fan. You have to save me. I'm not sure if you know this, but the man next to me is an ancient vampire. You need to kill him. He's evil."

"It's too early in the morning for me to deal with this, Dad," Luke grumbled.

Angelica's eyes widened and her head turned slowly in my direction. "You're the hero's father."

I smirked. "Yes."

"And an ancient vampire."

"Yes."

"I'm going to need time to process this." She turned to the other women. "Did you know about this?"

They all nodded, starting to find what was happening amusing.

Angelica possessed the astounding ability to get herself into trouble with nearly every decision she made, so what she said next didn't surprise me. "So, the hero's harem knows his father is a vampire."

Their amusement vanished.

"I think I need more information, because none of this makes sense."

I folded my arms and leaned back. "Vampirism is a curse until you kill your first innocent."

Angelica frowned. "I thought it was until the first time they fed."

"Most of the time, the first time a vampire feeds is the first time they kill an innocent, which is where the confusion comes from."

"What does that have to do with anything?"

"I've never killed an innocent. I've never completed the curse and lost my soul."

"And that matters why?"

"Because it means I can only eat and kill Unseen, and I'm not half as evil as I should be."

"You seemed to have no problem breaking all those people's legs."

"What people's legs?" Mara growled, climbing to her feet.

"Dark cultists," I clarified.

"Oh, I don't care." She sat back down and returned to her eggs.

Angelica glanced at Mara and then back at me. "You kill evil things. That's why the hero and his harem don't care what you do."

Diva gritted her teeth. "We aren't his harem."

"Girlfriends, concubines, you service his lusty appetites. I read the articles."

Luke snorted into his oatmeal.

That was the wrong thing to do.

All three women turned as one and glared at him.

Ice formed over his clothing as Sharani cleared her throat. "Is there something you would like to add to the conversation, hero?"

"Danger, Will Robinson," I whispered so softly only he could possibly hear me.

He chuckled, involuntarily. Then, realising what I had done, Luke started running for the door. It was not the fun and games kind of running either. He moved so fast only I could follow him.

The women were out of their chairs and after him before he was halfway out the room.

Angelica didn't know what to make of their actions, watching them race off with an open mouth. "What just happened?"

"They aren't sleeping with him."

"What?"

"They aren't sleeping with him, and they're all happily married, to other people. They're a little touchy about the rumours surrounding their party, and they like to take their frustrations out on my son."

"Why?"

"Because he's terrible at dispelling those rumours. Every time he's tried, he's only made it worse. They want him to get a wife to finally end the talk, but he refuses."

"Weird. Why am I here? I mean I understand why you needed me for everything else, but you don't need me anymore."

"Yes, I do."

"Wait, you actually want me to become your familiar."

"Yes.

"You said you didn't want me."

"Then I made you stronger."

"Now you want me?"

"Yes."

"I don't buy it."

"Strength is important to me. However, it's not the only thing. You are loyal to your friends. You are amusing. But most importantly, you're comfortable around me."

"You want me because I don't flinch every time you say something."

"I can count on one hand the number of people I have met who fit into that category."

"And that makes me a good choice for a familiar?"

"I recently spent a decade asleep, because there was no one around to wake me up. I need someone who is loyal to me to help me stay active. That's impossible for most."

"Because they're terrified of you, hate you on sight, and would rather stab you than wake you up."

"Yes."

My honestly seemed to surprise her. "Would you have made this offer if I didn't kill all those people?"

"No."

"Would you have let me die if I had said no to becoming your familiar?"

I shrugged. "I was planning to eat the Unseen. Whether or not the others continued with the ritual after I left would have been up to them."

"So that's a yes."

"That's a yes."

"What will happen to me if I say no to becoming your familiar?"

"You were part of a cult intent on sacrificing a girl so you could gain her attributes. I'll hand you over to the authorities and let them deal with you."

"But I turned against them."

"After you knew you were being sacrificed. Before that you were uncomfortable but content to go along with the ritual."

Her situation dawned on her. "They're going to hang me."

"Most likely."

"My choices are become your familiar or face the gallows. Would you let me make a run for it?"

"No."

"How long do I have to think about it?"

"Until I finish this paperwork."

I picked up the pen and began filling out the forms. I wrote at a relaxed pace; one a normal person would write at. Angelica had seen my speed, so she realised I was giving her time to think. When I put down the pen a few minutes later, she had come to a decision.

"I'll become your familiar."

"You need to *want* to become my familiar for the bond to work."

"But I don't want to become your familiar."

"You have a choice between becoming my familiar and certain death. To you, becoming my familiar represents life. It represents new sunsets and freedom. It represents a reprieve from the consequences of your actions."

"Why are you doing this?"

"Because you fit my requirements. Because you are strong. And because you got a raw deal in life, being born to psychopaths who dragged you into their depravity and convinced you it was normal. You might not deserve a second chance, but you deserve half a chance."

"Be honest: How evil are you?"

"Less evil than people fear, and more than I would like. I *did* feed you a human heart, after all. The thought of doing that to anyone, before becoming a vampire, would have been repugnant to me. Now I have no qualms about doing what is necessary."

"You said I would need to kill hundreds of people."

"They will be Unseen or people like the ones you killed last night."

"Wait, I just have to kill assholes?"

"A lady shouldn't swear. But yes."

She grinned. "I can kill assholes. I can kill a whole lot of assholes. You really should have led with that."

"Noted."

"Okay, you convinced me. What do we do now?"

"Now, you drink my blood." I pulled back my sleeves, exposing my wrist.

She looked around. "Right here?"

"Why not?"

"Where are the candles? Where's the dark altar? Where's the chanting? You're a lord of the night, have some self-respect."

"I sit at the table of my enemy in full view, surrounded by their strongest while anointing another, as they watch on, powerless to intervene. Hiding in the shadows, surrounded by sycophants, pales in comparison to such a display."

She blushed. "Say that again, but slowly."

I blinked, then realised what she was implying. "What kind of books have you been reading?"

Her blush turned a deep crimson.

Freaking teenagers.

Embarrassed that I knew what she was getting at, she quickly grabbed my wrist to hide her face.

I was not happy about the next words that came out of my mouth, even though they were technical instructions. "Bite down hard and drink deep."

Her teeth penetrated my skin. The instant her tongue touched blood, her jaw clenched, and she reached bone. I slammed my fist into my chest, stimulating my heart to beat, once for her, once for me, and once for the bond we forged. As the third beat faded, her jaw unclenched.

I pushed her head away and wiped her saliva from my wrist with a napkin.

Angelica sat frozen for nearly a minute, before finally speaking. “When does it happen?”

“When does what happen?”

“The rush of power.”

“You’ve been reading the wrong sorts of books. The familiar bond doesn’t give power.”

“What does it give, then?”

“Protection. Demons, vampires, and creatures of evil will smell my blood within you and leave you be, fearing retribution.”

“Is that why familiars are always commanding armies of darkness?”

“Yes. You speak with my authority now.”

She started grinning again.

I could see the thoughts running through her head. “You may only use my authority to protect yourself and innocents from harm.”

“Of course, whatever you say.”

She was still grinning.

She didn’t understand what she had given away. “I’m going to give you a command and then you can try to speak.”

“What?”

“Be silent.”

She stopped moving. After a few seconds panic set in as the horror of what she gave away so easily collapsed around her, becoming reality. She was completely at my mercy.

“You may make noise now.”

She started breathing again. “What the hell was that?”

“To a new familiar, their vampire master’s words are *absolute*. *Any* instructions I give you will be performed to your very best ability.”

Her gaze dropped to the table, and she whispered, “What have I done?”

"You have chosen life." I climbed to my feet. "Let's go see what class choices you've unlocked."

She remained in her seat.

I turned and looked down at her. "Angelica, I would prefer to give you as much freedom as possible, but that can easily change if you make matters difficult for me."

She rose to her feet. "You lied to me."

"I withheld the truth, so I suppose I did lie to you. The compulsion will fade with time. In a decade, my words will only bind you while you remain in my presence."

"And outside your presence?"

"They will have no more effect on you than the oath you made to me last night."

The thought of eventual freedom seemed to calm her. "You said something about a class."

"Yes, follow me." I led her through the building to the class hall. "What class would you prefer?"

She glanced at me and then at the stone. "You're giving me a choice?"

"People need to feel a connection to their class. Parents who force their children to take their class often find they don't live up to their expectations. Conversely, children who pick a class because they think it is their calling tend to excel and gain access to rarer skills."

"Shouldn't you have asked me what sort of class I wanted before making me your familiar? What if I want to become a baker?"

I chuckled. She was as easy to read as an open book. She craved power, and the security power gave.

She didn't like me laughing at her. "Is it all right if I become a necromancer?"

"Yes, but you have more options than you think."

"Why?"

"Because you performed the reaping ritual. Your flesh is a conduit for evil, power, and magic. You will have access to classes that are pure abominations. So don't take a class until you have my permission."

Angelica walked over to the class stone and place her hand on top. "Do you want me to read the list?"

"Only those that you find relevant."

"There are a lot of classes here. How is evil baker a class?"

"It's an Unseen class upgrade to the baker class. It allows them to mix poison into bread without it affecting the flavour."

"It's creepy that you know that."

Behind me a woman cleared her throat. "Excuse me, your Dark Eminence, but I was told you wanted to hand in a mission."

I turned around and offered her the mission statement I'd written and then explained what had happened the previous night. Her gaze kept sliding to Angelica and her unauthorized use of the class hall, but she didn't say a word. She would most likely bump this up the chain of command the moment she left.

She interrupted me halfway through my explanation. "You left a wagon loaded with occult material in the middle of the street!"

"It's out front."

"Hells below, I need to secure that immediately. Excuse me, your Dark Eminence." She turned and ran for the door.

I turned around and focused on Angelica. "You find anything interesting?"

"What's a hell knight?"

"A class that will immediately condemn your soul to Hell. Practically every class with the word Hell in the name will do the same."

"Which ones won't."

"Hell breaker, hell raiser, hell hunter, hellish architect, and hell singer."

"None of those are options and I'm almost entirely certain you made up the fourth."

"You're evil and they're good; of course, you don't have access to them."

"What's the reaper class?"

"It's a class that allows you to temporarily steal the attributes of those you kill. Not a bad class, power-wise, but the souls of those you kill will haunt your every step until you die. You need to be truly evil for it not to affect you, and you don't fit that category."

"What about a death knight?"

"Half-necromancer, half-knight. Strong class, but you need to pick a path. If you try to invest in both, you end up being weaker than both a necromancer and a knight."

"I kind of like the sound of that. I could be a necromancer, but still wear armour."

"Is that appealing to you?"

She nodded.

"If you want, you can read off your options, and I can sort them into that category for you."

She took me literally, reading every class on her list. Not because she was slow, but because she was a teenager and trying to find the limits of what I would allow. Before becoming a vampire, that would have bothered me, but I had nothing else to do with my day, so I waited and watched her become more and more annoyed as I didn't say anything while she read off classes like accountant and butcher.

An hour later, she reached the end of the list, turned, and forced a smile onto her face. "I hope that wasn't too boring for you?"

"No. I'm fine."

"Good…good," she said through gritted teeth.

"You've got three options. Death knight, necromancer legionnaire, and imperial necromancer."

"Only three options? The list was huge!"

"Working with death magic isn't inherently evil. It might make you colder and more calculating, but it won't make you evil. There were about twenty other options on that list that fit your requirements, but every one of them was inherently evil in nature and would corrupt you over time. In less than a year, most of them would leave you as an Unseen."

"And the rest?"

"It would happen almost immediately."

"Which one do you think I should take?"

"I would suggest the death knight class. The necromancy legionnaire is predominantly a class for raising large undead armies. The imperial necromancer is more for large-scale death spells. Neither of them is versatile, nor will they allow you to choose your own path."

"Let me get this straight. I just read that stupidly long list only for you to suggest I take the option that I said sounded right to begin with."

"Yes, now you can go forward knowing you made an informed decision."

"I think I hate you."

"Would you like to read through the list again to make sure you didn't miss anything?"

"No, I would not like to read through the list again."

"Good. You have my permission to take the death knight class."

A shiver ran through her a moment later. "Wait. How many attributes does this class give? Damn it. Why didn't I ask that first?"

"It gives twelve per level."

Her eyes widened and she started to giggle. "Did you say twelve?"

"Yes, but I would look at your base attributes, too. You might find them rather shocking."

She continued to giggle, but her gaze changed as she brought up her character sheet. Her mouth dropped open. "I'm a monster."

"Yes. *My monster*."

11

IT TAKES A VILLAGE

Angelica continued to giggle as she followed me around the guild. I went to the stables and collected the master storage chest, and then I headed for the courtyard in the centre of the complex. A dozen younger guild members were sitting around, studying in the early morning light. They got up and left the moment they spotted me.

All adventurer guilds had the same layout to make it easier for members to know where they were needed in an emergency, so I could hear hammering and other craft work coming from the right and the scratching of pens and the muttering of incantations to my left. Ahead, the training room was filled with sounds of people fighting.

I placed the chest on a stone table and indicated for Angelica to sit. She was clearly drunk on her own power. The cult she was a member of was a base chapter of what would have been a much larger cult. They were usually referred to as a sowing, because they were only presented with the first half of the ritual. This ritual allowed them to steal attributes from a sacrifice, before they moved on to sacrificing their children. They were never meant to know that they were being prepared for a much larger ritual -- one where they would become the sacrifice.

Connections and bonds in these sorts of rituals were important. The stronger the connection, the more attributes you could take from the sacrifice. Angelica didn't have as many attributes as she would if I had fed her a few dozen chapters of the cult, but she had significantly more than if I had used random strangers. She would one day rival Luke's party members in raw power, even if she lacked their skill.

The odds of someone being able to kill her while I slept were low, but they weren't zero. If she died before she managed to wake me, I could lose another decade or more. She was stronger than she had any right to be, but she wasn't strong enough for me to risk going back to sleep yet. I needed her to grow stronger before I would risk that.

Angelica continued to giggle as she sat.

"Tell me what skills you obtained."

She answered immediately, unable to fight my compulsion. "My racial skills were magic, enhanced physique, and darkvision. And my class skills were staff, war staff, armour, riding, death magic, disease resistance, necrotic resistance, and rapid healing."

"A potent combination."

She giggled. "Thank you."

"That wasn't a compliment. You played a very small role in becoming what you have."

"What do you mean?"

"Darkvision is not a human racial skill; neither is enhanced physique. You received them because you are my familiar. The same can be said for your resistance skills and your rapid healing."

"They're not death knight skills?"

"They are, but they are rarely obtained upon receiving the class, unless you come to the class at a much higher level. The death knight class is also unheard of as a first choice. You have the attributes I gathered for you to thank for that."

"You said the class gives twelve attributes. That makes it a second-tier class, doesn't it?"

"Yes, you are one class upgrade away from the top."

"What do I have to do to upgrade it?"

"From what I understand, unlocking the death lord class is not a matter of power, but skill. You will need to master *every* skill you have in order to assure its acquisition at level 10. I forbid you from touching a class stone without my permission."

She stopped giggling and began to scowl. "That will take years."

"Yes, but I will help you to the best of my ability. Would you like me to explain your skills to you?"

She nodded.

"Where would you like to start?"

"Why do I have two staff skills?"

"Because you are the luckiest kid in the kingdom. Most death knights come from the knight class, which means they usually use a knight-type weapon. They don't obtain the staff skill, which is a mage skill, until they become a death knight, and then they must switch between their weapons when they want to utilize their most potent magic. If they are very lucky, they will later obtain the war staff skill, and if they are even more lucky than that, they will be able to utilize some of their advanced skills with it."

"Isn't a staff a terrible weapon, though? Won't it bounce off armour?"

"If you only use it to hit things, then yes, it is a terrible weapon. However, with access to magic, you can learn to infuse your staff with magic, which makes it a very potent weapon, instead of a large stick."

"Is death magic an advanced skill?"

"Yes. Anyone who can utilize magic before they gain their class gains an advanced magical skill. But you already knew that."

She shrugged. "I wanted to see if you would give me an honest answer. What does advanced physique do?"

"Men are stronger and faster than women with the same strength and agility attributes. The advanced physique makes you stronger and faster than both."

She began giggling again. "It's an attribute-boosting skill. Those are insanely rare."

"Yes. Any other questions?"

"No."

"You don't want to know how to train your skills?"

"You're going to tell me anyway, so why ask?"

"Follow me, then." I picked up the chest and walked over to the enchantment workshop. Angelica quickly stepped past me and opened the door. It seemed like a behaviour someone had drummed into her, most likely violently by how quickly she acted.

The enchantment workshop was filled with all sorts of mages. They were mixing potions, enhancing materials, and writing up notes for enchantments. Enchanting was not simple work. The size of a breastplate changed from person to person, which meant they had to redo calculations for every item they made. It was a very math-intensive profession.

The few sounds in the workshop slowly went silent as everyone noticed my entrance. The head of the workshop hurried over as his people backed away.

He was a small, ancient man with deep, wrinkled skin and thick glasses. I'd heard somewhere his name was Oliver. "What are you doing in my workshop, vampire?"

"I am commandeering you and your staff until tomorrow morning. I have a project that must be finished before we leave. You will not be required to make anything you are uncomfortable with, and I will allow you and the crafting workshop to keep the excess materials."

He frowned. "What will we be enchanting?"

"Drake leather plate armour and a dragon bone war staff for a death knight."

"Will they be joining you on the mission?"

"Yes."

"Then I'll allow it." He turned and began pointing at enchanters. "You, you, you, not you Bartholomew, you, you, and you."

When he had gathered his enchanters, we made our way to the craftsmen's workshop. The craftsmen's workshop was the opposite of the enchanters: Men and women hammered away at metal, while leather workers shouted at each other, and glassblowers swore. The chaotic room quickly went silent as they noticed our presence.

The woman in charge hurried over, glancing at the old man behind me. "I'm Nina, head of the crafting workshop. What can I do for you?"

"I am commandeering you and your staff until tomorrow morning. You have a day to make and enchant drake leather plate armour and a dragon bone war staff for a death knight. You may keep the excess materials."

She looked past me. "You're going along with this, Oliver?"

He nodded. "The death knight will be fighting the lich."

"I'll be fighting what!" Angelica shouted.

I ignored her. "The dragon bone I have is from a red dragon and not suited for a death knight; are you familiar with the process of death enhancement for dragon bone staffs?"

The woman nodded. "You make an oversized, hollow staff, enchant the inner hollow to convert the bone to dracolich bone, and then fill the centre with quicksilver. The enchantments on the outside are used to strengthen the bone by drawing in death magic and death aura, which the quicksilver stores. When the staff reaches a point you are comfortable with, you empty the quicksilver and sand away the original enchantments and enchant it with your preferred enchantments. How do you plan to enhance it? You will need a massive source of both energies to make this work."

"I can provide the death aura, and the lich's city will provide the death magic."

She began to smile. "You're willing to provide *yourself* as a source to enhance the staff?"

"Yes."

"Would you be willing to provide blood for the enchantment?"

"Yes, but I would have to watch you the entire time." Blood was a potent magical reagent, and it could very easily be used against me.

She turned and began yelling at people, telling them to get other people. Then she turned back to me. "How much dragon bone do you have?"

"A dragon's worth."

"Would you be willing to part with it all?"

"Why?"

Nina glanced at Oliver and smiled. "Tobil holds some of the greatest minds in the kingdom when it comes to understanding death magic and the undead. With access to dragon bone, ancient vampire blood and aura, and lich death magic, we could craft a set of weapons and armour for a death knight that would potentially propel our skills forward by several levels."

This was an interesting opportunity. "I take it you would want us to return once the armour and weapon are enhanced, to complete them."

"Yes. If you successfully kill the lich, there will be no need for us to remain here any longer. But with greater skills, we could serve the kingdom to a much greater degree in other places."

"Why do people keep saying we're going to kill the lich?" Angelica asked again.

"It's what we are doing next, and yes, you are coming." I said glancing over my shoulder at her, before turning back. "She's new to her class, but has absurdly high attributes. It still seems a little soon to give her such powerful equipment."

The crafter began to grin. "How high?"

"Angelica, tell her your attributes."

Angelica answered through gritted teeth. Everyone stared at her with wide eyes. Several took a step back.

"And her level?" Nina asked.

"She only received her class this morning."

Nina's eyes widened. "Skills?"

I listed them off.

"I can work with that. If we don't focus on what she has, but rather on what she *doesn't* have, she should never outgrow the set. It will even continue to grow stronger with her, if we incorporate more of your blood into the materials."

"That still seems excessive. I would prefer she grow into her power, naturally. I don't want her to be reliant on her equipment."

"Make her train without it, then."

With that simple solution, the argument was settled. "You may make what you wish. How much blood will you need?"

"The more you give, the better we can make it."

"I'll need to find more Unseen, then."

I UNLOADED the dragon's entire skeleton while the crafters took Angelica's measurements. When they were done with her, I took her to the training room, answering her questions. She didn't want to fight the lich. There was only one lich around, and she knew that it was likely suicidal to attack it. I pointed out that I didn't plan on dying, and that if we did survive, she would come out of the fight with a world-class set of armour. This did very little to reassure her, until I mentioned that she would also likely level a great deal, too.

The training room fell silent as we entered. The silence stretched as they stared at me with uncertain eyes, gripping their training weapons fearfully.

"Does this happen every time you enter a room?" Angelica asked.

"Only when you're with me." There were several teachers present, so I raised my voice. "I'm looking for the guild's staff instructor."

A woman in a robe hurried over. "I'm the staff instructor. How can I help you?"

I pointed at Angelica. "You have until tomorrow morning to train her in the staff and war staff skills to the best of your ability. Do not treat her gently. I expect you to push her to her absolute limits. She will be joining us against the lich."

"She has two staff skills?"

I listed off her skills and her attributes, then added, "You will likely need a cleric with you. She is unaware of her strength."

Then I turned to Angelica. "You will do everything she tells you to do that is related to your training. You will train to the best of your ability, and you will not ask for breaks, nor slow down. You may defend yourself if the need arises, or if another innocent would come to harm. You may stop for breaks only when the needs of your body become pressing."

Angelica scowled. "You're compelling me."

"Only to greatness. I will see you tomorrow morning, where you will be allowed to sleep for several days and relax while we travel. Is there anything you need to say before I go?"

"Where are my siblings?"

I glanced at the instructor. "Where would the children of dead cultists be taken?"

"They would be rounded up by the guild for investigation and interrogation. If they pose no threat and were not complicit in the cult's activities, they will be handed over to family or friends willing to take them. If no one can be found, they will be taken to another town and handed over to the orphanage."

Angelica opened her mouth to protest.

"I will make sure your siblings are cared for, and they will join you for dinner."

She smiled her first honest smile. "Thank you."

"You're welcome. Now, you need to start training and I need to take care of this, so I can go hunting."

Unseen were attracted to evil. The villages that surrounded Hellmouth were filled with them. The same applied to Tobil. Evil flowed from the lich's city, corrupting the landscape and infecting everything. We were three and a half days' travel from the former provincial capital, but everything was still sick. Plants withered, crops grew poorly, and the stench of death hung heavily over it all.

I scoured the town of eighty thousand, running in and out of every public building I could find. Several groups of adventurers followed behind, accepting the Unseen I found. Clerics would make a small sphere of holy magic at the tip of their finger and press it against the Unseen's forehead, causing them to writhe. When they had confirmed the Unseen were who I claimed they were, they bound them and added them to the other prisoners.

A few hours later, I sat in the craftsmen's workshop while Oliver fussed over a syringe, hands glowing with mystical light. Extracting my blood was a difficult process. Overcoming my body's regeneration was hard. My regeneration caused my blood to rush back into my body, when given the chance. Only the old enchanter could perform the necessary steps to extract it.

I watched as my blood flowed into the enchanted syringe. As Oliver pulled the needle free, my hunger roared its ugly head. Replacing a vial of blood was not a simple matter for me. To a vampire, their blood was their power, and regenerating it was not easy.

Two adventurers rushed forward with a bound and panicking Unseen. My hand caught her by the throat, and she crumbled to dust. My hunger dropped to a less dangerous level but didn't abate.

"Another," I growled.

The pair standing at the door rushed forward with an elderly man. He crumbled to dust.

"Another."

A third crumbled, finally causing my hunger to retreat.

"Your hunger has increased again," Oliver commented. "Should we take a break?"

I shook my head. "The last break didn't change anything. Continue."

He shrugged and began preparing another syringe. "How many meals do you have left?"

"Eighty-three."

His eyebrows rose. "You've eaten *hundreds*."

"I found three hundred and forty-eight in town. The guild master is interrogating the local bishop."

"It's a pity that more clerics aren't willing to sacrifice their holy strength."

He was talking about clerics being willing to use their holy magic on everyone who entered and exited a town or village. Using holy magic to attack innocent people weakened a cleric's power. Enough misuse and they were essentially powerless. Very few clerics were willing to give up the power to raise the dead and mend broken bones with a wave of their hand to act as a security system.

"There was an attempt to force the matter several centuries ago," I said, remembering something I had read.

"I'm aware. Heaven sent an angel who smote the guild responsible." He plunged the new syringe into my arm. "How many do you think you will need to provide the death aura?"

"You would know better than me."

"I have no clue. There has never been an attempt to capture the death aura of an ancient vampire."

"There are nearby villages I can visit."

"You must be aware that news of the Unseen disappearing will eventually get out. You might find prey becoming scarce in this province in the coming years."

"I only need to eat every few weeks if I take no injuries."

"Still, you should consider building a larder. The guild would help you. The chance to remove Unseen from our society is not something we would pass up."

"It seems like too much trouble."

"You could have your death knight manage the larder."

That made the matter far less bothersome. "I'll consider it."

Hunger roared within me again, and the adventurers rushed forward with my next meal.

Nina walked over and grinned at the bowl filled with my blood as an Unseen crumbled to dust. "How much do you need, Oliver?"

"A fifty-fifty ratio for the quicksilver would be best. A couple of syringes worth for the enchanted ink and to build a focus. How much do you need?"

"More. We're making blood bone."

Oliver frowned. "You know how to make blood bone?"

"No, but Azula does."

"What method is she using?" I asked.

"Ether infusion."

That was a costly method, but it was also the most effective. "You'll need to send adventurers to the nearby villages and towns and have them gather the people there, if you want that much."

"You're proposing a purge," Nina said.

"Do you object?"

"No, I'll mobilize the guild immediately."

I COULD TRAVEL MUCH FASTER on foot than the wagons could move, so I arrived at all the nearby villages and towns before midnight. With the guild gathering the people for me, I quickly went through the massive crowds, tossing the Unseen to the waiting adventurers. They then proved to all the witnesses that the people I chose were Unseen and transported them back to the guild in Tobil.

Luke and his party were waiting for me in the lobby when I returned. Bound Unseen were packed into every room and hallway of the guild, filling my ears with panicked heartbeats. It was lovely.

"We need to talk," Luke said.

I treated the Unseen with the concern they deserved, which was none, walking over them as though they were carpet. "You'll have to follow me if you want to talk; I'm busy."

Luke and his party followed, walking over the Unseen with the same disregard. "We want to know what you intend to do with Angelica."

"We also want to know why you are going to such great lengths to provide her with this insane armour," Mara said.

"You're going to leave when this is over. When you leave, I'll have to return to the place where I became a vampire, so I can finally sleep and prevent myself from going mad. I need someone to wake me, or I will sleep for years. Angelica will be that person."

"And the armour?" Mara asked.

"That was the craftsmen's idea. I only wanted them to provide her with a simple set of drake armour. They saw an opportunity to raise their skill levels, and they convinced me to allow them to provide her with something better."

"Why give her such powerful armour?" Luke asked. "Why not take it for yourself?"

"Can't."

"Why not?" Mara asked.

"Same reason a sorcerer can't make a wand from their arm bone, even though it should theoretically provide the perfect wand."

"Similarity interference," Diva said.

"I have no idea what that is," Luke said.

"It uses *his* blood, so the enchantment will go haywire if *he* tries to use it."

I nodded as we walked into the craftsmen's workshop. I took a seat next to Oliver, who was fast asleep in his chair, and nudged him.

"What, oh you're back," he muttered, blurry-eyed. "Give me a moment. Oh, hello, Hero, have you come to donate blood. too? I'm sure Nina and her people can find some way of incorporating it into the armour."

Luke glanced at me. "I'll think about it."

Mara glared at him. "No, you will not."

"It would tilt the scales to the side of good," Oliver explained. "A vampire hero and his human hero son have the right sort of symmetry for this type of magical creation."

"You're making armour for a death knight," Mara spat the words with disdain.

"A death knight is not inherently evil," Oliver replied.

"Yet most death knights are."

Oliver sighed, like a man who had had this discussion many times. "While it's true that at least ninety percent of death knights take the dark path, it is also true that some do not. The opposite symmetry exists in the knight class, with one in ten taking a less-than-ideal path. Neither class is good nor evil, they are merely tools we use to fulfil our objectives. It just so happens that the tools of a death knight are more suited to those who prefer evil."

Mara turned her focus to me. "We read your mission report and what you did to Angelica to make her so powerful. You've created a monster."

"I don't deny that. But I will point out that she is *my* monster."

"For now."

"If she becomes a problem, you are welcome to kill her."

"She's already a problem. She was a cultist."

"Angelica is not evil. She is misguided and self-centred, but she could be a force for good. If I'm to make this world safe for my family, I need people who will work with me."

"You want me to believe you're trying to make the world a safer place, because you care about people."

"A *safe* place. Not a safer place. And I couldn't care less about 'people'. I care about *my family*. If others benefit from the safe world I create it, neither pleases nor upsets me."

"That has to be the most self-centred reason I've ever heard for saving the world."

"Yet it is all the motivation most need to make it better."

"He's got a point," Oliver said.

"He does not."

"As someone with children of my own, I can promise you he does. I do my work to keep *them* safe, to let *them* live happy lives. I don't do it for people I've never met, yet they benefit. There is no evidence to support doing good for your fellow man can't come from self-centred motivation. It does not need the unambiguous selflessness the church teaches. If it did, very few would ever do any good in this world. I am living proof that the opposite is true; so kindly take your misguided philosophy and keep it to yourself, or leave this workshop."

Mara gritted her teeth.

Luke frowned and crossed his arms. "How will giving you my blood help you? From what I've heard, only evil can be performed with it."

Oliver picked up the syringe and indicated for the adventures at the door to bring the first meal forward. Then he placed the needle in my arm and began his work. "Your father is a creature of evil, though he possesses very few of the actual qualities. There is a chance that this evil quality could be passed along in his blood, causing the armour to become corrupted over time. The bonds between you of blood, love, and class would allow us to fuse your bloods together, and thereby weaken this trait and strengthen others that are preferable, preventing potential corruption."

Oliver pulled the needle free, and the adventurers rushed forward with my meal. As the fourth Unseen crumbled, I waved away the adventurers coming forward. They carried the blubbering mess of a man back to the entrance.

Luke continued to frown. "Would my blood only be used to stabilise the negative consequences of his?"

Oliver shook his head as he finished adding my blood to the enchanted bowl. "No. Your blood would also greatly enhance the materials and the enchantments we lay upon it."

"Is that a side-effect or the intent?"

"Both. Changing the base materials changes what we can create. With blood from both of you, we would do the most we could with what we are given. To do less would negate our chances at gaining levels. And I believe that the sum total of the potential benefits from including your blood in addition to your fathers with any restrictions is less than not including your blood at all. The craftsmen in this workshop make the best weapons the kingdom has for fighting undead. With more levels, we can do better than we already do, supplying more adventurers with greater weapons for killing undead."

Luke nodded, his mind made up. "How much blood do you need?"

THE SUN WAS RISING by the time they finished drawing blood. Oliver took all he had gathered from the two of us to the enchanters' workshop, and under our gaze, he began processing it into the reagents Azula needed. I had eaten more than *a thousand* Unseen during the blood extraction; the process had resulted in a mild hunger that would not lessen no matter how many Unseen I ate.

It was concerning, even though it was tolerable.

With the changes to the armour, we were not going to be leaving at sunrise. Angelica had screamed and cursed at me when I informed her of that fact. I could still hear her muttering curses at me as her training continued.

The enchanters spent the entire day working on the reagents, before handing them over to Luke and me to carry to the craftsmen's workshop. Oliver had been true to his word, striking several enchanters who tried to pilfer my blood for personal research.

Luke and I crossed the courtyard, with the last of the Unseen under guard, and entered the other building. The craftsmen looked at us with excitement and heavy bags under their eyes as we approached Nina with the reagents.

She gave me a tired smile and then bowed to Luke. "Thank you for giving us this opportunity, Hero."

"Oliver made a convincing argument."

"I can only imagine. Now, I don't mean to be rude, but we need to get moving. The crucible is primed, and the mages are going to begin to pass out if we do not begin shortly. We have completed the blank armour and staff. Angelica confirmed that the armour was uncomfortably tight and that the staff was much too wide to be practical. The materials have been rushed through all the necessary processes, requiring many expensive reagents, but they are ready for the ether infusion."

"We could have stayed for another day if it would have saved money," Luke said.

I began heading to the crucible. It was the large, enchanted stone table, with the staff and armour floating above it. "You're making the wrong assumptions about crafting magical gear, Son."

He frowned as he followed. "I am?"

"Yes," I explained. "Only common magical gear is made slowly. The most powerful magical gear is made as quickly as possible. The reagents and enhanced materials leak magic during the binding process; the longer you take, the weaker the final product. They have every mage in town in the rooms below us providing the mana needed to stop the items from leaking magic and to force the magics to fuse."

Nina's eyebrows rose as she took the vat of blood mixture from Luke. "You understand crafting?"

"Not enough to *do* what you are doing, but enough to *understand* what you're doing."

"An academic interest, then."

"You could say that."

She waved over another woman. She was a short, freckled, grey-haired woman, with small delicate hands. "This is Azula. She'll be performing the infusion while I stabilise the bones."

"You altered their structure," I said, looking at the equipment.

"Since you had the entire skeleton, we ground down the bones and concentrated the dragon's essence into the set you see before you," Nina replied, as they began setting up.

"Risky choice."

"Would someone dumb it down for those of us who haven't read the entire guild library?" Luke muttered.

"You ever heard of a weapon and armour set called dragon's might?" I asked.

Luke frowned. "Isn't that set sort of mediocre?"

"Depends on what dragon you make it from and how old the set is. The sets grow stronger with age. By concentrating the dragon's essence into one set of armour, they gave it another growth property while making the material and the wearer stronger."

"You just said *another* growth property, didn't you?"

"If I'm not mistaken, there are *four* growth properties to this armour."

"It's only three," Nina said.

"I'm including the dracolich transformation growth property."

"That's technically a temporary growth property."

"Which makes it a growth property."

"You've been reading Yorick's work, haven't you?"

"Is there a problem with that?"

"The man never got out of the academic stage of the craft. He's a menace."

"His work is several stages above his competition."

"That madman's genius stretches the realms of what is theoretically possible, but he's never created a single method for how his creations would be crafted in the real world. If he hadn't restructured and simplified how they teach advanced crafting, he never would have contributed anything of substance to the field."

"That one achievement is more than most ever contribute."

"But less than he could have, which is why I have a problem with him. Now, stop bothering me; I need to focus."

Luke and I stepped back, taking a seat against the wall, where we could see everything they were doing.

Luke nudged me. “How can one set have three growth properties? My armour only has two, and it’s the best the whole kingdom has.”

“It’s *living* armour; yours is inert.”

“Dumb it down.”

“Your armour grows stronger because the enchantments on it can draw more power from you as you gain strength. It also grows stronger, because the material it’s made from can infuse more magic into its structure over time. It’s like a battery that gains more charging capacity each time you charge it.”

“And the set they’re making?”

“It’s different. It was made from something that was once living; and with magic, you can trick it into *thinking it’s still alive*. Dragons grow stronger as they age, so the armour does too. By infusing blood into the bone, they give it the ability to level, too.”

“The armour can gain experience?”

“Yes. Angelica will receive a steep reduction in the experience she gains wearing this set, but it will make both her and the set stronger for it.”

“And the last growth property?”

“It’s the same as the one your armour contains, but designed for a death knight instead of a hero. Technically, the armour won’t have that property until after we kill the lich, because the material needs enhancement to finish the conversion property, so it will never actually have four growth properties.”

Luke looked at the equipment floating in the air. “People said it was foolish of me to wear growth armour.”

“Most of the time it is. Growth armour is generally weaker than regular magical armour. However, that’s why it’s called *growth.* The armour you wear is weaker than what you could otherwise acquire for another five years; then it will be just as strong; a decade after that it will be a little stronger. Two decades later it will be significantly stronger. When you are old and wrinkly, people will talk in hushed tones about your armour.”

"It's like you always said. 'The younger you start making sacrifices, the easier life is.'"

"I told you that so you would share with your sister."

"It's still true."

"Only if you add the word, '*worthwhile,*' before sacrifice. There are many sacrifices you can make in your life that will eventually make it easier, but you need to make sure the sacrifices are worthwhile."

"Not this again. I'm not getting married."

"I want grandchildren."

Luke snorted.

"Life is slipping through my fingers, Son. I don't know how much time I have left. The grave calls me."

Luke began to laugh.

"Would you be quiet? We are trying to work here," Azula shouted.

AFTER THEY FINISHED CREATING the base materials for the armour and staff, the pieces went to the enchanter's workshop for the enchanters to imbue the first layer of enchantments, which would cause the armour to transform from red dragon blood bone to dracolich blood bone. The enchantments needed to go inside the armour plates, on the unreachable, hollowed out sections of the items. This was a fast process for the staff, but an extremely slow process for the much thinner armour, so it was another day before they were done.

Once that was finished, they returned the armour to the craftsmen's workshop. The craftsmen injected the quicksilver reagent into the staff and armoured plates, sealed it, and returned it to the enchanters to finish the external enchantments. Then they called me over to the craftsmen's workshop to fill it with death aura.

Everyone and everything had an aura. However, that aura was

rarely strong enough to do anything. As an ancient vampire, my undead nature gave me a powerful death aura that made death magic stronger and easier to control in my presence. Transferring that death aura to the armour would stabilize all the death magic that the armour would absorb and facilitate everything the enchanters and craftsmen had done to it.

Oliver grinned as he held the staff. "These external enchantments are designed to draw in death magic and will not harm you. We intentionally didn't include anything to draw in your death aura, because the quicksilver reagent was so potent, we were confident that it could draw it through the medium unassisted."

Nina shakily held out a crystal orb filled with more of the quicksilver reagent. "The hollow sections of the staff and armour will need to be sanded to remove the original enchantments. When that occurs, we will need more reagent to fill the space. Making another batch won't work, so we've made this focus for Angelica to carry with her. If you return, the focus will then be broken down and the reagent added to the armour and staff."

"I'm aware," I said.

Nina rubbed her eyes and yawned. "Sorry, I've had far too little sleep these past three days. Who knows what is beginning to blur together. Do you know we are using the focus to charge the items with your death aura?"

"No. Is there any particular reason?"

"We want to regulate the flow of your death aura. It's probably unnecessary. We designed the enchantments to survive a great deal of stress, but we're being cautious since this is all new territory."

"It's fine. We can begin when you're ready."

Oliver waved over a pair of adventurers holding my meal and Nina handed me the orb. The moment I touched it, it felt like I was crossing a stream. Power rushed out of me, flowing into the orb at breakneck speeds.

"Food!" I roared, panicking.

I WAS close to mad from hunger by the time the orb had finished extracting enough death aura. They had given me all the Unseen that were left while it drained me, so I exploded from the building, leaping up walls to flee the town. The nearest sources of food were several towns away, due to our purge, and I had to run wide around settlements to stop myself from jumping on the first person I saw.

As the first Unseen crumbled to dust hours later, a prompt appeared.

Your Willpower skill has increased to level 16.

Concerned with how close I had come to succumbing to my hunger, I began to consider Oliver's suggestion that I build a larder. Then I continued hunting.

Still hungry but unable to change the fact, I walked into the training room a few hours later to find Angelica still going at it. Her instructor sat against the wall, exhausted, while Angelica fought against another opponent. A group of clerics stood to the side, providing healing spells as needed, allowing the two to go at each other without restriction.

Adventurers watched from the side, making bets. Others watched purely for academic purposes. I made my way to her instructor and sat. "How did she do?"

The tired woman smiled. "Level 8 in both staff skills. Level 5 in armour. Level 3 for her rapid healing. And level 12 for her enhanced physique. She hasn't slept. She's barely rested. The harder I push her, the harder she becomes. However, if she ever sees me again, she's going to try to kill me."

"No, she won't."

"She hates me more than any student I have ever trained."

She believed her statement to be true, which concerned me. I didn't need Angelica distracted by vengeance. "Do me a favour. Tell her this and *only* this when you end this session: 'I have done all I can to train you so that you can survive what you will face. I only hope it's enough, and I'm sorry I couldn't push you harder.'"

"I overheard one of my old instructors say something similar to one of her students when I was Angelica's age. She only trained the best, but one of the girls at the academy lost her family to a werewolf attack, and she was intent on revenge. She taught her, despite her lack of talent, treating her as brutally as I have treated your familiar. I thought her methods harsh, but it was out of concern for her safety. Is that why you did this?"

"Yes. She's going into something that would terrify someone with a thousand times her experience. She will likely die."

"You could leave her behind."

"She doesn't deserve such a consideration. This is her penance. This is how she finds redemption."

"You want to redeem her?"

"She can't travel freely as a wanted criminal. The local lord has already agreed to pardon her actions in the cult if she should survive the battle. If she returns, she will be free before the law and more capable of fulfilling my will. You may end her training now."

The instructor left her seat and commanded the two to separate. Then she took Angelica aside and told her what I had told her to say. I watched as Angelica's face darkened with rage, but she was incapable of reacting. Leaving her angry at the woman I had told to instruct her served no purpose and would only distract her. When we returned, those words would change her disposition. She would never like her instructor, but she would be grateful, and grateful was better than hateful.

Angelica stumbled toward me when her instructor was done. Deep, heavy bags lined her eyes. Without the immediate fear of violence, there was nothing that could propel her to action. Still, she had grown stronger from the mistreatment. I could smell it in her blood.

"I'm going to kill you one day," she said, miserable and filled with rage.

"I have spent the past three days working on your armour."

"I don't care."

"It is the most powerful set of death knight armour this kingdom has ever produced."

"I don't care."

"And if you return from this mission, it will receive enchantments that make it unequalled by anything crafted by human hands."

"I don't care."

"A lot of people worked very hard to make this for you."

"I don't care."

"They are waiting outside to present it to you."

"I don't care."

"You will *pretend* to care. *I don't care* that you are angry with me. *I don't care* that you hate me. They spent sleepless nights and exhausting days working while you trained, in order to forge you a set of equipment that will be with you for all your days. If you cannot show gratitude to the people who have worked so diligently to save your life, you will *pretend* to show gratitude, and you will do so to the best of your ability."

"When can I sleep?"

I climbed to my feet. "You may rest and eat as soon as this is over. Now follow me."

I headed for the door. Angelica trudged behind me, teetering on her feet woozily. I slowed my step and caught her elbow to steady her. She was very close to passing out. The adrenaline was fading, and that hormone was the only reason she was still awake. I pushed the door open.

The thirty craftsmen and enchanters stood in the middle of the courtyard, to either side of a set of beautiful blood-red armour and matching staff.

As we approached, Oliver stepped forward, holding out the staff to Angelica. "It is my honour to present you with the staff of the Crypt Keeper set."

Angelica slowly held out her hand, unable to muster the strength to move quicker. The instant she touched the staff, she stood straighter, and colour returned to her cheeks.

Oliver collapsed.

I grabbed the staff and yanked it from his grasp, before she did permanent damage.

Nina turned to Azula, while enchanters rush to Oliver's side. "What just happened?"

"Vampiric touch," I replied, having recognised it instantly. "It wasn't that much, maybe a week off his life, but he was already exhausted, so he collapsed. You might want to hit him with a healing spell and let him sleep it off."

"I feel better," Angelica said, giving her full attention to the staff she was holding.

"You just sucked a bit of his life force out of him, so I'm not surprised.

"Wait. This staff has *vampire powers*?"

"It's *not* supposed to," Nina said, glaring at Azula.

"Stop glaring at me," Azula snapped. "No one has *ever* made blood bone from ancient vampire blood. He had to massacre a *thousand* Unseen just to supply us with the necessary blood. This is a *completely unique* set. Did I *expect* some of his vampiric nature might transfer over? No. Am I *surprised*? Also no. We knew we didn't fully understand what we were creating when we made it, which is why the unluckiest of us received two whole levels in all our relevant skills."

Angelica stared at her staff and began to smile. "My staff has vampire powers."

"It has a lot more than that. Would you like to try the armour on?"

Her smile grew.

12

SELF-CARE AND OTHER PREPARATIONS

Mara kept turning her head to look over her shoulder and glare at Angelica's snoring form lying in the back of the wagon. This prompted a member of her party to tell her to keep her eyes on the road and added to her frustration. We were behind schedule, which meant it would take longer for Luke and his party to reach the next province and cause the people there to suffer. On an intellectual level, Mara understood the time we had spent waiting for Angelica's armour to be completed was a net gain, but on an emotional level she only saw dead people. Dead people who had died to make a death knight armour.

With the completion of Angelica's armour, we had swiftly left Tobil. To a pessimistic person, the time we had spent there to help the craftsmen level would be a good trade as we were traveling to our deaths. But Mara wasn't a pessimist. She believed their party was destined to save the kingdom and that there was too much work left for them to do to for the lich to kill them.

Mara's behaviour was tolerable, but my son kept giving me nervous glances.

"What's troubling you?" I finally asked.

"You look sickly."

"I'm hungry."

"We can stop at a village on the way for you to hunt?"

"It won't make a difference. Making so much blood drained me. I need sleep."

"What about blood?"

I paused. "It might work. It might not. I'm not willing to take the chance."

"Are you in fighting form?"

I chuckled. My boy was concerned. "Hunger doesn't affect my strength."

"I meant headspace-wise."

"I'm a little compromised."

"Only a little?"

I nodded.

"Good." His shoulders relaxed, ever so slightly. "In that case, we need to talk about your misuse of party loot."

All three women groaned as Luke and I began haggling over the value of the dragon bones against everything else we'd acquired. I tried to argue for a straight value trade, but Luke countered with an unauthorised use charge, which stuck. I ended up losing twice the value of what the dragon bones represented on paper.

Our parties needed to set a precedent, and he pointed out that it would work in my favour if they ever did the same to me. Seeing the logic in such an argument, I accepted the price of my misbehaviour, loudly and obnoxiously mourning my lost loot.

A few hours later, Luke sat with his back to the wall, watching Angelica sleep. Mara had traded positions with Diva, and she and Sharani were fast asleep on the opposite side. The enchantments built into the wagon meant their breathing and occasional snorts were the only sounds a person would hear.

"She seemed to be happy with the set they made for her," Luke said, eventually.

"She was high," I replied. "The rush from losing the worst of her pain and exhaustion left her euphoric."

"She wasn't happy?"

"She was, but the feeling was exaggerated by the effects of the staff."

"I have to ask this. Is the Crypt Keeper set safe with her?"

"I'm not sure. I'll know by the time we return."

"How will you tell?"

"By the way she looks at it."

"What?"

"You don't put a gun in a child's hands; they tend to think it's a toy. That's the way she looks at her equipment for the moment. The city will change her attitude towards it, or it won't."

"And if it doesn't?"

"Then I'll take it from her."

"Just like that?"

"She needs the armour to survive the city. Day-to-day life is another matter."

"It's growth armour. It won't grow without her."

"She's young. She'll grow out of her immaturity, at which point she can have it back."

"Why didn't you tell her about the pardon?"

"It will distract her."

"You don't think it will motivate her?"

"No. She's used to making others deal with her problems for her. Her parents. Her friends. Me. I don't need a familiar that uses others to fix her problems for her. I need one strong enough to do it herself. She still thinks she's the small, weak girl her mother was going to sacrifice. She's not. If she can survive the lich, she will come out with a different understanding of herself."

"You're throwing her into the ocean and telling her to swim or die."

"Yes. I don't have the luxury of being patient with her. It's difficult enough to show the interest in her that I already have."

"Curse of Sloth?"

I nodded.

"She knows her siblings are safe, right?"

"Yes. I'm not sure if she believed me, though. It might do her good to hear you repeat it when she wakes. Worry will distract her."

Luke sighed and ran his hand through his hair. "I don't like what you're doing to her, Dad. You're treating her like a tool, an object to be used as you please, only to be discarded when you have no use."

"She is going to live a hard life, following me around. No one will trust her. No one will give her the benefit of the doubt."

"Just because the world will treat her poorly doesn't give you the right to do the same."

"You know what she was doing when I found her?"

"Yes. She was being a stupid kid trying to live up to her shitty parents' expectations. If you keep treating her the way you've been treating her, she's going to be the monster Mara fears. And I'll be the one who must put her down."

He was right. "I'll do better."

"Don't do better. Do your best. I don't like killing people I don't have to, Dad. You have a chance to make my guilty conscience one person lighter. Please don't make me have to kill her because you aren't willing to put in the time and effort. My life is hard enough without you adding to my problems."

A sad smile touched my lip. "I'll do my best."

THE FOLLOWING DAY, I gently shook Angelica awake. We had stopped beside a stream with a hollow. Angelica hadn't bathed since before we met, and the smell was bothering the others.

Angelica groaned as I continued to shake her. "You promised me you would let me sleep as long as I wanted," she muttered.

"You've slept for an entire day."

"Doesn't feel like it."

"You only need to wake long enough to bathe and eat; then you can go back to sleep."

She finally rolled over and opened her eyes. "There's food? Why didn't you say so? I'm starving."

"Bathe first."

"I'm not that bad." To prove her point she smelled her armpit. Her nose wrinkled with disgust. "On second thought, I could use a bath."

I offered her my hand to pull her up.

She ignored it, climbing to her feet alone.

"There is a fresh set of clothes on the crate over there, along with a towel and a bar of soap."

She blinked away sleep as she turned to see where I was pointing. "Those aren't my clothes."

"I went through your home, but your clothes weren't suited for battle, so I had the craftsmen make some that were."

"I'd prefer my own clothes while we travel."

"If you look out the back, you'll see we're beyond the border. We'll be running into wild undead soon. You need to be ready to fight for your life. If you survive, you can wear your clothes on the way back."

She scowled but took the clothes. "Is this a gambeson coat?"

"Yes. Both stylish and practical."

"You can't be stylish without hair," she muttered, running her hand self-consciously over her bald scalp.

"There are hair growth potions in the crate beside you."

She glanced at me, surprised. "You bought me a hair growth potion?"

"Didn't have to. My son is balding."

She giggled, before remembering how much she hated me. "The hero is balding."

"He takes after his mother's side of the family."

She lifted the crate lid. "Which one is it?"

"The one labelled 'Emergency Potion'."

She went through several potions. "They're all labelled 'Emergency Potion'."

"He buys in bulk."

She giggled again. "How many do I need?"

"Each potion will give roughly a finger's length of hair."

"Where specifically?"

"Everywhere. You might want to look in that crate over there before you use them."

She went to the crate and opened. "These are mine." She began riffling through. "Where did you find my brush? I've been missing it for months."

"Your sister's bedroom."

Her gaze tightened. "Which one of them do I need to murder?"

"Not the one younger than you, but the one under that." I hadn't been interested enough to learn their names.

"Celia. That little worm helped me look for it."

"You might want to collect your things. The food will be ready shortly whether or not you are, and my son likes to eat."

Angelica quickly collected what she needed and leapt out the back, running for the stream. I went to join the others. There was a perfectly serviceable kitchen in the wagon, but Luke said he wanted to grill, and had pulled out a charcoal barbeque, that looked like the one I'd had back on Earth.

I walked over to the horror show he seemed to call barbequing. "You need to flip that steak."

"Mara only eats it well-done."

"And she calls me a heathen."

Luke chuckled. "Did I see Angelica running off with my hair potions?"

"Yes."

"Did you warn her not to drink them?"

"No."

"She's going to have hair *everywhere*."

"Self-care is soothing. It gives you a sense of control."

"There is nothing soothing about foot-long leg hair, Dad."

"Speaking from experience?"

"I may not have read the label the first time I used them or the second time."

I chuckled and then began to scowl. "You're murdering that steak."

"It needs another minute for Mara to eat it."

"You should consider kicking her out of your party."

Mara turned and glared at me. "I heard that."

"You were meant to. This is a crime."

"You still seem to care about steak," Luke pointed out.

"Maybe. Maybe I just still care about injustices being committed before my eyes."

Luke laughed while he flipped the inedible steak.

"She's not one of those people who puts ketchup on her steak, is she?"

"No, I would kick her out for that."

"I heard that."

"You were meant to."

We both chuckled.

In moments like this, the years we had lost faded into the background and it was just me and my boy. Not me and a hero whose father had slept away the last ten years, forcing him to fight through this world alone.

"Can they make a decent hamburger bun in this world?"

"Better than back home."

"We should have burgers and beer before you leave."

Luke smiled. "I'd like that."

"Your other steaks are leaving medium-rare territory and approaching medium-well."

"It's intentional."

"Then I've failed as father."

"Butchering skills aren't as sterile as back home, and diseases and parasites are different. You need to cook your steaks a little more to make sure they're safe. Believe me, you only need one bad experience to change your views."

"The meat is clean. I can smell it." All but one of the steaks were flipped in less than a second. "I thought you said you were a changed man."

"I lied. This world a cruel place and medium-rare is God."

We both laughed.

MARA PULLED the wagon over to the side of the barren road and climbed into the back with the rest of us. Yesterday, Angelica had stayed awake long enough to bathe, eat, and get a haircut to tame her blonde mane and foot-long eyebrows. After that she'd immediately gone back to sleep, waking up early this morning. This was partly due to enhanced physique skill. Her body had gone through a substantial transformation, causing her to take much longer to recover. She had been a thin girl when I met her; now she was very close to gaunt. That would change with more food.

Mara pulled out a map and placed it on the table. "We need to go over the plan and everyone's capabilities before we go any further. This is the city of Kindling. Before its destruction from the hellmouth invasion, it housed close to thirty million people. The lich, Contessa, has made no secret of the fact that she has taken up residence in the old governor's palace, so that will be our target." Mara pointed to the outer wall around the city. "This is the west gate. It will be our point of entry. We need to travel down this main road to this side street, which will provide the most cover and the safest route to the palace. However, because of the closeness of the buildings, we will have to deal with more attacks from above. Speed is our friend. There are over two million undead in the city, and the longer we take to reach the lich, the more time they have to engage us, so we won't be stopping for any reason."

Angelica grumbled, scowling at the map.

"Information on the lich's capabilities is limited," I added. "It is incredibly likely that the undead will remain animated after her demise. Do we have a fallback point if we suffer heavy injuries once we succeed?"

Mara pointed to a small building near the palace. "This is the old treasury building. There is a vault below ground that can provide us with some security if we can reach it." She reached into her pouch and pulled out an amulet. "Opening the door isn't instantaneous, so we will have to hold the corridor for a while."

"What's the plan if we get separated?"

"If we are separated on the way in, we will regroup at this building, here. If we are separated on the way out, it's every man for himself. Head for the wall and hope you make it."

I glanced in Angelica's direction. She was fidgeting. "You can move faster on foot than you can in the wagon. Your chances for survival will improve if we're separated on our way out. Don't stop to engage in battle unless you have no other option. Mobility is your friend."

She frowned. "Why would it be safer on my own?"

"Undead are not typically known for their speed. There are exceptions, but for the most part you can outrun them."

Mara flicked her gaze to Angelica. "With Luke and Vincent taking point and clearing the undead in the street, the three of us will have to be up front countering threats from the top of buildings. The canvas over the wagon has powerful shielding runes stitched into it, leaving only two possible points of entry. You will remain at the back of the wagon and deal with anything that attempts to enter through the rear entrance."

"I can't do that alone," she whined.

"You don't have a choice," Mara said. "Your armour makes you a threat to the party. If we touch you, we'll weaken."

"That's not my fault."

"I made you strong enough to reach the palace," I said. "So, stop whining. The only threats that will reach the wagons will be ones Mara and the others deem too weak to waste a spell on. Your equipment is designed to consume death magic, so even if the undead get their hands on you, they will immediately begin to weaken as you grow stronger. Which reminds me, if you see an opening to grab the lich during battle, I'm commanding you to take it."

She stiffened. "I don't want to fight the lich."

"I have to agree with her," Mara said. "She has no place fighting the lich. She doesn't have the experience or the skills she needs for such a confrontation."

"But she has the equipment."

Luke frowned. "You want her to vampiric touch a lich."

"Her equipment is designed to absorb the lich's magic. Between its need to absorb death magic, in order to convert the base material to dracolich blood bone, and having my blood at its core, its storage capacity for death magic is unparalleled. The lich is a conduit to her army, storing her excess mana within them. If Angelica manages to grab Contessa and hold on, the undead closest to the lich should crumble. It will significantly improve our survival chances."

"And kill her," Luke said.

I shrugged. "It might. It might not. While she's absorbing its magic, Contessa will be cut off from using it. She will only have her raw strength to depend on to escape Angelica's grasp. And after her armour has reached capacity and transformed, Angelica will be immune to death, necrotic, and fire magic, limiting the methods the lich can use to kill her."

"Wait, her armour is a trump card," Mara said. The time she had spent around Luke had changed her, making her occasionally throw out Earth lingo.

I nodded. "The craftsmen built it to give us a chance. Its current form is designed to weaken the lich and its army for us."

"I'm going to die," Angelica whispered.

"You died a week ago, Angelica. You live because I allow it. And I do not intend to spend your life fighting this lich. Do your best to stay alive while you assist us."

Her mouth fell open. "Did you just command me to live?"

"Yes. It will improve your chances."

"Can you command me not to be afraid?"

"I can no more compel you to not be afraid than I can compel you to harm those you love or kill yourself. There are limits to our bond."

"Great, then I'm leaving." She climbed to her feet and started walking towards the back.

"Stop." She stopped walking. "I may not be able to command you to kill yourself, but I can command you to follow me into battle and spend your life to save mine. Return to your seat."

Angelica marched back to her seat and sat, scowling at me. "Fine. What do I do when we reach the palace?"

13

ONE DOES NOT SIMPLY WALK INTO A LICH'S CITY

"You drugged them," Angelica said as she tried to shake Luke and the others awake.

"Obviously," I replied, going through the crates and taking out what we needed. Mara's plan was never going to work. Neither was the plan I proposed. The lich was too prepared and too powerful. But I needed my son to *think* it would work. It was the only way he would let his guard down, so I could save his life.

"Why would you drug them? We're about to reach the city."

"Their plan wasn't going to work." I finally found where Diva was keeping the holy smite potion and added it to the potion bandolier. "Get your armour on, Angelica."

Angelica pulled her armour from the storage crate and began undoing the buckles. "When are they going to wake up?"

"They're not."

"How are we going to do this without them?"

"We'll improvise."

"That's not a plan."

"Neither is trying to fight our way through *millions* of undead." Angelica was struggling to put on her armour, so I walked over and assisted, pulling the straps tight. "Their plan would have killed us."

"You don't have a plan, *which is worse.*"

"You and I have an advantage over them, Angelica."

"What advantage?"

"You have performed the reaping, and I am an ancient vampire. We reek of evil. Alone, without them, we can walk through the gate and reach the lich without ever drawing our weapons. We will not arrive in the city as invaders, but as honoured guests."

"And then stab them in the back."

"Obviously."

"I don't like it."

"It's not your place to like it. It's your place to help me achieve my goals. Now, raise your foot; I'll help you with your boots." Angelica continued to grumble as I finished helping her put on her armour. "Test your range of motion."

She quickly flowed through a few simple exercises designed to make sure her armour was in the correct place. It was.

"Where's your armour?" she asked.

"I'm wearing it."

"That's a leather coat, not armour."

"My pants and coat are made from the skin of an ancient vampire that was far stronger than I am. It is resistant to magic, immune to non-magical weapons, and regenerates any damage it takes."

"Is it cursed?"

"Yes."

"In that case, I hope it hurts."

"It's not that sort of curse."

"Pity."

When she was ready, we climbed out of the wagon. I grabbed the summoners' horn sitting on the crate at the back and blew a long, sharp note. As the sound faded, eight ethereal figures appeared around us.

They were men and women, former guild members, whose spirits had remained in this world to protect their allies. They clutched intangible weapons and looked at me with disgust.

"We do not serve your kind," the nearest one said. He was a strong-jawed man with a heavy, two-sided battle-axe.

"Look in the back of the wagon." The ethereal man walked over to the wagon and glanced in the back, unconcerned by my presence. "I need you to take the hero and his party to safety. They are bewitched and in an enchanted sleep. They need a cleric to purify them. Can you do this?"

"Will you be with us?"

"No."

"We will do this task."

"The nearest town is Tobil, and three days from here. Follow that road, until you reach civilisation, and then use the map I placed on the driver's seat."

He held out his hand. "Our horn."

I passed it over. "Keep them safe."

"We serve the light," he replied.

The figures all made their way to the wagon and then climbed aboard. Two immediately began fussing over my son and the others, while three raised spears and took up defensive positions, going entirely still. The leader climbed into the driver's seat and picked up the reins. He dropped the brake and flicked the horses to get them moving.

I watched them leave until the sounds of the wagon had faded into the petrified forest. Then I turned to Angelica. "Let's get moving."

She lifted the blood-red visor on her helmet. "It's stupidly hot in this armour."

"You need to raise your armour skill then."

"It's also hard to see."

"You need to raise your armour skill then."

"Why are you making me die uncomfortable?"

"Because I'm a sadist. Now walk."

"You can't really expect me to believe they're just going to let you walk in."

"Your cult invited me in."

"That was different."

"How?"

"You were an honoured guest."

"Because you thought I was a vampire."

"Well, yes."

"And if you had known what I really was?"

"Then you would have been offered the maid and maybe a couple of the leaders' kids as an appetiser."

"Why would you expect it to be any different here?"

"Because it's the lich, Contessa!"

"The minions of Hell have a hierarchy. My standing is higher than that of a lich. I will be invited in and treated with respect, so long as I show respect in return."

"And me?"

"You will have to fight her minions and establish your place. Try not to kill anyone."

"Why?"

"Because then the other challengers will show the same lack of restraint."

"What's stopping them from trying to kill me from the beginning?"

"Killing the familiar of a guest like me would be in poor taste."

"So, nothing."

I chuckled.

"I'm glad someone finds it funny."

WE ARRIVED at the city gates just before sunset. Undead lined the tops of the walls. Rows of skeleton knights stood before skeleton spearmen and a smattering of mages. They stretched as far as the eye could see, unmoving and unchanging, waiting for a threat to appear.

Zombified drakes flew through the air, circling the city with zombified mages on their backs.

We made no attempt to hide our approach as we left the petrified forest, walking directly down the road that cut through the barren dirt landscape, towards the massive gate.

The earth here was dead; nothing lived. Not even bacteria. This was the most lifeless place I had ever seen, and it felt like home.

A revenant, a hate-filled man that had died and clawed his way back to the living to possess his own corpse, flew in riding on a dracolich. He landed beside our path and bowed from the saddle. "My master sends her greetings, your Dark Eminence, and invites you to visit her palace."

I'd been instructing Angelica how to behave for the past few hours, so she immediately replied. "My master accepts her greeting and returns his."

"Quiet, worm," the revenant spat.

Angelica didn't hesitate, leaping across the distance and swinging her staff toward the revenant's head. It raised its arm with contempt to block her blow, only to scream as the death magic and what little life it had left was ripped from its body. Her staff shattered his arm and slammed into his body, knocking him from his saddle, only for her to land in his seat.

"This is mine now," she spat. "Do you agree?"

The revenant barely had the strength to whisper back, "Yes." Power flowed from the revenant to Angelica as it gave up control of its mount. The dracolich, which had been bristling at her proximity, relaxed.

"Get off before you kill it," I warned.

Suddenly realising she was sucking the death magic out of her new mount, she placed her gauntlet onto the saddle and vaulted off, flipping mid-air and landing on her feet.

"Come," she said, running a few steps to catch up with me.

Behind us, the dracolich plodded along, ignoring the revenant as it slowly pulled itself toward the city with its one good arm, unable to stand after what Angelica had done. In the distance, the gates began to open.

When we were far enough away not to be overheard, I whispered. "You performed perfectly."

"Only because you have me so bound with compulsions that I can't do anything else," she hissed back.

"Treat this as a learning experience. Should you master these skills, there will be no need for me to compel you in the future."

"This is etiquette training all over again."

"I'm glad you have experience to draw from."

"I hated etiquette training."

An open carriage pulled by undead horses arrived at the gate as we approached. Another revenant climbed out and stood to the side, bowing as we walked up.

"My name is Delk. My master has sent me to entertain you while you travel to her palace, your Dark Eminence."

I ignored him, walking past and climbing into the back of the carriage.

Angelica stopped before him. "My master thanks yours for her consideration."

The revenant gazed past her to the dracolich, deciding whether he wished to challenge. He paused, then decided against taking such action, accepting a lower place in the hierarchy. "I will pass along your words." He held out his arm invitingly. "Please, after you."

Angelica walked past him and took a seat on the opposite side, making room for the revenant. A few seconds later, the revenant joined her.

Its gaze dropped to my bandolier filled with potions, fixating on the holy smite potion. "I must apologise for my shortcomings, but this lowly one is unaware of who you are."

Angelica moved to answer, but I waved her away.

"I am new to the night, barely a decade old."

The revenant didn't miss a thing. "You were born during the hero alignment, under the rites of deconsecration."

"You've heard of it."

"My mistress boasts an occult library that is without equal. My knowledge of the dark rites is respectable, which is why I am most impressed. Few can claim to have killed a hero."

"That screaming simpleton was only a hero in name. To brag would be in poor taste and lessen the accomplishments of others."

"Your humbleness inspires me. Might this lowly one ask why you are here?"

"There is another hero traveling through the province. His party has cut a swath through the countryside pushing back all who walk in the night. While I slumbered, my scourge thought to please me, by offering me his head. He showed them the sun for their stupidity."

"That is unfortunate."

"Don't be concerned. Those sycophants were my steppingstones to immortality. I would have done away with them long ago if I could, but alas, my nature prevented me."

Delk gave a dry, wheezed chuckle. "You have come for my master's assistance."

"I'm not sure if I want to kill this hero or leave him be."

"He could be a threat."

"If I killed every potential threat, I would soon be strangling babies in their crib for all eternity."

He gave another wheezed chuckle. "Some of us lowly ones would enjoy nothing more. But I can understand that you might be too busy for simple pleasures."

Angelica's dracolich flew above, gliding through the night, as it searched for prey that would never appear. As the dead city passed us by, wandering skeletons and zombies stopped and bowed as we approached, having sensed our presence, forcing them to show unconscious reverence. There were signs everywhere of how wealthy the city had once been, but it was a hollow shell of its former glory.

As the silence stretched, Delk tried to fill it, but his attempts at entertaining banter were dull. I quickly lost interest, and the ride continued in silence. Delk didn't take offense, content as I was to wait out eternity. I found this city filled with the aimless dead peaceful. The world of unending silence felt *right*, like I could retreat to the earth and sleep peacefully for eternity.

It was a shame I'd have to burn it to the ground.

DELK LED us through the palace to his master's study. It was a slow process, because every other hallway, some undead creature would challenge Angelica. She had quite the collection of trophies, including an undead servant. I watched with mild amusement as she knelt over her latest victim and reached for the undead knight's belt.

"I like this buckle," she said. "I'm taking it."

She then tossed it on top of the pile the undead servant was carrying. The creature was a complex zombie. It looked alive and had a rudimentary ability to think for itself, making it likely some necromancer's early attempt to make a zombie that could pass unnoticed in public.

Delk began walking, and I followed. "Would you be interested in selling your familiar? My master would appreciate the chance to study a specimen that has been through the reaping ritual."

"Perhaps. The offer would have to be substantial. Finding loyal servants who don't need to be protected is such a chore, after all."

I had warned Angelica that they might make an offer for her if she impressed them. I also warned her that I would have to consider the offer to maintain our cover.

"That is not such a difficult challenge when one can make them."

"I would be more impressed by your statement if one of your master's creations had managed to harm my familiar. As it stands, you leave me wanting."

"Perhaps a tour of the court is in order, then."

"I'm not opposed to this."

We turned a corner. Halfway down the richly decorated corridor, a pair of guards stood before the door. They were like Angelica's servant, complex zombies, only more impressive. There was intelligence behind their gaze and substantial strength in their bodies. I could sense strong death aura coming from behind the door they were guarding.

"This is impressive work," I said, stepping past Delk and approaching the guards. I followed the contours of their muscles and the colour in their complexion. By all physical appearances, they seemed to be alive. I could even hear a heartbeat. "How intelligent are they?"

Delk stopped beside me. "As intelligent as you wish. Though more intelligence requires more effort. This pair took close to a year to craft and train."

I stepped back. "They impress me less now."

Delk waved his hand, and the guards opened the door. I followed him inside, but the moment Angelica tried to enter they challenged her. I left her to deal with them as I walked behind the revenant.

Before me were two dozen corpses, spread across as many tables. They were either in the middle of being autopsied or in the middle of being reanimated. The majority of them were human, but there were a few beasts and other creatures. There were also lesser demons among them, creatures that weren't fully dead, despite being cut open and having their flesh peeled back.

I passed an elder vampire whose skin had been flayed several times, and placed against the wall in identical cut- outs. "Help me, Master," it moaned, reaching out a skinless hand.

I kept walking.

At the far end of the laboratory stood the lich, Contessa. She had the appearance of a beautiful woman with soft brown hair, though her eyes released a thick black smoke that floated to her head and tried to form a crown. She wore a long, white satin dress, speckled with blood and entrails, and she carried a knife similar to a scalpel in her hand as she cut into a screaming lesser demon.

She didn't look up as we approached, continuing her work. "I must apologize for my lack of hospitality, but I just received a fresh shipment, and the needs of my work require me to be rude, so they don't spoil. Is there any way I can make amends for this offence?"

I considered her offer and the appropriate response. "I'm told you have a rather interesting library. I would not object to reading while I wait for your hospitality."

Her lips tweaked at the corners. "Did Delk tell you to say that?"

"He mentioned the library, but the interest is my own."

"You're an academic."

"I'm barely worthy of the title, but perhaps that will change shortly."

"I look forward to hearing your insights. Few in my domain go to my library willingly."

"I will leave you to your work."

I turned on my heels and spotted Angelica walking into the room followed by her servant. She saw me walking towards her and stepped to the side, waiting for me to arrive so she could follow. Two pools of blood marked the ground outside the door, but neither of the zombies were dead. That was good, because I had a feeling I was going to need her. The lich was far more powerful than I was led to believe.

The aura coming from her concerned me.

She was close to becoming a lich queen.

14

THE EDUCATION OF THE PREPARED

If the guild's library was a repository on how to kill evil, then the lich's library was a repository of the application and uses of death magic, told through the inconsistent ravings of madmen. Contessa had a particular fascination with zombification, the process by which dead flesh was made to mimic the living. It was a very small field in a larger subject, but half the books were devoted to this field. Most of the tomes in the library were research notes made by necromancers or other liches who had jotted down their ideas and the results of their experiments.

Of the fifty thousand volumes on hand, I had to guess only a thousand of them were what I would define as a book. Very few necromancers seemed to be willing to take what they had discovered and condense it into a concentrated form that was easily digested by others, preferring instead to move onto their next experiment. It meant that much of the library was devoted to failure and extremely hard to follow.

While that was frustrating, studying the collective failures painted a picture of what was and was not possible for necromancy.

I'd even discovered a way to extend my family's lives if I couldn't turn them into vampires safely. One of the books had mentioned a creature called a body snatcher. It was capable of moving souls between bodies, which would effectively make my family immortal if I could find one.

Several hours after arriving, I walked past the table where Angelica sat, and placed an open book in front of her. "Start reading here and continue reading for the next ten pages only." I'd been passing her anything I found that was relevant to her class and education. The book I had handed her was written by another death knight and described the process by which one could unlock the death lord class. The author had also mentioned an interesting secret vault that was hidden inside a secret vault in the king's Northern Royal Library.

She put the necromancer guide I'd given her earlier to the side and picked it up, reading without commenting.

"Are you hungry?"

She nodded, tilting her helmet forward.

I reached into my coat and handed her a wax paper package, filled with dried fruit, nuts, and meat. She opened the package, lifted her visor, and began nibbling on the contents while she continued to read.

I returned to reading.

A few hours later, I lifted my head and sniffed the air, running the scents around me through my awareness. A few seconds later, a skeleton knight escorted the most peculiar creature into the library. She looked human, yet she wasn't. She was so subtly different that I didn't know what to make of her, yet her eyes glowed with the same soft, white light I had come to associate with those that were favoured by Heaven.

As a rule, liches were not able to procreate. They were the embodiment of animated death, a reflection of the living world; yet the girl who entered was the lich's daughter. She appeared to be roughly the same age as Angelica, with long black hair and pale features, but her dull, glowing gaze reminded me of those who were eternal. There was a dry husk quality to her skin and cheeks that was not found among the living.

She walked over to Angelica and hugged her without saying a word. She was like a child without fear. Angelica froze, unsure how to act. The hug cost the girl a little of her lifeforce, as Angelica's armour drank it in, but she didn't seem to care as she made her way to me and did the same. Something inside me softened as her arms wrapped around me.

Whoever this girl was, she was good.

Someone who needed to be protected.

I decided then and there, I would protect her.

The moment she released me, the feeling faded, taking the compulsion to protect her with it.

She walked to a shelf and collected a book, then she sat at one of the tables, and began to read with the slow disinterest only the undead could show. Yet she was not dead. She was very much alive. But alive in a way I had never encountered or read about. Her heart beat faintly and irregularly, and it was several minutes before she took a breath.

From the moment she arrived, the concentration of death magic in the library began to recede faster. It was nothing like the way Angelica's armour worked; that was like pulling a plug in a bathtub. This girl was more like the slow vanishing of oxygen from an enclosed space. I watched her while I read, but nothing changed. The girl read, and the death magic slowly dissipated.

An hour after she arrived, I walked over to Angelica and picked up her books. "Follow me." I took the books to the other girl's table and placed them beside her.

She didn't look up or acknowledge my presence as I pulled out the chair next to her for Angelica. "You may chat if she engages you in conversation. Otherwise continue to study."

Angelica sat and wordlessly went back to reading.

I returned to my search, pursuing the shelves at leisure.

As the minutes passed, colour returned to the girl's cheeks, and she lost her pale complexion. Her heart rate slowly sped up, along with her breathing, and the dull gaze in her eyes faded. The changes were interesting, but they didn't confirm my theory until she noticed Angelica.

She slowly turned her head, as if perceiving Angelica's presence for the first time. "Hello." She spoke quietly, almost nervously.

Angelica's visor was still up, so I saw the grin that spread across her face over being freed from my compulsion. "Hi," she said, cheerfully putting her book aside.

The lich's daughter seemed to have the ability to process death magic for energy, but the drawbacks of this power were the undead qualities I noticed. I'd placed Angelica next to her, because her armour reduced the nearby death magic to zero. I'd expected this to make the girl sicklier, not improve her condition. I was under the assumption that the lich was trying to breed a human that was immune to the effects of living in a location filled with death magic, but I seemed to be wrong.

Losing interest, I went back to reading. After a few hours, the two of them walked over.

I finished my current book and placed it on the shelf. I picked up the next and spoke without looking over. "Hello, Davina."

"You know my name," she said.

"I overheard your conversation."

"That makes sense. Would you like some help finding what you're looking for? The library is difficult to navigate if you don't know how everything is organised."

I paused, running her offer through how an ancient vampire should act. "That's acceptable."

"What are you looking for?"

"Books, condensed information on a given subject, rather than the inconsistent ramblings that seem to be the majority of what I find."

"That's simple enough. Where would you like to start?"

"Let's begin with basic necromancy and work our way up to more difficult information."

Davina took off, crossing through the library, ignoring the lower bookshelves until she reached the far wall. She grabbed the ladder and carried it to the back corner, climbing to the top shelf. Angelica followed behind, happy not to be studying.

"Catch," Davina said, and began tossing books to Angelica. "Mother reorganises the library every few years, depending on what's relevant to her research. Basic necromancy is never relevant, so it's always in the most difficult place to reach."

I began reading and immediately smiled. This was exactly what I was looking for. The books talked about the fundamentals of magic and their applications to necromancy. They were the link I'd been looking for between the theoretical and practical.

"If you'd like, we could collect the books you want and bring them to the table for you," Angelica offered, seeing an opportunity to get out of more study.

OVER THE NEXT EIGHT HOURS, they collected every book the library held that was relevant to what I needed to know. Then the skeleton knight collected Davina and marched her out of the room. By the time she reached the door, the pale features and dazed look had returned, which I found curious, because it implied that her ability to absorb death magic was extremely powerful.

I made a pile of books that I felt were relevant to Angelica's education, and commanded her to read them, until she needed to sleep. Davina returned the following day, with the same vacant gaze, and gave us both hugs. Angelica tried to engage her in conversation but found it impossible until the death magic had left her system. What followed was an animated conversation that I found rather intriguing.

"You're immune to necromancy," Angelica said.

"Sort of. There are side effects."

"Is that why you sat there reading like you were a zombie?"

She nodded.

"Why aren't you a zombie right now?"

"I don't know. I'm rarely *aware* two days in a row."

"That sounds terrible."

"There are benefits."

"Like what?"

"I age slower."

"Really. How old are you?"

"I'm not sure exactly, because I don't know what year it is, but at least three or four centuries. I've probably only been *awake* for about sixteen years of my life though."

"It's not really a benefit, then."

"I still learn while I'm unaware. I've read everything in here and remember most of it. That means I don't need to study when I'm aware."

"What do you do with yourself when you don't study?"

"Practice magic, mostly."

"What's your class?"

"I don't have one. My mother won't let me take one."

"You practice magic without a class? I did that, too. I'm not very good, though. I was never able to form a core, just move my mana around."

"I can't form a core, either. It has something to do with my condition, but I've managed to create a mana network to perform spells."

"Is there any point without a core?"

"You don't technically need a core to cast spells. Your core just holds excess mana. You can use the mana your body naturally generates to empower spells without it. It just takes longer."

"A lot longer."

I put down the last of the relevant books the library held. I now had a thorough grounding in magic, necromancy, and the occult.

The guild information mostly discussed how to *disrupt* these practices, not *perform* them, so I was now more aware of how to do both.

I could see how to disrupt dark magic *and* how to reinforce it so others couldn't tamper with it. Progress from here would be slower. I'd need to dive back into the research notes in order to push the boundaries of what I knew. But the information between these walls was worth the effort.

There was power here. The kind of power that would keep my family safe. I would have it all.

I climbed to my feet and walked over to the girls' table, intending to cause a little trouble. "Thank you for your assistance, Davina. You have offered me knowledge; now I'll do the same in return."

She frowned.

"You were aware today and yesterday, because of the armour Angelica is wearing. It's absorbing the death magic around you, stopping your body from absorbing it. The reason your condition is so severe is because you live in a high-death magic environment. If you wish this affliction to pass, you will need to leave."

She trembled. "You…you know what's wrong with me."

"Your body absorbs death magic and breaks it down for energy. The side effect of this process is the undead-like state you fall into. However, living in a death-magic-rich environment is not necessary for your survival. Your body is perfectly capable of living the way a normal human would."

"I could be aware all the time?"

"Yes. Now, I would like more books. Specifically on vampires."

IT TOOK four days for the lich to finish with her research. With my higher agility, that was enough time for me to comb through her collection and gather everything I thought would be relevant. I was not opposed to reading more, but I was now much more familiar with the world of the occult than when I'd arrived. I had all the information I needed to guide Angelica's growth and my own.

Contessa leaned back, lounging on the couch beside me, looking over the edge of the balcony to the courtyard below. Undead legions fought against one another, tearing each other apart for her pleasure. "I'm told you have a hero problem."

I waved my hand, rejecting her comment and relaxed into the armchair. The room behind me was a large sitting room, designed for lounging. A set of double doors lay directly at my back, putting me in a compromised position, which I was sure was intentional. "The province has a hero problem. Personally, I see opportunity."

"You want more territory."

"Yes."

"I'm not interested in territory."

"I suspected as much."

"You did?"

"You've been here since the war and made no attempts to expand your border. Either you have everything you need, or you lack ambition."

"Which do you think it is?"

"You are on the cusp of becoming a lich queen, so you don't lack ambition."

"Was that flattery?"

"Respect."

"I would have preferred flattery."

"I imagine you would prefer a great many things. I take it you're studying the effects of the hellmouth on the local population."

"Why would you say that?"

"Your library gives the impression you're trying to craft a living vessel. A powerful shell that can host your powerful soul."

"All liches pursue power."

"Yes, but they do so in the traditional sense. You seem to be fixated on living flesh."

"Undeath has its limitations." She ran her fingers down the side of her face and throat before stopping at her stomach. "This shell can create life and possesses few of the weaknesses an undead body offers."

"Yet it is fragile as any mortal body."

"For now."

"What is your end goal?"

"You."

I frowned, not understanding her intent. "Me."

"Yes. Before they step into their primordial might, ancient vampires possess the peak of mortal flesh. My goal is to replicate this power in my own vessel."

"Have you had the opportunity to study my kind?"

"No. Elder vampires are the best I have secured."

"Is that why your court is surrounding us?"

She chuckled. "Well, you do present the most delightful opportunity to extend my research."

I gave her a bored expression as I followed their approach, sensing them through the walls. "But at such a high cost. You will undoubtedly survive our confrontation; however, I cannot say the same for your court. My familiar can hold her own against some of the lesser members, and I will destroy several before you manage to overcome me."

Angelica lowered her visor, as she backed up to a wall inside the room behind us. Her eyes began darting about as she gripped her staff.

"Their loss is regrettable."

"But the reward is too great for you to pass up."

"Exactly."

"Have you considered asking for my participation?"

"I don't need your participation."

I chuckled. "You're as short-sighted as your library suggested."

She sneered. "I am a pioneer."

"You are a scared little lich barely willing to push the boundaries of your craft. You focus your research in only the safest places for fear of creating something more powerful than yourself."

"What you call fear I call prudence, and it has served me for centuries, allowing me to push further than any before me."

"Your research stalled two decades ago, and you know it."

"You have fixed that issue for me."

"Peeling the flesh from my bones will only confirm what you already know and offer you a template to replicate my power. It will not give you what you truly seek."

"But I will grow closer, and I am content with that."

"If you are content with inadequacy, inadequacy is all you will ever achieve."

Everything happened at once.

The stone wall behind Angelica exploded as a pair of gigantic fleshy arms reached through and embraced her. The flesh monstrosity screamed as her armour sucked the life and death magic from its undead flesh. A pair of revenants leapt over the balcony, going for my throat. I caught the first while it was in the air, and threw it at Angelica, who raised her staff like a spear and impaled it through the skull, like a biker hitting a guard rail at a hundred miles an hour. The second received my sword through the head, falling into two lifeless pieces.

That was the point where the bone claw reached down from above and impaled me with its spear-like fingertips, and the entrance to the room exploded inward. Contessa made her second mistake as she raised her finger and launched a lance of pure necrotic magic directly at Angelica's armour, which absorbed it gratefully.

I swung my sword above me, removing the arm that held me, and launched myself at the dozen fodder necromancers rushing through the doorway. Every one of them were Unseen, and I was hungry. I exploded out the other side of their formation into the hallway, leaving a wall of dust, and jammed my sword through the helmet of a ghost knight, to reach the revenant behind it.

Then the rest of her court arrived, landing on the balcony and tearing through walls.

There were eight in total, including the one holding Angelica. My instincts warned me, the undead death lord was the biggest threat, followed closely by the lesser lich, her husband and Davina's father. There was also a dracolich capable of changing its form into a nine-foot-tall skeleton that wielded a bone club, that I had to worry about.

I rushed the two Unseen necromancer court members, forcing my way through their barriers with Slaughter. A single touch on my blade was all it took, and they crumbled to dust.

Behind me, Contessa swore.

I didn't pay attention, going for the two zombie members of her court that thrummed with life. They were the culmination of her centuries of research into zombies, a death lord and an arch-necromancer, one male and one female, both capable of procreation. The life force drained from them just as quickly as the Unseen, but they did not turn to dust, instead becoming withered husks animated by death magic.

I tossed them at Angelica, who caught them in her arm to suck the remaining magic from them.

Then I pulled out the holy smite potion and leapt into the middle of the room, raising it above my head. "Do you want to negotiate, or should I make this interesting?"

Contessa scowled as she held up her hand to restrain her court. "You expect me to believe you will take actions that might kill yourself."

I grinned at her. "I'm not the one afraid of death, Contessa."

She glanced at her creations melting in Angelica's grasp. Then turned her gaze on the dust that was her former Unseen servants. "Few use vampiric touch as a weapon; most consider it a parlour trick. It takes dedication and self-restraint to master it, and not many can overcome the hunger or find the motivation needed. I have miscalculated."

She was trying to buy time to think.

I shattered the potion, filling the room with an explosion of holy magic. The zombies and the flesh monstrosity fell apart under the holy assault, freeing Angelica. She leapt. Contessa recoiled as the holy magic burned through her flesh, only for Angelica to wrap her body around her. Her flesh began to wither as the life and magic were sucked from her.

I was left dealing with the undead death lord, the lesser lich, and the body-altered dracolich. All three were reeling from the effects of the potion. I crossed the distance and bisected the lich, destroying its physical form before swinging my sword in an arc and removing the undead death lord's head. I followed up, by sheathing my sword in its neck, leaving Slaughter to devour the life and magic that kept the cursed soul animated.

The lesser lich was dead for now but would come back that moment it could get to a spare body. There was no changing that. If the sword did its job, the undead death lord wouldn't be back.

I tackled the dracolich as it stumbled, knocking it in Angelica's direction. She was on the ground with Contessa in a headlock. Her hand snapped out and grabbed the massive skeleton's ankle as it passed. The creature dragged them with it as it moved, blinded by the holy magic. I leapt to my feet, locked my hands together, and jumped, bringing my fists down on its skull.

The skull shattered.

The dracolich began to stumble around aimlessly. The death magic it would normally use to reform its skull was being absorbed by Angelica's armour. Outside, the legions of dead were collapsing as the death magic that animated them was returned to Contessa to hold her form together.

I knelt beside Contessa and stripped the last of her life force from her body. The lich's skin instantly took on a mummified quality, leaving it completely defenceless and unmoving.

I turned my gaze to Angelica. I could see the panic in her eyes. "Drain the dracolich until it's dead and destroy Contessa's body the moment she begins to move. I'm going to make sure that the undead death lord remains dead."

IT TOOK Angelica's equipment fifteen minutes to glut itself on Contessa's death magic. The transformation to dracolich blood bone was a hungry process, and hundreds of thousands of undead had perished in its transformation, leaving the city and palace as silent as the grave. Further growth would be slow as the dracolich nature of the armour could only reinforce itself so quickly, but her batteries were topped up, so it wouldn't slow down for several days.

I was lounging on Contessa's couch, entertaining her daughter Davina when Contessa finally returned in a fresh new body. Based on its smell, it was clone of her previous one, which meant she wouldn't have to adapt to it. I had found Davina wandering aimlessly through the halls. Her undead minder had crumbled to dust, leaving her without direction. She found the story of my fight with her mother entertaining, giggling mischievously as I describe the way she withered under Angelica's grasp.

Davina had always suspected her mother was not being honest with her when it came to her condition and was fully aware of her evil nature, yet powerless to do anything. Revealing the truth of her condition had endeared me to her, and we were fast approaching friendship.

Contessa wandered through the rubble wearing a powerful black silk robe, stitched with thousands of small but powerful runes. The head of the equally powerful sceptre bounced off her palm as she approached. "You are in my chair, vampire."

"You were indisposed," I replied, lazily.

"You have gutted my court and purged my house."

"You opened our negotiation, and I presented you with my counteroffer."

"Now, I have the upper hand."

"You assumed so last time, too."

She paused, considering my words. She was risk-averse, a type-A personality that always needed to be in control. I had shattered her expectations. Now, instead of fleeing, I remained for her to find me. To someone like her, it meant I held hidden cards. It meant I was still in control.

I was, of course, bluffing.

Without Angelica's armour to drain her, and with no more holy smite potions, we were entirely at her mercy.

"What are your terms?" she eventually asked.

"What are your requirements?"

"I need to dissect you, submitting your flesh to every conceivable form of harm. Samples, reactions, reductions, everything you can possibly imagine will be done to your flesh as I search for the secrets of its creation. Finally, I will need to know your limits."

"You mean destroy me."

"Yes."

"That will be off the table."

She scowled.

"Is there anything else?"

"Unlikely. I can study what I need with samples."

"You have a very limited imagination. You play this much too safe."

"Your terms."

"I would like you to study how my bloodline, physique, and regeneration are strengthened. I would also like access to all your research, not the dead-end fluff you keep in the library. Your true research and personal library."

"For this you will submit yourself to my experiments?"

"Yes, but I would also like you to answer a question for me."

"What question?"

"Why did you abandon experimenting on your daughter? The results were promising."

Contessa sneered. "That creature is an abomination. She was

supposed to be the perfect vessel, a body that could contain endless amounts of death magic. Instead, she consumes and purifies it."

"And yet her mana regeneration grows stronger from doing so," I pointed out.

"Becoming mindless in the process."

"I read your notes. She was completely mindless for nearly a century. It was only after consuming more death magic that she became aware."

"If you read my notes, then you know that growth is limited. Each stage requires significantly more death magic to increase her mana regeneration. That would be acceptable, but she is unable to form a core and cannot be used as a vessel."

"Perhaps, but she would make an exceptional familiar."

Contessa paused. "You want to study her?"

"Yes."

"Would you be willing to share your notes? I have no interest in taking this line of research further myself, but I would be interested to know the results."

"That can be arranged."

Contessa turned to her daughter. "You belong to the vampire now. Serve him as you would me." Then she turned back to me. "Is that all?"

"I will, of course, need to read your research before you begin."

"That can be arranged. Now, excuse me. Many of my research subjects were freed because of your trickery, and I must gather them up."

Contessa turned and fled the room.

Davina remained in her chair frozen. A few more seconds passed, and the shock faded. "I'm free," she whispered. A single tear ran down her cheek, and then a smile bloomed. "I'm free," she shouted. "I'm free. I'm free. *I'm free!*"

"I wouldn't say that."

Davina gave a giddy laugh. "A decade spent serving as your

mindless familiar is nothing, compared to the centuries I've spent under that monster."

"True."

"Also, you can't harm me as your familiar. She could."

"What?!" Angelica shouted.

I smirked. "Did I not mention that?"

"No, you did not. And I don't believe it. You tried to kill me."

"That was training."

"I almost died."

"You were at least another day away from death."

"Says you."

"I am an authority on all things dead and dying, so you should trust me."

Angelica scoffed.

Davina climbed out of her chair and walked over to my couch, kneeling beside me. "I'm ready."

"You have to *want* it."

"I know. I want this. I want to go to places that aren't filled with the dead. I want to walk among trees that aren't petrified and hear the chattering of life as the wind blows through the leaves. I want this with everything I possess; and if I have to serve you to achieve this, I do so gladly and with an open heart."

I offered her my wrist. She needed no instructions. She was an old soul trapped in a youthful body. She held centuries of knowledge within her head but had yet to live. She bit into my wrist. Her jaw clenched a moment later and I struck my chest. Once for her. Once for myself. And once for the bond we were forging.

15

IMPROVISING

The problem with improvising a plan is that everything can quickly get out of control. You might find yourself chained to a table while a lich cuts into your body without empathy or compassion. That's what happened to me.

Contessa took an unreasonable amount of pleasure in hearing me scream and beg for mercy as she used powerful enchanted instruments to peel away my flesh and fillet my organs. Overcoming my regeneration also overcame my pain tolerance, so there was no safety blanket. Only torture. The kind reserved for the denizens of Hell, where mercy was a forgotten construct, and mortality a thing you wish they still had.

Being on her table might have been a fate worse than death, but it was an easy trade to keep my son alive. So, I endured.

You have mastered your Willpower skill.

The sight of that prompt offered me little comfort. The pain did not lessen, and Contessa did not stop. All it did was prove to me that I would do *anything* for my family.

The hours blurred into days, and then those days lost their

meaning. Contessa would stop to check her notes or write something down, leaving me half-gutted on the table. The only respite she offered me was when she needed to recheck her work, removing her instruments and allowing me to heal, so that she could begin again. Those brief moments of salvation brought my sense of time back into focus, until the intolerable pain made it vanish once more.

And then suddenly, Contessa's hands flashed across my body as she yanked out her equipment, tossing it onto the table beside her. My flesh began pulling itself back together, stitching bone and muscle like a ripple across a pond.

"Is it over," I whispered, voice hoarse.

"No, only postponed. The hero and his party have shown up at my wall. I need to take care of them."

"How long?"

"Nine days. I have completed my preliminary research and begun on what you requested. You may read my notes."

"I feel good," I said as my body finished repairing. "Better than when we began."

My hunger was still there, but some of the weariness that had come from it was gone.

"I noticed your regeneration was compromised by my work, so I experimented with methods for improving it. A solution of elder vampire blood mixed with human blood injected directly into your muscles and organs was most effective. The effects, however, are only temporary and will quickly fade."

I rolled off the table and walked over to her research notes, reading through them. "How did you confirm vampirism is a demonic parasitic infection?" I asked, before reading the answer. "'Metamorphosis, beginning with corruption of the blood, progressing to the muscles and organs, before escaping these systems and moving freely through the body.'"

"The demonic parasites within you are large enough to view with a basic magnifying spell," Contessa replied.

"This invalidates your research hypothesis."

She thought that vampirism made the human body stronger, but it appeared to be the opposite. The human body never got any stronger, only the demonic parasites. Her research pointed towards a primordial vampire merely being a vampiric parasite that had finished growing and erupted from its human host.

I could hear her gritting her teeth. “It would seem so. However, further study is required. If I can find the mechanism by which these parasites strengthen you, I could create undead parasites to mimic this.”

Her research was fascinating, and I quickly found something else to catch my attention. “The larger parasites are immune to sunlight, silver, and garlic. Why do I still suffer from these, then?”

“You are playing host to all three stages of the infestation. Only the earlier stages are susceptible and succumb to exposure. The third stage survive and repair the damage. When you are no longer exposed, they reproduce and reinfect you with the earlier stages.”

“Efficient.”

“Extremely.”

I put down the first book and picked up the second. There were eight in total, each filled with notes and observations of the things she had done to me. I began reading the next.

“Don’t let me keep you,” I said.

Contessa scowled. “Your little game has emptied my court and crumbled my strongest defenders.”

“That is not my problem.”

Contessa reached behind her and held up another pair of books I hadn’t seen. “This is the knowledge you seek.”

I paused, letting my hunger and anger enter my tone. “Are you trying to renegotiate our deal?”

“No. I am merely pointing out that you will not receive further information without my assistance. These two tomes might be all you learn unless you help me.” She offered me the books. “I will be in my throne room with the surviving member of my court, waiting for the hero and his party. Assist me or remain impartial. But know that if I perish, you will gain no more knowledge."

I took the books from her. "You're being awfully dramatic for someone with your power, Contessa, but I'll consider it."

The lich nodded and turned to leave.

"Of course, you won't object to me eating a few of your human minions. You understand, I need my strength if your injections will soon fail me."

Her shoulders tightened. "You are a petty, vindictive little parasite, vampire. You know I have plenty of stock for my research in the dungeons below, yet you prefer my minions because it costs me."

"I can't let you be the only one having fun, Contessa. You laughed more than your fair share during your research and replicated your results more than was strictly necessary."

She cackled at being caught out. "You misunderstand me. It is your most endearing quality."

"I have books to read."

"And I have a hero to kill."

As I watched her walk to the door, thoughts raced through my head.

THE FIRST THING I did when I finished reading was hunt. Contessa kept a single cult of necromancers near her, so there were fewer than twenty left to choose from. Thankfully, they were even more evil than your average necromancers, so only two survived my little purge. An elderly gentleman who invited me in for tea and biscuits and a cold young woman that swore the moment she saw me.

This left me on the other side of the palace in a section I'd never visited. But a vampire's nose is a beautiful thing. With it we can navigate sections of a building we've never even entered. I followed the scent of traffic back to more familiar territory, and then used it to track down Angelica.

She was staying with Davina.

"Don't you know how to knock?" she shouted, sloshing bathwater around, as I entered the room.

Davina giggled and dropped into a curtsey. "How may we serve you, your Dark Eminence?"

"The hero and his party are coming. I need you both dressed and ready for battle immediately."

Angelica launched out of the tub, grabbing her towel and rubbing herself dry, as she ran towards clothes. "Stupid compulsion," she complained.

"I keep telling you, fighting it only makes it stronger," Davina said, slowly walking towards her wardrobe. "As long as you work towards his request and don't push back, you can take your time." She began looking through her wardrobe. "No, that won't do. The colour is terrible."

As she continued to examine her wardrobe, I cleared my throat. "What are you doing?"

"I'm trying to find something suitable to wear. I don't have armour or necromancer's robes, because I've never needed to fight outside of training." She pulled out a black dress. "What do you think of this?"

"The skirt is too long. It might get caught or cause you to trip. Do you have trousers?"

"No." She turned back around. "Something shorter."

"Do you have a needle and thread?"

"Obviously."

"Get them for me. I'll adjust your clothes appropriately."

As she ran off, I looked through her closet. There wasn't much to work with. Her shortest dress reached her ankle, and most covered her neck. They weren't expensive or fashionable, mostly made from recycled materials, such as curtains. Palace curtains, but still curtains.

I selected a black dress with slightly thicker material and some sort of silver embroidery and started cutting.

Davina handed me her sewing kit, and I got to work on fixing the loose edges, making small folds and hand-stitching it all. With my agility, it was faster and more accurate than a machine.

"Who taught you how to sew?" Davina asked.

"My wife."

Sandra loved Halloween and would go all out on the kids' costumes. The first year Luke was old enough to go out, I found her half-asleep in the kitchen at 3AM making coffee, so she could stay awake long enough to add all the details she wanted. After that night, I learned to sew so she wasn't so exhausted at work. It became a sort of yearly tradition where I did the simple bits and she handled anything too complex.

"You're married?"

"Not anymore."

"Did you eat her?"

"No."

"You don't have to be ashamed; a lot of vampires eat their wives and kids."

"I didn't eat her." I flicked out my work, examining what I'd done. I touched up a few loose threads and then flicked it again. It was passable. "Here you go."

She looked at it and screwed up her face. Then she patted me on the shoulder. "At least you tried."

"You're not half as funny as you think you are. Go get dressed."

"I need help with my armour," Angelica called.

Getting dressed in plate armour was a two-person job. You could do it alone, but it took much longer. I ran my gaze over her armour as I approached. The smooth, blood-coloured bone plates had taken on a dull appearance, compared to before their transformation. In the past, the colour had expressed life, blood, and fire. Now it expressed the sickly decay of hot infection. It was true dracolich blood bone, radiating death and fire magic in equal parts.

The moment I touched the first piece, I knew something was wrong. The armour was hungry, starved for sustenance. "What happened?" I asked.

"Don't be mad," Angelica replied.

"What…happened?"

"I needed to get out of my armour, but you weren't here."

"And."

"And I might have asked Davina to help me. She sort of sucked all the death magic out of it. She didn't take long, but all the death magic was gone by the time she was done."

I filed that interesting piece of information away for later.

"What happened to Davina?"

"She slowly mummified before my eyes. I didn't know what to do, because you were busy being tortured, so I put her on the bed. When I woke up the next morning, she was fine. Do you think we can-"

I placed my hand over her mouth, so she didn't say it aloud, and nodded.

She relaxed.

I pulled my hand away and finished buckling her up. "Davina, are you ready?"

I turned to see her dressed and waiting. I had shortened her dress to below the knee and added a cut down either side, so she could run and climb without obstruction. I'd removed the sleeves and dropped the neckline from the bottom of her chin to her collar bones, adding a small slit down the back so the thick material could move.

"Wow, you should be a dress maker," Angelica said. "I can't believe you managed to turn her horrible wardrobe into something like that."

Davina stuck out her tongue. "I happen to like my wardrobe."

"So do nuns."

They both giggled.

I went to find my sword.

"It's in the crate," Angelica said.

"Why's it in a crate?"

"It tried to eat me after I took my armour off."

I pried open the lid of the crate, pulling out nails, and grabbed Slaughter. I opened my hunger to it, consuming the small traces of life it had managed to gather, without mercy or care for its wants. It wasn't a sentient sword, so I didn't bother trying to reason with it. I just fed upon it until it was too weak to pose a threat.

Once I was satisfied, I belted it on. "Do you have your focus?"

Angelica ran to a chest of drawers and retrieved it. "Here it is."

I took it from her and walked over to Davina. "Guard this and stay within a few steps of Angelica."

"Are you-"

I covered her mouth and nodded. "Are you okay with this?"

She nodded.

"Don't say a word about this."

She smiled.

16

DING DONG THE LICH IS DEAD

Contessa suffered from the same affliction from which all undead suffered: an inability to perceive the relevance of time. The destruction of the local undead population had not troubled her once I handed her what she wanted, causing her to only recall the bare minimum of the undead to maintain the palace amenities. Without the living members of her court to remember more than these simple needs, nothing had been done.

Now she was desperately recalling skeletal mages and undead drakes to fortify her defences, causing the undead to surge towards the palace from all directions, moving too slowly to make a difference.

Luke and his party had broken through the defensive lines, thanks to Sharani's pet elemental, and they were now battling their way past the palace gate. Without my intervention, it would have been impossible to make it this far. The city's defences had been too thick, too well-layered. Sheer numbers would have overwhelmed us. Luke and I might have escaped, but the others wouldn't have.

By the looks of it, Luke's party would reach Contessa's throne room and her revenants in a matter of minutes, cleaving their way towards her, which would ultimately end in their demise. Being here had taught me much about my weaknesses. I was powerful in a one-on-one sense, but I was not an army. I could still be overwhelmed; and when this happened, a powerful individual could snipe me, killing me with ease.

Contessa had lost the ability to do that to me or Luke when she lost the undead at the palace. Her remaining forces were mostly cannon fodder -- good for fighting soldiers; terrible for fighting a hero and his party. She would have to engage them herself, with the last member of her court. She was a coward by nature, so she would hold back from fully engaging until the lesser lich was destroyed.

Sacrificing her lich husband would barely annoy her.

I watched from a tower window as Luke and his party reached the entrance to the palace and were confronted by a sea of revenants. The sentient undead were not Contessa's creations, so they had not suffered from the effects of Angelica's armour. They were the last true threat the palace held. Mara raised her staff and holy magic crashed over them, quickly followed by Diva's fire.

A wave of necrotic smoke exploded from the entrance, revitalizing the revenants. Mara stood in the middle of their party with her staff raised, surrounding them in holy light, holding back the attack.

"Good," I said. "Contessa has joined the fight. Let's go assist her."

I scooped Davina up in my arms and began running down the stairs. Her physical attributes were all within the normal range for an unclassed human, so it would take her nearly ten minutes to reach the throne room without assistance. Angelica ran ahead of us, knocking aside any undead who got in my way, allowing us to reach the door near the back of the throne room in only a minute.

I put Davina on her feet and pushed her towards Angelica. "Remember your orders."

"Die gloriously," she replied cheerfully, incapable of being unhappy, even in the face of death.

I chuckled as I stepped past them and opened the door to the sounds of battle. Revenants were scattered across the throne room, suffering holy magic burns, howling in pain, as they cowered. Others were still on their feet, throwing spells and swinging blades. Diva and Sharani were countering most of them, as Luke cut a path forward. Mara was busy engaging the lesser lich, hurling massive bolts of holy magic at its shield, while maintaining a barrier around their party.

Contessa was seated on her throne, hurling lances of necrotic magic any time she saw an opening.

I strolled into the chaos, like it was a beautiful, moonless night, stepping around the cowering revenants as I made my way to her throne.

Her gaze briefly landed on me as I stopped beside her. "I didn't expect you to come."

There was a barrier around her throne. It was a mystical shield made from many magics. It made her practically invulnerable while inside. Neither Angelica's armour nor Slaughter would easily pierce it.

"It would be rude not to help. After all, you are clearly going to win."

"I need the cleric dead. You are insufficient to kill the hero, but I can safely join the field if she is gone."

"I'll need her defences weakened. Can you perform the necro night spell?"

Contessa raised her sceptre and unholy night engulfed Luke and his party. I drew Slaughter and launched myself from the dais, leaping over the battlelines and entering the abyss. I was just as blind as they were, only knowing where I was when Slaughter pierced their barrier and I was bathed in holy light. I caught the barrier with my foot as I cut my way through and pushed off, blurring across the distance, and knocking aside Luke's sword, before catching Mara and leaping back into the darkness. I sheathed my sword as I placed my thumb against her femoral artery, drawing just enough life from her to leave her unconscious.

I landed at the back of the dais a moment later and dropped Mara's limp form on the ground. Then I appeared next to Contessa's throne. "Done."

"You didn't kill her."

"I like to play with my food."

Contessa gave a throaty chuckle, as she stood and dismissed her spell. The unholy darkness vanished as she walked forward, exiting her barrier. Power filled her sceptre, and Luke charged towards her, trying to cut a path fast enough to save them from death.

Slaughter flashed from its sheath, blurring through Contessa's arms, causing her to lose control of the magic she had summoned. My hunger caught the life coursing through her body, and she withered to a husk, as the explosion from her spell's backlash threw her over her throne, and into Angelica's waiting arms.

Davina mummified in the space of a heartbeat as the death-devouring hole inside her connected to the focus in her hands, amplifying the armour's magical absorption property.

I threw a health potion across Mara's face and then proceeded to put down any revenant in the vicinity, before coming up behind the lesser lich, who didn't know what had happened, to hack through its knees and elbows. Its dismembered body appeared at Angelica's feet a second later, and her boot landed on its head, draining the death magic from it.

Without anything important left to do, I proceed to end more injured revenants, before closing in on those attacking my son. It didn't matter that they didn't have Mara anymore. Luke, Diva, and Sharani were more than a match for revenants not supported by liches, so much so, that by the time I was done putting down the injured, most of the survivors were in the process of fleeing. The only ones still fighting were too close to run.

I dealt with the fastest cowards, while Luke finished off those that were closest, and Diva and Sharani killed everything in between.

As the last revenant collapsed, Mara began climbing to her feet. I was between her and Angelica before she could get her bearings and do something stupid.

Her gaze landed on me after a few seconds. "You," she hissed. Then she tossed me the holy symbol I had left in the wagon.

I caught it and slipped it over my head. "Happy?"

"No." She glanced past me to Angelica and raised her hand.

I stepped in the way. "I wouldn't do that."

"Get out of my way."

"I mean if you want to be responsible for unleashing millions of undead on the countryside leading to untold amounts of death and destruction, go right ahead." I stepped aside. "If it was me, I would wait for Angelica's set to finish absorbing all the death magic the lich has accumulated over the centuries, so that didn't happen. But you can do what you like."

Mara scowled but lowered her hand.

Luke walked up behind me and threw his arm over my shoulders. "You're an asshole and I hate you. But I'm glad you're all right."

"Language."

He snorted. "How much can she absorb?"

"The real question is how much *Davina* can absorb. She's the real limiting factor in all of this. Angelica finished transforming her armour the first time we fought the lich, which is the only reason you got in here."

"You're not getting more than 35% of the loot."

"I soloed the boss."

"While we provided a distraction."

"I killed all the mini-bosses."

"Who's Davina."

"The mummy-looking one."

"Is she undead?"

"No. She can metabolise and break down death magic. It comes with side effects."

"Like turning into a mummy."

"Yes. Also, don't kill her. She's my familiar."

He paused and sucked in a breath, grip tightening across my shoulders. "Dad, I'm starting to get concerned. I'm noticing a trend."

I had no idea what he was talking about. "What?"

"Hero summoned to another world, followed around by a handful of cute teenage girls. You're turning into an anime protagonist and building a harem."

I snorted. "As a vampire, I'm not a sexual being."

"Neither are most anime protagonists. It doesn't stop them from having a harem." He pointed two fingers at his eyes and then mine. "You're walking a thin line, old man. Next thing you will be trying to do is justify this because one of them is several centuries old and only looks like a teenager."

His statement horrified me. "Oh, God, I *am* an anime protagonist."

His face lit up and he started to grin. "Wait, the new one is really a centuries-old woman trapped in a teenage body?"

"No, it's worse. She's a centuries-old woman trapped in a teenage body with the life experience of a teenager."

Luke's entire body shook as he roared with laughter. "You're so cliché."

"Tragically so."

"Do you mind explaining what's going on," Mara said through gritted teeth. "You seem to have a plan."

"Angelica is syphoning death magic from the lich into her armour. Davina over there was an experimental creation of the lich who attempted to make a human that would thrive and grow stronger in a death magic-rich environment. Instead, she created a human that would feed on death magic and purify it as she grew stronger. Her body's hunger for death magic is even stronger than the armour's hunger, so with her holding the focus, Davina can draw away the death magic from the armour, basically allowing the armour to feed until she can't take any more."

"What's her limit?"

"Theoretically, there isn't one. Her body converts death magic to attributes. The cost grows exponentially, but if there is no limit to the growth, only a higher cost, she could potentially cleanse death magic *from the entire world*."

"She's a saint."

"No, saints can cleanse *all* dark magics. She can only cleanse death magic. The lich tested that."

"Does she possess an unusually cheerful and helpful disposition despite her circumstances?"

"Yes, but that's a side effect of not being affected by death magic."

"She could also be a saint."

"A saint wouldn't consort with the forces of evil."

Mara paused. "True. Though technically you're not evil."

"Plenty of the people here were."

"There are people here?"

"Only research subjects and a pair of necromancers that aren't Unseen yet."

Luke growled and let go of my shoulder. "Where are they holding them?"

"Somewhere down below. I never bothered finding out."

"Are they safe?"

"Unlikely."

Luke continued to scowl but didn't move to leave. You couldn't run off to save people in a situation like this. People were a liability. They painted a target on you and slowed you down. If you gave in, you were only going to put them and yourself in danger.

I patted his shoulder. "If you need something to do, there are still undead in the surrounding corridors. I can guard the entrance if you cover our backs."

Luke nodded and gathered Diva and Sharani. They took off at a slow run.

"Watch your back," I warned. "The lesser demons she was studying might have gotten free."

Luke replied by slamming his sword through a revenant waiting behind the door and tossing its lifeless corpse in our direction.

Mara walked over to Angelica and studied the two liches she was holding. "Contessa seemed to trust you. Why?"

I chuckled. "I let her cut into me for over a week."

"You could hear his screams from the other side of the palace," Angelica said, shuddering.

"Torturing doesn't normally lead to trust," Mara said.

"She was studying vampirism. I was research."

Mara blanched. "Why?"

"She needed to be distracted after we gutted her defences and court. Letting her cut into me seemed like the best way. I expected you to arrive a week ago."

"You knew we were coming back?"

"I knew Luke was. What took you so long?"

"The spirit guardians got lost. It took them a week to find Tobil."

That wasn't surprising. They were warriors, not teamsters. If they hadn't been my only option, I wouldn't have used them.

"Why did you do it?" Mara asked.

"Coming here was suicide. My son was walking to his death, but I couldn't change his mind. So, I changed the plan."

"You could have talked to us."

"No, I couldn't have. You don't trust me, Mara. You likely never will. If I had told you I was going to walk into this city and dine with the lich to undermine her, you would have thought I was setting you up. You're the sort of person who needs to see proof first. I had to prove that I could control my hunger. I had to prove I was only eating Unseen. And I had to prove I would undermine the forces of evil without oversight."

Mara sighed. "You hurt him, you know."

"I know."

"He thought you abandoned him. He thought you were dead."

"I hate that I hurt him, but the alternative was unacceptable."

"He needs to hear that."

"He will."

I walked over and grabbed the lesser lich out from under Angelica's foot. It made several feeble movements but was so thoroughly drained of magic that it couldn't do anything else. I dragged it away from Angelica and held it down.

"Do you know how to tether a soul?" I asked.

"I'd rather perform a banishment."

"I'd prefer if you let Angelica shatter its phylactery."

"Why?"

"One of the methods for unlocking the death lord class is killing powerful undead. Also, they might be storing loot where they keep their phylactery."

She groaned. "It's always about loot with you two."

ANGELICA SWUNG HER STAFF, bringing it down on Contessa's phylactery. The large cut amethyst shattered into a million pieces, scattering across the gold-covered floor like purple ice cubes. Trapped souls howled as they were freed from their torment, rushing through the air towards the spare cloned bodies Contessa had left lying on the enchanted tables. Mara bathed the room in holy light, cleansing them, and causing them to fade as they moved on to their afterlife. The holy light also caused Contessa's spare bodies to crumble to dust. Without her soul to empower them they were extremely fragile.

It had taken nearly an hour to reach Contessa's phylactery, and that was after waiting eight hours to kill all the undead. Finding the secret passage and then getting through the vault was not easy.

I walked over to my familiar and patted her on the shoulder. "Angelica Lich Bane, it is my pleasure to inform you that you have fulfilled the requirements of your pardon."

She lifted her visor. "What?"

Luke chuckled. "My father organised a pardon for your crimes in Tobil. Participating in killing the lich was the condition."

A bright smile lit her face. "I'm not a criminal anymore."

"There is still some paperwork, but no."

She turned to me still smiling. "And you're going to free me from being your familiar."

I snorted. "Nice try."

"Please."

"No."

"Pretty please."

"No."

She sighed. "It was worth a try."

"It's time to go hunting," Luke said. "We need to finish purging the palace and rescue any survivors."

"Angelica, stay here and protect Davina." I tossed her my storage pouch. "Also, collect the loot."

I'd placed Davina's mummified body against the wall. Her fingers were locked around the focus, which was a problem because her flesh was so dry it had become brittle. I'd have to snap her fingers off to remove the focus from her grasp, which wasn't something I wanted to do, because I didn't know if healing magic worked on her. It also meant that Angelica couldn't kill any undead without prolonging Davina's undead state.

"I bet I can kill more undead than you can," Luke said.

"One percent of the loot says you can't."

"Make it bragging rights."

"Deal."

We spent the next day purging the city. Thousands of undead creatures had flocked to Contessa's service. The smartest ones had fled when they saw her horde collapsing around them a second time, but most had no true sense of time, so they had gone to collect their things. I got lucky and found an undead death knight raiding the treasury with its minions. Gold wasn't useful to undead creatures, but it was useful to the living, and most of the times, it was easier to pay a thief or slavers to collect what you needed, rather than do the dirty work yourself.

Even without the undead at the treasury, I still would have won. I'd had more time in the city and I understood how the undead operated, so finding them and putting them down was much easier for me.

"Remember that time you bet you could kill more undead than me, but you couldn't," I said a few days later, as we rode out of the city in the back of the wagon.

Luke chuckled, while he sat on Davina's coffin. "I maintain my position that demons counted."

The wagon had been loaded to capacity with powerful magical or cursed items that couldn't be put in storage. Leaving the cursed objects behind was no different than leaving radioactive waste, and Mara had spent most of her time tracking them all down. She hadn't even looked at the other loot as she made sure the city was safe.

As we passed through the gates, Angelica swooped down on the back of her dracolich, startling the survivors in the other wagon and causing her dress to flair. I could hear her laughing above as she encouraged it to go faster. The beast had survived the lich's demise, because it was linked to her. Her undead servant had not. Luke had killed it during his rampage through the palace.

"She's going to be scary when she grows up," Luke said, watching her fly off.

"I'll keep her under control."

"I hope so." His gaze dropped to the dead landscape. "It's going to take generations to heal this place."

"Maybe not."

"You have a plan?"

"There is a lot of death magic in this land. Davina could use that magic to grow stronger."

He smiled. "Not the worst use of your time, but I'm not sure the church will be happy."

"They're never going to be happy where I'm concerned. But

that's fine. I don't care what they think. Only what you think. I'm sorry I drugged you."

Luke snorted. "No, you're not. You're sorry you *had* to drug me."

"It was the only way to keep you safe."

"I understand."

"Do you?"

"You're not the only one who's abandoned his party to solo a suicide mission."

I smirked. "How did they take it?"

"Not well. Now that I've been on the receiving end, I can understand why. But I've also been on your end, so I'm more forgiving."

"You're not going to hold it against me?"

"No. But I won't be so trusting going forward."

"I'd be concerned if you were."

"What happens now?"

"I need to rest. After that, I'm not sure. It depends on if the guild can convince the king to allow me outside the province."

17

CHILD OF THE GRAVE

Oliver gleefully rubbed his hands together as Azula opened the crate containing Angelica's armour and staff. Nina stood beside the old man, just as excited. They hadn't expected us to survive, let alone be successful, but they had held out hope. The next stage of the enchantment process would potentially gain them even more levels than they had already received, and they were excited for the challenge ahead.

The return trip to Tobil was uneventful. Mara was off working with the clerics to purify the weaker cursed objects while the others dealt with the survivors. Angelica had given her instructor a tearful hug, thanking her for her training, and had then raced off to find her siblings.

"Where's the focus?" Oliver asked.

I opened the coffin next to me and pointed to Davina's hands. "She's got it. We can't get it back until she recovers." I moved to close the lid.

Azula stopped me, grabbing the lid as she dropped to her knees. "Fascinating. Do you mind if I study this creature?"

"Yes."

"It's human, isn't it."

I felt my eyebrows rise. "You can tell."

"The undead are my specialty."

"We share the same speciality," Nina said drolly.

"Then you should be as giddy as I am, instead of drooling over the armour. Do you have any idea how much death magic is contained in her?"

Nina pulled out a monocle and held it before her eye. She took a step back. "It's a bomb."

"No." Azula traced her finger across Davina's stomach. "It's too stable to be a bomb."

"How is that possible? There is too much death magic."

"My guess would be that her flesh is immune to necrotic effects. It soaks in death magic and then breaks it down. Right now, it's overwhelmed her life force, leaving her in this state."

"Can you accelerate the breakdown?" I asked.

Azula shook her head. "Doing anything while she is like this would be unwise. She might turn into a bomb."

"What about normally?"

She nodded. "I'd be interested. Why do you ask?"

"I need to do some research on the undead. I'm looking for assistants."

"I'm not interested."

"I have the lich's library and research notes."

All three froze.

Oliver cleared his throat. "How large was this library?"

"There are fifty thousand tomes' worth of occult information, outside of the lich's personal library. It should only take me a month to read it all. I'm going to condense it into usable material for the guild, but the original work will remain with me."

The three shared a look.

"I might be interested in working with you," Oliver admitted, taking off his glasses to clean them. "My sight is fading, and fine motor control is going with it. Retirement from active work is fast approaching, and studying for the next generation was always my plan. Do you have suitable facilities?"

"My familiar will purchase the estate where I was turned, and the lich's loot will pay for the academy I want to build. I would be willing to fund your facilities, but I'll leave you to think it over." I turned to Nina. "Do you have apprentices I could borrow?"

"What for?"

"I've got cursed gold and silver that needs purifying."

Anything that spent enough time around undead and demons who caused widespread suffering and horror took on a minor cursed quality, causing sickness. This wasn't a major problem, as clerics could easily cleanse these minor issues away if the item or building was important enough to warrant it. The rest was usually destroyed. In the case of gold and silver, the easiest solution was to reforge it in a consecrated crucible. The act of changing the materials' form was enough to remove the curse's effects; using the consecrated crucible was just to be safe.

Nina nodded. "How much do you have?"

"The silver will fill this room several times over. The gold might do it once."

Nina turned her gaze to the massive workshop. "I don't think our facilities are big enough to manage that."

"I only need my share, after guild and kingdom taxes."

"While that's less, it's still significant."

I shrugged. "The final work on the armour is going to take a few weeks, so they have time."

"It shouldn't take more than a few days," Oliver replied.

I reached into my storage pouch and retrieved a set of six books I'd found in Contessa's personal library. "Have you heard of the death lord Arthur Dragon's Bane?"

All three froze again.

Oliver's mouth dropped open as he gazed at the books. "The Treaties of the Infinium. You don't."

"I do."

As one, they all reached for the books.

"These were destroyed," Nina whispered.

"Not in Hell," I said.

None of them hesitated, taking the books and beginning to read. For a normal person, their actions would be insane. However, they possessed classes that made them aware of curses and spell traps, so they knew when something was safe to touch better than anyone.

"What else do you have?" Nina asked.

"All sorts of lost knowledge and hidden secrets. The kind you won't find anywhere else."

"I'll get you those apprentices," Nina said.

"Why do I have to go?" Angelica grumbled, a few days later, while Luke and his party loaded the wagon. She had just come from the mayor's office, where he had handed over her preliminary pardon, and she was in one of her moods.

"As a vampire, I can't buy the estate, and you need to have the governor sign your pardon papers to make them official."

"Couldn't I just fly there and fly back?"

"Do you really want to arrive in Hellmouth on the back of a dracolich without the hero to vouch for you?"

"Probably not."

"If you're concerned about your family, I can take care of them for you while you're gone."

"I don't want you anywhere near my family while I'm gone."

I shrugged. "Fine."

"Do I get travel expenses?"

"If you behave. Luke has my money."

She grinned.

"Remember to join the guild while you're there, so you don't have to go through the training. If you want more money, you can take a few quests on your way back."

"I don't have my armour."

I rolled my eyes. "You have a dracolich. It can eat most mid-tier quests for a snack."

She glanced up, watching the undead dragon circling above, and smiled. "I'm going to be rich."

I left her to her daydreams and walked over to Luke. We'd had burgers and beer three times since getting back, saying everything we needed to say. He was a man now, not the boy I'd raised, and sticking around with his old man would just slow him down. "You got everything?"

"You mean everything you stole," Mara growled.

"I hope not."

Luke chuckled. "I think we've got everything. Both stolen and fairly gained."

"Good. Remember to deliver my letters."

Luke sighed. "You honestly think Riker will let you open a guild on your estate?"

"It gives the guild the perfect opportunity to monitor me. He'd be stupid not to take it."

"I'm not sure why you suggested Tora as the guild master. She hates you."

"Which means she will jump at the chance to keep me in line."

"And give you access to her husband."

"Angelica needs someone to train her. Sir Brandon can help her in the beginning and knows the right people to help her later. They also know me. I trust them not to plot behind my back. I can't say that for others."

"I'll come and visit when I get the chance."

I smiled. "I'll be waiting. And if you ever need somewhere safe to sit out the apocalypse, I'll be ready."

"The king's not going to like that."

"The guild won't either, but they'll have to deal with it. I'm not going back to sleep, and I'm not going to let you spend the rest of your life fighting evil. I want grandchildren."

"Sorry, I didn't hear that last part."

"The grave calls me, Son. I'm old and weak, and my dying wish is to bounce a little you on my knee."

"I think I can arrange that with a shrinking potion."

I laughed. "I would love to see you fight like that."

Luke chuckled. "It would be nothing but crotch-punches."

"There goes the mighty hero, smiting evil one crotch-punch at a time. The ballads write themselves."

"Knowing my luck, I'd probably get a skill for it."

"We can't always get what we want."

"That's easy to say when you didn't go up twenty-two levels."

I winced. "Twenty-two."

"On top of the fifteen levels I got from the quest with you. I'm beginning to think you're bad luck. I've never leveled this quickly, before I found you."

"It can't be all bad."

He shrugged. "I got quite a few rare skills."

"See."

"All of them revolve around killing you."

"And other undead and demons, I imagine."

"Yes, but I get the feeling they're meant for you. This isn't the first time I gained a skill I needed, before I killed something."

I could see he was struggling, so I wrapped my arms around him and hugged him tight. "I'll never hold it against you if you have to put me down. I love you."

"I know. It doesn't mean I have to like it."

"But it does mean you don't have to feel guilty. You don't have to beat yourself up or hate yourself for what you might need to do. If you have to raise your sword, you won't be killing me, only something that is wearing my face."

"Thanks."

I stepped back. "I'm proud of you and the man you've become."

He smiled. "I'm proud of you, too. I'm proud I can say my father became a vampire and fought off his hunger to keep his soul. That he killed the lich, Contessa, and helped people."

"And ate a whole lot of Unseen along the way."

Luke chuckled, noticing the others were waiting. "I guess I should get going."

"Send my love to your mother and sister if you see them."

"I will."

"Safe travels."

Luke climbed into the back of the wagon, and I watched them leave, already missing him.

I'D GIVEN the master storage box to Mara to return to the Hellmouth guild headquarters, not because I regretted taking it, but because the lich also had one. The same went for most of what I had stolen. I had no use for it now that the lich was dead, so giving it back didn't bother me.

Dividing up all the loot we'd recovered had taken over a day. The guild assessors had to come in, evaluate it all, and gave a price.

Mara had tried to destroy the lich's personal library, even as the guild's craftsmen protested. I said it would be coming out of her share, which hadn't stopped her. So, I handed her the rarest and darkest volume and had her listen from the other side of the room as I repeated the entire volume, word for word. She made me do it with another volume; only then would she accept that she couldn't expunge the information from the world. In the end, Luke and his party took most of the magical items and left me with the library and the bones I scavenged.

I also kept the lich's research equipment, her robe, her husband's staff, and the recently uncursed altar Contessa used to create her undead, but the rest of the items were of little interest to me. The guild paid 60% of the items' value, and I walked away happy.

The treasury and most the banks had evacuated before the city fell, but that still left millions of people with their personal savings. Even after all the taxes, I was incredibly wealthy, which was good, because it was going to be expensive to pay for the academy I wanted to build.

I made a few marks on the chalkboard, as I changed the size of the library, adding more space. Pieces of paper covered the table as I organised the knowledge I had absorbed over the last month, condensing it into the design for the perfect academy.

The guild had rented me a suite so I could work in a place where I didn't unsettle the other guildmembers. Apparently, an ancient vampire muttering to himself in the middle of the tavern while scowling at random drawings put people on edge. Yet, they had no problem with Oliver cackling as he read The Treatise of the Infinium.

Work on the armour had completely stopped as the craftsmen poured over the books, expanding their skills and knowledge. That didn't bother me. I wasn't in a hurry.

I was making another alteration when a heart that had not beat in over a week gave a little thump. I glanced at Davina's coffin in the corner of the room. "It's about time." I turned back to my work.

It was another day before she came around, and her reaction to waking up in a coffin was not what I expected. "Not *this* again." A second later, the lid of the coffin exploded. Davina coughed and spluttered as wood dust poured over her. She sat up, looking around. "Oops." She spotted me. "I thought I was buried alive and had to dig my way out again. I'll clean up."

I picked up the chalkboard and knocked it against the side of the table, removing the dust. "Please do."

She grinned. "We survived."

"Thanks in no small part to you."

She leapt out of the coffin and ran to the window. "Where are we?"

"The adventurer guild in Tobil."

"Can I go exploring?"

"Maybe in the morning. Everyone's asleep."

"Where's Angelica?"

"She's in Hellmouth."

"What's she doing there?"

"Purchasing the estate where I was turned, joining the guild, and getting her pardon signed by the governor."

"Why aren't we with her?"

"We weren't needed."

"Can I go for a walk?"

"No."

"Why not?"

"You're too fragile." I paused after saying that and looked at the coffin. "How did you pull that spell together so quickly?"

"I don't know. Last time it took ages."

"We should probably find out."

"How?"

"By unlocking your class. Any thoughts on what you want?"

"Necromancer."

"You'll have access to better classes."

"Doesn't matter. I want to be a necromancer. Going through the class upgrades gives more skills."

"At the cost of attributes."

"Skills are more useful and valuable."

"Only if you have the capacity to utilize them… which I guess you do."

She marched across the room and locked her arm with mine. "Lead the way, your Dark Eminence." To anyone else, her cheerfulness would have been infectious.

"One moment." I pulled my arm free and walked over to her

coffin and retrieved the focus. She was waiting at the door when I turned around. "You may only take the necromancer class."

She giggled. "You're not very trusting."

"Angelica set a precedent."

We made our way through the sleeping building to the guild's class hall. Davina let go of my arm and rushed over the moment we arrived, overcome with excitement. She slapped her palm against it and began reading off her choices, but only the ones that were relevant.

I began to frown. "Are you ignoring the dark paths?"

"No. There haven't *been* any so far."

"Tell the truth."

She laughed. "I am. There haven't been any."

"You don't happen to have saint as an option?"

"Let me check. No. I do have something called a *necrosaint*, though."

"Take it."

"Why?"

"It's a fusion of the saint class and the necromancer class."

"But I want to be a necromancer. You said I could be a necromancer."

I paused. "I did say that, didn't I. I rescind my last order. Would you be willing to wait for me to get someone?"

"Sure."

I woke up the desk clerk, who screamed, waking up the woman next to him. When he calmed down, he gave me directions to the guild's class specialist, who also screamed when I woke her. When I explained why I was waking her, she ran out of the room with only her blanket wrapped around her.

People were in the hallways with naked blades, likely due to all the screaming. She pushed through them, shouting over questions that she had to get to the class hall. The adventurers took this to mean that was the source of the danger, and by the time we arrived, they had surrounded Davina. Multiple barriers covered her, while other mages gathered magic for spells and warriors followed her movements, ready to leap forward and cut her down.

"Hi, everyone," she said excitedly. "I'm Davina. Thank you for coming to my class ceremony. I really appreciate the support."

The class specialist pushed through the crowd. "Pipe down, you lot," she shouted. "Hello, Davina. I'm Gwen the guild's class specialist. Your master has asked me to assist you in choosing a class."

Davina smiled. "That's all right. I'm going to be a necromancer."

Gwen returned the smile. "While that is lovely. I'm told you have access to a class called *necrosaint.*"

"I don't really want it."

"Even if you don't take it, I would appreciate a chance to know more about this class." Then she turned to the nearest adventurer. "Go get me a pen and paper."

The man frowned. "Is there no danger?"

"I didn't say that."

I reached into my storage pouch and handed her a pen and paper.

"Thank you." She turned back to Davina. "Please read every class choice you have from the top."

Davina glanced at me.

I nodded. "Tell her everything honestly and leave nothing out."

Those further back realised they couldn't get closer, so they ran off to get better equipped. When they returned, they replaced those in the room, who went off and gathered their equipment, before returning. The guild master turned up before they arrived and took a spot beside me, listening, ready for a fight to break out. I'd gained a bit of a reputation for causing mayhem at the Hellmouth headquarters, so they weren't taking any chances.

When Gwen was finished writing down Davina's class options, she began asking questions. These questions varied from her diet to her childhood, to her opinions on certain topics. Hours passed, and those on guard changed several times.

Gwen eventually sighed. "I'm afraid you have to take the class."

Davina frowned. "Why?"

"By your own admission, you're different to most people. You have some sort of strange ability to cleanse death magic. This ability is not evil. It seems to be the opposite. All saints have access to other classes, and like you, their class options are always good or neutral. There have been *five* people with what we refer to as hybrid saint classes over the *entire* history of the guild. Each of them had some unique circumstance like you. Two accepted this class. Three did not. Those three eventually became monsters. One was stopped before she could kill more than a few dozen people. The other two massacred several towns and cities. While this isn't proof that taking the hybrid saint class is necessary, it does strongly suggest it."

Davina sighed. "Is it a hybrid of the necromancer and saint classes?"

Gwen frowned. "Who told you that?"

Davina pointed at me.

"How did you know?" Gwen asked.

"Educated guess," I said.

"So, you assumed from the name."

"Educated guess," I repeated.

She folded her notes and turned back to Davina. "The vampire is likely correct. Most of your options have a necromancy focus. There is a very small chance that the class *isn't* a necromancer saint hybrid."

That caused a few eyebrows to rise and the guild master to comment. "How would that even work?"

"The saint class is a healing and cleansing class. Hybrid saints have this capacity, but in a smaller area. She will likely be able to heal necrotic wounds and cleanse undead curses, along with performing all the usual acts that necromancers are known for."

I frowned. "If she's not a true saint, will she be able to upgrade her class?"

"Yes, but it's a technical yes. Hybrid saints are a prestige class, so they receive three skills every tenth level."

I turned to Davina. "The choice is yours. Necromancer or necrosaint, you decide. I've got things to do." I turned to push my way through the crowd.

"Wait!" Davina shouted.

I glanced back. "What?"

"You can't leave my class ceremony."

"Hurry it up then."

She looked at the faces around her. "Does anyone have a coin?"

Several people groaned; several others facepalmed.

A roguish looking man pulled a coin from his pocket. "Heads, you take the necrosaint class. Tails you take the necromancer class."

Davina grinned. "That works."

He flipped the coin.

I fought the urge to laugh as I saw heads on both sides. He caught it in the air and slapped in on the back of his hand. "Heads. You take the necrosaint class."

"Two out of three," Davina said.

He shrugged and repeated the process. "Heads."

"I want to see that coin."

He fumbled, switching out the coin in the process.

Davina looked at both sides of the coin and flipped it herself. It came up heads. She sighed. "Fine." Her eyes moved as she manipulated a list none of us could see.

A tear in the fabric of reality appeared directly above her, as she accepted the necrosaint class. Holy light rushed through, bathing the class hall with warmth and filling everyone who saw it with peace, as a nine-foot-tall angel descended from Heaven through the portal. It landed behind Davina and placed its perfect hand upon her head, completely covering it.

For the briefest moment, its gaze landed upon me. There was no judgement, no fear, just a quiet sorrow as if seeing me reminded it that it had lost something precious.

"Use my power well, child of the grave," the angel whispered.

"And know Heaven is watching." The angel crumbled to golden dust as the power fled its body, entering Davina.

The gateway immediately closed, cutting off the light and removing the sense of peace. Tears flowed down my cheeks, uncontrolled and unrestrained as my soul mourned the death of an angel.

"What have I done," whispered the tearful rogue as his two-headed coin fell from his fingers.

18

THE ASCENSION OF EVIL

Over the next few days, everyone who had witnessed the angel's death quietly packed their bags and left. They went in ones and twos, with despondent eyes. The guild no longer felt like home to them, and the town only reminded them of what they'd witnessed. I was not immune to this effect. I wanted to leave and never return, but leaving wasn't an option. Now that Davina was awake, the craftsmen could finish Angelica's armour.

The three master craftsmen came to my suite to show me their plans for the enchantments and the final alterations.

Oliver went first. "Arthur Dragon's Bane's armour was an abomination and a perversion of all that is good. We'd be unleashing a nightmare if we attempted to recreate it, but there were aspects of it that we can take. Specifically, the class enhancement enchantments."

"You changed them," I said, looking over the designs.

"Yes. We made them stronger."

"How?"

"By not cluttering them up with layers of enchantments designed to tear people's souls out. There is a *holy* set of enchantments underneath all its unholiness."

Azula nodded. "The most powerful unholy relics and

enchantments are always created from a holy source. It's the perversion of the good at their core that gives them so much power, and Arthur Dragon's Bane's armour was no exception."

I scanned the schematics. "You linked the class enchantments to the growth properties. Will that work?"

"We think so."

"You *think* so?"

Oliver shrugged. "The original class enchantments were linked to a growth property that fed on human souls, so it's reasonable to conclude that the class enhancements can grow stronger. However, we don't recognise several of the runes, so we can't know for sure whether it will actually work without using souls as a fuel source."

"Which runes don't you recognise?"

Oliver pointed them out.

I searched my brain for the relevant information and then opened the storage chest and removed several forbidden books, flipping to the sections they needed. "Here's what they do. You probably want replacements. They're all demon runes." I scanned the schematics again. "And these ones. That one is a curse." I grabbed a pen and drew another rune beside it. "You can replace it with this." I saw something else I could change and corrected it. Which showed me something else.

Oliver stood beside me with a growing frown as I changed more and more of the designs. Finally, he couldn't stand it any longer. "You can't add a condensing equation there! Do you have any idea what sort of reagent you would need to use to stabilise it?"

"Powdered lich phylactery suspended in ancient vampire blood and fortified with ancient vampire ashes."

He snorted. "That would be overkill."

"I mean, we could use something weaker, but it's what I've got on hand."

All three of them froze and turned to stare at me.

"Did I not mention that?"

"Only the first two," Oliver said.

Nina turned to Azula. "With ancient vampire ashes we could add a death lacquer to the finish."

Azula scoffed. "Instead of doom veins."

"You can't add doom veins to blood bone."

"You can to dracolich blood bone."

"Theoretically."

"Everything we have done has been theoretical. Why stop now?"

Nina nodded, conceding the point. "Why not both? There should be more than enough ashes."

"The doom veins will radiate death magic, eventually breaking down the death lacquer."

"Not if Oliver syphons it off, to power his enchantments."

"You think he has the skills to pull that off?"

"I most certainly do have the skills to pull it off," Oliver growled. "I just need the right reagents, which are apparently exactly what I have to work with." He turned to me. "You don't have anything else up your sleeve, do you? No dark phoenix feathers or lich king bones?"

"How much do you need?"

They stared at me across the table.

I opened my storage chest and removed the box of loot that I'd I failed to mention to Luke and the others. The contents of the box were something Mara would have cleansed on sight, which is why I had kept quiet. There had been other boxes filled with demonic and less powerful but extremely evil undead materials that I'd handed over just to keep her from getting suspicious.

I opened the lid and placed it in front of them.

They leaned back.

Azula scowled. "Please, don't take this the wrong way, but do you mind putting that unholy, cursed box away?"

"In a moment. You need to verify the contents."

There were numerous smaller cases, bottles, jars, and vials inside the box, each carefully labelled. I pulled them out one by one and showed them to the craftsmen, letting them confirm that the contents were authentic. Then I put the box away.

Azula sighed. "Don't let anyone touch that box. They'll immediately turn into an undead abomination."

"I figured."

Azula paused. "It would make sense you could tell."

"Can you use any of it?"

They nodded.

"Good."

"I'm guessing you got the box and its contents from the lich," Oliver said.

"Is that a problem?"

"No. Also yes. Most of the content of that box is a controlled substance. The rest of it has an immediate destruction order placed upon it by the church and crown."

"None of the materials inside the box are inherently evil, only most of the applications they can be used for, correct?"

They all nodded, uncomfortably.

"Would it make you more comfortable to properly dispose of these materials by incorporating them into my familiar's set, rather than leaving them in my care?"

"It would make me more comfortable to just dispose of them, period," Nina said.

"There is an ancient vampire between you and such an outcome. In that scenario doesn't it seem wiser to take the available path rather than the impossible?"

"This must be what making a deal with a demon feels like," Oliver said. "You're desperate enough to accept, but you know you're damning yourself to Hell for doing so."

Azula chuckled. "Don't be dramatic. We aren't doing anything we weren't already doing. We're just breaking the law a little."

"And supplying an ancient vampire with the perfect opportunity to blackmail us," Oliver countered.

"Think of all the skill levels you will get and all the good you can do with them," I said.

"Okay, I hear the deal with demon part now," Azula muttered. "He's definitely going to blackmail us into coming to work in his academy."

I smirked. "Azula, you three have been giddy as schoolgirls since I arrived. The small amount of information I've handed to you and your staff had you all cackling like madmen. Be honest with yourselves: Do you really think you can turn down the opportunity I'm offering you?"

They squirmed under my gaze.

"You know what I am. You understand how I think, and you know the limitations on what I can feel. You know that the *only* thing I care about in this world is keeping my family safe. So, you also know that I want you and your staff to be all that you can possibly be, because it helps me achieve this goal."

"We also know that you will cross lines we won't cross," Nina said. "For you the ends will always justify the means."

"Then make sure I have the tools I need so I don't have to cross those lines."

Oliver sighed. "Sadly, you've summed up exactly what we've all devoted our lives to."

"We stand on the line, so others don't have to walk across," Azula said.

"We accept the night, so we don't become it," Nina said.

"But we never serve it," Oliver said.

"We never serve it," Nina and Azula echoed.

"Then we have that in common," I finished.

THE DEATH of an angel is enough to make a vampire weep. Nothing I witnessed since coming to this world was close to that experience. It was a moment that would haunt me for all eternity. So, I didn't push

Davina. I gave her space and let her adjust to what had happened. When I was human, that would have been a decade or more for her to grieve. As a vampire, it was only a week.

Davina walked out of her room and gave me the same brilliant smile she did every morning, before curtsying and saying, "Good morning, your Dark Eminence." She turned, heading for the door.

She had taken to exploring the town and the surrounding countryside. Some days I escorted her, other days I paid an adventuring party who hadn't witnessed what happened to keep her safe. She was fascinated by everything and everyone, taking delight in all that she saw and did. She was vibrant and full of life, a soothing presence on even the weariest of souls.

"We need to talk," I said, pushing aside my pen and paper.

She pivoted without a word, walked to the table, and took a seat.

"How are you doing?"

She gave me a sad smile. "I was wondering how long it would take you to bring it up."

"Are you upset?"

"No."

"Everyone else who was there is."

"Including you?"

I nodded.

"Don't be. It's what it wanted."

"Is it?"

She nodded. "It made a choice. A choice that no one else would have made, but it is a choice that it decided for itself. I'm not upset by this. I think that's part of why it was willing to give me its power. If it had done the same for anyone else in that room, it would have ruined them. It would have crushed them with guilt. But not me. Because I respect and accept the choice it made."

"If you said that to anyone else who was there, they would try to kill you. They saw a being of infinite kindness and compassion give its life for what can only be described as a corrupt and wretched soul by comparison."

"Do you regret asking me to take the class?"

"Yes."

"Do you hate me for accepting?"

"No. I pity you."

"Why?"

"Because it left you a burden that no soul should carry. A debt that cannot be repaid."

"There is no debt. Demons require debts. Angels only give freely and without restriction. It saw a chance to do good and accepted the cost, with peace and contentment."

"How do you know?"

She touched her heart. "Because of what lies in here. It is not greed, envy, or anger, only kindness, caring, compassion, and peace."

"Would you like to be freed from my service?"

She smiled and then slowly shook her head. "No. I'm exactly where I'm supposed to be. It would not have given me its grace if it were not so."

The turmoil in my soul calmed. "In that case, you need to get to work. I would like to know your attributes and your skills."

Davina proceeded to list off a rather appallingly low set of attributes, until she reached her mana regeneration.

"Did you say, 2,862?"

"Yes. I can generate enough mana with a single breath to empower a mid-tier spell."

"Bypassing the need for a core."

She nodded. "I also get the feeling I don't need to be concerned about falling into an unaware state from being in a place like where you found me. My body metabolises death magic far more quickly and in greater amounts than in the past. It would now take a powerful direct hit from a necrotic spell to affect me, and the effect would be minimal and short-lived."

"Is this due to your class or your constitution?"

"My constitution. I had this impression immediately after waking up."

"Since you can't form a core, I'm banning you from investing your attributes into your mana regeneration."

"That's fine, I wasn't planning to invest in it anyway."

"Your skills?"

She grinned. "Racial skills are prodigy, magic, and advanced physique. Class skills are death magic, ritual magic, runic magic, death curse-breaking, cleansing death magic, staff, and mage armour."

"That is a potent combination for a necromancer."

"I would have preferred create undead, instead of the curse-breaking skill. I have about five decades of study that is going to waste without it."

That was a curious objection. "You aren't complaining about the cleansing death magic skill?"

She shook her head. "I think it might help me with my constitution."

"That's a reasonable assumption. Do you need me to explain any of your skills?"

She laughed at the absurdity of my offer. "No."

"Are you aware of how the prodigy skill works?"

She continued to laugh. "It can only be trained during your first training session with a new skill, and it improves based upon how far you can push your skill's level during that session. I'll have most of my skills mastered by the end of the day."

"Get to it then."

She grinned and jumped to her feet. "I've been waiting a week for you to say that." She turned, about to run for the door.

"Hold on." I went to my room and came back holding her mother's robe and her father's staff. Neither object was cursed anymore, and each one complemented her class perfectly. They were growth items and family heirlooms, created with the intent of making the most powerful necromancer imaginable. They would respond to her the way they had for her parents. "I kept these for you."

She made one of those high-pitched squeaking sounds teenage

girls make when they see a member of their favourite boy band. And then raced across the room and snatched them from me. She completely forgot I was there, as she ran from the suite into the hallway, and began shouting for help wanting to know where the laundry was done.

I walked across the room and closed the door, pausing for a moment. "I probably should have told her not to practice necromancy inside the town." I considered going after her to tell her. "How much harm could she cause?"

I closed the door.

LUKE HAD EXPLAINED that having the hero class was different to other classes. All your actions were taken into account as a hero, so you could end up receiving utterly useless skills if you did too much of a mundane task. For this reason, he didn't clean his clothes, make his bed, or haggle for anything but loot. His love of barbequing had caused him to gain the cooking skill and then the grilling skill, and his thirst for beer had given him the inebriation skill, so he was exceptionally careful about everything he did.

Which is why I had waited for Davina to take her class before visiting the guild's class hall. There were a handful of training skills that I wanted to gain. They would eventually make my minions more powerful, which would keep me safer, so I had waited until I improved my chances.

It was late in the day when I walked into the class hall and placed my hand on the stone. The golden dust that had fallen from the angel, a material called *celestial sunlight*, had absorbed into the stone, consecrating the room and causing a soft, warm glow to radiate from the space.

Congratulations, you have leveled your hero class.
Your class has leveled.

Your class has leveled.
You are now a level 7 hero.

Your class has unlocked new skills:
Death Magic
Create Undead

You have 40 attribute points to spend.

"Two freaking levels. Is this a joke?" I touched the stone again, but nothing happened. "Are you serious," I growled. "You give Luke twenty-two levels and all I get is two? I was freaking level five!"

Nothing changed as I kept tapping my hand against the stone like it was the bell at an empty hotel desk.

"On top of that, you give me two skills I don't even want. Why the heck would you give me two skills that require something I haven't used? My mana regeneration is zero."

Someone started ringing the guild's alarm bell. I could hear dozens of heartbeats skip and then accelerate as everyone dropped what they were doing and rushed to gather arms. I was out of the class hall and at the front desks before the third strike. The guild rules were clear on this. Participation in an emergency was mandatory for all members in the building, whether or not someone was visiting.

The young man striking the bell jumped as I appeared.

"What's the emergency?"

"There's some sort of disturbance over the guild."

I rushed outside and looked up. A vortex of death energy a hundred meters across floated in the air above the guild growing by the second.

"Davina!" Her name came out as a roar.

19

NEW DIRECTIONS

At sunset, three and a half weeks after she left, Angelica dragged herself into the guild's tavern. She was covered in weeks of dirt and sweat, and hadn't eaten in days, but was otherwise uninjured. She dropped into the seat across from me, tossed a pile of letters at me, as she grabbed the remaining half of the apple pie and the bowl of whipped cream I'd been saving for Davina. She inhaled the food, making it disappear in less than a minute, and then reached for my glass of milk.

I pulled it away. "Order your own."

She pouted. "But I'm thirsty now."

"That's your fault, Angelica."

She raised her nose at me. "The correct way to address me is Countess Angelica Lich Bane, peasant.

I gave her an unimpressed look. "That's the last time you attempt to make someone use the title I handed to you or call someone a peasant. Now order your own."

She continued to pout as she called over one of the staff, ordering a jug of milk, and several bowls of stew. Then she noticed Davina. "She's awake. What's she doing?"

Davina was standing at a chalkboard on the tavern's stage,

writing lines. Without a guild master, no one at the guild had the authority to punish her, but there had been enough complaining that I knew if I left her unpunished, everyone would ask for something extreme the moment the new guild master arrived.

"She's writing lines."

Angelica squinted. "'I will not create death voids in town. I will not create death voids in town.' How many times does she have to write it?"

"From dawn until dusk, until we leave."

"What's a death void?"

"A very complicated and powerful spell that can kill an entire town."

"And she created one."

"She thought she was being clever."

Angelica looked around. "Everyone seems to be fine."

"That's because she's as clever as she thinks she is."

Seeing that Angelica wanted to know the story, I explained how Davina had gotten the bright idea to master a bunch of her skills simultaneously, in order to master her prodigy skill. She had hundreds of years of knowledge and practice performing magic without a class or core, so she could master magic and death magic any time she liked. Instead of doing that, she had pushed herself in a way that no normal person would. She'd performed the death void spell as a ritual using only runic symbols, which was something only a master necromancer would attempt.

The massive death void, which had hung above the guild, had gathered all the latent death magic in the surrounding countryside, cleansing the land, before she collapsed the spell into a concentrated sphere the size of a marble *and ate it*. The act caused her to master her magic, death magic, ritual magic, runic magic, staff, and prodigy skills *simultaneously*, while giving her levels in her cleansing death magic skill. It also left her mummified for half a day and gave her another dozen points for her mana regeneration.

The only reason the guild hadn't locked her up was I'd managed to convince them that she had been performing a *cleansing* ritual for the town. The fact that most could tell that the air was cleaner, and the plants and people were healthier, supported my claim.

"So, now she's writing lines," I said.

"This is so unfair. She performs a necromancy spell that can kill everyone, and she doesn't even get arrested, while I have to fight a lich to be pardoned for being part of a cult."

"She did the town a service and was in complete control the entire time. You were going to have someone sacrificed so you could gain their attributes. It is not the same thing."

"Says who?"

"Says anyone with moral fibre. Now where have you been?"

"Sorgin Mountain Range?"

I kept my annoyance from entering my tone. "That's on the other side of the province."

"The guild there pays a hundred gold an ogre head after taxes, and you said I could take a few quests for spending money."

"Those quests were supposed to be on your way back here."

She smiled, trying to win me over with charm. "You didn't specifically say that."

She needed to practice more. "It was implied."

Her smile turned into a mischievous smirk. "That's your fault."

"How much did you make?"

"Ten thousand gold pieces. They cut me off after I killed a hundred, for some reason."

"Monsters have territories. If anyone but a hero exterminates a species, something else moves in. Ogres are dangerous when their numbers grow too large, but they keep a lot of other nastier threats in check."

"I'd rather have more gold."

I ignored her comment. "I gave you freedom and you chose to abuse it. How much money do you think you should hand over for you to understand that isn't a productive choice to make?"

She cringed. "None. I'll behave."

"But will you learn your lesson?"

"Please don't take my gold. I have to look after my brothers and sister. They're orphans. You killed our parents, and the mayor confiscated my family's property and assets."

"I know for a fact you are still allowed to live in your parents' house."

"Walls don't fill bellies."

That was true. "I suppose I could let you give all your money to them."

"They only need a quarter of it," she said immediately. "They don't eat much."

"That might be true, but they also need clothes and shoes, expenses for their education, money for healing, and someone to take care of them."

Angelica groaned. "I can give them half."

"Half of everything you make until they're old enough to fend for themselves seems fair."

She began to choke.

"I mean, that is the sort of thing that would make you learn your lesson." As her eyes filled with hopelessness, I threw her a lifeline. "I would, of course, consider anything you spent on your household to be part of this expense if they were living with you."

Angelica paused running my offer through her head, figuring out all that ways she could abuse it. I didn't care about the money, but I had noticed a rather bad trend with her personality. She didn't work well in isolation. She tended to become more selfish and self-centred. This didn't happen when she was around her siblings, so I needed to keep them around to calm her darker impulses, so Luke wouldn't have to kill her one day.

"Would furnishings be included?"

"Yes."

"Then I would go as far as 40%."

"*Half*, Angelica."

She groaned. "I promise not to abuse my freedom again."

"You misunderstand me. This is your punishment for this instance. Should you do so again, you will consider this to be a little slap on the wrist by comparison."

Davina finished wiping off the chalkboard and walked over, taking the seat next to me. "Hi, Angelica." Her gaze dropped to the empty pie dish. "You said you would save me half."

"Angelica ate it."

"You let her eat it," Davina complained.

"Yes. She hadn't eaten in a few days."

Davina frowned and turned to Angelica. "Why haven't you eaten in days?"

Angelica blushed. "Everyone ran screaming whenever I landed in a village to get something to eat."

I sighed. "Go to the chalkboard and write this a thousand times. 'I will not land my dracolich in the middle of a village and scare everyone.'"

Angelica leapt out of her chair and raced to the chalkboard.

I picked up the pile of letters Angelica had tossed at me when she arrived and started going through. Several of them were from Luke, confirming that he had done what I asked. One was a writ of ownership for the manor and land around where I was turned, signed by Angelica and the governor, making her the countess of the estate. Another was my neutrality papers, confirming my status with the guild. Another was my paperwork confirming my membership to the guild.

Another letter was from a talented geomancer, called Augustus, who had seen my request at his guild and wanted to take on my academy project. Enclosed was a list of his qualifications and his reason for wanting to accept my project. His reason basically amounted to him being ambitious and knowing that he likely wouldn't be given a chance at a project for another two decades if he turned it down like everyone else had. He was willing to risk being eaten, in order to become a senior geomancer before he reached his fifties. Augustus, however, was only one geomancer, and I needed dozens.

The final letter was written on enchanted paper using gold as the ink. It was a summons from the king. I was to present the attached letter to the guild master in Hellmouth and then proceed to the capital with all possible haste. Where I was to tell no one of my nature and report to the king directly. He wanted me to provide an undisclosed service, and the letter hinted at the fact that I might be allowed to move freely through the kingdom if I did so.

"Anything interesting?" Davina asked, as I put down the last letter.

"Potentially. It looks like we'll be heading to the capital when Angelica's armour is done."

"I thought you needed to rest."

"That will have to wait."

TEMPTATION IS A BEAUTIFUL EMOTION; it can lead honest people to make all sorts of wonderful and stupid decisions. The temptation to use the forbidden materials in my box was too much for the master craftsmen to endure. They rationalized their actions the way I wanted them to, by incorporating them into Angelica's set, thereby removing them from the potential clutches of evil.

It was almost too easy.

Bolts of death magic that behaved like lightning surged through the craftsmen's workshop as Azula and Nina harnessed the power trapped within the dark materials. Davina stood to the side, redirecting the wanton power to flow back to its source, causing a ring of concentrated magic to spiral above the forging table.

I raced around the room with Slaughter, cutting down dark, undead abominations that sprang into being from the bones I'd scattered across the floor. They were death elementals, created from the pure death magic that was freed from the breaking down of the powerful materials.

The craftsmen's need to do good compromised their common sense, making them risk it all, as they found a way to dispose of everything taken from Contessa in the most dangerous manner imaginable.

Terrified workers ran between the forge and tables, adding reagents as Azula called for them, stepping around the creatures that pulled themselves together from the bones I'd scattered across the floor. Mages stood at the edge of the forge's workshop, chanting and holding a barrier so the effects wouldn't spread through the town.

All the mages from the nearby guilds had been mobilised to help in the creation of the armour and were collapsing from mana exhaustion quicker than I would have liked.

Angelica fought against a spiked bear death elemental, trying to duck under a swipe of its claw. She was wearing borrowed armour and wielding a borrowed staff, struggling to keep up with the creature without her set. The bear's claws struck her chest, sending her flying across the room to collide with the mage's barrier. "Fuck," she growled, pulling herself to her feet.

"Language," I said.

"Bite me," she shouted, charging back in.

I delivered a lazy cut with Slaughter, banishing another elemental and scattering its bones, and then I appeared behind another that was in the process of forming. I struck it down before it could finish, and I moved on to the next. The bones I'd scattered were a conduit for death magic, a way to give the chaotic energies form without losing control.

We had already done this to make the reagents they were using, and we would have to do it again for the final enchanting process. That was fine with me. The bones I supplied were all from the most powerful undead death knights Contessa commanded, and this process was refining them, strengthening them, making them into the perfect material to craft a legion of truly powerful minions.

Contessa had been too fixated on her research, preferring to invest her power in a horde of undead creations that required little effort and slowly grew stronger, rather than taking the time to craft powerful undead. Her courtiers had been the result of her research, not an intent to make something strong enough to keep her safe.

I wasn't going to make that mistake.

My class was pushing me towards creating undead minions. Creatures that would serve me loyally. Skills were too important to neglect. With my inability to level quickly, they were my only choice for gaining power, other than making my familiars stronger. So, I would push them to the extreme, master them, and create a world that was safe for my family.

A FEW DAYS LATER, the master craftsmen and enchanters stood around the table wearing tired grins as they went over Angelica's set with a fine-toothed comb. There were thirty-three who had participated in the project. They'd all mastered their general skills during the creation process, whether it was in crafting and/or enchanting, along with many advanced skills. A few also mastered more specialised skills, propelling their skills forward to undreamed-of heights. Those who hadn't been so lucky still received a handful of levels in their specialized skills, which was no small feat.

They would all leave Tobil, far more capable than they had entered. The kingdom's undead were going to find themselves at their mercy for the foreseeable future, and my family would be safer for it.

These men and women had the capacity to make real change. The equipment they supplied from now on would be significantly better than before we met, saving the lives of guild members, and causing the demise of their enemies. Within a few years, their work would sit in a thousand different hands and kill tens of thousands of foes.

Oliver put away his monocle and sighed. "It's everything we were hoping for and so much more."

"Explain," I said. "What do you mean, *more*?"

He ran his finger across his bald scalp. "I mean everything we attempted to incorporate has been incorporated and in a stable manner. The set will give her access to all death knight skills and allow her to train them with increased efficiency. Any skill she already possesses and has mastered will have its maximum level increased by one, and both traits will grow stronger as the set's growth potential develops, expanding when she gains the death lord class."

"Is that all?" Angelica asked.

Several people's gaze turned murderous.

Angelica took a step back. "I mean you made it sound like this was going to be *legendary* armour."

"It's *much* more powerful than that classification," I said. "So shut your ungrateful mouth and listen, before I let these nice people murder you."

The craftsmen chuckled.

Oliver smirked as he nodded his thanks. "Beyond the effects the armour has on your class, which are substantial, it also gives you authority over the undead. Mindless undead weaker than you will not attack you, even if commanded. Mindless undead substantially weaker than you will accept *your* commands, as if you were their master. Sapient undead will suffer similar effects, so much so that as you are, you could command a vampire to do whatever you like, if it were in your presence."

Angelica's gaze darted to me, and she began to grin.

I snorted. "You would find it difficult to command even an elder vampire as you are. But you can test my patience if you like. However, I promise you that you won't like the results."

"What else can the set do?" Angelica asked, finally interested.

Seeing he had an attentive audience, Oliver perked up. "Defensively, there are three layers of barrier spells built into the armour. Arrows and spells will be deflected around you, and anything that is powerful enough to get through will be blocked by the third barrier. Offensively, the gauntlets allow you to throw burning necrotic bolts without the need to cast a spell. Your staff will also allow you to create a burning necrotic wave without needing to cast the spell. In addition, any strike you deliver, whether with your staff or your body, will unleash burning necrotic energies, strengthening your blows and making you more deadly."

"How deadly?"

"You could kill an unarmed man with a tap of your staff. You can also reinforce the burning necrotic bolts and burning necrotic wave with your own mana to make them stronger."

"I'm going to be an even bigger monster," she whispered.

I smiled. She was finally strong enough for me to risk going back to sleep.

"Nina, would you like to take over?"

"There's more?" Angelica asked, excitedly.

Nina nodded. "While wearing the set, you will be immune to fire, death, and necrotic magic. The blood bone is also now tough enough to make you impervious to unenchanted blades and claws. Enchanted blades are still problematic for now, but the barrier enchantments Oliver laid make them less concerning. Weighted strikes should be your only weakness, as these enchantments will save you from most spells."

"What about life magic?" Angelica asked. "Isn't that normally death magic's weakness?"

"That's only if the enchantments are purely death magic or unstable. This set contains neither of those weaknesses as it was originally crafted from red dragon bones. For this reason, we haven't incorporated any unholy materials in its creation, so it doesn't have a weakness to holy magic, either."

"Are we forgetting anything?" Oliver asked, with a small smile.

Azula grinned. "I think so."

"I doubt Angelica wants to hear anymore," Oliver said, dryly. "I believe our work wasn't up to her standard."

"I'm sorry, I'm sorry," Angelica said in a rush. "I want to know everything. This is the best set I've ever heard of."

The craftsmen gave another chuckle.

Nina smirked. "I mean, it would be a shame not to mention the strongest feature."

"Would you like to do the honours?" Oliver offered, enjoying watching Angelica's frustration.

"No. I wouldn't dream of doing that. It's mostly your work, after all."

"I'm sorry for not being impressed."

Oliver held his hand up to his ear. "I'm old and didn't catch that."

Angelica groaned. "I'm sorry for not being impressed by all your hard work and skill. I promise I will never be like that again, and I will tell everyone I meet how brilliant and intelligent you all are."

Oliver grinned. "We'll hold you to that. As for the most impressive part, we have incorporated *three* growth properties into your set that all boost your attributes, skills, and the power of your equipment. So, everything we've described to you is your set at its weakest and least desirable stage."

"But you just described a legendary set."

Oliver only smiled in reply.

"What will it be when it's stronger?"

Nina shrugged. "That is something you will have to find out for us, because we're not entirely sure what we've created for you."

20

THE ROAD TO HELL

The craftsmen spent the next three days training Angelica, teaching her how to use her equipment safely. They'd built the set to cause unimaginable destruction, meaning that she had to pay attention, or she would easily hurt others. Angelica didn't take their training as seriously as I would have liked. She paid attention, but not enough to please me. So, on the third day, I collected her two younger brothers and three sisters and added them to the training field.

She only made one mistake.

That mistake would have cost Angelica her little brother Samuel's life, if I didn't take the burning necrotic bolt in the chest for him. After that, she begged me to take them away. I didn't. I had found her weakness, and I was going to exploit it. With far more focus, she returned to her training, eventually passing the craftsmen's minimum standards. So, on the morning of the fourth day we headed for Hellmouth.

With their new levels, the craftsmen were returning to Hellmouth to equip others, so we joined their wagon train, and Angelica continued her training in the back of an empty wagon Nina had put aside for her.

Two days into the trip, Angelica tossed down her latest attempt at controlling her set's vampiric touch ability. The withered plant was bone dry and deep brown. I'd pulled it from the ground less than ten minutes prior. "Can't you compel me to do it properly?"

Davina glanced up from the book she was reading. Her education was deeply rooted in the occult, so when it came to more standard practices, she wasn't anywhere near as educated as she would like. "Vampiric compelling doesn't affect your thoughts and wants, only your motor control. We can be compelled to hit someone. We can't be compelled to *want* to hit them. The armour is reacting to your *wants*, *not* your physical action, so his Dark Eminence can't help you."

Angelica scowled at me. "You could try."

I paused and considered her request. She had been attempting to control the vampiric nature of her equipment for the past two days without success. Her siblings had motivated her before, so they were likely to do so again. However, killing several of them to help her train would only leave her too distressed to be useful. It would also be wrong. My *memories* told me that, even if I didn't *feel* that anymore.

"Do you prefer cats or dogs?" I asked.

"What does that have to do-"

"Answer the question."

"Dogs."

"When we reach Hellmouth I'm going to search the city for the cutest puppies I can find. Each morning you will have to pick one up wearing your armour. Whether or not you suck the life from it is up to you."

Angelica looked at me with open horror. "You want me to murder puppies."

"The cutest puppies I can find."

"That's so evil."

"No. It's motivating. Now practice."

Davina stared at me. "You're not seriously going to have her murder puppies, are you?"

"Making her practice on her siblings is too cruel. This was the best alternative."

Panic swept across Davina's features, and she turned to Angelica. "He's serious."

"I know he's serious."

"Let me help you."

"Wait, you can help me? Why weren't you helping me before?"

"You need to learn how to work things out for yourself, but I can't allow him make you kill adorable puppies to do so."

"I'm listening? What do I have to do?"

"You should try draining the life out of those plants as fast as you possibly can. If you can make the effect stronger, you will gain a measure of control. Then you have to work on controlling how fast you strengthen the draining effect. Eventually, you will develop the ability to reduce the drain as well as increase it."

Nina leaned back in her seat to talk to me without taking her gaze from the road. "You have a unique teaching style."

"You don't sound like you disapprove."

"Considering what her equipment is capable of, I don't. Do you mind coming up here so we can talk?"

I climbed to my feet and stepped over the back of the chair, taking a seat beside her at the front of the wagon. We were traveling through the mountain range where we'd found the earth elemental. The air was crisp and cold. The cliff walls bathed everything in shadow. "What did you want to talk about?"

"How serious was your offer?"

"You need to be more specific. I've made several offers recently."

"You handed everyone who worked on Angelica's set an untitled book containing more knowledge on how to kill undead than any book any of us have ever seen, and you said you were opening an academy to educate the next generation in the fight against evil and we were welcome to join as teachers and students. How serious was that offer?"

"Completely serious. I've been studying the guild library and teaching methods and have found them to be unacceptable."

"Why?"

"You rely on the church too much."

"You have a problem with the church?"

"No. I think they do a lot of good."

"Then why do you think we rely on them too much?"

"Because the majority of the guild's instructions for fighting the undead involve the words: 'And then have your cleric hit it with holy magic.' Very few undead cannot be put down without holy magic. The guild's over-reliance on clerics, and their low numbers as a class, limits the guild's ability to deal with these threats on a larger scale. Adventurers can be trained to fight undead and demons without a cleric in their party, so they should be."

"That's a big claim. Do you have any proof?"

"Do you know Hector the vampire hunter?"

In the upper echelons of any field, everyone tended to know each other.

"That's one example."

"Yet no one else fights vampires without a cleric in the party. He's proof that not only can it be done, but it can be done well."

"What about those threats that need a cleric?"

"There are signs that can warn you you're in over your head. The guild doesn't usually teach these signs, because the party always has a cleric when fighting undead or demons. This is a mistake and has no doubt led to many unnecessary deaths."

"Are you going to teach people *how* to fight?"

"The guild already does an adequate job of that. I would prefer to teach people *when* to fight and *what method* to use."

"Few will want to come to your academy. You're a creature of darkness, so the church will likely oppose this academy, too."

"The academy doesn't need to educate students. It needs to

educate *teachers*. Adventurers who can take what they learn to their guild and teach others. The information I want to share is only known by a select few, people who are grizzled and angry and no good for education, only for killing evil. Those who want to learn will come because we're the only place teaching this sort of information."

"You could write another book."

"I will, but it's not the same."

"No. It's not. Will they be studying the occult?"

"They will have to. A rudimentary understanding is necessary."

"That knowledge is dangerous."

"So is magical knowledge, but magic stores will gladly sell a fireball spell to any child who walks through their door."

"Studying the occult corrupts people."

"You and I both know that's not true. Common occult knowledge is perfectly safe; only specific, advanced knowledge corrupts those who study it. Yes, you might be able to summon a demon with this common knowledge, but the knowledge itself isn't corrupting, and anyone who would willing summon a demon is either desperate or already corrupt."

"There are a lot of desperate people in the world."

"Do you think these people would be coming to my academy to study?"

She shook her head. "There are easier ways to learn what they need."

"But no easier ways for those who want to *fight* them."

"Why do you want to fight evil so badly?"

"My son has got it into his head that he will fight evil until the day he dies. The kingdom is in turmoil. The guild is a shadow of what it once was. Unseen run freely through every village, and evil rules the wild places. This needs to change for him to relax. So, I'm going to make it change."

"It won't be easy."

"Nothing important is ever easy. That's why we put it off until the pain it brings us can't be ignored. I've watched my son suffer every day since we were reunited. He puts on a brave face for the world, but he's scared. He's sad. And he's a little miserable."

"How can you be sure?"

I tapped my nose. "Every emotion has a scent. I wasn't so good at reading the differences at first, but I've got the hang of it now."

"I wish I could trust your words."

"Because I offer exactly what you want to hear."

"Yes."

"Demons and good people always do."

"Which are you?"

"I'm both."

THE CARAVAN HAD STOPPED at a marked campground, half a day from the city of Hellmouth. People were busy putting away everything they had used to make dinner and preparing for the night. We were in open country surrounded by grassland and wandering herds. With major threats a thing of the past, thanks to Luke, everyone had decided to save money and stay in the open instead of behind walls.

Angelica and Davina were practicing frantically in the back of the wagon behind me trying to improve her control, before the puppy murder deadline. And I was sitting comfortably with my back against the wagon wheel, trying to deal with a rather amusing and slightly horrifying problem.

"So, you want me to eat your little brother," I said to four-year-old, Nathanial, who was holding Michael, his two-year-old bother's hand. Michael clearly had no clue what I was and was happily standing before me picking his nose.

"He ate my sausage," Nathaniel said petulantly, rubbing his greasy hand through his blonde locks.

I tried not to smile. "That's not a good reason to try to feed him to a vampire."

"It was my sausage! I was saving it." He said it like he couldn't understand how I didn't deliver the death sentence immediately. He didn't know what he was asking for. I could tell.

"Nathaniel, Michael, it's bedtime," a woman called in the distance.

The two turned their heads in the direction of their mother's voice.

Their father, Nathaniel senior, walked around the back of the nearby wagon and froze for half a second when he spotted me, then he walked over and scooped up his kids. He had worked on Angelica's armour, so we had spent some time together, and my presence didn't terrify him completely anymore.

He sighed as he held his son. "I told you boys not to bother Vincent."

"Michael ate my sausage!"

His father gave a tired nod. "That wasn't very nice, Michael."

Michael's only response was a giggle.

"It was naughty. And naughty boys get eaten by vampires, like you said."

Their father continued to smile for half a second, and then the reality of what his son had said sank in. Horror transformed his expression. "Did you bring your little brother over here to be eaten by the vampire?"

"He was naughty. He ate my sausage!" Nathaniel's four-year-old brain couldn't understand why his father seemed to be upset with him. Naughty boys were eaten by vampires, after all. And they just happened to have a vampire nearby.

My children had a five-year gap between them, so they had never been as close as these boys. Luke didn't want to be stuck playing with his baby sister. She had still followed him everywhere, despite his protests. However, I could still see this happening to them when they were their age, which is why I found it so amusing.

"Parenting is tough, right?" I empathized with a fond grin, remembering happier days.

He nodded, gave an exaggerated sigh, and walked off, carrying his boys in his arms. "We are going to have a long talk about this with your mother."

"But she gave him my sausage. It's not fair."

"Wait, it wasn't your sausage?"

"It was mine. I claimed it."

"Whose plate was it on?"

"Michael's, but I claimed it, so it's mine."

"You tried to feed your brother to a vampire, because he ate his own sausage."

"It was my sausage!"

I began to chuckle, more amused by their childish antics than anything else I'd seen while traveling. The urge to eat them had never crossed my mind. Neither had I been overwhelmed by exhaustion from simply listening to them. They had offered me nothing that could help my son, yet they held my full attention. Maybe Hector was right, and I needed to open an orphanage to stay active, but the thought of making any child grow up around a cold, undead creature was repugnant. I wouldn't make myself do that, even to stay awake.

"Maybe I could be a babysitter or go into childcare," I said to myself. "Do they even have preschools here? If they don't, I could open the first one. I'll call it Little Sucker. The slogan would be, 'I promise not to drink their blood'."

Oliver wandered over a few minutes later while I was chuckling to myself and making up absurd names and claims for my imaginary preschool. "We might have a problem."

I glanced in his direction. "The mercenaries?"

They had ridden into the campground while I was talking to the boys and had made very little effort to prepare for the night ahead, despite the fading sun.

Oliver nodded. "Some of them are wearing cursed items."

"Slavers?"

"They don't have the wagons. I'd guess soul reapers."

Soul reapers didn't care about a body, only a person's soul. Souls were the currency of Hell, and you could buy a lot with them, if you were willing to take them. "This close to Hellmouth?"

"The hero is gone, and the countryside is safe. Patrols are less frequent than in the past. Soldiers have been sent to more dangerous territory."

"Leaving this area open for a surprise attack."

"Yes."

"This won't be the only group, if you're right."

"Which is why I came to you."

"Does the guild still have the twenty gold bounty on soul reapers?"

"Last time I checked."

"Good. Tell Angelica that I might have found her some live test subjects to practice on."

"Nasty way to go, but no worse than they deserve."

"I'll go see if these mercenaries are who you think they are. Tell my familiars to join me as soon as they're ready."

I pushed myself to my feet, dusted the dirt off, and made my way through the camp towards the mercenaries. There were eight caravans staying in the campground, which amounted to close to six hundred people. The mercenaries had close to a quarter of that number, which gave them a clear advantage against any resistance. Without combat skills, attributes rarely mattered.

The mercenaries had parked their horses in a line. Some were feeding and watering them, while others had started cooking over enchanted flat stones. Only three tents had gone up so far, and it only looked like they had another three with them, unless they all had storage pouches, which seemed unlikely.

I ran into the first Unseen before I entered their camp and met the second the moment I did. I didn't get much further before someone stopped me.

The man was cleanly dressed and freshly shaven. His armour was well-kept, and his sheath seemed to be freshly oiled, so he gave no impression that he was anything more than a respectable mercenary. He wasn't Unseen, and he didn't wear any cursed items. "What do you want?"

"I'd like to speak with the leader of your company. Do you mind pointing me in their direction?"

"Sure," he turned and pointed over his shoulder. "The big tent; you can't miss it."

I made my way over to the tent, spotting more Unseen, and noticing a pattern. The Unseen belonged to the group of mercenaries who had storage pouches and better equipment. This equipment wasn't well-cared for, despite its value, showing obvious neglect. In total there seemed to be fifty-seven that fit this description, out of the hundred and sixty. Not all of them were Unseen, but most were.

The other hundred mercenaries all wore altered uniforms. Until recently they had all had a crest stitched onto their chest; now they all had fresh patches on their right arm.

No one was standing guard outside their commander's tent when I arrived, which suggested that they weren't here to cause trouble, another thing that didn't make sense. I raised my voice slightly, seeing the runes stitched into the fabric, "Could I have a moment of your time? My camp is the one next to yours."

"Come in," came a gruff reply.

I pulled aside the flap and entered a well-lit interior. A mat had been placed against one side, with a rug, and bedding for two on top. A chest sat at the back of the tent and a desk that could clearly be broken down sat to the right. A middle-aged man in a clean shirt sat behind the desk, ignoring his paperwork and looking at me.

"I'm Gregory. How can I help you," he said, offering me his hand as I walked over.

"I'm Vincent. My caravan isn't from around here and didn't recognise your company's colours, so they wanted someone to come over here and chat to put everyone's mind at ease."

"Where are you from?"

"Tobil."

"Border town, you're far from home."

"Hence why we don't recognise anything."

He chuckled. "I'd be surprised if you did. We used to be called the Crimson Dragons, but with the hero pacifying the land, contracts dried up. With everything so safe, work became hard to come by, and my company couldn't afford to continue. I sold up last week and merged my company with one owned by a noble. I got to keep my command and the best of my men under me. The rest got work under their other commanders, so I can't really complain. In the end, we didn't have to uproot our lives and move to greener pastures."

"Must have been a big company."

He nodded. "Almost a private army. Three thousand strong when they got here. Bought out a dozen companies since, so it's close to twice that now."

"They're not local?"

"Moved here to take advantage of the hero. Wherever he goes, property values rise and people are safer. Makes for profitable trading, from what I'm told."

"That's unfortunate."

He frowned. "Why?"

"I came in here thinking you were all soul reapers. But you're just a desperate victim."

He chuckled. "Buddy, you need to lay off the drink."

I reached into my coat pocket and accessed my storage pouch. I placed my letter of neutrality in front of him. "I believe you know what this is."

He glanced down, and then did a double-take. He read the letter and paled. "You're a-"

"Concerned citizen," I said calmly. "I'm just thankful you have noise-dampening spells on your tent."

"Are you going to kill me?"

"No. I'm here to help you."

"Help me?"

I pointed to the letter. "You have in your camp fifty-seven individuals who were part of this other company, correct?"

"How did you know?"

"I have eyes. Half of these individuals are Unseen."

"That's preposterous. I witnessed their testing myself."

"Testing performed by your people. I noticed you have a cleric on staff."

"Well, no. My wife is a combat cleric. They brought in their own cleric. But I witnessed the tests."

"Was your wife there?"

"It's just a formality."

"And?"

"And she was at a training session."

As what I was saying sunk in, I continued talking. "I'm traveling with several master craftsmen who specialise in undead enchantments and craftsmanship. Some of them also specialise in curses, and it was the cursed items your company were carrying around that caused them to ask me to intervene. I am working under the assumption that these new members of your company are soul reapers. Would I be correct in assuming that they are the strongest members of your command?"

He swallowed. "They told me they wanted to make an elite fighting force."

"No. They wanted to harvest as many strong souls as they possibly could."

"What are you going to do?"

"I'm going to save you."

He frowned. "I need proof. I can't just take your word for it." He picked up my letter of neutrality and handed it back.

"Will one be enough?"

He nodded.

"Will your wife listen to you?"

He snorted.

"I mean in an emergency."

He nodded.

"Tell her to make a holy attack against the individual I point out. When they fall screaming, order your men to sit down and make sure they listen. My familiars and I will take care of the rest."

He swallowed. "When do you want to do this?"

I stood up. "Now."

"You're not dressed for battle."

I snorted. "I don't consider this a battle."

If he could get any more pale, he would have. His legs shook as he stood, but he walked with me outside his tent and called over his wife. He whispered a set of instructions in her ear with what sounded like a secret code and her face turned grim.

She looked at me and nodded.

I pointed to a man tending to a pair of horses.

Holy light engulfed him, burning him to a crisp in a flash, showing his wife wasn't a woman who did things by half measures.

Gregory put his hand in his mouth and gave a shrill, sharp whistle that stopped his soldiers in their tracks. I was gone before he started giving orders, grabbing the nearest Unseen and draining her of life, as I moved on to the next.

"Everyone under my command, get your ass on the ground and sit this instant!" Gregory roared. "Don't trust the new members. They're Unseen and soul reapers."

"Angelica, Davina, kill or cripple the standing members," I shouted, as I killed another Unseen. "Ignore the ones without storage pouches!"

The soul reapers under Gregory's command pulled weapons, but Gregory's men and women did as he said, dropping on their behinds, drawing blades to protect themselves.

Davina ran into their camp hurling bolts of necrotic energy at anyone who looked like a standing threat, killing them instantly. Angelica rushed through as a red blur, slamming into a dozen who had been in a group when the violence started.

I left that side of the camp to them and rushed to the other side, crippling those that weren't Unseen and eating those that were.

The fight was over before it started.

Screams filled the air as I finished on my side and circled back, arriving seconds before two of Gregory's men were run through. A few of the soul reapers had tried their luck and sat down. I showed them just how stupid that was, before I met up with Angelica and Davina. "Angelica, move the injured to the big tent as fast as you can."

"But I'll kill them."

"That doesn't bother me, but I'll let you keep the twenty-gold bounty for everyone that makes it."

She leapt towards the nearest screaming mercenary and grabbed his shattered arm. "Don't die," she pleaded. His flesh began to wither. "No. No. No. I want that money." The withering slowed but didn't stop. She ran for the big tent dragging her screaming victim.

I turned to Davina. "Go tell Oliver it's taken care of."

She nodded, picked up the edges of her mother's too-big robe, and started running.

Gregory's people stared at me with horror as I walked back to his tent. He and his wife were back-to-back, telling each other what they could see.

"Is it over?" Gregory asked.

I nodded.

"I need more proof," his wife said.

I pointed out half a dozen Unseen that had survived Davina and Angelica's attention. One by one, they all became crispy. As the last one dropped, his wife also hit me with the same spell.

Her surprise at the ineffectiveness made me chuckle. "I never killed an innocent and only eat Unseen. Holy magic doesn't even tickle."

She raised her hand to try again, but her husband caught her wrist and pushed it down. "Please don't antagonise the ancient vampire that just purged the strongest members of our company like they were field mice, honey."

"I need a drink," she said.

"After. We need to talk about the rest of our people."

"Finally made it," Angelica shouted happily, over her screaming, sickly looking captive. "You owe me twenty gold." She raced off to try again.

I walked over to the captive and snatched the storage pouch off her belt. I opened it and then upended it, pouring the contents across the ground.

"Sacrificial knife and soul repository," Gregory's wife growled. "They're soul reapers." She spat on the woman and turned to me. "The rest of our people are out there. We can give you their locations. The entire company is on the move tonight. We were told we were meant to be guarding a treasure caravan, and the whole company was being mobilized as a distraction. We're spread out across all the campgrounds around Hellmouth, so they're probably planning to summon a demon horde to attack the city from all directions."

Gregory nodded. "I can write you notes. My men will trust you without question if you hand one to them, and they will get you to the other company commanders. Where are you going?"

"To get my sword. If they're summoning demons, I'm going to need it. I'll be back shortly; have the notes ready."

"Can we stand up now?" the man who had pointed out his commander's tent asked as I passed.

"Did your commander say you could?"

"Shutting up and staying seated, sir."

"Good soldier."

"You wouldn't happen to be the hero would you, sir?"

"I'm his father."

"Shit, if you're his old man, he must be a monster."

"You got it the wrong way around. *I'm* the monster. *He's* the hero."

"Well, you're not like any monster I've ever seen, sir."

I chuckled all the way back to the camp. People were armed and surrounding the wagons. They relaxed slightly as I walked past, pointing back to where Oliver was talking to Davina.

As I was passing a wagon, two little heads popped out from behind a flap. Each of them was holding a sausage and grinning happily.

Nathaniel's eyes lit up when he saw me. "What happened?"

"I took care of some naughty little boys."

21

RAMIFICATIONS

Trying to reach everyone in time was a mistake; even with a dracolich and my impressive speed it was an impossible feat. The twenty-four companies the soul reapers had broken into were spread in all directions, making the furthest away a day's travel by wagon from where we began.

An impractical area to cover.

We headed straight for the guild headquarters in Hellmouth, landing on the roof in the middle of the city, waking everyone. Riker was furious at our intrusion; then he was furious for an entirely different reason, mobilizing the guild and sending runners to the governor. The city's defence forces were mustered in less than fifteen minutes, with runners heading for the guild halls and barracks in nearby towns and villages.

We stayed long enough to give a warning and mark out which companies we were claiming for ourselves, then we were off to enjoy the slaughter.

It was a very profitable night.

Two days later, at dawn in the guild tavern, Angelica stood in front of me, armed for war. Her dull, blood red armour moved with the contour of her body as she danced from foot to foot with nervous tension.

Davina was whispering encouraging words as Nina and Oliver took notes from the side. Angelica had found ample opportunity to learn to control her powers over the last two days, as neither the guild nor the authorities objected to me using live Unseen as test dummies.

In my hands, I held out the cutest most adorable puppy I had been able to find. He was chubby and soft, with a constant little doggy grin that caused his tongue to hang out the side of his mouth. Every teenage girl I'd walked past on my way back to the guild had released an uncontrolled, "Awww," as they saw him.

"Please don't make me do this," Angelica begged, close to tears.

I scratched the little guy behind his ears, making him bark happily.

An unrestrained, "Awww," came from Davina, before she turned to Angelica. "Don't let him win. You can do this." To show her faith, she put her hand on Angelica's armoured shoulder.

Nothing happened to her.

Angelica took a deep breath and cringed. "I've got this." She stepped forward and picked up the puppy.

Nothing happened to him.

I let her hold him for a minute and then took him back, cradling the adorable little guy in the crook of my arm.

A huge smile spread across Angelica's face. "I did it!"

Before she could begin to celebrate, I said, "Tomorrow, you hold him longer."

Her smile vanished. "I have to do this again?"

"Yes. Every morning until you can hold him all day without him dying."

Her horror was nearly amusing, but the little guy's life was on the line, so it wasn't actually funny. I was going to be a bit upset if she failed to control her armour and killed him. It seemed I had a soft spot for puppies.

I walked over to Davina and handed her the puppy. "Look after Test Subject One."

"That's a terrible name," Davina replied, cuddling him to her chest.

"Don't give him a name," Angelica whined.

"Go practice controlling your vampiric touch if you're concerned for his safety. You've got another day, before you do it again."

Angelica raced off toward the training room.

Nina looked over from where she was taking notes with Oliver. "Do you think she was at her limits?"

I shook my head. "She got the hang of controlling the hunger yesterday. She could have played with him half the morning without harming him."

"Does she know?"

I shook my head. "She would slack off if she did. She doesn't get that luxury until she's in complete control."

"Prudent."

"There you are," Gregory shouted.

I turned around, seeing the clean and well-groomed company commander walking towards me. I hadn't seen him since we flew off into the night, but I'd heard he was asking around about me. "What brings you to the guild, Gregory?"

"You do. Walk with me?" I fell in beside him and we began walking towards the entrance. "I wanted to thank you for what you did for my company. You saved a lot of good people. We owe you."

I didn't do it for him. I did for the loot and the chance at gaining an easy meal. "You're welcome."

"I've been asking around about you. Ancient vampire saving people is the kind of thing that doesn't let you sleep until you get answers."

"You seem to be well rested."

He chuckled. "Your traveling companions were forthcoming. The guild master and Sir Brandon filled in the blanks. You seem to be a good man."

"I like to think so."

"You have a no-nonsense approach to evil."

"Keeps life simple."

Holy magic engulfed me as I exited the guild's entrance onto the street. Helen, Gregory's wife, grinned at me. "Just checking."

I rolled my eyes.

A second later a dozen other holy magic spells hit me from all directions. The street was packed with mercenaries, men and women that we'd saved from being sacrificed in their sleep. I recognised every one of them, having separated them from the soul reapers. They were the people and friends Gregory had asked me to save. The former company commanders stood in front of their people, beside the clerics who had just tried to incinerate me.

"Being extra careful," Helen clarified.

As one, they all saluted.

Then in one voice they said, "I pledge my life and my soul to the hero. Let his path be my path and his fate be my fate." The clouds hanging above the city parted and holy light bathed the mercenaries.

A feeling I hadn't felt in a decade filled my chest as a bond was forged between us. It was a bond that I had no control over. A bond that had to be made freely, by those who felt the call to serve me. A bond that made me responsible for them even if I didn't want to be.

It was very annoying.

Gregory stepped in front of me glowing with holy light and dropped to his knee. "We are yours to command, Hero. From this breath until our last."

Behind him the others took a knee. Only the clerics remained on their feet. They were also the only ones not to say the oath.

"You realise I don't live in Hellmouth."

Gregory grinned. "Our business prospects have dried up of late, Hero. No one will trust mercenaries who joined soul reapers. Even if they did so unknowingly."

"You're broke and need work is all I'm hearing."

Anyone in earshot chuckled.

"I'm not hearing a no," Gregory replied.

The chuckling turned to laughter.

"A simple thank you would have been sufficient."

Everyone found this hilarious.

Gregory stood up. "I heard you're looking for geomancers. There are three dozen in our ranks, trained in building combat fortifications. Same number of combat mages. And a dozen clerics who will travel with us despite what you are. We've got fifty knights. The rest of us are warriors. We're five hundred and eighty-three in total. Not an army, but enough to guard your estate."

"I'll take the geomancers."

"We're a package deal."

"Figures."

"What the hell are you doing in front of my guild?" Riker shouted right behind me. He was in one of his, 'Why do I have to put up with a vampire?' moods.

"Building an army against my will."

He paused, running what I said through his risk assessment filter, and finding it tolerable. "Well, do it somewhere else."

"Guild rules allow guests."

"Guild rules also allow me to stop you from filling my guild with mercenaries."

"They're not in the guild."

He scowled. "Will it hurt if I stab you?"

"It will itch a little."

"Take your business somewhere else."

"Since you've finally got enough free time to badger me and my guests, look into this for me." I passed him the letter from the king.

He swore and marched off.

Gregory seemed stunned by the guild master's reaction. "What the hell did you give him? I know Riker's reputation. That man doesn't back down for anything."

"Letter from the king. It's not important." I looked past him to the people still kneeling. "You can get up now."

"Does that mean you're going to take us?" someone shouted.

"I guess so."

Gregory grinned. "Just like that?"

"No, not just like that. You did your research. You knew I needed geomancers and that my estate likely needed guards. You saw an opportunity and then made sure it was safe, talking to the right people and hitting me with enough holy magic to prove I wasn't a fake. *That's* why I said yes. You've got a good head on your shoulders, *and* you're not willing to make the same mistake twice. Common sense is not as common as people think, and it's something you should always keep around."

"I still figured you would take longer."

"You have a couple hundred more than I needed, but I can work with that. Besides, your oath doesn't give me much of a choice. I'll be compelled to take care of you if I don't actively do so."

Gregory knew that. "We're a little short on funds."

"I bet you are."

"Is that a no on an advance?"

"That's a bring me your accounts and a list of your debts. I'll work over the numbers. I'm going to need the attributes and skill levels of my people, too."

"Your people?"

"You swore yourselves to me, body and soul. You're my people, whether I like it or not."

Gregory sighed. "It will take weeks to go through it all."

"If it's not finished by lunch then you couldn't bring me everything fast enough. If you think I can fight fast, you'll realise its nothing compared to how quickly I can do paperwork. Apparently, vampire accountants are a thing."

ANGELICA WHINED the entire short walk from the training room to the class hall. "I don't see how this is fair. I had my class first, yet you're letting Davina level before me."

"Davina has mastered over half of her skills, including her cleanse death magic skill. She would be massively overqualified for her next class upgrade if she didn't have a prestige class. Letting her level has no draw-backs."

"But I was first."

"Master your skills; then we can talk."

Davina giggled and patted Angelica's armoured shoulder. "Can't you just be happy for me?"

Angelica pouted for a second and then nodded. "I'm being a bad friend, aren't I?"

"I would have said, 'Spoiled brat,' but that's true, too."

She tried to kick my ankle.

She missed.

We turned a corner and entered the class hall.

Davina happily skipped over to the stone and placed her hand on top. She grinned. "I received bonus skills."

"What level are you?"

"Level 37."

"Got the class upgrades?"

"Yep."

"Good. Tell me in order what skills you got."

"I got necrotic magic at level 5. The level 10 upgrade gave me life magic, barrier magic, general resistance, and the war staff skill as a bonus. Level 15 gave me death strike and life strike as a bonus. The level 20 upgrade gave me healing magic, protection magic, cleansing magic, and disease resistance as a bonus. Level 25 gave me necrotic strike. Level 30 gave me life enchantment, magical resistance, damage resistance, and summon life construct as a bonus. Level 35 gave me mana manipulation, and holy strike as a bonus."

"How did you get so many advanced skills on top of all those bonus skills?" Angelica whined.

"Class upgrades count as a reset point for skills," I said. "The skills she got, before and during the class upgrade, can receive upgraded versions. She had three class upgrades, so she got to specialized skills quicker than most."

"What do you want me to invest my skill upgrades in?" Davina asked.

"Magic skill, unless you had something specific in mind."

"Why not prodigy?"

"Prodigy is more useful to those of us who aren't actually prodigies. You mastered most of your skills by performing a single highly complex and difficult spell while giving yourself all sorts of limitations. You perform so far beyond your skill cap that it seems pointless. By comparison, raising the tier of your magic skill will boost everything you can do."

"Most of these skills are related to life magic. I've never studied life magic. I might not be as suited to life magic as I am to necromancy."

"And if that turns out to be true, you can invest your later skill upgrades into prodigy. Until you master your new skills, it's not like prodigy is going to make a serious difference."

"That's true. Magic it is." She made the changes and pulled her hand away. "Are you going to see if you leveled?"

"Might as well."

Congratulations, you have leveled your hero class.
Your class has leveled.
Your class has leveled.
Your class has leveled.
Your class has leveled.
You are now a level 11 hero.

Your class has leveled and unlocked new skills:
Kilij
Create Undead Skeleton

Enchant Undead
Enhance Undead Creations

You have reached level 10. You can upgrade one of your existing class skills.

You have 120 attribute points to spend.

"What the hell," I said as I upgraded my prodigy skill.

You have upgraded your Prodigy skill to tier two.
This skill can be upgraded one more time.

"Did you level?"

"Four times. This makes no sense."

"I have a theory," Davina offered.

"I'm willing to listen to anything at this point."

"You don't gain the same benefit from fighting evil and monsters that others do."

"Why?"

"You're evil and a monster. You're fighting your own side."

I paused, thinking it over. "That makes a painful amount of sense. And if you're right, I leveled four times because of all the non-Unseen soul reapers I brutalized, instead of killed."

She nodded.

"Well, that's annoying."

"You're still a hero. You should be able to level by doing non-evil fighting deeds."

"That's even more annoying."

"What skills did you get?"

I told her.

She groaned. "I want to create undead skeletons."

"Why?"

"No one respects a necromancer who doesn't have an undead horde."

"It's a status symbol to you?"

She shook her head. "It's proof you're an uber-powerful necromancer. Without it you have to cause complete carnage for people to believe you. And I don't like causing carnage."

"You can still create undead without the skills."

"It's a full-time job managing them that way."

"Go ask Riker if you can cleanse the city of death magic, if you're looking for street cred."

She grinned. "Do I have to tell him how I'll do it?"

"He probably knows by now."

Her face fell.

"You did it half a dozen times on our way here. He'll take the risk."

"You think?"

"They're on a Hellmouth. Cleansing the city of death magic is something they will want."

Davina skipped out of the room.

The moment she was gone, Angelica continued complaining. "This is so unfair. You're letting her perform dark rituals in cities and I can't even level."

"You've got a puppy to save. You're too busy to level."

22

ORGANISING THE TROOPS

Blocking a river wasn't something the guild typically did, so it took almost a week to pull enough people together. Riker had to act in secret, rather than make a public announcement, which is why it took so long. If he could have done it faster, he would have. He was happy to see me leave his province.

The king going to the guild instead of the governor suggested he didn't trust his administration. The guild didn't involve itself in politics, only in fighting evil, so the king requesting their involvement also suggested something was seriously wrong, as it implied that there was evil in the king's administration.

"Who's the geomancer you have talking to my people?" Gregory asked.

Gregory and the other company commanders had taken to traveling in my wagon. They wanted to get a feel for working with me so they could react appropriately. The last thing you needed in a chain of command was a leader whom people didn't understand was joking or understating.

Their people were riding their horses behind the convoy. I'd decided to bring them along with me for two reasons. I wanted their mages to learn how to block rivers for me, and I wasn't going to pay them to sit around doing nothing.

"Augustus will be the one who will direct the building spell for the academy."

"Bit young, isn't he?"

"He's the best I could find."

"He's perfect then."

The commanders all chuckled. They were used to relying on what they could get, rather than what they wanted. Sometimes the reason was lack of money; other times, the right people weren't available.

"Any thoughts on how you want to structure us?" Gregory asked.

I reached into my storage pouch and passed him the plans I'd drawn up.

"This says I'm in command."

"I asked around. The other commanders all voted for you."

Gregory grinned at the dozen individuals sitting around us. "Thanks for your support."

"We voted for the person we thought the boss was least likely to eat if they had to deliver bad news," Taylor said, with a roguish smirk.

Her company had been one of the smallest before they were bought out. Only those who had been with her when I reached their camp survived. The people the guild and governor sent didn't have my skills for seeing evil, and the fighting had been bloody in other places.

Gregory chuckled. "Thanks for your confidence, then."

Gregory and the other commanders had only brought the people they trusted to the guild when they made their oaths. Most who fit that description weren't willing to commit themselves to serving a vampire -- even a vampire hero. So, what had begun as a thousand became five hundred. It was far more than I expected to join from such a small number.

Gregory's people were the best of those that had come, with an average level in the mid-twenties. He spent more on training and equipment. This was why he ended up broke so quickly. It made him a good choice for a commander, and the others knew it. They would rather serve under a man who would empty his own pockets to keep them alive, than one who wouldn't.

"The chain of command will be simple," I said. "Gregory will oversee everyone. Five commanders will oversee a hundred troops each. Each commander will have two lieutenants in charge of fifty. Units will be broken up into ten-person groups, with a sergeant in charge."

"We've got more than five hundred," Gregory pointed out.

"Scouts and other specialised units will fall outside of this command structure."

Gregory nodded. "It's simple. Makes sense. I like it. You been in the military?"

"My brother was. He talked about nothing else from the time he was twelve until the day he died."

"Sorry to hear that."

"He knew the risks. I respect his choice."

Everyone here had lost friends and family to their trade. They knew what it was like. They didn't dwell on it for more than a few seconds.

Gregory continued reading and frowned. "You made a mistake in the training budget. There's an extra zero."

"That's not a mistake. I don't need warriors. I need knights. That's your budget to make it happen."

Gregory began to grin. "We could afford to hire a dozen master knights with this budget."

"Don't look for a swordsmanship master, nor an armour master; I've got those covered."

"That's most of my men. We won't spend half of this budget."

"You will. You're going to be drinking recovery potions like wine. If my name doesn't become a curse on your lips within a week, I'll consider you all masochists."

"Want to bet?" Gregory said, far too confidently.

"What's your swordsmanship level?"

"Ten."

"If you put in everything you have, I'll have you at seventeen by the time we reach the capital."

"Bullshit," Taylor said.

"Language."

She snorted. "There is no way you can have his level that high in two weeks. Not while traveling."

"I'll bet you all ten gold per sparring session that I can. No limits on what you want to bet."

"In that case, I bet a million gold."

I held out my hand. "It's a bet."

She looked at my hand. "You can't be that sure of yourself."

"Chicken."

She looked around her and realised the other commanders were all smirking.

"*Bock. Bock. Booock*," I clucked, egging her on.

That did it. She grabbed my hand and shook. "You better be good for it."

"Fair point. The limit is ten million total."

"I'll bet a million," Gregory shouted, over the other commanders.

"You can't bet on your own failure. But I'll give you a thousand gold if you succeed."

Gregory grinned. "That works for me."

"I'll bet a million."

"Deal."

"I'll bet a million too."

"Deal."

"Put me down for a million."

"Deal."

One by one they all bet a million gold, until only one was left. She was the oldest commander, a woman named Erin. She had a thick set of scars down the right side of her head that looked like claw marks. "I'll bet ten gold he succeeds," she said calmly. "Any takers."

"You really think he can do it?" Taylor said.

"He's too sure of himself."

Taylor scoffed. "I'll take your gold."

They shook.

"When does the training start?" Gregory asked.

"We'll have your first sparring session when we stop for lunch."

A few hours later during the lunch break, Gregory collapsed, gasping for breath and holding his side, leaving his sword on the ground. Helen hit her husband with another healing spell as the mercenary crowd roared their approval, cheering his valiant attempt to fight me. He hadn't held back and had been fighting too fast for most of them to follow. From their perspective it had been a close match. One where their commander only lost because I had limitless endurance.

The other commanders sat dumbfounded, able to follow what had happened. They had witnessed not only our skill difference, but our attribute difference, too.

"How did you do?" I asked.

"I leveled," he gasped.

"You leveled from *one session*," Taylor said in disbelief.

"*Twice*," he finished.

The commanders stared at each other in horror.

"We're going to have to spar like that," Taylor said in disbelief.

"A hundred thousand times," Erin replied cheerfully. "You can hand over the gold now, if you like."

INSTRUCTING the commanders on swordsmanship gave me something productive to do while we travelled. Gregory sorted out who oversaw what by the end of the day, so the following morning, all seventeen officers filled the back of my wagon and spent the next two weeks listening to my lectures on swordplay.

When we stopped for lunch, Gregory and I would spar until he collapsed. Then I'd pick on someone else until he recovered enough to go again. We did the same in the evenings, so by the time we rolled into the capital, anyone who had the swordsmanship skill had reached level seventeen. Gregory was eighteen. With my prodigy skill at the second tier and limitless stamina, training people to seventeen was straightforward, but their progress still surprised me.

Something was going on with Gregory and his men, something I didn't understand.

As our caravan unloaded everyone outside the palace gates, Gregory got his people into formation. I hadn't organised anywhere for everyone to stay, so I'd elected to bring them with me. They all wore clean clothes and had polished their armour and equipment. They glanced nervously at the palace walls as they got their mounts into position.

Angelica sat atop her dracolich and would have looked positively intimidating if she wasn't carrying a puppy. Instead, she looked like she was going through a phase.

Davina stood beside me, dressed in her mother's robe and carrying her father's staff. The robe was too big for her, making her look like a kid in her mother's clothes. "Quite the imposing entourage," she said with a giggle.

"It sends the right sort of message."

"And what message would that be?"

"Stabbing me in the back won't be as simple as killing me."

"You sure this won't be considered an invasion?"

"Countess Angelica Lich Bane is allowed to travel to the capital with an escort of up to two thousand, with an average level of sixty. These men and women are under her employment."

"Does she know that?"

"She didn't read the papers I told her to sign."

Davina giggled. "You have an odd habit of holding to the letter of the law while crushing the spirit of it."

"Thank you."

"We're ready, sir," Gregory said.

"We'll give them more time to react."

The palace guards were in the process of full mobilisation. There were already a thousand on the wall above the gate, but more were coming every second.

Last night, we'd camped outside the city gate while we waited to be inspected.

The capital was built on a massive plateau, which had been transformed by tens of thousands of geomancers over generations, raising its height, and making it nearly impregnable by land. The wall surrounding the city was less of a wall and more of a cliff face. There were monsters that would have no trouble climbing a vertical cliff, so there was a wall with towers at the very top, with layers of offensive and defensive spells to welcome anything that reached that point.

Once we were inspected through the city gate shortly after dawn, we spent the first half of the day travelling to the city centre at full speed. A hundred million people lived in the capital. Fed by druids who could grow crops overnight and supplied with everything else by the enormous kingdom they controlled. So, it was no surprise that the palace was twice the size of Manhattan.

A functional city within a city.

Despite the mobilisation going on above us, they never closed the gate. Wagons appeared at the checkpoint. Their contents were inspected, and then they were waved through.

Eventually, an official came to talk.

He was a fat, middle-aged man wearing silk slippers and a sorcerer robe. His two assistants walked behind him, both young and attractive women who glanced at the dracolich nervously, though the nervousness didn't enter their scent.

He stopped before me, because I was at the head of our group. "I am Rupert Metrin, Keeper of the Eastern Gate, and servant of our most illustrious King Linus Ironheart. How may I be of assistance?"

I passed him the summons.

He read it through twice. His expression didn't change, which warned me he wasn't as soft as he appeared. The summons stated that I was an ancient vampire and that all precautions had to be taken upon my arrival. The fact he didn't so much as blink when he read that meant he was tougher than anyone I had come across so far.

He met my gaze when he finished reading. "You wish me to allow your entourage entry?"

"I would like to keep my familiars with me." I pointed to Davina and Angelica.

"And the soldiers?"

"Let me introduce you to my familiar, Countess Angelica Lich Bane. They're her guards."

He gave a dry chuckle that didn't reach his eyes. "Most amusing. I'll allow them through." He turned to his assistant on his right. "Please go and tell the third, fifth, and eighth legions to mobilize to escort the king's guests." He turned to the one on his left and handed her a seal. "Please inform the king's chamberlain that the king's guest has arrived from Hellmouth."

Both women turned and broke into a run, blurring with their speed. I put their levels somewhere around eighty, making them former members of the dungeon legions.

"I'll walk you in," Rupert declared.

I fell in beside him.

Gregory called for everyone to march, and they began to follow.

Rupert turned to Angelica as we walked. "Please keep your dracolich grounded inside the palace walls. The defensive enchantments will automatically kill you if you leave the ground."

Angelica nodded.

Rupert turned to me. "I don't mean to accuse you of anything, but what is the creature she's holding?"

"A puppy."

"I had to check. I once saw a mimic that had learned to pass itself off as a little old lady."

"How did you manage to find it?"

"With a great deal of difficulty. It moved around a lot. We had to follow a trail of disappearances and ask a lot of questions. Eventually, enough people mentioned seeing a little old woman with a hooked cane and a grey shawl that we started taking it seriously."

"How many people did it get?"

"Thousands. We're not sure exactly how many. We know it operated in the city for decades, moving from one side to the other. Never acting out. Never drawing attention to itself. We had to pore through records, but there is evidence that it might have been here for over a century."

We began walking through the gate tunnel. "I notice you haven't asked me any questions."

"It's not my place to ask the king's guests questions, only make sure everything is secure."

"In that case, would you be willing to play guide? My familiar is bursting with questions."

"I have no objections."

Davina rushed forward and grabbed his arm. "What's that?"

Rupert began explaining, quickly realising I wasn't understating her interest. He seemed to be a history buff because he knew a story about every building we passed, happily sharing everything he knew with Davina.

No carriages arrived to transport me, but the street was cleared of traffic as soldiers marched in as escort. Three thousand highly trained killers from the dungeon legions with levels that were also around sixty walked in time with us. The commanders of the legions were the real threat, though. They were called Old Monsters and they were there for me, and for my familiars. They were warriors who had survived hundreds of battles gaining levels beyond a hundred. I got the strong impression that I wouldn't win a fight, not without having to drain the life from them, which would cost me my soul.

I still had 120 attributes to spend, and I toyed with the idea of putting them into agility, so I could keep up with them. I decided against it, only because I wasn't sure it would be enough.

As my gaze left them, it fell on the splendour surrounding me.

I'd visited the Forbidden City once, while doing humanitarian work in rural China. The palace reminded me of it. Only on a much larger scale. The buildings were all fifteen storeys tall, with arched bridges spanning the gaps. You could go from one side of the palace to the other without ever having to visit the ground, which I realised was the point. The ground was for outsiders. The world above was for the elites. The rulers of this kingdom. Servants walked on the ground while they watched from above.

Davina's curiosity supplied me with a constant stream of information. I had read anything I could find on the capital and palace. So, I knew the buildings we passed, but the details Rupert shared were not the sort of details you would find in books. They were the kind of details only locals knew.

It was the middle of the afternoon before we reached the inner palace. The walk had been brisk, but that didn't matter when you had so far to travel.

An envoy waited for us at the gate. Behind them, the inner palace guards lined the courtyard. They made the elites of the outer palace look like chumps. Every one of them had reached level eighty.

An elderly man in a silk robe came forward, leaned over his cane, and smiled. "I'm Godfrey, the king's chamberlain. Your familiars are welcome to join you for your audience. My assistant will show your familiar's guards the palace where you will be staying, so they may check its security before you arrive."

I nodded.

Godfrey turned to Rupert. "Forget everything you learned."

Rupert nodded, turned, and began walking back to the gate.

Godfrey glanced at Angelica's dracolich. "Is the creature tame?"

I nodded. "It's not a natural dracolich."

"Then she will have no objections or safety concerns sending it with her guards."

Angelica leapt off the dracolich's back, startling the puppy awake, who howled in protest. She turned to her mount. "Go with Gregory, and do what he says. *No flying.*" The dracolich turned, looked at Gregory, and somehow expressed disappointment, before looking back at Angelica doing its best to mimic the puppy's behaviour.

"I think it's waking up," Davina said.

I frowned. "That's supposed to be rare."

"It could be her set. Undead wake up faster around powerful sources of death magic."

"Is there a problem?" Godfrey asked.

"No," I said. "Angelica, be firmer with it and give it clear instructions not to harm anyone unless Gregory says so."

Angelica did as I said, and the dracolich turned and walked to the commander, dragging each foot to express its dissatisfaction. If it had lips, it would have been pouting. Godfrey's assistant walked over to Gregory, and the two started talking.

Godfrey waved us forward, and we followed him into the inner palace. Guards shadowed our every step as we passed through three separate courtyards and halls, before arriving at the largest and grandest. Godfrey explained the significance of each hall as we entered, and how they were used to host different guests. The halls were mostly ceremonial, but they did hold certain significance.

War, for example, could only be declared in the third hall. Law changes for the lowborn were declared in the first hall, and law changes for nobility were declared in the second. The fourth hall was unique in that the king's authority was absolute within. It was the only place where he could order anything to be done, whether legal or illegal.

The guards stopped at the entrance, and the doors closed behind us. The hall was a hundred metres long, capable of hosting thousands. It was empty of all but the king and his personal guard.

Godfrey led us down the long carpet, stopping at the foot of the dais.

The king was in his fifties, with deep, tanned skin and grey streaks through otherwise-flawless brown hair. He was a handsome man, devoid of the physique you would see in a warrior, but his body radiated power. His family had bred the most powerful sorcerers for generations, and his skill and power were unrivalled in the kingdom, for his age. That was an important distinction. He wasn't the most powerful sorcerer in the kingdom, just the most powerful *for his age*.

"I'll keep this short," King Linus said, his voice holding none of the power his body did. "I think the Pope is an Unseen. You will evaluate him for me and kill him if my suspicion is true."

23

THE NECROSAINT

Your average cleric doesn't know they're looking at a vampire unless they're trained to notice. Pale skin is pale skin, after all. And if the vampire can walk comfortably in sunlight, then the normal assumption is Irish, or whatever this world's equivalent was. Indifference was the reaction I'd become accustomed to because of this fact. However, indifference was not the reaction I received when I walked through the door of the church's head cathedral beside the King.

Outside my control, my fingernails transformed into claws and my fangs descended. My pale skin took on a corpse quality that was dry and scaly as my cheeks hollowed. Then holy magic rained down on me in a concentrated beam that didn't stop.

"You failed to mention this part," I said, calmly standing within the holy light.

"I told you the cathedral was the most well protected building against creatures of evil in my kingdom."

"I thought you meant it was full of clerics."

The clerics chose that moment to start hurling spells at me. Paladins drew swords and blurred forward, only to be knocked down by the King's guard.

Davina stood beside me, gazing around, ignoring the violence. "It's so pretty. I love it here. Can I go exploring?"

The architecture celebrated the beauty of life and all things good. The paintings, tapestries, and statues complemented this by displaying the best in humanity. It all meant nothing to me.

A paladin was knocked unconscious, landing near my feet, and spraying blood across my leather pants. The smell made me salivate. "You going to tell them to stop?"

The king shook his head. "I have no authority here. I'm waiting for an archbishop to appear, so I can explain the situation."

Another paladin managed to sidestep the king's guards fast enough to throw a knife. I caught it before it went through my eye. It exploded. Shrapnel bounced off of Davina, Angelica, and the king's barriers, leaving them unharmed, as my hand pulled itself back together.

The king suddenly grinned, spotting someone he could speak with. "Archbishop Jannette, how wonderful to see you."

Archbishop Jannette wore a thick, ornate robe and carried a gold sceptre. She was in her late sixties, with grey hair tied in a bun and soft, wrinkled skin. A dozen clerics flanked her as she raised her voice and began chanting in a commanding tone. The clerics joined in weaving their magic with hers to make a truly powerful holy spell. They no doubt knew other magic, but holy magic was a cleric's main weapon against evil. They rarely used anything else.

Apparently, Archbishop Jannette didn't know this fact about clerics. A hair-thin beam of holy and light magic split me in two, cutting me head to tail. My two halves pulled themselves back together immediately, but it was still enough to make me say, "Ouch."

Seeing how ineffective her spell was, the archbishop decided to turn to the king. "What is the meaning of bringing the abomination within these hallowed halls, Your Highness?"

The fighting continued, and the clerics didn't stop throwing spells at me.

"The abomination, as you so eloquently mentioned, is my guest. He and his familiars killed the lich, Contessa, in the Hellmouth province, ridding this world of an old evil. As he has not taken innocent life and his soul remains, I promised him that the pope would attempt to cleanse him of his curse."

Jannette paused and then scowled. "That is within your rights as this land's sovereign. Stay your hand, people." The clerics and paladins immediately stopped. The holy light radiating down on me from above, did not. "We should move quickly. The cathedral defences will weaken the longer the creature remains. Mika, go with my voice, and summon the archbishops and holy paladins to defend the pope."

"Is that really necessary?" King Linus asked.

Jannette nodded. "Evil will go to great lengths to gain influence within these walls. Sacrificing a knight to take a general is something we have come to expect."

Jannette turned and led us through the cathedral. It was a massive building that housed and educated the kingdom's entire next generation of clerics and paladins, so we didn't reach the pope for fifteen minutes. A congregation of thirty archbishops and holy paladins all armed for holy war waited outside the pope's secondary throne room, in a dazzling array of costumes and armour.

As we approached, a trio broke away from their group and started walking towards us: an elderly pair of archbishops, one male, one female, and the youngest of the holy knights, a handsome, blond boy no older than Davina and Angelica. They all shared the same glowing white eyes and were staring at Davina.

They bypassed the king as if in a daze, stepping around me and the holy light that was still trying to kill me, to fall to their knees at Davina's feet. As one, they picked up the hem of her mother's robe and pressed it against their lips.

Power burned through their lips, flowing into her robe like a tsunami, crashing over it and changing it with its passage. The fabric transformed, bleaching a holy white, taking on a hallowed property.

The robes' silver arcane sigils and runes transformed, reconfiguring into a new pattern, becoming a deep, abyssal black that drank in light. Her staff transformed next, causing the bone to take on the same deep black of the runes on her robe. The runes and arcane sigils on the staff took on the holy white colour, making a stark contrast between robe and staff.

Power thrummed through her items, raising Davina's threat level substantially. They were *saintly* items, *holy* items, *consecrated* items. Blessed with abundance.

"I renounce all vows and devote myself to the service of *the necrosaint* from this breath until my last," they said as one, with tears in their eyes.

Davina's smile would have made the dead sit up and pay attention. She reached down and touched the elderly man and woman on the forehead. "I name you Father. I name you Mother. For you will raise me and teach me from this day until your last as my mother and father should have."

Davina's touch restored their youth, shaving seventy years off their age and causing her skin to wither and take on a mummified quality.

Next, she touched the young boy's forehead. "I name you Friend. For you will walk with me and guard me all my days as only a friend can." The change this time was subtle, so subtle I couldn't sense what it was, but there was a difference. He went from being someone who *might* concern me to someone who *did*.

Archbishop Jannette stared in awe. *"A saint."* She dropped into a bow. The rest of the congregation followed.

"*Half* a saint," Davina clarified. "And you don't have to bow."

Jannette didn't raise her head. "Why do you travel with the abomination?"

"Because I was his familiar before I became a saint."

"Say the word and we will gladly die to free you from his will."

"He already offered."

"Wait!" Angelica shouted indignantly. "You offered her a way out. Why didn't I get this offer?"

"You can't be trusted to make decent decisions. You're also not a saint."

"Half a saint," Davina corrected.

Jannette remained bowing. "Can I ask why you didn't accept your freedom?"

"*Heaven* had no issue with me being his familiar, so *neither* do *I*."

There were several sharp breaths at this statement.

"You are young, perhaps," Jannette started.

"I'm 384 next month."

"Excuse me?"

"Death holds no power over me. You look at me now and see a talking corpse. But that is only because I have taken Father and Mother's death upon myself to cleanse it. By the end of the day, I will be myself, because death holds no power over me."

"You can heal ageing."

"I can cleanse death. They are not the same. Now raise your heads and continue. The cathedral's defences are weakening."

Jannette nodded and straightened back up. The congregation followed. Most ignored the holy light enveloping me, choosing to stare at Davina like she was the second coming. I took note of those that didn't. It seemed suspicious.

Davina's Mother, Father, and Friend moved to stand behind her, having changed sides the moment they saw her. After seeing the holy transformation from their devotion to her, I wasn't surprised. They had blessed her, sacrificing all their power for Heaven to intervene on their behalf in a way they could not. Heaven had intervened and then chosen to return their powers, reaffirming their actions were Heaven's desire, and cementing their path in the only way that mattered to them.

The archbishops opened the door at the end of the hallway and entered.

An elderly man with a kind smile and smoking black eyes waited, sitting on a small throne. The archbishops formed a line based on rank before him and bent their knee and kissed his ring. The king took his place behind the holy paladins and waved me back, motioning for Davina to stand behind him, followed by the archbishops and the holy knight who had sworn themselves to her, leaving me at the back of the line followed by Angelica.

When Davina reached the pope, he didn't let her take his hand and kiss his ring. Instead, he apologised for *not* being able to renounce his vows and serve her, which pleased the archbishop and holy paladins.

When it came to my turn, he welcomed me with a loving smile. "Your courage to hold to the path of the righteous is valiant, Vincent. Do you come seeking redemption?" He held out his hand.

I took his wrinkled fingers between mine as I met his smoky gaze and bowed. "Always." He crumbled to dust as his life force rushed through me.

I wish I could say popes were a better meal than your average Unseen. I mean, it seemed like they should be. But sadly, he was nowhere near as good as the kid I ate.

I had a fraction of a second to savour my meal and then I was fighting for my life, blocking holy swords, holy hammers, holy axes, and one holy scythe, if you will believe it. The holy paladins were out for blood, and the archbishops were throwing all the magic they could.

A small flick of her hand was all Davina had to do to calm her people. Then she walked from archbishop to archbishop and quietly explained that I kept my soul and my immunity to holy magic by only eating Unseen. She pointed out the holy symbol hanging around my neck, as I fought, to illustrate her point.

Angelica couldn't keep up with one holy paladin, let alone the two she was fighting. She only survived the first few seconds because her equipment outclassed theirs by a lot. The following seconds were because Davina sent her holy paladin to protect her.

The boy had to be the genius of a generation, because he fought the much older fighters to a standstill, trading blows so he didn't cripple them.

The rest of the holy paladins surrounded the king and his guards but made no other move against them. Their pope was dead. The last thing they wanted to do was start a war between the church and the state, throwing the nation into turmoil and allowing evil to flourish. If they were going to kill him, it would be planned and swift, and then they would move to seize the throne before his body cooled, the way it had been done in other kingdoms.

My fight didn't go nearly so well as the boy's. I'd like to say I fought them to a standstill for ten minutes and only then succumbed to overwhelming power. But the truth is, the archbishops' spells created all sorts of openings, which the holy knights took advantage of, pinning me to the wall in less than thirty seconds. One guy did lose a pinkie finger though, so it's not like I didn't give as good as I got.

Just because they had me pinned, it didn't mean they stopped hitting me. Magic bombarded my body, tearing me apart, only to regenerate, and be torn apart again.

I screamed through most of it, catching brief flashes of Davina talking to archbishops. One by one, they stopped throwing spells, before walking to a holy paladin and explaining what they had learned. The tension slowly eased out of the room. Then, the grief and horror took hold.

The paladins pinning me down didn't remove their weapons, despite learning why I had eaten the pope, which I would have respected if their weapons weren't enchanted with all sorts of magic that hurt like crazy.

A set of enchanted chains was brought in, and I was bound. Only then did they remove their weapons, shoving me away like I was filth.

"I hope you understand that I did what I had to do," King Linus said to the congregation. "You were being led by an Unseen. I could no more make that accusation than you could make the same against me. Clean your house, so I don't have to."

I snorted. "That's rich, coming from you."

His gaze swept to me. "Explain your meaning."

"I counted at least two dozen Unseen on my way to your inner palace and three once I got there."

He frowned. "They're inside the palace."

I nodded.

He scowled. "What a fucking mess."

"Language."

The King stared dumbfounded over being corrected. One of the archbishops had to cover his mouth to stop from laughing. Finally, he remembered how to speak. "Will you return him to my care?"

"He has to be executed," Jannette replied. "He killed the pope."

"I killed an Unseen."

She frowned. "True." She looked around the room. "I'm open to suggestions."

"Trial of purity," I offered. It would be a truly abysmal experience, but it would clear my name in all ways that counted with the church.

Several people hissed.

"That is a barbaric, heinous practice of the past," Jannette hissed. "It comes from a time when evil walked these halls."

"Evil does walk your halls. And it's the only way you can be sure. If it makes you feel better, I'd also like to know for myself if I can pass."

"Very few come out with their minds intact."

"Demons don't suffer from torture. We just go on living. Trust me, I know."

Jannette paused.

"He can see good and evil," Mother said. "Whether we go through with this, we should ask for his endorsement for succession."

"We cannot trust the words of a vampire for succession," one archbishop shouted. He was a thin, elderly man who had been one of the last to stop hurling magic at me.

"You would say that." My words caused several hands to drop to their weapons as the paladins eyed the archbishop. "He's not Unseen. No one in here is. He's just not good enough for me to notice. Only nine of you have the glow of a good soul, and three of those follow Davina."

Jannette sighed. "Point them out please."

"You can't allow this," said the same archbishop.

"The truth will come out in the trial of purity," she replied. "Go ahead."

I lifted my manacled hands. "You, you, you, you, you and you."

The king's guard pointed at his chest. "Me?"

"Yes you."

"But I'm not a cleric."

"Most good people aren't." He stared at me blankly. "There's a story in a holy book where I come from. The son of god points to an old woman who's giving a few tiny coins to the church and tells his disciples that she is giving more than the rich man beside her. Because she has so little to give it counts for more. You might not have holy powers to do good on the scale they can, but you give more of what you do have. Heaven sees and says you're better than these men and women who wave their hand and heal the sick."

"We can't trust this creature."

"If it makes you feel even worse, Mr. I Don't Trust The Guy Who Eats Unseen, every cleric who has renounced their power in favour of performing small holy spells on people entering and leaving a city to weed out Unseen has the glow of a good person. They chose *service* over glory, like you're *supposed* to."

Every member of the church inhaled at once.

Mother gave a weak smile. "That's not meant to be public knowledge."

"Anyone with the evil eye can see."

"You misunderstand. They are the best of us. We do not want to see them corrupted by those who feign devotion."

"That seems like a mistake. They can't hold high positions in the church, because they can't fight evil."

"We go to them when we need guidance," Jannette explained. "They keep us on the path."

They were the church's conscience. "Angelica, you're forbidden from sharing that secret."

"How long will this trial of purity take?" the king asked.

"It will take as long as it takes," Jannette replied.

I turned to Davina. "Make sure Gregory uses this time to train my people. And make sure Angelica doesn't slack off. You're in charge. Angelica, you have to do what Davina says."

The holy paladins picked me up and carried me off to be tortured to the point of insanity to the sound of Angelica complaining about how she was supposed to be the senior familiar, because she was a familiar first.

24

SEVEN MONTHS

I was slamming my head against a stone wall to fight the insane thirst raging through me when the trial ended. The acolytes, who had volunteered to be the living temptation, filed out of the sunlit prison cell, and the holy paladins dragged in a terrified Unseen. She was dust before they got two steps through the door.

"More," I croaked.

"Follow us, then."

Instead of going into a rage, I took control of my hunger and did as they said. They led me to another cell packed with people of all ages, even children. The survivors watched me knock on the door a minute later.

The holy paladin looked through the barred window. "You missed a few."

"They're not Unseen."

His eyes scanned the faces, and then he nodded. "You pass."

The survivors calmly got to their feet and dusted themselves off. Then it clicked. "They're acolytes."

"Clerics with vows of poverty," the nearest woman replied, placing her hand on the shoulder of a young girl. "I have never felt so safe in the presence of a vampire as I did just now. Starved and half insane, you never looked at me as food from the moment your gaze met mine. You are only a threat to the wicked."

"Or those who get in my way."

"That was made very clear to us during your trial," the holy paladin replied as he opened the door.

Davina burst through the opening and leapt at me engulfing me in a hug. "I knew you could do it."

Everyone in the cell bowed.

"Aren't you happy to see me?" she asked. "Hug me back."

"I'm not a hugger."

"You hug your son all the time."

"That's different."

"Because you love him, but you don't love me?"

"Yes."

"Then humour me."

I patted her back twice, only so she would let go. She squeezed properly at that point, and I felt my back click.

"You spent your attributes."

"Yes."

"Good. Now let go."

"No. Your soul needs a hug."

I sighed, as something inside me eased, and I hugged her back. My hunger disappeared, and the exhaustion fled. The animalistic urges I felt, that wanted me to tear the people around me apart with my teeth, vanished. "Thanks, kid."

"Angelica killed the puppy," she mumbled into my chest.

"I'm sorry to hear that."

"Twice."

"Twice?"

"I can resurrect people and puppies, now. And break curses. And heal injuries. And smite things. I'm amazing."

"I'm glad you used your time efficiently."

"You were gone a long time."

"How long?"

"Seven months."

"No wonder I'm still starving. Do you want to get out of here?"

"When you finish crying."

"I'm not," I noticed the tears on my cheeks.

"I'm very good at healing."

"Thanks, kid."

Davina was true to her words, hugging me until the tears stopped. I had no idea why I was crying. I didn't feel upset. But my body relaxed with each tear shed.

She grinned at me as she stepped back and took my hand to keep my pain at bay, leading me from the cell. "They have a new pope. She's one of the people you endorsed. She purged the church, tracking down a bunch of Unseen clerics outside the city who were working with the old pope. She also demoted a whole lot of clerics and archbishops who were participating in financial corruption and other crimes. They're all excommunicated or fighting on the frontlines."

"That's good." I meant it. The church did a lot of good in this world, and I needed it to be strong and unified if I was going to make this world safe for my family.

As we left the dungeon, her archbishops and holy knights fell in behind us. Davina led me to a room where the other archbishops and holy knights were all waiting, only letting go of my hand at the last moment.

My hunger and exhaustion immediately returned.

The archbishops stripped me naked and bathed me with holy water, before dressing me in white. It was the final step of the trial of purity. The complete endorsement of the church.

The new pope washed my feet.

The pope was the last to finish, and when she returned to her chair, she sighed. "You did us a great service, so I thank you, though I know you didn't do it for us or Heaven, but for your family. However, despite all the good you did, you remain a vampire corrupted by a human soul. Your intentions are pure, that is without question, but your methods for achieving these pure intentions borders on the heinous. You have little regard for human life. Your philosophy of right and wrong is warped. And you hold little compassion, caring, or kindness. You are not evil. You are not good. But you are an abomination. Should you make the decision to leave with the necrosaint, we will have no choice but to excommunicate her and all who follow her."

"She made her choice."

The pope met my gaze, lips trembling. She stepped out of her chair and dropped to her knees. "Please, don't make me do this. I'm begging you. She is touched by Heaven, and it will break my heart to act against her."

Her display didn't move me. "If you had faith in her, you would have faith that she would tell you if she was compromised. This is your choice."

The pope froze and then smiled with understanding, climbing back onto her throne. She turned to Davina. "If you follow him, you will be excommunicated for the next decade. At which point, you may be reinstated."

Ten years would ensure she could speak freely outside my presence.

Davina grinned. "See you in a decade, then."

I looked around. "Where are my clothes and sword?"

"I took them to the palace so the church wouldn't try to destroy them," Davina said as she walked to the door. "Angelica put your coat on her punching bag for a while and tried to tame your sword."

I nodded to the pope and followed Davina out. "Was she successful?"

"No, but she's in complete control of her set's vampiric touch now."

"You bet she couldn't do it, didn't you."

"Of course. You told me not to let her slack on her training."

"How's she doing, skill-wise?"

"She's made a lot of progress. I found the most handsome

instructor I could. She trained from dawn to dusk for three straight months, before she caught up to the gap between them. Progress has been slower with her new teacher."

"Have you trained her in how to use magic?"

"Not in a significant way. Her equipment will outperform her magical talent for decades, so I focused on building up those skills. She's ready to become a death lord."

"How are Gregory's people progressing?"

"Outstandingly. Luke went ballistic when he discovered what happened. He threatened to work independently unless the king gave your people the very best hospitality. We've had Old Monsters training them day and night. Gregory and his people have been broken down and rebuilt from the ground up several times over. The knights are ready to become death knights, and his warriors are ready to become knights."

"Death knights. That seems too fast and mildly impossible."

"They swore themselves to the hero. Your strength and skill are their strength and skill when they act in your service. The more desperate they are, the more they can draw on your strength and skill. The Old Monsters have pushed them to the point where I've seen them heal broken bones instantly, which only let them push them harder. The palace guards have taken to calling Gregory and his men Young Monsters, because they've all mastered swordsmanship, *whether or not* they have the skill."

I frowned. "Anyone feeding?"

"No. But half developed a weak magical talent for death magic, which is why they can become death knights."

"And the other half?"

"A normal death magic talent. They've also been gaining attributes like they were teenagers. No more than twenty in any place, but no less than ten, either. The king is becoming concerned about their progress. Your bond is much stronger than the typical hero bond."

"I can't imagine that is something that he would share with you."

Davina smiled. "I have eyes and ears all over the city. There is little of significance that I do not know of."

"Do any good with that knowledge?"

"She has made a great many powerful enemies," Mother offered.

"A lot of good, then."

Mother smiled and nodded. "She doesn't like to boast; nor does she like us to boast on her behalf. But I can say, I have been very happy with my service."

Davina blushed.

"Anything else I missed?"

"Angelica's dracolich is sapient now. She named herself Delila Morgana Frostwing the 3rd and won't reply unless you use her full name. Having to deal with a clone of herself has softened Angelica's pettiest tendences."

I chuckled.

"Nina and the others wrote to ask when we were coming back. They've decided to accept your offer and have been gathering instructors and resources for the academy."

"I hope you sent them money to secure their services."

"Do I need to dignify that with an answer?"

"You did terrify an entire town into thinking they were going to die."

She blushed again. "I was overexcited and didn't understand the limitations of life with the living."

"What else happened?"

"Luke reached level 87, and his companions can't keep up with him in a fight anymore. I believe he was attempting to gain enough personal power to storm the cathedral and wrestle you from their grasp."

"He's leveled a lot faster since we were reunited. Do you think it has something to do with me?"

"Yes. He's gained some of the experience you didn't, I believe."

"Is that possible?"

"He's your son. That's a powerful magical connection. You also ate a little bit of his life force, which would theoretically strengthen the bond."

"You ate your son's life force," Father said horrified.

"We were arm wrestling for loot, and he cheated first."

"You think that justifies your actions?"

"He chose to continue."

"He chose loot over life," Mother said, appalled.

"I'm proud of him. A man like that will go through any dragon to get to its hoard."

"That's a bizarre justification, but strangely makes perfect sense for what would make a good hero," Father said.

"We can't all have self-sacrificing motives in the face of fear."

Mother and Father nodded, which surprised me.

"Anything else happen?"

"Not really. The rumours about your son's harem grew worse after his recent attempt to quell them. People are now saying, 'Like father, like son'. Though they look on him more favourably because there isn't such an age difference."

"You made that up."

Davina giggled. "Just seeing if you were paying attention. Your son told me to tell you that, 'You have too many anime protagonist tendencies,' whatever that means."

"It means he thinks he's funny."

We reached the front entrance to the cathedral and walked out into the sun. More than a thousand clerics and paladins stood in formation with twice as many acolytes behind them. As one, they bowed.

Davina stepped forward and enhanced her voice with magic. "The pope has chosen to excommunicate me for following my master. I cannot return for a decade."

"I renounced all vows in service to the necrosaint," they replied as one. "Where she goes, I follow."

"Your army is bigger than Angelica's," I said.

"She's very upset by that. You'll only upset her if you mention it."

"Why doesn't that surprise me?"

I NEVER GOT a chance to see the palace where I was meant to stay. It was nice. What you would typically think of when you thought of a palace, not the monstrous thing the king called a palace. Think Dutch palace in the 1800s and you will get a good picture. It was a gigantic building with hundreds of rooms capable of housing thousands. Beyond a curious look to assess its defences as the carriage rolled up, it didn't interest me.

Gregory had his men in formation in the front courtyard when I arrived. They had changed out their weapons while I was gone, so everyone had a kilij on their hip, even the mages. They saluted as I stepped out of the carriage, before Davina and her entourage followed.

"We welcome the hero," Gregory roared. "And hope he does not find us wanting."

Every voice joined his cry, adding to the volume, and causing the windows to rattle.

My eye dropped to Gregory's hands. "I notice you're holding a spare kilij."

Gregory tossed it to me. "Thought you might want to see our progress for yourself, sir."

I caught it by the grip and flicked the sheath aside. "We'll see."

Gregory cleared his kilij fast enough to knock my incoming blade up and over his head, causing it to miss rather than pass through his skull. It was a very risky move that required a lot of skill, because a mistake cost you your life. His commanders drew their kilijes and charged me.

Behind me the archbishops started casting buffing spells on Gregory's men, and then things got interesting. They fought me six at once, and when one took an injury or was about to collapse, they traded off. The fighting was vicious and violent, and Gregory's people didn't pull their blows, nor act with any concern for my safety. Working together, they got inside my defences, overwhelming my agility with skill and numbers.

Cuts appeared along my clothing.

I still had time to shout corrections, chastising anyone who failed to deliver a strike they should have made. They weren't the sorts of mistakes a swordsmanship master would make. They were beyond that level now, but they still had room for improvement. That didn't mean I wasn't impressed. Any six of them were a match for me in pure skill, overcoming the attribute difference, including the mages -- which was unheard of.

By the time I reached the last in line, I'd been fighting for hours, and my borrowed clothes had long since fallen away in shreds. Gregory's men were not above stabbing a man in the crotch, which I considered a mark in their favour. Neither were they above using dirty tactics; everything was open to use, as it should be in a fight.

As I stepped away from the last exchange I smiled.

You have mastered your Kilij skill.

They had pushed me hard, so hard that I'd learned from the experience.

Gregory walked over as my opponent collapsed, gasping for breath. "Do you find us wanting?"

My men watched in anticipation.

"There is room for improvement, but none of my people are found wanting. If any ask who serves me, I will reply, 'Only the best.'"

They roared their approval, shouting and jumping on one another in their enthusiasm. They had seen me fight their commander all the way here and seen how much he improved. To be recognised for the same improvement was all they'd wanted.

Recognising their improvement cost me nothing and earned me their loyalty, which is why I had been less scathing than I could have been.

Gregory grinned. "Good. Now do you mind putting pants on."

"I'm comfortable."

Gregory chuckled. "It's up to you, but your next fight's not going to be the sort that you want to do naked."

At the edge of the crowd, the dracolich crashed into the ground and roared at me. Angelica sat on its back, wearing her dull blood red equipment, humming with magic.

Davina ran over and tossed me my equipment.

I leapt, catching it in the air, landing a moment later fully clothed, with Slaughter on my hip. I started walking towards Angelica. Everyone scattered, running as fast as they could, until there were at least fifty meters between them and us.

The dracolich had grown a few feet taller since I'd seen it last, and it roared at me again as I approached. "I am The Dracolich Delila Morgana Frostwing the 3rd, vampire-"

I glared into the dracolich's empty eye sockets and released my hunger.

"-and you may call me anything you like, good sir. I hope this fun and friendly sparring match does not get too out of hand."

"You're supposed to be fierce and intimidating," Angelica hissed.

"Fuck that. I don't want to die again."

"Language."

"Sorry, sir. I will refrain from swearing in your presence-"

I intensified my hunger, releasing a little more control.

"-or anyone else's from this day forth."

Having established the pecking order, I turned to the rider. "Angelica, hold nothing back. That's an order."

The dracolich opened its jaw, and black burning death engulfed me, looking like dirty diesel smoke. I charged through it and delivered an uppercut that closed the dracolich's mouth.

I caught her head as she reared back, letting her pull me up, and launched myself feet-first at Angelica, only to be cut in two by her necrotic magic-coated staff. Her staff spun, cleaving through me three more times, before she dispelled the magic and knocked me aside.

I spun mid-air and landed on my feet, skin and flesh pulling back together. She had cut through my armour like it wasn't even there. I needed an upgrade.

I drew Slaughter. "You've got my attention. Now let's see how long you last."

The dracolich bucked, trying to throw Angelica off her back. "Screw this."

Angelica kicked off instead of fighting to remain on her mount and backflipped, landing on her feet.

Her dracolich jumped and flapped her wings to fly to the roof of the palace. "If you live, I'm sorry, Angie."

"Remind you of anyone?" I asked walking forward.

"Too much." Angelica charged, taking advantage of her longer reach.

Whoever had been training her was a real monster. She had mastered the war staff and staff skills beyond the normal limits, and I found myself struggling to keep ahead of her, without using my now-slight agility advantage. Then she started using her equipment properly, and I found myself fighting against her vampiric touch, having to counter her hunger with my own without going so far as to drain the life from her.

Burning necrotic bolts harassed me, blocking my vision so she could land strikes. She used the barrier spells in her armour to deflect blows rather than take them. And she threw kicks whenever they gave her an advantage.

It was vicious. It was violent. And it was an actual challenge. Without her set, she wouldn't have been a concern; but with it, I was beginning to worry.

Two hours later, she was exhausted, spent in every way you could be. She was only still going because someone had trained her to fight until she died, and everything was coming reflexively from her skills. I needed to see how far I could push her. How far she could go.

I also wanted to know if I could make her resort to trying to compel me with her armour or if she was now wise enough to not make that mistake.

To my surprise, she didn't try to compel me.

25

THE SOUL PARADOX

Even after seven months of torture, the King wasn't done with me. As the sun rose the following morning, Godfrey was waiting at my palace gate with a summons. Luke was out in the field, battling evil and cleaning up the kingdom, so I had no excuse or reason not to go.

An hour later, I entered the fourth hall. Angelica and Davina flanked me, each with their own entourage of guards. I didn't expect the king to try to kill me. He needed me. After that, he might try, but I wasn't sure. He had no problem abusing his tools, but I didn't think he was the sort to break them intentionally.

He seemed to have re-evaluated our threat level, because his guards had tripled since my last visit. "I'm told you have made a full recovery from your trial," he said, the moment I reached the foot of his dais.

"Demons only suffer at the torturers' hands during the process."

"How convenient for you." There was no sympathy in his eyes, no empathy. He didn't care what had happened to me anymore than I did.

"Did you invite me here to exchange pleasantries? Because I have other business to attend to."

"Insolent demon," he spat.

I scoffed at him. "*Insolence* is allowing someone who helped you to be tortured. *Insolence* is trying to make them do your bidding the morning after they are freed. *Insolence* is all you deserve."

A sneer crossed his face. "You will show respect, or I will *make* you show respect."

"You will receive respect only when your motivation is not so obvious, and your moral fibre is not so lacking. You want me to purge your palace of Unseen. You are going to try to sway me with the fact that it will help end the evil in your kingdom. When that doesn't work, you're going to try to sway me with loot, likely a fifth of all they own. You will, of course, lie about this amount and give me a pittance, which is why I will not accept this offer. You will then ask me what I want, and I'll tell you the Northern Royal Library. You will complain, and I'll point out that you have three copies of every book in that library and can easily make another. You will argue that the Northern Library contains only the most illustrious copies and ask if I will accept the lesser versions instead, which I will decline and inform you that I will also be claiming the copies *before* I begin the purge. You will then ask me, as a show of good faith, to go through the inner and outer palace guards and point out all those who are of good character, before you hand the library over. You will claim this is because you want to know those of good character, but you will gently push these individuals out of the palace to places not under your direct control, because you don't need tools with a conscience, but you do need good people to keep your kingdom safe."

His anger was obvious. Not because I'd treated him like he was a child, but because I'd *shown* him that he was one. A demon who had only met him twice knew his motivations and his thought patterns better than his own advisors.

The selfish and petty-minded were an open book to demons, and the king was both. Power and glory led him. He wanted to be the king who rebuilt his nation. He wanted to be the king who ushered in a new era of safety and prosperity.

His goals were admirable.

But he had a saviour complex.

He could just as easily lead his kingdom to ruin as to salvation. He wanted to cut himself off from evil, but at the same time he wanted to cut himself off from good. That was only a winning strategy if he could maintain control, but he couldn't. No one could.

His reign would end with his kingdom either a little better or a little worse than it started. If real change occurred, it would not be because of him. It would because of people like my son. People who went out and did good, despite what others wanted.

King Linus took several deep breaths and forced himself to calm down. Despite his bluster, he didn't want to fight me. He didn't want to risk me losing my soul, not because it would make me a monster, but because he would lose me as a tool, and he was in desperate need of my talents. Unseen roamed his palace. "I find it strange you would choose my library over other rewards."

"Knowledge is liberation. It is freedom. It unshackles us from our limitations and lets us grow. A blacksmith looks at a fallen tree and sees charcoal for his forge, a carpenter sees a chair and desk, a bowyer sees bows, a fletcher sees arrows, and a papermaker sees paper. Each one of us have our potential limited by our knowledge. We make up for this weakness by building communities to share this burden so we can grow beyond our individual potential. I do not have this luxury. I am alone in this world, unloved and untrusted. For me to grow and thrive, I must become a community unto myself. That is why I want your library."

"You seek power."

"In every form. Now do we have a deal?"

"By your own admission, I am removing one threat only to create another."

"I have no interest in your throne, but you cannot say the same for the threat I will remove. So, you will choose the lesser of these evils, passing the price of your actions off to another."

"You think so little of me."

"Don't try to patronize me. You're wise enough to know that if the throne is compromised, it will lead to widespread disaster. Enriching a local terror is nothing compared to allowing one that can stretch across your entire kingdom."

The king smirked, somehow amused by my patronizing. "So, I am left with no choice but to accept your terms."

"For the good of your kingdom."

"In that case, I accept your terms. The palace will be locked down when you leave this hall, and Godfrey will accompany you during your exploits, making note of all those you consume."

"You have no interest in questioning the Unseen?"

"Guilt by association is enough. You may leave."

I didn't disagree with him. It was easier to pull the tree out by the roots than spend time and resources trimming away the sickness and hoping you caught it all.

Godfrey fell in beside me as I headed for the exit. His cane tapped against the stonework with each step. "The inner palace guard is assembled and ready for your inspection."

"I'm going to the Northern Royal Library to collect my loot. I don't trust your king not to secretly strip the restricted section while I inspect his troops. My familiars will remain on the premises, with my master storage chest under guard until the inspection has been performed. Then we will begin to clean your king's household. I trust you have no objections to this."

Godfrey frowned. "I'll summon a carriage."

"I'll meet you there."

LIBRARIANS ARE FUSSY PEOPLE. That goes double for any who work in private facilities where you can't borrow their inventory. To the worst of them, the books become their children, and the idea of a vampire running off with their children is enough to kill them. Sometimes literally.

The head librarian had a heart attack when I informed him that the king had given me the contents resting in his hallowed halls. Davina arrived with Godfrey in time to save him. By then I had kicked the visitors out and made sure the staff were all where I could see them.

The Northern Royal Library was the greatest repository of knowledge that the kingdom had. It covered everything from history, to crafting, to magic, to the occult and religion. It did not pander to egos of others, filling its shelves with books written by men and women who thought the world needed to know about their exploits; *facts* lived here. There were gaps in the collection, but there were gaps in every collection. The half a million books would give me the grounding I needed to understand this world and the tools I needed to change it.

Gregory's men moved through the library, collecting normal books and adding them to my master storage chest. Angelica was doing the same with the books in the restricted section, walking behind the head librarian as he disabled the protective enchantments so she could access the works.

I had already dragged him down to the secret vaults, hidden behind false walls, under the library, and read the forbidden texts held within. These were books that could not be copied by mundane means. Their knowledge needed powerful materials to contain them safely and even more powerful magic to keep them in place. I couldn't walk out with them even if I wanted to.

Godfrey was surprised I knew they existed. And then grew concerned when I asked the head librarian to open the secret vault that was hidden *inside* the secret vault.

One of Contessa's books had mentioned the doubly secret vault. The writer had been driven insane by the knowledge he'd read there, referring to it as his 'dark awakening'. Godfrey's alarm diminished slightly as I ignored the cursed texts and focused only on the higher magic hidden within. We both knew that the king had not intended to give me access to the knowledge, but his word was law in the fourth hall, so until he rescinded the order, I was free to read.

Which is why I began reading the moment I reached the vault and didn't stop until I had taken everything of value.

The power contained in the runes and diagrams tried to liquify my brain as I read, but I healed too quickly for it to kill me. To a lesser demon like myself, higher magical knowledge, the kind reserved for true demons and angels, was *sustenance*. It empowered us. It changed us. It made us stronger. It brought us closer to Heaven and Hell.

At least, that was how it was supposed to work.

I was currently dealing with the side-effects of discovering what all academics discover at some point. Just because something works in theory, doesn't mean it works in practice.

Davina stood behind me with her hand on my head, directing the power surging within me as she attempted to stabilize my condition. When I had stumbled out of the vault, my flesh had been melting off my bones, pooling at my feet, only to be reabsorbed by my body, so the process could begin again. Trapped within me were runes and diagrams my flesh could not contain. Instead of empowering me, this knowledge was killing me.

"Any idea what's wrong, yet?" I hissed through gritted teeth, barely able to speak. "I'm supposed to be growing stronger."

"Do you want the bad news or the worse news?" Davina asked, before answering her own questions. "Your soul is interfering with your demonic ascension. The process is corroding it."

"Are the vampiric demonic parasites trying to evolve into something that can feed on my *soul,* instead of growing stronger?"

"That's what it looks like."

"Can you reinforce my soul?"

"I am. It's slowing the corrosion."

I considered having her remove my soul temporarily, but that wasn't a solution. If they evolved into something that could feed on my soul, the moment it was back the process would begin again. And while it was gone, I was going to be dangerous. *Too* dangerous.

Strengthening my soul wasn't working, and changing it to make it toxic to them would only lead to disaster. People who screwed around with their soul rarely came out in a better place.

With an understanding of what was going wrong with me, a solution presented itself. "Get me to a guild."

Davina carried me to the carriage as I gave her instructions, explaining what I thought might have changed, and then we sped through the palace streets. Godfrey shouted down any guards that tried to stop us, getting the carriage from one side of the palace to the other in short order. Davina flashed our guild tokens as she dashed through the door with me in her arms, carrying me into the class hall.

My strength was fading, but the moment my fingers touched the stone sitting on the pedestal, I knew I might survive.

Congratulations, you have upgraded your race to ancient vampire variant.

You've unlocked new racial skills:
Demonic Mutation

"Bind me," I whispered weakly.

Davina smiled. "By your will, your Dark Eminence."

VAMPIRES, at least before the primordial stage, were not demons. They were people infested with demonic parasites. Contessa taught me that. When they took their first innocent life, Heaven judged them, and the demonic parasites would kick their souls out the door to face that judgement, leaving an amoral consciousness behind that only lived to service its desires.

In these earlier stages, the demonic parasites were not supposed to evolve. They were a curse, a gift to humanity from Hell for the express purpose of corrupting us for all eternity. They were not supposed to be more than that. They were not supposed to be less. But like all demons, they were unhappy with their place in the universe. Their nature dreamed of the day they would be more than what they were.

When I gave them the opportunity to grow stronger, the little demons tried to kill me for my audacity, evolving into something that could consume the soul that had been the frustration of their existence. But change is a double-edged sword for a mindless demonic parasite. By changing their nature, they were changing mine. With the demonic mutation skill unlocked by the forbidden knowledge, the mindless demonic parasites were able to change and grow stronger, but they also opened themselves up to manipulation.

And I fully intended to exploit this weakness.

There are many reasons practitioners of the magical arts summon and bind demons, and there are many reasons those demons let them. It could be for power, knowledge, or slaughter, pursuits demons are happy to facilitate, as they appreciate watching mortals be corrupted.

The art of summoning a demon involves a name, a true name, and spells crafted specifically to contain demonic energy. For this reason, vampires before the primordial stage cannot be summoned. They are mindless parasites without identity residing in mortal flesh, which makes them able to walk freely through demonic binding circles.

Only if the vampire is willing to sit happily within your binding circle, or is tied up with chains, would such actions have any effect. The summoner could then bind the demonic parasites within them, and command them to sleep, stripping the vampire of their vampiric power. The vampire would then die a mortal death, unable to live without a beating heart or flowing blood.

This was the only power summoners had over vampiric parasites, because vampiric parasites could not change. They could not become something else.

Then they tried to eat my soul.

Davina carried my body from the class hall and performed a demon binding in the middle of the guild's lobby with the assistance of her archbishops and holy paladin. She bound the demonic parasites within me and commanded them to stop eating my soul. Then she took a break to gather her thoughts, leaving me on the lobby floor as wayward power ravaged my body.

"The parasites have to evolve," I wheezed weakly, struggling to focus.

"I'm aware of that," Davina replied. "But the matter remains, you are only among the living because you are a vampire. If they evolve into anything else, you will die."

"Could you not command them to evolve into something we could cleanse?" Father asked. "We could heal his body and give him life."

"He's suffered too much mental trauma for a human mind to deal with," Davina replied. "He'll go insane, if the knowledge he read doesn't immediately make his head explode."

"Then why don't you just command the parasites to become stronger?" Mother asked.

"Vampiric parasites already have a mechanism to grow stronger, and it's a peak demonic trait incapable of evolving, which is why we have vampires, elder vampires, ancient vampires, and primordial vampires. Ancient vampires have the demonic parasites in the first three stages within them. Each one interacts with the body in a unique way, causing the noticeable difference in power." Her eyes lit up. "I can use that."

"How?" I croaked.

"By making them perform separate parts of a task. They were evolving to feed on your soul. I need to make them also evolve a stronger mechanism to repair and strengthen it. It will give them the mindless satisfaction of feeding on your soul without them realising they're making it stronger."

"Too much hunger," I whispered. The life force necessary to do something like that would be insane. I'd be eating every few hours.

"I could have them evolve to feed off your magic to compensate."

"No mana regeneration."

"Spend your attributes."

"Not enough."

"Have you done the math or are you being stingy?"

"Math."

She scowled at me, clearly thinking I was lying.

"Unholy magic is good for feeding off souls, horrible for restoring them," Father said. "Regular magic would be more efficient."

"Souls," I whispered.

Davina frowned. "You want them to evolve so you can consume souls?"

"Nibble."

"Thank the Heavens you said 'nibble'," Father muttered. "I was about to raise my first protest since renouncing my vows."

Mother folded her arms and frowned. "Souls are your area of expertise, Father. May I hear your justification?"

"Souls can be injured. We call it trauma or heartache, depending on the cause. We can recover from this. We can heal. Heaven would not object to punishing the Unseen in this way, but it would object to him consuming their souls, so they do not face justice. That objection might extend to them sending an angel to smite him."

Davina paced back and forth. "A mutation on your vampiric touch ability that allows you to harvest fragments of an Unseen soul, combined with making your vampiric parasites capable of feeding on your magic, should be enough for them to repair and strengthen your soul, which should make it possible for you to contain the knowledge you've read. I can't promise there won't be any side effects, but you shouldn't turn into an emotionless killer before the sun goes down."

"Do it."

Congratulations, you have upgraded your ancient vampire variant race.

You've unlocked new racial skills:
Ancient Vampiric Soul Regeneration
Ancient Vampiric Soul Strengthening

You have upgraded one of your racial skills:
Vampiric Soul Touch

+120 Mana Regeneration

26

INSURANCE

It was late in the afternoon before Davina got me back on my feet. My plan to grow more powerful hadn't worked. I'd overlooked key details and almost lost my soul. I would need to be more careful going forward and hold myself back from diving into every opportunity that presented itself, no matter how fleeting it might be.

I was almost entirely certain I would hold to this new rule, until another opportunity presented itself. My nature made it difficult to judge the consequences of my actions, and my current exhaustion and hunger left me easily distracted. Both of which were now much worse after my demonic parasites' transformation.

Godfrey wanted to head to the parade ground immediately, because the king's guards had been waiting for hours, but I told him I needed to hunt. A ravenous hunger burned through me. I was almost as hungry as when the church finally fed me. It wouldn't take much to push me over the edge.

I didn't feel well.

I wasn't weak, my body didn't allow weakness, but I was compromised with a weariness that made it hard to focus. My willpower had reached its limit, unable to push through the hunger and weariness with ease.

Godfrey didn't back down, reaffirming his position that we should go to the parade grounds, until I told him I couldn't promise I wouldn't attack the guards. Only then, did he agree to let me hunt. Following behind and writing down names.

The hunt barely helped.

After a dozen kills, the ravenous hunger had only become a gnawing hunger. The pressure inside my head lessened, but the headache didn't go away. I had gone too long without rest. Dealt too much punishment to my body. Today was only the most recent incident in a long chain of punishments.

The grave called me home.

I could feel a pull drawing me back to where I was turned. I had ignored the demands of my body for too long, and madness was approaching. If I didn't return soon, there would be no coming back for me. I'd become a ghoul. So, I went to inspect the guards, hoping to hurry through the process so I could leave.

After I had inspected the guards, I collected my loot from the library and ordered Davina to take everyone and head for the first river and wait for me there. I told Angelica to go into the city to facilitate my exit. She named an expensive hotel we had seen on our way in, and I told her I would catch up. Godfrey got everyone through the gate, and then we began the purge.

I stumbled through as quickly as I could.

There were half a million people living in the outer palace, and all were under house arrest. We went from building to building hunting Unseen. The palace guards ushered everyone into groups, who invited me in. Most of the time, I gave them a cursory glance, pointing out anyone with the glow. Occasionally, I got to eat.

Godfrey was slow, tedious, old, and suffered from the weakness all mortals suffered: a need to sleep. That turned the outer palace purge into a week-long experience that made the mental haze grow thicker.

When the outer palace was cleansed, we moved on to the inner palace. Security was better, so only a handful had wormed their way in. They went the same way as the others.

The call of the grave only grew stronger as time passed; eating did nothing for me, and I was only growing hungrier. I could feel the life force burning inside me, but my vampiric parasites were too exhausted to consume it, allowing it to build into an inferno within me.

It was a relief when Godfrey and I left the last building and entered the king's home to deliver the results.

The end was in sight.

The king's staff were absent as we walked through the entrance, having been part of the last inspection. None were Unseen, but Godfrey's relaxed posture had suggested he knew that already.

The inspection had been a formality.

My brain felt foggy as we climbed a set of stairs to the third floor. It was impossible to focus on what Godfrey was saying. It was taking everything I had left not to turn and run for my grave.

A door opened halfway down the hallway as we reached the top. Eight young men between the ages of eighteen and thirty exited the room, laughing and joking with one another. One of them spotted Godfrey and waved cheerfully, causing the others to turn and look.

They *all* had smoky black gazes.

A week of feeding on any Unseen I saw, and no small amount of brain fog, had conditioned me to react in only one way. They were dust before I stopped to consider whose house I was in and the fact there were no servants around. The especially pleasant zing that came with their lifeforce snapped me out of my stupor.

I turned, seeing Godfrey's horror.

Everything came back into focus, and I had him by the throat before he could open his mouth. We were downstairs and in an empty room a few seconds later.

I pinned him to the wall and very quietly whispered. "Who did I just kill?" I needed to hear the words, before I did anything drastic.

Tears ran down his cheeks as he feared for his life. "The crown prince and his brothers," he whispered, barely getting enough air to speak.

"They were Unseen."

"It doesn't matter."

"I know," I said contemplating how much danger Luke was in. "Does he have any other children?"

"Five daughters."

After he replied, I remembered I knew that. "I'm taking the oldest one that survives as insurance. If his army sets foot in the Hellmouth province, his heir dies."

"You can't."

"The only alternative is I kill him before he kills my son in retaliation. The ramifications of such an action would be the end of his dynasty and give rise to a monster that would terrorize this nation. But I'll make that choice. Can this world survive *four* vampire heroes without souls?"

He shuddered, eyes going out of focus. "Fourth floor, east wing. Their suites are next to each other."

I already knew that. I could hear their heartbeats. I pulled out my strongest sleeping potion and poured it down his throat. Then I finished cleansing the king's home.

The king's daughters didn't rush to the door when they heard it open, too used to servants coming and going. It made it easy to see them before they saw me. Four of his five daughters didn't make it; only the youngest survived.

When I visited the queen, I found out why.

Black veins crisscrossed her once-delicate features as she lounged on a sofa. A second face made from shadows rested over her flesh. The books I had read on how the evil eye worked told me she was a *body snatcher*. They were notoriously difficult to find because they weren't harmed by holy magic. Having a houseful of Unseen made sense now. She had replaced the children with her minions. The youngest was too young to survive the transition which is the only reason she had been spared.

I wrote a note to the king and left it in her ashes. Then I copied the note and placed it in Godfrey's pocket. The servants weren't Unseen, but it didn't mean they were uncorrupted.

I opened the sleeping princess's bedroom door and walked over to her wardrobe, throwing her clothes into my storage pouches. I added anything else that she might need and then walked over to her bed.

She looked like her mother, with delicate features, but didn't have her blonde hair, taking after her father with chestnut brown. She was a little younger than Angelica when I met her, fifteen almost sixteen, which annoyed me.

"Luke is going to make a harem joke about this," I muttered as I threw her drugged body over my shoulder like a sack.

I made my way through the palace, leaving via a door in the kitchen, timing my movements between the guards. The moment I got outside, I started running. I moved from building to building in a blur, listening for heartbeats, and manoeuvring around them.

I reached the inner palace gate without being noticed. But that presented another problem. I had it on good authority that I would survive going over the wall and through the defensive enchantments. The issue was my insurance would not. With stealth no longer an option, I sprinted through the open gate.

The normal palace guards couldn't match my speed, but they were quick enough to see me. The alarm was raised in under a second. If I could have felt dread, I would have.

The Old Monsters were coming out to play.

Old Monsters were born in battle. They were warriors who had survived the dungeon legions, thriving in an environment that others barely survived. For them the dungeons were a steppingstone to true power, not the end. When the hellmouth opened, it had been Old Monsters who closed it.

There were three grey and grizzled Old Monsters waiting for me at the eastern gate when I arrived. Three full legions stood behind them, ready to die to stop my escape. The warning bells had beaten me here. Rupert, the Keeper of the Eastern Gate, stood beside them, dressed in sorcerer robes. He had a staff in his hand, and lightning crackled between his fingers. A visible barrier covered the exit behind them.

I slowed as I approached.

Fighting wasn't an option. Rupert was cunning enough to understand why not. It was why I'd risked this gate. I kept a thirty-metre gap between us when I stopped.

Then I lifted the princess's head and held it up. "Do you know who this is?"

Rupert nodded. "My cousin, princess Carolyn."

"Do you know what I've been doing in the palace this past week?"

"Eating Unseen."

"The queen was a body snatcher. She got the royal family, but not this one. She was too young. I ate the crown prince and his brothers before I realised who I was eating. You may use a cleric to verify she is not Unseen."

Rupert raised his hand and shouted. "Clerics, engulf the vampire and the princess with your most powerful holy magic.

Holy magic bathed us, leaving us unharmed.

"Are you confident she isn't Unseen?"

Rupert nodded. "You killed all her siblings."

"And the queen. She's the only heir to make it out uncorrupted."

He frowned, thinking through the ramifications. "The king will want your head. If he can't take it, he will take your son's. So, you have taken his heir."

I wasn't surprised he knew about Luke. I'd been counting on it. "Mutually assured destruction."

"In another age they called it diplomacy. You are undoubtedly willing to kill her if we try to stop you, but you have every reason to keep her alive and happy once you gain your freedom. Protecting the royal family is our purpose. Since you hold the heir's life in your hands and can assure her safety, I have no other option but to allow you to pass." He smirked. "You are quite the diplomat. Open the gate and let him through!"

He waved his hand and the barrier disappeared. A moment later the gates began to open, and the legions parted.

"You are no doubt aware you have killed me," Rupert said. "I'll be executed for this."

"He's your king. You chose to serve him."

"No offer to take me with you?"

"I smell your children on you. You won't let them take your place."

"No, I won't." Rupert smiled. "Look after my cousin for me. If you can teach her to be like your son, the kingdom will be a much better place for my children."

He stepped to the side, and the Old Monsters backed up.

As I walked past Rupert, I heard him whisper, "I pledge my life and my soul to the hero. Let his path be my path and his fate be my fate." Nothing happened, showing he didn't hear the call. He grinned as I looked his way. "It was worth a shot."

He'd been trying to force me to save his life, which likely would have forced me to give up his cousin.

I passed through the gates. The moment they closed behind me, I broke into a run. I needed to reach the hotel Angelica was staying at and get out of the city.

ANGELICA HAD SET herself up at the most expensive hotel in the city and was in the middle of a massage when I kicked in the locked door, sending woodchips flying.

She was off the table and armed before I entered. "I have to pay for that, you know."

"Get in your armour and grab your stuff, we're leaving *now*."

I put the princess on the nearest couch as the handsome masseur dashed out the door. Angelica dressed in a flash and then blurred around the room, throwing her stuff into her storage pouch. Then, she went for her armour. I was next to her, jamming pieces into place and tying straps and belts so quickly that she was ready for war before the masseur began yelling.

I could smell the injuries I'd caused the princess during my flight across the city, so I pulled another health potion from my storage pouch and tossed it down her throat. Then I threw her over my shoulder again.

"Who's the girl?"

"Princess Carolyn."

"You kidnapped the princess! Why?"

"I ate her siblings and mother. I needed insurance."

Angelica grabbed my coat and pulled it aside, looking for the holy amulet. "Okay, so the royal family were Unseen. That would explain why the kingdom has gone to shit."

"Language."

"Bite me. We need to get out of the city. Follow me."

She broke into a sprint, and we were outside at the stables in half a minute. Her dracolich was lounging in a wagon stall on a mountain of pillows, while a dozen terrified staff scrubbed and polished her bones and moisturized the skin on her wings.

"I have to pay for this," Angelica shouted at her.

The dracolich waved away her comment. "It's worth whatever it cost you."

"Get out of the stall; we're leaving," I growled.

The dracolich was up and out so fast that it caused several injuries. "Yes, your Dark Eminence, always willing to serve no matter the inconvenient timing."

"What's that on your back?" Angelica shouted.

"My new saddle. Do you like it? It's designer, one of a kind. You could build a house for how much it cost you."

The blood red saddle was made from some sort of snakeskin. It matched Angelica's armour perfectly, creating a nice but expensive symmetry.

"I have to pay for that."

"Get on," I growled.

Angelica immediately leapt onto the dracolich's back. I landed behind her a second later.

"In the air *now*. We're going to Davina. Cross no natural river or streams."

The dracolich beat her wings, rising in the air and knocking the scrambling staff over. "You're not the only undead creature that can't cross running water here." She cleared the building and picked up speed. "Who's the meat bag?"

"Princess Carolyn," Angelica replied.

"You spoil me, Angie." The dragon squealed. "I'm so excited. I promise to feed and walk her. I'll make sure she brushes her fur and cleans her claws."

"I told you not to call me that," Angelica moaned.

"But it's a nickname and it's so cute."

"The princess is mine," I growled.

"Yes, sir. I fully understand, but if you ever need a princess sitter, I'm available."

Angelica looked over her shoulder as the city flashed by below us. "You're doing a lot of growling over there. You also don't look good."

"I need rest."

"Are you sure? You look worse than when you arrived, and that wasn't that long ago."

"I feel worse."

"Did you eat a princess?" the dracolich asked.

"Yes. Why?"

"You might have gained a royal bloodline. You normally need to keep them for a while and be nice to them to improve your chances, but sometimes you get lucky. Alternatively, you can eat a whole lot of princesses, but that's wasteful. Actually, ignore what I just said. Girl monsters eat princesses. Boy monsters have to eat princes."

"I ate eight of those."

"That's very wasteful, but you will definitely have a royal bloodline. You're going to slowly feel worse for a few days and then you will get better."

"I appreciate your insights."

"Since you clearly have a royal bloodline, could I have the spare?"

"No."

"But I just told you secret dragon knowledge."

"All you told me is I'm going to feel progressively worse for a few days and then get better. It changes nothing."

"I told you how to unlock a royal bloodline."

"True. What do you want as a reward that isn't the princess?"

"Can I sleep in your treasury?"

I paused, considering her request. "If you don't break anything."

"I'm not a mindless beast."

"I'll kill you if you steal anything."

"Common dragon rule for allowing another to sleep on your hoard."

"You can sleep in my treasury when it is built."

"Can I eat intruders?"

"Yes."

"Can I leave the door open to encourage them to come in?"

"No."

"Can I disseminate the knowledge of the size and value of your hoard in villages and towns to encourage the unscrupulous to come and try to steal it?"

"No."

"Can I tell other dragons about your hoard, so I can steal their hoard while they try to claim your hoard?"

I started to grin at the opportunity. "How are we dividing the loot? I'm doing all the heavy lifting here."

"You can't talk to dragons as an equal, so I'm clearly bringing more to the table. Seventy-thirty."

"You think you deserve thirty. It's my hoard you're using as bait."

"I meant you get thirty."

"Did you?" I snarled.

"Angie, stop him! The evil vampire's trying to take my hoard."

"Stop calling me Angie, and I'll take your side."

"What?"

"If you want to make a hoard, you have to stop calling me Angie."

"But it's such a cute nickname."

"Those are my terms."

"Fine, I'll take thirty."

Angelica choked. "You're choosing my nickname over a hoard."

"I like you more than gold."

I could feel Angelica grin. "What about princesses?"

"No way. I'm going to be a royal dracolich."

"Would you eat me if I was a princess?"

"No."

"You know, if we wanted, we could always just kill the dragons without his help."

"Then we could keep all the hoard for ourselves. Angie, you're a genius."

Lost loot flashed before my eyes. "I accept seventy. No takebacks, no cutting me out of hoards."

"That's cheating," the dracolich roared.

"You got a problem with that?" I challenged.

"No, your Dark Eminence."

We quickly left the capital behind, flying for a few hours before spotting Davina's campsite in the distance. They had set up camp at the first impassable river, waiting for my arrival. The dracolich had an even stronger sense for natural running water than I did. Casually navigating around the streams and rivers, passing over still ponds and lakes, to take shortcuts. I could sense running water only a hundred feet away, under normal conditions. Up in the air, that sense was stronger, but not enough to do anything the way she could.

She banked at the last second, flared her wings, and dove. The sun sat behind us, blinding any who tried to look in our direction. It was a standard dragon hunting tactic and their preferred way of landing. Dragons were vulnerable on the ground, so they gave themselves every advantage.

A warning horn blew as we approached the ground. I watched everyone pause to listen, and then go back to what they were doing. We landed in an open field next to the camp, and I leapt down with the princess over my shoulder.

"Thank you for flying air dragon. Please remember to tip your pilot as you leave."

I chuckled. I'd been wondering if she had spent time around Luke when she said, 'meat bag.' This confirmed it. I reached into my storage pouch and tossed her a gold bar.

She started dancing from foot to foot. "It worked just like he said it would!"

I started walking away, heading for the white tents.

Angelica caught up a second later. "She's such a fan girl."

"Of my son?"

"Yes."

"Why?"

"Heroes and dragons are natural enemies, so being able to train against one is better for a dragon than being trained by those Old Monsters. He helped her strengthen her dragon skills, and she's been worshipping him ever since. She's a ditz, but she's incredibly powerful for her age and size. Before they trained together, she couldn't breathe death fire."

"Do you think it will work if we train?"

"It's worth trying, but you might gain dragon-slaying skills from it. Luke did."

"I'll pass, then. Go tell Gregory to break camp and get him up to date on the situation."

"You expect the king to come after us?"

"Not with his army, but we should expect assassins and an extraction team."

"Old Monsters?"

"Yeah. The king will only send his best."

"I'll get everyone moving." Angelica dashed off, becoming a red blur.

She had grown while I was gone. She wasn't where I wanted her, but she was closer. A little more training, a few years for her to mature, and no one would be able to kill her while I slept. I'd been able to rest without worrying about no one waking me up for a decade.

By the time I reached the church's outer camp, they were already breaking down tents and packing away their supplies. They didn't salute, nor do more than give me a cursory glance. They weren't my people. They were the saint's.

I meant nothing to them.

Davina's tent wasn't hard to find, mainly due to its size, and she was waiting out front when I arrived. "Who are you carrying?"

"Princess Carolyn. The abridged version is her mother was a body snatcher who corrupted all her siblings. I ate them. Now the king wants me dead. She's insurance."

The archbishops hissed behind her, speaking together. "The pope."

I looked past Davina to the pair. "The former queen is likely the one who corrupted him, but I can't confirm this." I returned my focus to Davina. "We're moving out immediately. The princess is your responsibility. I want you travelling with your strongest people, in the middle of Gregory's camp. I'm expecting assassins and an extraction team in the next day or two. Wake her up and tell her what happened once we're moving."

Davina frowned looking me over. "You don't look well. Did you gain a royal bloodline?"

I wasn't surprised that she knew about royal bloodline transference. "Maybe. Maybe, I just need to sleep."

"We'll stop at a guild along the way to check. There's a lead coffin in the tent behind me. It won't let you sleep, but it will ease your discomfort."

I smiled gratefully. "Thanks, kid."

27

THE SURGE

Silence was a welcome change. The constant sound of heartbeats, rushing blood, insect wings and a hundred thousand objects in motion faded as I closed the lid above me and lay back in the coffin. All that was left was my hunger and a deep ache in my bones.

With nothing to push me forward, I could let time pass without me. I barely noticed when they loaded the coffin into a wagon. I didn't notice when we crossed the river.

Davina left me alone until we reached a town with a guild. I was only out long enough to visit the class hall and then I was back inside the coffin. The prompt floating before me, drew my attention to the world.

Congratulations, you have upgraded your race to ancient royal vampire variant and leveled your hero class.

Your class has leveled.

Your class has leveled.

Your class has leveled.

Your class has leveled.

Your hero class is level 15.

You've unlocked new racial skills:
Royal Vampiric Authority
Royal Constitution: Sorcerer Sovereign

You have upgraded some of your racial skills:
Royal Vampiric Soul Touch
Royal Vampiric Aura
Royal Vampiric Thirst
Ancient Royal Vampiric Physique
Ancient Royal Vampiric Bloodline
Ancient Royal Vampiric Soul Regeneration
Ancient Royal Vampiric Soul Strengthening

Your class has leveled and unlocked new skills:
Negotiate
Create Undead Skeleton Spearman
Create Undead Skeleton Knight
Create Undead Skeleton Mage

You have reached level 15. You can upgrade one of your existing class skills.

You have 80 attribute points to spend.

I didn't know how my royal status changed the effects of my racial skills, nor what the new racial skills did, nor why I had leveled again. I only knew how the royal constitution worked. The sorcerer sovereign bloodline was public knowledge. The king and his family remained in power because the advantage their bloodline gave them made them the undisputed magical power in the nation.

Usually, people had to increase the tier of their individual magical skills the same way they had to increase every other skill. With the sorcerer sovereign skill, that changed. The specialized skill improved magical control and growth similar to the prodigy skill. Unlike the prodigy skill, the sorcerer sovereign skill also increased the tier of all magical skills when you upgraded its tier. With three tier upgrades, the royal family would have all their magical skills at tier three, before they had to upgrade skills individually.

It was a monstrous advantage. A monstrous advantage that I couldn't use currently, so I upgraded my prodigy skill instead.

You have upgraded your Prodigy skill to tier three.
You cannot upgrade this skill further.

Gaining the negotiate skill amused me, and I was looking forward to developing it. The create undead skeleton spearman, knight, and mage skills had practical applications, but they did not excite me. They were just a piece of the puzzle. They would help me make the world safer for my family, but they wouldn't do it alone.

I added the eighty attributes to my mana regeneration, to help ease my hunger, bringing the total up to two hundred; and then I let the world fade.

+80 Mana Regeneration

I expected us to stop when the sun went down. The horses couldn't run easily in the dark, and it was better to let them recover for a full day tomorrow than have them run at half-speed during the night. We didn't stop, however, pushing forward until around midnight.

Davina opened my coffin shortly after the wagon stopped moving. "I assume you're wondering why we kept going?"

"Not enough to ask."

"We're outside a dungeon town. They're fighting off a dungeon surge. They've got five thousand soldiers, a thousand guild members, and three thousand mercenaries. But it's not enough."

"You want us to help them."

"Yes, but I knew you wouldn't allow it without a secondary

reason. Gregory's people aren't strong enough to take on Old Monsters. They have the skill levels, but they need the attributes to match. There's only six of us who can really keep up with anyone tough enough to be labelled an Old Monster, and that isn't enough for your plan to work. A dozen of them will cut straight through us."

Her reasoning was sound, so I climbed to my feet. "We train until dawn." I leapt out of the back of the wagon and spotted Angelica waiting for me. "Have you decided if you are taking the knight or mage path for your class?"

"Months ago. I'm a knight, not a mage. Seeing how much time Davina spends studying really put me off being a mage."

"Go to the guild and become a death lord. Distribute your attributes appropriately for the knight path."

"Finally!" She was gone in flash.

We were outside the entrance to the dungeon, next to a large fortress with a massive gate, which acted like a cork in a bottle. If the surge pushed too close to the surface, the dungeon legion's commander would shut the gate and seal the monsters in. This was only a temporary solution as the monsters would eventually break through and begin attacking the countryside.

Gregory was off to the side of the wagons, giving orders to his commanders in front of a map his wife held up.

They were outlining a battle plan.

"Do we know what we're fighting?" I asked as soon as I joined them.

"Everything, by the looks of it," Gregory replied. "The legion got pushed out of the dungeon fortress last night when something big and ugly came up from the abyss, and they've been fighting in the tunnel ever since, falling back as needed. They have to push forward and reclaim the dungeon fortress to fight effectively, but they lost most of their heavy hitters."

Davina walked up beside us. "I've instructed my clerics to treat the wounded. The acolytes can't participate in this without being massacred, so they're assisting the clerics. My paladins are assembled and ready to engage; just give the order."

I took the map from Helen and glanced at it. "They're a mile and a half from the dungeon fortress, fighting in tunnels. Do the dungeon effects extend that far?"

Dungeons were the only place where you leveled without needing a class stone. You couldn't evolve your class when you were down there, unless you had a prestige class, but you could keep track of your progress as you leveled. If you reached a level 10 milestone, you could go to a class stone and upgrade your class, so long as you didn't level again before you got there.

"It does," Helen said. "The green line *here* shows when it stops."

They were close to being pushed out. We needed to act fast. "In that case, we're going with a simple wedge formation straight up the middle. Angelica and I will throw aside any soldiers who get in our way. Once we hit the monsters, the two of us will take apart the mini-bosses, while you roll over the monsters. Davina will provide support to your men."

Gregory frowned. "Shouldn't we coordinate with the others?"

"No. We're only here until dawn. We have enough to hold the line and cut our way to the fortress. Send someone to inform their leadership that we'll get them back to where they need to be. Any questions?"

"My men are ready to upgrade their classes."

"Rotate everyone back when they reach a milestone. Have wagons ready to run them to the guild and back. It's the only break they're going to get."

"What about the princess?" Davina asked.

"Keep her with you." I tossed her one of my storage pouches. "Her battle robes and staff are in there."

Helen scowled. "Do you honestly believe you can cut your way through a dungeon surge?"

"Yes. Now let's get moving. We're wasting starlight."

EXHAUSTED MEN and woman drenched in blood that came in an array of different colours rested against the tunnel walls, repairing clothes, and performing field maintenance on equipment. The fighting could be heard up ahead as we passed by their weary forms. I was glad they had enough discipline to leave a wide corridor down the centre, allowing wagons to roll past and hand out food or pick up the injured. It made it easier to reach the frontlines.

As we marched, paladins stepped out of our formation to place their hands on anyone with superficial injuries, healing them instantly. Then they returned to their position.

People didn't take notice of me as I passed, but they took notice when the dracolich did, backing up and staring wide-eyed. Not even an army of paladins could ease their tension.

Angelica was waiting for us, when we reached the back of the fighting. Now that she had leveled, she radiated power to an extent where I felt like I was standing before an equal. "Their commander didn't listen, so I beat him to a bloody pulp like Gregory told me to. His second in command was more accommodating. They're ready to split."

"Good. What level are you?"

She raised an eyebrow. "Did you know there are classes after death lord?

I frowned. "There shouldn't be."

"Royal death lord. It's a prestige class. Every ten levels I gain another rank in prestige and three more skills. I'm level 53. I think I'm strong enough to order you around now."

"Not yet."

She frowned. "You sure?"

I met her gaze. "You want to play that card before you're sure you'll win?"

She smiled and lowered her visor. "Let's go level, then."

"Form up," I roared, cutting through the cacophony of battle. The thirty-deep line of soldiers in front of us began to part.

The tunnel was just over two hundred meters wide and close to a hundred high. The ground sloped downward, heading further into the earth and monster territory. We had the high ground, but that didn't mean much where you were fighting monsters that generally started at two metres tall.

Angelica and I charged ahead, running through the gap as it grew. Lances of pure fire flew through the air, striking down a large insect crawling along the tunnel walls, while shards of ice tore through anything that could fly. The soldiers at the front fought a wall of creatures with sharp teeth and claws, desperate to push forward and escape the dungeon.

Against her orders, the stupid dracolich flew over our heads, reaching the front first. A torrent of death fire poured from her jaw, engulfing the horde below, as she attempted to show off. Then she passed the point where the air was contested and got swamped by flying creatures. Claws tore into her wings as creatures landed on her, trying to pull her from the sky.

Angelica and I leapt, jumping over the last five rows of soldiers. I drew Slaughter, cleaving through a bear-like monster and unleashing my hunger. It collapsed to dust, momentarily waking me up.

"Save me, Angie!" the dracolich shouted as she fell from the air. "I'm too pretty to die!"

I blurred, tearing through the surrounding monsters, consuming their life and magic to make a hole. "Go save your stupid dragon," I ordered.

"Thank you," Angelica shouted, blurring forward and twirling her Crypt Keeper staff like a weed wacker. Blood and flesh flew in all directions as she mowed down anything in her way faster than I could. The problem was there were so many dungeon creatures that the gap she created immediately closed.

By the time Gregory and the others caught up, I had made little progress. Every monster that collapsed into dust was immediately replaced by another.

Gregory saw the problem the second he reached the front. "Stop eating them. We need the bodies to slow down their momentum. Help us form our lines? Where the heck is Angelica?"

"She's saving her stupid dracolich," I replied, decapitating something that looked like a bull and a dingo had a baby. As its body dropped, I cleaved through a horse-sized slug.

Wherever a body dropped, the dungeon monsters feasted, taking a handful of creatures out of the fight as they chose food over violence. Seeing the obvious advantage to this, I started dashing through the monster lines, cutting down the largest of any five I saw.

Gregory's men and the paladins slowly spread out to take over the frontline, and then we began pushing forward, climbing over the dead one body at a time. Because of their low levels, it took us two hours to reach Angelica and her dracolich. The pair had hunkered down against a wall and were killing anything that came close. The dracolich's wings were shredded, and they were being swarmed from all sides, fighting just to keep their ground.

"I need to get to the guild," Angelica shouted. "I'm holding at sixty."

"You said you got a prestige class?"

"I might get something better."

I doubted that would happen, but it was worth checking. "Rotate out, then."

The cowardly dracolich took that to mean she could leave. "Come on, Angie, let's get out of here."

"Not you. Get behind the lines and provide fire support."

"But I've been fighting for hours. My claws are a mess."

"Get in position," I growled.

"Yes, your Dark Eminence. Always willing to serve, until Angie can take you down a peg."

"We need to talk," Gregory roared at me over the battlefield sometime later.

I turned and cut my way towards him, draining the life from the creatures. They gave little sustenance compared to an Unseen, but with how many there were, that didn't matter. Life force blazed inside me as I leapt over the frontline and landed before Gregory. "What's the problem?"

"We're gaining levels too fast. Three out of four of my men are about to need to head to the guild, because they're approaching their milestone. The rest are already on their way. The paladins are holding most of the line, but they're going to need to switch out soon."

"No, they won't. They only have one class after paladin, and only a few will be ready for it."

"They still can't hold the line if we lose four hundred of my men."

That was true.

"Where's the military commander?

"Look for the big flag. She'll be under it."

I leapt, jumping over our lines into the gap behind us, sprinting across the expanse to where the military had kept their lines. We'd only pushed forward a few hundred meters, but that gap was covered in corpses. The mess frustrated me, and I unleashed my hunger as I ran. The corpses crumpled to dust, clearing the tunnel, causing dungeon monster cores to litter the floor like gems.

You have leveled your Royal Vampiric Aura skill to level 5.

The life left in the corpses was negligible, but the skill levels were nice. I leapt over the soldiers' lines and landed at the foot of the flag.

A handful of men and women were looking over a map. They were used to dealing with people with high attributes, so they didn't look up. The dungeon legions were renowned for their strength. "Which one of you is in charge?

A gruff-looking woman holding a staff turned to me. "I am now."

"You will move your people forward and hold the line. I need to rotate too many out to visit the guild."

She scowled. "You should have come to us earlier. We have mobile military class stones with us. What do you need?"

"Advanced sorcerer in all the forms you have. Knight and then death knight if you have it."

"We have knight class stones. But you need a death lord to upgrade a knight class stone to a death knight class stone, and they only last for a decade. We haven't had a death lord in our ranks for a century."

"I've got a death lord you can borrow. How long will it take to get me that stone?"

She frowned. "We would be keeping the stone."

I respected her decision to clarify loot distribution. "You need an army for mobile class stones. I don't have an army. It's no use to me. So, how long?"

"Not long. I'll have runners summon the mages to begin preparation and collect the knight class stones. Where do you want us to set up?"

"Behind my line."

"I'll get it done." She turned and hurried away.

The man in heavy armour beside her scowled. "Who are you people? Your soldiers don't have high levels, but they fight with a kilij like they were born holding it."

"Does it matter, if we can get you back to the fortress?"

He turned and spat. "The fortress is a death sentence. Some ancient evil woke up and started ascending from the abyss. Whatever it is, it displaced all the regional tyrants. We dealt with the dungeon boss two days ago. Then we dealt with another creature just as powerful. Then another. They kept coming until an abyssal floor boss reached the fortress. It can't come any higher, but it won't go any lower, either. It's afraid of what's down there. It's sitting outside the fortress surrounded by dozens of creatures powerful enough to be dungeon bosses, slowly growing weaker as it treats the others like foot soldiers."

I'd read a lot about dungeons. They weren't really a threat, so I hadn't thought much about them. The creatures that lived inside dungeons could only survive in a magic-rich environment. They didn't consider humans a food source because the mana content in their flesh was too low, and if the ones that could survive in the dungeon level, the highest level, ever reached the surface, they died within a day. Those that lived in the lower levels, called the abyss, would die as quickly as a person without air.

So, the only time the dungeon monsters ever came to the surface was when something powerful moved, destabilising the food chain and terrifying the weaker creatures into a suicidal charge to escape.

They had their own eco-system, and normally they were happy to stay there. This was being caused because a lower floor boss got scared by something else and moved up to escape. It would die from lack of mana, but until it did, the mad rush wouldn't end.

"I'll deal with the lower floor boss."

"Your funeral. We're not moving our men out of the tunnel until it's dead, though. Doesn't matter if you reach the fortress."

"Just make sure your people are in position then."

WITH CLASS STONES NEARBY, Gregory's people were able to cycle out and back in immediately. With their new class skills and levels, we were able to move forward faster. The added speed taxed them, but the more they were taxed, the stronger they became, drawing on our bond. If someone was injured, they were pulled back and patched up, only to be shoved back into the fight half-healed. By the time they reached the front, they had fully recovered. I saw dozens survive injuries that should have killed, bleeding slower than was normal or ignoring things like having their skull split open. If any died, Davina was there to pull them back into the fight.

I quickly learned the power of a saint was not to be trifled with.

At one point, Davina was only given a foot. The man made a full recovery after his body parts tore themselves from the flesh of dead monsters and came back together under her command. When I asked her what she had done, she said it was mixture of death magic and life magic. Death to pull him back together the way a skeleton knight would, and life to resurrect him. Her archbishops stood behind her in awe, muttering to themselves about the implications, while Princess Carolyn threw bolts of lightning against anything that flew, protecting her kingdom and releasing her grief upon an enemy she could kill.

There were so many heavy injuries and deaths that at one point only half the force had armour. Davina noticed before I did and fixed the problem by casting a massive summon bone armour spell, using the magical bones of the dead monsters. The armour was only temporary, but it encased them in a layer of protective bone, and those who had become death knights grew stronger from the armour change. Death magic covered their blades as they pushed forward, unafraid and uncaring. As the warriors that had become knights reached their next milestone, they became death knights and leapt into the battle, summoning the same death magic.

Their progress was insane.

"We've reached the end of the tunnel," Angelica roared several hours later from the corner up ahead.

She'd begun fighting further forward to slow the surge, after her third and last pointless trip to the guild. Her efforts allowed me to slow the surge further, so that those behind us weren't fighting against a wall. We'd only been making quick progress in the last fifteen minutes, as the last of Gregory's men gained the death knight class.

"Prepare to hold the tunnel without us," I roared.

"We're ready," Gregory yelled back.

I glanced back to see a wall of soldiers rushing forward, cutting through the dungeon monsters with abandon. I could see the exhaustion in their eyes. They wanted out. And if that meant one big push to the holding grounds, nothing was going to stop them. Despite the rush, their formation didn't break, and they quickly moved to fill the entire tunnel, taking the place of the paladins.

Seeing their determination, I stopped controlling my hunger and cut a violent line through the sea of monsters, opening a dusty gap that they could fill. It took us five minutes to clear the last three hundred metres, and then they held, letting the paladins reform their lines.

The paladins knew how to fight in formation, but they weren't experts. Usually, paladins operated in small groups like adventurers, only fighting like this when they were defending a wall, so no one thought less of them. This wasn't their battlefield.

Angelica and I retreated behind the frontline, so she could catch her breath. She immediately downed a recovery potion while I assessed our situation.

The back of the dungeon fortress filled the tunnel, completely blocking it. Monsters poured from the gate and windows like water from a leaky pipe, finding any way to get through the obstacle and away from what was on the other side. The structure was unharmed, and so heavily enchanted as to be almost indestructible, which was the only reason the monsters hadn't torn it apart to escape.

On the map I'd seen, the fortress was shaped like a triangle, with the back being the point closest to us. The main wall was several hundred meters beyond what I could see through a long tunnel filled with monsters.

"Davina, you coming?"

"Do you need me?" Davina asked. "I don't like bugs."

"Angelica might."

Angelica turned to glare at me. "Why am I going?"

"Because you haven't leveled in over an hour."

"I'm level eighty! Do you have any idea how insane that is?"

"Exactly, you reached the dungeon limit. These creatures are fodder to you now. You need a proper challenge."

"And you think a proper challenge is a dungeon boss that climbed up from the abyss."

"Shows I believe in you."

Her eyes widened with surprise. "Fine. I'll kill your stupid dungeon boss."

"That's the spirit." I glanced at the archbishops behind Davina. "You can't come." I nodded to her holy paladin. "You should survive. You can come. Recover and prepare. Call me when you're ready to go."

I leapt over the frontline, landing in the middle of the horde. I dissolved my way to the gate of the fortress and stopped, cutting down anything that tried to push through, easing the pressure so my men could catch their breath, eat a few mouthfuls, and drink. It was ten minutes before they called me back.

"I'm taking point," Davina said as we pushed through our lines to the front. To illustrate why she was so confident, she exited the frontline and raised her hand. A wall of corrosive death streamed from her palm, dissolving anything it touched. Her holy paladin moved to cover her back, and Angelica and I covered the flanks.

After a few seconds, Angelica turned and glared at Davina behind her visor. "If you could do this the entire time, why did we just spend most of the night fighting our way through all that?"

"Everyone needed to level," Davina replied, raising her staff to hurl a bolt of concentrated necrotic energy at a centipede monster that was tough enough to make it through her wall alive. "I didn't want to steal anyone's experience." Bolts of necrotic magic burst from her staff, gunning down anything her wall couldn't reach.

With Davina on point, we had a surprisingly uneventful walk through the fortress.

Halfway through, her paladin stopped guarding her back and walked over to me. "I don't believe we have been formally introduced, your Dark Eminence. I am Toran."

"Vincent. What can I do for you?"

"Were you aware the necrosaint was this powerful?"

"Yes. You weren't, I take it?"

"I assumed her condition limited her. Her Heaven-blessed mana regeneration is mighty, but what I see here is beyond my comprehension. She doesn't have a core."

"You aren't well-versed in magic, I take it."

"I thought I was."

"A typical mage uses ten times more mana than the spell requires the first time they cast the spell. Most mages never master their skills, so they never master casting their spells without wasting mana. Davina has. Beyond that you will notice that Davina's necrotic wall is only finger-thick. She's reduced the thickness to conserve mana, reinforcing the corrosive capacity of the wall to compensate. She's only using half the mana that a necromancer would typically need for the spell, even if they had mastered the spell."

"Then I'm unneeded."

"She's fighting below her capabilities. Creatures like this aren't a concern, but a powerful creature will overcome her before she can gather enough mana to empower stronger spells. Put another way, if you weren't needed, I wouldn't have invited you."

"I will conserve my strength and guard the necrosaint against greater threats."

"Shout if you need help."

"I will."

He went back to guarding her, looking for threats that he needed to be concerned about.

When we reached the end of the tunnel, I signalled for everyone to stop. The courtyard beyond the tunnel was filled with creatures pushing forward, trying to escape. The press of bodies forced them into Davina's necrotic wall, creating a never-ending meat grinder.

The wall and gatehouse were a hundred metres away. It was thirty metres tall with turrets spaced every fifty metres. The wall was close to five times the width of the tunnel, but the enchantments built into it would empower the dungeon legion defenders if they could reach it. However, creatures currently crawled over it, through it, or above it in an endless stream.

"Davina, what level are you?"

"I'm level 72."

"Wait here until you reach level 80. I'm going to scout ahead."

I leapt through her spell and started running across the monsters' backs, moving too fast for them to harm me. I headed for the wall and used the monsters crawling over it as steppingstones to reach the top. I drew Slaughter and cut my way to the parapet and surveyed the battlefield, cutting down anything stupid enough to get close.

The dungeon was a massive cavern riddled with tunnels. The far side was five kilometres away and roughly the same width. Glowing purple crystals filled the centre of the cavern, where a massive centipede, as fat as the body of a 787 jet and four times as long rested in the middle, surrounded by bus-sized versions of itself. Any time a monster came near them, one of the smaller ones would raise their head and send out a firehose of acid, dissolving the threat.

Fifteen minutes flew by before anything changed.

A creature that looked like an amalgamation of a gorilla and a porcupine burst from one of the far tunnels and roared. It was the size of King Kong, towering above the monsters around it, crushing them underfoot as it charged for the crystals. More of its kind streamed out of the tunnel behind it.

That wasn't the interesting part.

The interesting part was it could *speak.* "With me, brothers," it roared.

I was off the wall and running towards it the moment the words left its lips, racing across the backs of monsters to reach it before it died. I managed to reach it before it reached the centipedes, and I leapt, landing on its elbow. I caught its fur in my fist and threw myself to its shoulder to scramble up.

I needed a few questions answered. This was the second abyss floor boss to enter the dungeon, which suggested a larger threat. "Large creature who can talk. What are you running from?"

The massive gorilla immediately stopped running and raised its fist, halting the others.

"Who speaks to Gorgath?"

"I'm on your shoulder."

It turned its head, pointing a massive eye at me. "Demon, what is your business in the monster realm?"

His body trembled under me as he spoke. It seemed to be able to sense that I could kill it. "What are you running from?"

"Ants. Their queen succumbed to age."

"Now they're on the warpath, I take it."

"She was sapient, like myself, which is a rarity among her kind. Her empire reached through a dozen levels of the abyss. Without her to keep her children in check, they have returned to their bestial nature, ignoring treaties and pacts. They now spread, eating everything in their path, laying eggs and growing their numbers as their nature demands. We have come up here to rest and recover, so we can make the march to safer lands. This land will not find its equilibrium for many generations."

"You have been most accommodating. As a thank you, I will spare your life and remove the pest sitting in the crystal garden for you."

"Gorgath thanks you for his life and the lives of his brothers who would have perished in the struggle. We will wait for you to clear the field."

I leapt from his shoulder and raced back to the fortress, leaping over the wall, and cutting my way to the tunnel. Davina was holding her barrier, wearing a bored expression.

"Are you level 80 yet?"

"Almost."

"Good enough. We need to kill the big bad and then get out of here."

"Aren't we going to take the fortress?" Angelica asked.

"No. This isn't a small surge that will be over in a week. This is a multi-year calamity."

Monsters bred quickly, so when Gorgath said generations, he meant rabbit generations.

"How do you know that?"

"I had a conversation with a floor boss from the abyss."

"You can't have gone into the abyss that quickly."

"He's up here. I told him we would clear the floor boss that got here first as a thank you for his help."

"Why do we have to fight the boss from the abyss for them if we're not even going to retake the fortress?" Angelica whined.

"You need to level."

IT WAS SURPRISINGLY difficult to kill the centipede. I could drain the life out of something my size in a fraction of a second, but something that large turned me into a leech instead of a dragon. Davina and Angelica were done with the smaller ones before I had killed it, so they helped me finish it off.

"Why didn't you just cut its head off?" Angelica asked, as we walked back through the dungeon fortresses tunnel.

"I might need to fight something that big again someday. I need to know how long it takes to kill it with my vampiric touch."

"We helped you finish it off, though."

"Exactly. Sucking the life out of something that large isn't smart."

"Couldn't you have worked that out sooner?"

"And let you miss out on the chance to level?"

"You were stalling!"

I chuckled. "It got you both to level 89, didn't it?"

Angelica was still fuming when we reached the frontline. The fighting was thicker than when we left. The monsters getting through the windows had been allowed to build up, making another press. The dracolich lifted her head as we approached and incinerated the rear ranks. Angelica and I walked through unaffected while Davina redirected it around her and her paladin with a barrier.

The ranks parted, letting us through.

Gregory was waiting. "We're ready for the last push."

"Fall back."

"Fall back, sir?"

"This isn't a normal surge. A sapient ant queen died, and now her empire is eating the abyss. It might be years before it slows down, and all sorts of abyssal creatures are coming up here for a rest. I'm going to go back and inform the army, so they will be ready to replace you."

"This is going to spread, isn't it, sir?"

I nodded. "Every dungeon across the kingdom will be facing the same threat within a month."

"As above, so below."

"What's that?"

Gregory sighed. "It's an old saying, sir. It means the world up here reflects the world below us. Their queen died. You ate the royal family. Both will cause chaos, upending peoples' lives, and recreating empires."

"You're too superstitious."

"I did almost die twice today, sir."

"What's the average level?"

"Early sixties, sir. We had a surge just before you got back. Some jumped five levels. But only those of us who swore the oath. Everyone else slowed after reaching forty. My wife is quite upset that I'm leaving her behind."

"I told you you're bleeding experience you can't use," Davina whispered while passing by.

I turned and caught her wrist. "You think?"

She nodded. "Only way to explain how they leveled that much. You're fighting above your level here, giving you an experience multiplier. If that experience is being passed off unfiltered to those below you, then your ability to kill as fast as you do could account for the difference."

"We're staying, then."

"Seems wise. But they might run into the same issue that Angelica and I did and stop once they reach eighty, though."

"Dungeon limit."

She nodded.

I turned to Gregory. "Ignore my retreat order. We're staying until you reach level eighty. I'm going back in."

IT WAS late in the day when the last of them hit the dungeon limit. The paladins had faded before then, unable to keep going. They didn't have the levels or the endurance. Gregory's men did. But they would have collapsed before noon if the clerics hadn't finished treating the wounded and come to buff them.

"We're pulling back," I told the military commander further down the tunnel. She was clutching her staff and glaring at me. "You can't hold the fortress, and you shouldn't. This isn't a normal dungeon surge. The sapient queen of a dozen-floor-spanning ant empire died a few days ago, and her bestial subjects have begun eating everything around them to grow their numbers. They're going to be spreading in all directions. Abyssal floor bosses are coming up here to recover before running somewhere else. This isn't going to be an isolated incident. You have to warn the other dungeon legions to fall back and build fortifications in the tunnels."

"How did you come by this information?"

"I intimidated it out of another sapient abyssal floor boss."

"Likely story. We will hold the line until we receive other orders."

That was a bad call. It would lead to millions of deaths and the world becoming less safe for my family. "Will a royal command from the heir work for you?"

She snorted. "Sure. I've got my authority amulet in my pocket. If you get the king or his heir to give that order, I'll pass it along."

I was back in two minutes with Carolyn.

"Who's she?" The commander asked.

"The heir."

"The heir is the prince."

"The prince died yesterday."

She frowned. "Even if that were true, she's still too young."

"He wasn't the only one. This is princess Carolyn. The only surviving member of the king's children, making her his heir." The princess was white as a sheet as I yanked her forward. "Give them the order."

She swallowed.

"If you ask them to rescue you, they will die pointlessly." I turned to the commander. "Get your amulet out."

She frowned at my words but opened a pouch on her belt and removed the amulet all high-ranking military officers carried.

Carolyn took a deep breath. "I order you to hold the line here until the countryside can be evacuated. You will send your fastest runners and command all dungeon legions to begin building fortifications at the narrowest point before the dungeon entrance, giving them permission to draw on any resources that are necessary to make this happen in the fastest conceivable way. They are to prepare for a yearlong surge and are given permission to call in reinforcements and resources as needed."

The commander's amulet glowed the entire time Carolyn spoke. The commander had dropped to her knee the moment it lit up. "I hear your orders and obey, Your Highness. I overheard what he said, and I would gladly lay down my life and the lives of my legions to win you your freedom."

I was behind the commander's back before she realised I had moved.

The princess saw the commander's surprise and confusion at my disappearance and gave a resigned sigh. "That won't be necessary. A rescue is already in motion. I will not throw your life away needlessly."

I picked the commander up by the scruff of her neck and shoved her toward her people. "That means go follow her orders." She froze when she realised I'd gotten behind her without her seeing, and she quickly scampered away when I released her.

I turned to the princess. "Congratulations, Your Highness. You just saved millions of your subjects' lives."

She couldn't hide her disgust. "And all I had to do was follow the orders of the monster that ate my family?"

I paused and then shrugged. "I guess we're doing this now then."

"Doing what now?"

"Dealing with your misdirected anger. I reject your accusation that I ate your family. The creature that took your mother's body killed your family long before they ever crossed my path. It would be correct to say that I ate the people who killed your family, ridding the world of what would have been the start of an immortal Unseen dynasty and saving it from the disaster that followed."

Congratulations, you have leveled your hero class.
Your class has leveled.
Your class has leveled.
Your class has leveled.
Your class has leveled.
Your class has leveled.
You are now a level 20 hero.

Your class has leveled and unlocked new skills:
Create Undead Death Knight
Commander
Educator
Necrotic Magic
Study

You have reached level 20. You can now upgrade one of your skills.

You have 100 attribute points to spend.

"What just happened?" I asked myself as I upgraded my willpower skill and felt my exhaustion ease.

You have upgraded your Willpower skill to tier one.
You can upgrade this skill four more times.

"Are you honestly claiming you saved the kingdom by killing my family?"

My brain switched gears, back to the conversation. "Yes, they would have gone on to cause a reign of terror that might have never ended. I would call eating the Unseen pope saving the church for the exact same reason."

Congratulations, you have leveled your hero class.
Your class has leveled.
Your class has leveled.
Your class has leveled.
Your class has leveled.
Your class has leveled.
You are now a level 25 hero.

Your class has leveled and unlocked new skills:
Combat Educator
Instructor
Battle Commander
Research
Footwork

You have reached level 25. You can now upgrade one of your skills.

You have 200 attribute points to spend.

"You can't be serious. I wasn't getting experience because I wasn't recognising my actions as good." Testing the theory, I kept talking. "I came down here to reclaim the fortress, so the dungeon legions could fight more effectively and save lives. I then discovered what had the dungeon monsters so upset and realised the threat was bigger than anyone knew. I passed along the information, so the army could prepare. When they didn't believe me, I got the princess to order them for me, even though it risked me losing my soul if they tried to save her and I accidently killed one of them. I did this so I could save innocent lives and make the world safer."

Congratulations, you have leveled your hero class.
Your class has leveled.
Your class has leveled.
Your class has leveled.
Your class has leveled.
Your class has leveled.
Your class has leveled.
Your class has leveled.
Your class has leveled.
Your class has leveled.
Your class has leveled.
You are now a level 35 hero.

Your class has leveled and unlocked new skills:
Parry
Heavy Blow
Strategist
Thrust
Impale
Block
Dodge

Cleave
Occult Researcher
Occult Educator

You have reached level 35. You can now upgrade three of your skills.

You have 400 attribute points to spend.

"Stupid evil alignment," I muttered dismissing the prompt, and raising the tier of the willpower three more times, and feeling much better for it.

You have upgraded your Willpower skill to tier four.
You can upgrade this skill one more time.

"You want me to believe you're our saviour?"

I snorted. "I'm no saviour, princess. I'm a hero. I'm a hero that doesn't get experience from killing monsters or evil creatures, because I'm fighting on the wrong side. So, I only get experience from doing heroic deeds. And I got five levels from killing your family, because it was a heroic deed. So, take your anger and point it at the *real* monster who hurt you, not the one conveniently standing in front of you."

Her mouth dropped open. "You gained five levels from killing my family?"

"Yes. That's more than I got from killing the lich, Contessa, and as much as I got from killing the pope. But what we just did here was worth double what I got from them. Maybe more, if you consider higher levels requiring more experience. Maybe less, if heroic deeds give straight levels instead of experience. I don't fully understand how this works. Gosh, I'm hungry." I realised I was rambling and stopped talking.

"Your hero class gave you levels for *killing my family*," she said more quietly, shock overcoming her anger.

I sighed. "It did. I know that's not what you wanted to hear, kid. But I'm not the monster in this situation."

Tears fell from her cheeks as repressed emotions came to the surface. "I *told* my father that mother wasn't behaving like herself *years* ago. He didn't listen to me. Why didn't he listen to me?"

"Because you were a child. Adults don't always listen to children. It's not your fault. It's not his fault. It's the creature that killed your mother's fault."

"He could have saved them."

"I just told the local army commander that this surge was going to last a year and got scoffed at. Her reaction would have cost the lives of millions. Do you want to go execute her for her incompetence?"

She screwed up her face at the suggestion. "No. Why would she believe you? It's absurd."

"So are the logical steps between your mother not behaving like herself and her having being replaced by a body snatcher. If you won't execute the commander for not listening to my warning, don't hold yourself or your father responsible for what happened to your family." I walked forward and took her by the elbow. "Come on, we need to get moving. Your rescue team should be arriving shortly."

+100 Strength
+100 Agility
+200 Mana Regeneration

28

GETTING AWAY WITH IT

Because of Luke, the king had ordered his Old Monsters to train Gregory's men. I think they were watching when we exited the dungeon. The sight of the men and women, whom they had trained, all being level 80 must have made them reconsider their plans for how to rescue the princess.

They didn't attack that day.

They didn't attack the next.

Nor the one after that.

They gave us five days to get comfortable, hoping to lull us into thinking maybe the king had accepted my terms to take his daughter as a ward. It also might have taken them that long to gather enough reinforcements.

Who knows.

We used the time they gave us to travel during the day and raised forts every night. Four walls and a keep, stones formed into bricks, piled upon each other, and bound with magic so the whole thing didn't collapse.

The clerics, acolytes, and paladins that weren't required for my plan to work set up camp separately from us, to show they weren't involved. The church and state going to war was unacceptable, and I didn't expect the Old Monsters to fight them unless they were given no choice.

I made sure I gave them that choice.

The attack came at dawn.

I knew because I felt one of my men die.

I silently lifted the lid off my lead coffin and tapped the guard on the shoulder. "They're here."

"I'll spread the word," he said, before heading for the vault entrance.

Gregory and his people spent their days sleeping in the wagons, so they could spend their nights awake and on guard. They were ready and waiting. I walked over to the bed in the corner of the room. Princess Carolyn was wedged between Davina and Angelica. Both of my familiars felt the need to take up as much room as possible while they slept and were giving her very little space.

I shook Angelica's foot.

Her eyes opened immediately.

"Get dressed."

I did the same to Davina. She remained fast asleep. I tried a little harder, shaking her foot. She mumbled but continued to sleep. I walked around the bed and whispered in her ear. "I command you to wake."

Her eyes snapped open with a hurt frown. "Do you have any idea how horrible it is to be woken up by a command?" She whispered.

"I tried other methods. Grab your staff. They're here."

"How many dead?" she asked, holding out her hand.

I grabbed it and pulled her to her feet. "Twenty-three so far. They've taken the east tower unopposed."

Davina let go of my hand and reached behind the headboard for her staff. I dumped a sleeping potion over the princess, before transferring her to the coffin, and then turning to Mother and Father. They were seated in a pair of armchairs in the corner of the room. I nodded to the sleeping princess, indicating it was time for them to guard her.

Without a word, they walked over and began raising a barrier around the coffin, filling the vault with a gentle yellow light.

Angelica let out a frustrated grunt as she struggled to put on her armour alone. I rushed over to help her equip, pulling straps tight, and repositioning plates as necessary. The moment she was battle-ready, she rushed out of the vault door.

I glanced at Davina. "Stay safe."

She rolled her eyes. "Yes, your Dark Eminence."

"I mean it. No coming out to fight."

"That command is rather open to interpretation."

"That's because I trust your judgement."

She smiled as I walked to the vault door and entered the main keep. The fortress was an empty shell. A large hollow structure made to look like a keep. There were high positions for the mages and clerics to attack down or buff from, and the curtain-covered upper windows were all designed to crumble inward if someone reached them.

The keep was a kill box.

We just needed to get them inside.

Gregory nodded that everything was ready as I closed the door.

His men were lined up with their backs against the walls of the kill box, ready to fight anything in the middle. This was a stealth mission for both sides. The Old Monsters needed to get in without being detected, secure the princess, and hold the line while others got her out. They weren't going to use the door. And there was a dracolich on the roof, so the windows were the only option.

Right now, they were stripping my men in the tower and putting their equipment on. They would cross the open ground in full view and then scamper up the walls too quickly for the dracolich to react. When they arrived at the windows, they wouldn't be wearing their best equipment. And they wouldn't have time to change.

There would be no mages among them. Mages weren't suited to this sort of operation. They didn't have the skills or the right attribute distribution to creep into an enemy keep. Razing a keep to the ground they could do in a heartbeat, but that would likely get the princess killed. So, no mages.

I drew Slaughter.

This was going to be a difficult fight, which is why I had put a hundred more points into agility and strength, along with another two hundred into my mana regeneration. I needed to maim without killing. Leaving the Old Monsters compromised so my men could finish them off. If I went all out and killed someone that wasn't Unseen, I'd lose my soul. It wouldn't even matter if they were here to kill me and I was defending myself. Demons didn't get special considerations when they killed people. We'd lost the privilege by becoming demons.

I couldn't let that happen.

There were no other warnings before it started.

The dozen windows crumbled in at the exact same moment, dropping two dozen surprised Old Monsters into our midst.

I lopped the legs off the two falling from my window before they reached the floor, jumped off the wall, and descended upon another pair landing right behind them. As the grey-haired man's arm fell away from his body, he spun, delivering a kick to my face that slammed me into the wall thirty feet away.

By the time I landed, everyone was fighting.

Angelica had two pinned down, keeping them distracted so the death knights could cut them to pieces. I rushed through the fray, towards the nearest target, only to see her cut down before I could reach her. I changed directions only to see it happen again.

Gregory's men fought with abandon, unafraid of death. They had seen the saint resurrect a man from a foot. So long as she was with them, death couldn't hold them.

I watched men take mortal wounds to deliver injures with grins on their face. When I eventually found someone to fight, I barely had to help, cutting off a hand while they were distracted. It was over in less than a minute.

Two dozen Old Monsters lay dead on the floor, and five times as many of my own men were beside them.

"Secure the building," I shouted. The geomancers raised their staffs and the openings closed. "Clerics, heal the injured." I opened the vault door and received a blast of necrotic energy to the face. "We need resurrections. Get out here, Davina."

"That was fast," she said rushing past in a blur. She'd used over twelve hundred attributes to reinforce her body, so she was as strong as the death knights and a lot faster.

I turned to Mother and Father who were guarding the coffin. "Would you anchor the souls of my people, so they don't move on?"

They nodded their heads, holding hands. They dropped the barrier around the coffin and raised their staffs together. Power filled the building, encompassing the entire fortress.

"It is done," they said.

"Thank you."

I hadn't asked them to join the fight. Instead, I asked them to protect the princess and return her to the victor. They had sworn themselves to the saint, but they were people of faith. If I pushed them too far, they would push back. So, I only had them help in ways they were comfortable to help.

With her new levels, Davina was now stronger than the holy paladin who had been guarding her. Toran had stayed behind in the dungeon to train. He said he would be back when he was ready to perform his duty.

"Will you allow us to resurrect the kingdom's elites?" Mother asked.

"They will be resurrected. Whether they remain among the living will be up to them."

ANGELICA AND GREGORY wrestled the last Old Monster through the door and placed him at my feet, painfully twisting his arms behind his back to keep him in place. He was a grizzly bear of a man. Nearly seven feet tall with bulging everything. He had a long, rugged beard that was completely grey, like all the others'. Wrinkles lined his light blue eyes as he glared at me.

"Hello, Sir Trent. I must thank you for training my people so well. You did an outstanding job."

He chuckled. "They were Old Monsters waiting to happen. Beating the monster into them was one of my proudest achievements, even if it kills me. So, if you want to thank me, give me the princess and kindly die."

"I'll have to decline giving you such a reward. However, if you want to keep the princess safe, I would be willing to allow it."

He frowned. "What are you playing at?"

"Do you know what an oath brand is?"

He nodded. "Cleric magic. Like a slave brand, but the recipient has to *want* to keep the oath when they make it. When their oath is fulfilled, it vanishes."

"Good. I want you to take an oath that you will protect the princess from all serious harm and make no attempt to help her or others who would assist her in leaving my side, until I return her to the capital."

He shook his head. "You think I'm going to help you kidnap the princess? After dying to get her back? Just kill me again, vampire."

"Did you not listen? I said protect her from *all* serious harm. That includes *myself.* Should I turn on her and attempt to seriously harm her, you would be within your right to strike me down."

He froze. "Keep talking."

I explained how his oath would work. He would recognise Carolyn as my ward. Her protection would be his responsibility. My people were under me; so as long as they did not try to harm her, he would not touch them. If they did something that was morally objectionable to him, he was allowed to incapacitate them, only if the need was immediate; otherwise, he had to bring it to their commander's attention.

His only limitations were, he wasn't allowed to view us as enemies, nor act against us, nor help others act against us, and he wasn't allowed to help the princess escape, nor help others help the princess escape. It did mean that if the king sent other Old Monsters, he would have to fight against them, but he saw that as a way to improve the princess's safety, since I promised to give them the chance to make the same oath.

He asked the archbishops for advice at that point, wanting to know if he was being tricked by a demon, which was the first time any of them had thought of that. They answered honestly, saying that he had few options. This would see him through certain death in a way would allow him to fulfil his duty and keep his honour intact. He might be making a deal with a demon, but it was a demon that had the necrosaint's guidance, and she would not allow him to stray too far from the light.

It was interesting to hear their views on me. They were wrong. But they were interesting.

He agreed to give the oath.

Davina performed the spell and confirmed that it had taken, meaning that it was what he wanted. Angelica and the others released him.

He immediately punched me, knocking me across the room. As my head slammed into the far wall, I heard him chuckle. "Thought that might work."

Everyone stared at him, unsure what had happened.

I picked myself up, curious but not angry. "How did you manage that?"

He continued to laugh. "You can't be hurt by a punch, vampire, so I'm not really harming you. You might need to feed if I go all out, but minor injuries like punching your smug face don't cause any problems for you. So, I can punch you whenever I need to feel better."

His logic was sound.

"I need to train my unarmed combat skill at some point. You want to volunteer?"

He gave me a lopsided grin. "Now, *that's* a reward for training your troops."

"Glad you're happy." I turned to Angelica. "Go get the others." I turned to Davina. "You can wake the princess."

"What others?" Sir Trent asked.

"You didn't think you were the first one we resurrected, did you?"

"I was their commander."

"Which is why I figured you were going to be the most stubborn. I left you for last."

He sighed. "How many accepted?"

"*All* of them. It's lunch time. You need to go and deal with the Old Monster mages you've got waiting in the woods. Davina and Angelica will come with you, so no one dies for too long."

RUPERT, Keeper of the Eastern Gate, was in good spirits when he marched into our fortress a few hours later. He was at the head of a column of three dozen mages. He waved at me cheerfully when he stopped before me. "Nice to see you again."

"I take it you weren't executed."

"They needed volunteers for a suicide mission."

"Lucky you."

"Don't pretend you're not happy to see me."

I paused, thinking through his statement. My brain was growing foggier by the hour now that the danger had passed, making even simple tasks difficult. The grave called me home, and it didn't care that I had raised my willpower. I was very close to succumbing to madness. But there was too much to attend to. Rest had to wait.

I eventually found his statement to be true. "You are a competent, intelligent individual. It's better that you're alive than dead. I can use you."

"How cold."

"Your cousin is inside trying to convince her guards to help her escape. Please explain to her why that is impossible."

"I heard what you did in the dungeon."

"Which part?"

"The part where you had my cousin warn every dungeon legion in the kingdom that a nationwide surge was going to happen. Now that the second surge has occurred, her reputation is soaring. The common folk are hearing that her first act as heir was to reinforce the military at the nearest dungeon surge, only to uncover the threat to millions on the first day. She's fast becoming the most beloved member of the royal family of the last century."

"I take it you had something to do with the information spreading?"

He grinned. "You don't become a gatekeeper without knowing how to control the flow of information. Is it true you're starting an academy to teach people how to fight evil?"

"Yes."

"Would the princess be staying at this academy?"

I paused. "She could, if she could be convinced staying was in her best interest."

"Wonderful."

"You might consider mentioning that if she knew the signs to look for, she would have been able to recognise what happened to her mother."

His lips turned down with distaste. "That's a disgusting use of her mother's death."

"It's also true. You've all grown overly reliant on clerics. You've forgotten how to recognise evil without them."

Rupert frowned. "You can recognise a body snatcher without clerics?"

"Have them drink water with silver flakes. It gives them diarrhea."

"Seriously?"

I nodded. "They will run for a bathroom before they finish the glass."

"The queen got rid of the silverware and replaced it with gold."

"Now you know why."

Rupert sighed. "I'll tell her."

"Good luck. She has a sword."

"Who gave her a sword?"

"I did."

"Why?"

"She needs to learn how to use it."

"She's a sorcerer."

"Yes. But if you know how your enemy fights, then you know how to counter them. Good luck."

29

BACK TO THE BEGINNING

With the Old Monsters guarding the princess, there was nothing to stop our progress. I retired to my coffin, and no one disturbed me until we reached Hellmouth.

Nina and Oliver's teams had spent the past eight months making and enchanting equipment for fighting the undead, teaching the local guild craftsmen all sorts of new tricks, and helping them grow their skills. They were coming with us. They just needed me to pay for the equipment they required to run their operations.

Between buying Angelica's title of nobility, and the cost of building and equipping the academy, my loot had shrunk to a fraction of its former glory. I had less than a year of the capital necessary for maintaining the academy and to pay my guards. But there were a hundred ways to make money through the guild. So, I wasn't concerned by this.

Riker gave permission for a guildhall to be constructed in the small town that would be built around the academy, and Tora agreed to be the guild leader, which pleased Sir Brandon.

It took Gregory's men a week to pack up their households and say goodbye to friends. They knew the move was coming, so their wives and husbands had sold their properties months ago. The only thing left to do was purchase enough wagons and horses to make the trip.

When the week was over, everyone loaded their equipment into wagons, and we headed for the estate.

We reached the first of my detours a few days later.

In the early evening, I knocked on the door of a small, dirty house in the back corner of a small town. The elderly woman who lived here was not well-off. She had lost everything, including all but two of her eight children, when the hellmouth opened. She had come to this town to start a new life for her surviving children and ended up in waste management.

Rena's embarrassment over her mother's profession was likely why she had been so particular about being clean. They had been very well-off before the hellmouth opened, and becoming poor, on top of her mother's new profession must have traumatised her.

Her elderly mother opened the door and greeted me with a sad smile, eyes falling to the holy amulet around my neck. "You must be the vampire that was with my Rena when she died."

I gave her a sad smile, looking so haggard it was easy to tell I was a vampire. "Yes, ma'am."

"The guild said you wanted to share how she died."

"And learn how she lived." I handed her Rena's share of the loot.

She looked at the storage pouch and sighed. "This is full of gold isn't it."

"Yes."

"How much?"

"She helped kill an ancient vampire and a dozen elders. With the bounty, you never have to work another day in your life."

"Seems a poor trade for my Rena."

"It is."

"Do you know where she's buried?"

"Yes."

"Would you tell me where? I'd like to say goodbye."

I told her.

She wiped the tears from her cheek. "She would have preferred somewhere clean."

"You can move her, if you'd like?"

"Maybe. Maybe not. What she did in that room was her greatest achievement, seems wrong to take her away from that." The tension eased out of her. "You can come in and tell me how she died, and then I'll tell you how she lived."

I followed her in.

Two days later, we stopped in another village near the border of Angelica's estate. I entered a tavern that had seen better days. It was empty, despite being midday. The ghouls had ravaged the countryside here, so this wasn't the only business that was struggling.

Denton's wife had a new husband. He frowned when I walked up to the bar. "You're him, aren't you?"

I nodded.

"I'll get my wife."

I took a seat at a table while he went into the back.

A young girl, around ten years old, with light brown hair and freckles ran down the staircase a few seconds later. She raced through the room, wove between the tables, and stopped before me, wearing a big smile. Then she reached out and placed her hand over my heart. My heart thumped in response, once for her, once for me, and once for the bond that was forged.

I had no idea what she had done and sat stupefied.

"I dream about you," she said, cheerfully. "I watched you sleep every night, for the longest time. My dreams are much more exciting now you're awake."

"You dream about me?"

She nodded.

"Do you know why?"

She shook her head.

"Can you do anything else?"

She looked around quickly, seeing if anyone was nearby, and then bit her hand hard enough to draw blood. The wound healed over in seconds.

"I can also see the bad people," she whispered. "Do you want me to show you?"

I nodded.

She took me by the hand and dragged me around the village in the fading light, pointing out the Unseen through their windows along with anyone who had a cursed objects. Her parents were frantic when we returned. I understood why. A vampire had walked off with their child.

"Were you carrying Amelia when her father passed?" I asked when her mother finally calmed.

Sanna was an attractive woman in her late twenties. She would have been in her late teens when Denton died, maybe five years younger than him. "I don't see how that is any of your business?"

"Amelia dreams about me when she sleeps. She also has some of my powers."

"You're the sleeping man," her husband said horrified.

I nodded. "Her father's last act was to swear himself to me body and soul. The only reason I can think of to cause such a powerful link between us would be you carrying her when he made the oath."

Her mother pulled her daughter towards her, wrapping her in a protective hug. "You can't have her."

"She somehow created a familiar bond, just by touching my chest. Her link to me has been growing stronger since we met."

"You can't have her," Sanna repeated, a pleading fearful tone entered her voice this time.

I sighed, barely able to care about her distress. "I didn't come here to take your child. I came here to tell you how your first husband died and pass along his share of the loot. I'll be leaving alone."

Her husband frowned. "What's going to happen to Amelia?"

"I don't know. Our bond is stronger than the ones I share with others."

"You said the bond was growing stronger."

"It is."

"Yet, it's already stronger than the ones you have with others."

"Yes."

"Do you hold power over her?"

That was a good question. "Amelia, jump on the table."

She looked at her mother. "Can I?"

That was not the reaction I expected. I gave her another command. She looked at her mother for permission again. Her parents began to smile as I gave more orders, and she didn't respond.

"I have no power over her," I admitted. "Whatever this bond between us is, it doesn't make her mine. However, the fact remains, she has some of my powers. Powers that will make her a target."

Her father glanced at her and then met my gaze. "She claims she can see bad people."

"She can. When we walked around the village, she showed me all the Unseen and cursed objects. She was right *every* time. This ability is so rare that I was thought to be the only one to have it in the kingdom."

"She'll have to go to the church," he said.

Amelia began to tremble. She was terrified.

Her terror concerned me, enough to act. "Not necessarily."

"You can't have her," her mother repeated more firmly.

I had other options. "Would you consent to her to becoming Princess Carolyn's handmaid? Carolyn can keep her safe, until she is old enough to protect herself. Carolyn will one day rule this kingdom. With Amelia at her side, she could become a ruler like no other."

"I can meet a princess!" Amelia's face lit up, losing only some of her fear to distraction.

"Would you like me to get her for you?"

Her parents didn't know what to say to the offer.

Amelia did. "Yes, please."

I was back in ten minutes with the princess. Her guards entered the building ahead of her, checking it was safe, and then assumed positions inside and out. Carolyn sat in the chair I pointed to.

"You're the crying girl," Amelia said, excited and happy to meet someone else from her dreams.

Carolyn frowned. "Crying girl?"

"She dreams about me," I explained. "She must have seen you in her dreams."

"Are you a princess?"

Carolyn nodded.

Amelia frowned. "Where's your crown?"

"Only the ruler wears a crown." Carolyn turned to me. "Why am I here?"

"Amelia's father was the first person to swear the hero's oath to me. He made the oath while his wife was pregnant and seems to have created a link between me and his daughter. She has many of my powers, including the evil eye. She needs to be protected, but her parents do not want me to take her. I offered you as an alternative to the church. She would become your handmaiden."

Her guards took notice. I saw several of their gazes changed, before they moved to a position that would allow them to defend Amelia more effectively. The Old Monsters served the kingdom first and the king second.

Carolyn made a small gesture.

Rupert walked over and whispered in her ear. "Accept. She is the most precious child in the kingdom. Your father exchanged the royal library for a week of access to this skill. Her value as a future advisor is incalculable."

Carolyn nodded then she turned to Amelia's parents. "I am currently the vampire's prisoner."

"Is that why he picked you up and ran away with you after eating the bad people?" Amelia asked.

Carolyn gasped. "You saw what happened?"

"I dreamed about it."

"Tell me what you saw."

Amelia did not dream like other people. She saw my life in all its details. Heard what I said and what others said to me. She *remembered* it all, too. When Carolyn asked her what happened to me in the church, she cried, talking like she was in a trance. She had seen what the church did to me. She had witnessed unspeakable things no child should have to see. That's why she was terrified of them.

I left the table and collected Davina.

Amelia was still telling the story in the same tearful trance when we returned. Davina rushed to her side and scooped her up without me needing to say a word. Amelia called her, "the happy girl," and then collapsed unconscious in her arms.

Her parents didn't bat an eye, smiling as Davina held their daughter, like they were blessed. Davina had come into her power as the necrosaint, and people intrinsically sensed the good in her. This wasn't the first time I had seen this reaction.

Carolyn wiped the tears from her cheeks. "She confirmed what you said about my family. Was that why you brought me here?"

"I assumed she saw flashes. I didn't know she dreamed with detail. Her confirmation was unexpected. I brought you here because she needs to be protected. You were the best option available."

"What is she?"

"She's a child. But one with more potential than most."

"Her parents said you have no power over her."

"It appears I don't."

"Is she someone you will protect?"

"Yes."

"Why?"

"She is the daughter of the man who saved my life, and she is a child."

"Is that all?"

"It's enough."

"She likes you. She's not afraid of you. She says you only kill bad people and monsters, and that people don't trust you because they only see you do violent things. They don't see you slipping gold into poor people's pockets or explaining to little boys why they shouldn't try to feed their little brother to vampires."

"Is that a problem?"

"It means I will never convince her to work against you."

"It also means that if *she* ever tells *you* to work against me, you should do so with everything you have."

She frowned. "That is another way to look at it. And it would make me foolish not to accept for that alone. I'll take her as my handmaiden."

"Will we be able to visit her?" her mother asked.

"The vampire is building a town, and my guards require a place to live that is outside his direct control. If you are willing to move and run an inn, she can live with you."

Her mother frowned. "We can't afford it."

I placed two storage pouches in front of her. "You can afford anything you want. Your late husband didn't die in vain." I started to tell her the story of how her first husband died.

It was a story filled with betrayal, death, and a vampire trapped in a cell, half driven mad from hunger. It did not have a happy ending, but it was not a tragedy. Her husband died a hero with a smile on his face, having rid the world of an evil that he had no place ridding the world of.

WE REACHED the estate the following day, passing through the petrified forest. Undead creatures, spawned from the death magic hanging in the air, roamed the grounds around the once-majestic building where Sir Denton had lived. The discomfort that had built inside me eased as my weariness grew. The closer we got, the weaker I became. My body was spent. And the dead in me needed to slumber in my grave to return to the land of the living.

They carried my coffin through the ruins, down under the manor, through the tunnels, to the hidden rooms built inside the mountain.

Davina opened the lid and helped me stand. "You sure you want to sleep in that?" she asked, eyeing the sarcophagus Angelica was opening distrustfully.

I had been summoned and turned in this room, like the vampires I had eaten here. This was, quite literally, the *only* place for me to truly rest. The lead sarcophagus hadn't changed while I was gone, but I had.

I gave her a tired smile. "The grave calls me to it." The pull was like gravity. If I let go of Davina's hand, I would fall in.

Davina helped me stumble forward. Gregory's men stood around the walls, prepared to deal with anyone who would wish me harm. Everything was organised for the academy's construction, and there were Unseen ready for me to feed on when I woke. Nothing demanded my attention. Nothing pulled me from the grave. My body was weak. My soul was tired. It was time to rest.

Gravity took over as Davina released my hand. My feet left the floor and my body turned before I fell into the sarcophagus. The grave continued to pull against me, increasing my exhaustion.

Davina smiled. "Sleep well, your Dark Eminence."

Angelica began to slide the lid into place.

The world began to fade as my strength fled.

At the last moment Angelica whispered to me through her visor. "Release me from your service." The words reverberated through my skull, pounding against my psyche, trying to crush it with their weight.

I was at my very weakest, utterly defenceless to her armour's compulsion. The life was rushing out of me, and exhaustion was mounting. But this world had skills, skills that would not allow me to fall below their level.

"No," my fourth-tier willpower replied.

"Forget I said anything when you wake," she whispered, panicking and trying to compel me again.

"No."

She tried to close the lid, but my finger filled the gap.

"Angelica, I promised you that you wouldn't like the results of trying to compel me. You will spend this time while I sleep training your death lord skills with the same intensity as your first staff training session in Tobil."

"I didn't sleep for three days!" she shouted. "You could be asleep for months! I'll die!"

"Davina, bring her back if that happens."

"Can't we negotiate?" Angelica asked, hyperventilating.

"Goodnight, Angelica. Enjoy your time without me."

I pulled my fingers from the gap and slid the lid closed.

The world faded, and peaceful slumber took over.

The end.

Final Character Sheet

Race: Ancient Royal Vampire Variant
Class: Hero
Level: 35
Strength: 340
Agility: 520
Endurance: ∞
Constitution: ∞
Cunning: 240
Perception: 480
Recovery: ∞
Mana Regeneration: 400

ALSO BY BENJAMIN KEREI

UNORTHODOX FARMING

Oh, Great! I Was Reincarnated as a Farmer

Oh, Great! I Discovered How to Cultivate a Farmer in 52 Easy Steps

THE VAMPIRE VINCENT

Death Loot & Vampires

Made in the USA
Monee, IL
21 November 2023

47072726R00229